Date due is no longer stamped in library materials.

HARD LINE

HARD LINE

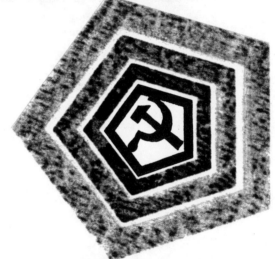

Richard Perle

RANDOM HOUSE
NEW YORK

All rights reserved under International and Pan-American Copyright Conventions.
Published in the United States by Random House, Inc., New York, and
simultaneously in Canada by Random House of Canada Limited, Toronto.

Library of Congress Cataloging-in-Publication Data

Perle, Richard Norman
Hardline : a novel / Richard Perle
p.   cm.
ISBN 0-394-56552-5
I. Title.
PS3566.E69154H37   1992
813'.54—dc20   91-51015

Manufactured in the United States of America

24689753

FIRST EDITION
Book design by Carole Lowenstein

For Leslie—
and to the memory of Jack and Martha,
and Sonny and Scoop

Author's Note

In the waning days of the Cold War, a remarkable summit meeting was held in 1986 in the countryside near Helsinki at the summer cottage of the Finnish composer Jean Sibelius, a place called Ainola. This is the story of the amazing events leading up to that meeting and a little-known episode that occurred there.

After long silence, I should perhaps explain why I have chosen to write this book now, and why I have written it in a novelistic style.

In the time I've been teaching, I have tried to convey to my students how policy is made at crucial moments in world history. My course, "Diplomacy from Munich to Ainola," has been well attended, especially by undergraduates. Some of them, at least, accept my account of events.

But I have been dismayed recently at the revisionist line that has come to dominate historical writing about the last stages of the Cold War. What is particularly galling is the claim made by the liberals of the period that the Soviet Union never really threatened the Free World, that the Pentagon overstated Soviet military power to justify huge military budgets, that *liberal* policies (of *restraint,* no less) led to the Western victory in the Cold War and the subsequent breakup, first of the Warsaw Pact and then the Soviet Union itself. In their view, the American president was at best a minor player and, more commonly, a mere bystander, haplessly witnessing events he neither understood nor influenced.

Others think the Ainola summit was irrelevant, that it changed nothing. But the whole course of history might have been different if that summit meeting had ended as the Soviets—and some Americans—wanted it to.

In the revisionist histories the concluding battles of the Cold War— seminal events such as the deployment of missiles in Europe, the beginning of strategic ballistic missile defenses, and the Ainola summit itself—are scarcely mentioned.

Ainola was the turning point; the preparation for it was crucial. Yet Ainola is perhaps the least-understood event of the period.

Ten years ago, before leaving Washington to take up a teaching position at Harvard, I made a visit to the Federal Records Storage Center in Suitland, Maryland, to review the files from my office during the last days of the Cold War, when I was assistant secretary of defense. I was astonished to discover how much of the documentary history of that period had been preserved. My secretary at the Pentagon had been meticulous in recording everything that went on. She had even saved early drafts of memos that were later revised extensively.

As I rummaged through the files—110 boxes of them—I remember thinking that some future historian would be able to reconstruct much of the sequence of events with which they dealt, but he couldn't possibly know or understand the private thoughts and feelings of the participants. This struck me particularly when I read a memo from the assistant secretary of state for European and Canadian affairs at the time.

It was dry as shredded wheat, in preferred State Department style. Its bland paragraphs gave no hint of the perfidy that lay behind it. It was yet another example of the State Department skillfully undermining the Department of Defense, as it had done countless times in those years.

The documents I had collected after the Kostiv affair were intact, all neatly labeled and ordered chronologically. Reading them again was like stepping into another century; with two million Russian emigrés having arrived in the United States in the years after the Soviet Union broke up and the Federation borders were thrown open, it is hard to believe that the Ainola summit was nearly canceled over a single Ukrainian seaman jumping ship in New Orleans.

I will undoubtedly be criticized for writing a novel rather than a history. My academic colleagues will argue that I should have put my evidence on the line so it could have been examined impartially by professional historians.

But it is not them I wish to reach. I want my readers, like my students, to understand how policy battles are fought. Like other conflicts of human will, they are struggles between people whose ideas and values, virtues and failings, determine the outcome. When you read in your morning paper "The White House has decided" or "The State Department has announced" some policy or other, remember: Behind the institutional anonymity there are winners and losers, careers made or broken, causes advanced or thwarted. These are the realities that get lost in the thicket of footnotes one finds in academic writing.

Also, unlike some of my government colleagues who have, over the years, written memoirs or given interviews to the press about privileged events in those days, I feel bound to keep faith with those who trusted me. I won't quote people who spoke to me in confidence, so the novelistic genre serves me well. Here, my invented characters say only what *I* wish them to say. None of their words can be held against them. I alone am responsible. And I can't be accused of having violated anyone's trust.

Moreover, much of the documentary material I found when I returned to Suitland last year was still classified. Many of the most interesting documents were Top Secret at the time they were prepared. And while there is no very good reason for them to be kept secret now, they remain officially classified. Their publication would violate the law. There are no Top Secret documents in novels.

Criticism from my academic colleagues troubles me not at all. I have grave doubts about the impartiality of professional historians and political scientists. Just look at how far the revisionism has already gone. For example, Stanford University Professor C. Edward Hartung is widely regarded as having written the standard work on the history of the deployment of medium-range missiles in Europe in the early 1980s. So-called professional historians fawned and cooed over his book. *The New York Review of Books* applauded when it won a Pulitzer. But in almost every respect it is tendentious and misleading. Hartung swallowed the Soviet line on one issue after another. To hear him tell it, the Soviet leader, not the president of the United States, was the architect of the proposal to do away with medium-range missiles. What a travesty! And his is not the only one, of course. One searches in vain for a book that gets the story right.

Since the passage of the Walters-Roberts Amendment to the Freedom of Information Act opened up the State Department archives five years ago, there have been no fewer than fourteen books dealing with the period in which I served in government, and all fourteen take the same revisionist line. I have watched with mounting dismay as a rich and complex history has been twisted and distorted to preserve the predisposition and outlook of a class of intellectuals who never wished to fight the Cold War and now claim to have won it. It was won, to be sure, *but not by them.*

If they'd had their way, we would have accommodated Moscow generously. They know little of power, less of evil. And of power in the service of evil men, they know nothing at all. That is why our Western academics (and the diplomats and journalists upon whom they exert great influence) take from a clever compromise the satisfaction that men of action can achieve only in victory. They are full of praise for the State Department compromisers who figure as heroes in their writings and seminars but have only disparaging things to say of the president and the secretary of defense, who somehow managed to prevail.

Many of my former government colleagues were kind enough to draft for me private accounts of events in which they were involved. I have drawn much from this material. I have also made generous use of the files in the Defense Department archives, although I have not quoted from any official papers. Instead, I have reconstructed critical documents from memory, sometimes reinforced by the recollections of others.

So, this book deals with events both real and imagined. But it is, most of all, a book about the struggle for a president's soul, a struggle waged by men he appointed to high office, some of whom shared his vision and sought to advance it, some of whom did not and undermined him at every turn. It is dedicated to those who stood by him—and won the Cold War.

—MICHAEL WATERMAN
Cambridge, August 1998

PART ONE

CHAPTER ONE

The White House, September 16, 10:45 A.M.

It was gray and unseasonably cold for mid-September. The black government sedan of the assistant secretary of defense made its way through the serpentine complex of concrete security barriers surrounding the White House and pulled up to the guard post at the Southwest Gate. Inside the car, Michael Waterman withdrew his Defense Department photo-identification card from his wallet, handed it through the car window, and waited while a uniformed Secret Service officer entered his name in a computer inside the bulletproof glass-and-steel gatehouse. Finally, the reinforced hydraulic iron gates swung open slowly and silently. The guard handed Waterman's I.D. back through the open window along with a laminated, numbered, black-and-white White House pass he'd wear on a chain around his neck for the duration of his visit.

"You're cleared for the Situation Room, sir," the guard said. "You know how to get there?"

"Yes." Waterman nodded, absently running his hand through thick dark hair graying at the temples. The car was already moving toward the green canopy in front of the basement entrance to the West Wing. Through the windshield Waterman saw a network stakeout camera crew in blue ABC parkas clumped behind the rope line on the North Lawn. It looked like rain, so their equipment was wrapped in black plastic garbage bags.

"I'm early for the eleven o'clock," Waterman said to the receptionist just inside the second of two sets of double doors. "If it's okay, I'll just wait here."

"Of course, Mr. Waterman," she said cordially, writing his name in a spiral notebook. Still, she glanced at the computer screen on her desk, confirming that Waterman was actually on the list for the meeting.

Waterman cracked a smile; he knew that previous National Security Policy Group meetings had been subject to gate-crashing and that the crashers had even more impressive titles than his own, or flag officer's stars on their uniforms.

Depositing himself in a red leather wing chair, Waterman crossed his legs, declined the offer of a paper, and idly peered around the reception area. The buff-colored walls were covered with huge color photographs. Most of them showed the president at his best—arms raised in the traditional two-fisted V-for-Victory wave, in front of a bank of American flags; others caught him in some private moment of joy, smiling as he did the nation's business with world leaders or members of Congress; still others showed him at work at the White House, discussing policy with his Cabinet. Indeed, the frequency with which Cabinet officers appeared in those photos, much of official Washington believed, spoke volumes about who was up and who was down at any particular moment. Waterman wondered whether the KGB analyzed the pictures in the White House corridors the way the CIA pored over the annual lineup of Politburo figures arrayed every May Day atop Lenin's tomb in Red Square.

Waterman's early arrival was, to say the least, uncharacteristic. His usual tardiness was a defect his wife grudgingly accepted, his subordinates suffered ungladly, and his bosses came to tolerate. Today, however, he hoped to steal a minute with the president's national security adviser, General Mitchell Wallace, before the meeting got under way. With luck, Wallace would tell him what the urgency was about.

There had been nothing on the schedule of Secretary of Defense James Ryder—SECDEF in government-speak—about a meeting with the president, so it couldn't be a policy-making session. There were no news bulletins about the type of crisis that would require the president's immediate attention—nothing in the CIA's daily Top Secret intelligence summary, the "NID," or National Intelligence Daily, which Waterman read every morning in his office over a double espresso. In fact, all Waterman knew was that he'd been called at nine-thirty by Bob Reed, a blunt, no-nonsense Defense Department staffer detailed to the NSC, and told to appear ninety minutes later in the White House Situation Room.

"What's it about? Why such short notice?" he'd asked.

"I don't know," Reed replied testily. "All I was told was to call you and Bennet, and that the president will be there."

"How the hell can you not know the agenda before a meeting with the president when you work a hundred yards away?"

Reed's tone became defensive. "Because I *do* work a hundred yards away, Michael. A hundred yards! In this business that's an ocean, or a continent. Don't give me a lotta grief. They don't tell me what they're thinking. You've been summoned to help carry the Pentagon's water. Show up. Be on time. Bye."

When the digital clock on the wall displayed 10:54:00, Waterman walked across the reception area to position himself to catch the NSC adviser coming down the stairs from his first-floor office on the way to the Situation Room. He hoped that Wallace would be early. If he came in at the last minute with the president, Waterman would miss any chance to learn beforehand what the hastily called meeting was about.

It annoyed him deeply that others—in particular his counterpart from Foggy Bottom, Assistant Secretary of State for European Affairs Dan Bennet—would probably know the agenda, while he'd been kept in the dark. Knowledge was power. The more you knew, the more you could use what you knew to expand your empire or advance your political agenda—or both. Dan Bennet would make it his business to know.

In the five years he had been at the Pentagon, Waterman had clashed repeatedly with Bennet. It was a surrogate war, meant to hide the real combatants: James Ryder, Secretary of Defense—Waterman's boss—and Bennet's boss, Secretary of State Anthony Winthrop. Since turf wars and ideological battles between principals on such a high level invariably attracted unwanted publicity, to which the president always reacted unfavorably, assistant secretaries did the fighting instead. Urbane guerrillas in dark suits, they fought not with AK-47s but with memos, position papers, talking points, and news leaks. It was unrestricted warfare; there was no rule book. And no two antagonists in this administration had gone at it more regularly than Michael Waterman and Daniel Bennet.

They were opposites in almost every way. Bennet was as tall and flamboyant as Waterman was compact and reserved. Indeed, at first Waterman—who had served a long apprenticeship on Capitol Hill, where aides often had greater power than senators but worked behind cloaks of invisibility—had contempt for Bennet's ostentatious style and extravagant wardrobe. But he'd learned from experience that while Bennet's Savile Row suits, bold striped Turnbull & Asser shirts with white collars and cuffs, floppy breast-pocket handkerchiefs, and antique cuff links gave him the look of a dandy, the man was a talented—and deadly—infighter, who used the system, as well as his influence with the secretary of state, to full advantage.

Damn Bennet anyway. Of course he'd know what this was all about.

Waterman had tried to deduce the morning's agenda during the eight-minute drive from the Pentagon to the White House. He doubted the sincerity of Bob Reed's professed ignorance. The logistics of any meeting attended by the president virtually required that the national security adviser know what was going on. And if Wallace knew, Reed knew: Wallace depended totally on his assistant. It irked Waterman that Reed's loyalties had so quickly shifted from his permanent employer, the Department of Defense, to his temporary employer, the National Security Council.

Still, it was to be expected. Working at the White House (even though Reed actually toiled in a ten-by-thirteen-foot cubicle on the third floor of the Old Executive Office Building) was heady stuff. Correspondence on White House stationery got faster reactions than it would on a DOD letterhead. NSC phone calls were returned more swiftly. Knowing what the president would say on national television hours before the broadcast began, sitting in the Situation Room, where issues of war and peace were decided—for a GS-13 (the equivalent of an army major like Reed), such perks of power were addictive.

But despite the circumstances, Waterman was relieved to have been invited here at all. Assistant secretaries were seldom included in meetings of the National Security Planning Group—reduced in government acronym to NSPG—unless they had something specific on which to report. Waterman may have been a sporadic guest on *Face the Nation, Nightline,* and other network political talk shows—not to mention that his name and likeness appeared in *The New York Times* and *The Washington Post* with regularity—but as far as NSPGs went, he was just another assistant secretary. So decreed Washington's complex, rigid caste system, which pigeon-holed by title, not capability.

At three minutes before eleven there was no sign of the NSC adviser. Waterman knew that if he waited much longer, he would not be in place when the president entered. Indeed, he might even bump into the president en route in the narrow passage that led to the Sitroom—an awkward moment best avoided.

Just then the outside door opened. In came Bill McCandless, the perpetu-ally rumpled director of central intelligence (DCI). McCandless, who seemed to Waterman uncommonly preoccupied, mumbled an unintelligi-ble "hello" and kept moving down the hallway toward the Situation Room, accompanied by the National Intelligence Officer (NIO) for Soviet Affairs, Hal Engel. A few steps behind Engel was Gerald Copeland, undersecretary of state for political affairs, a Foreign Service officer who had risen through the ranks of the diplomatic establishment despite a succession of disastrous judgments. Had Copeland been the chief loan officer of a suburban bank, he would long ago have been pink-slipped. Instead, the ruddy-cheeked bureaucrat carried a black diplomatic passport, held the rank of career ambassador, and was called "Your Excellency" overseas.

Still no sign of Wallace. Then, immaculately dressed in a dark gray chalk-striped suit worn over a gray, lavender, and black-on-white striped shirt with a polka-dot tie, a perfectly tanned Dan Bennet came bounding down the stairs from the first-floor offices. He saw Waterman and smiled. "Morning, Michael. Glad you could make it on such short notice."

Gotcha.

Waterman offered his hand and nodded noncommittally. "What's this all about?" he asked Bennet.

"The Russians want a summit."

Stunned, Waterman tried to keep his expression even. "Was there a letter from Novikov?"

"No." Bennet's answers were lean, offering as little information as possible. His studiously casual, smug expression, on the other hand, spoke volumes.

"So how did they approach us?" Waterman pressed.

"They sent word through a backchannel."

"When did we find out?"

"A few days ago," Bennet said vaguely, obviously pleased to confirm that such significant information had been successfully withheld from his rival. He glanced up the stairwell. "The secretary will lay it all out in a moment. We'd better go on in."

But we're not ready for a summit, Waterman thought. His mind churning, he followed Bennet down a short corridor past the White House mess. They stopped in front of the cipher-locked entrance to the Situation Room complex. Of course, he thought, it was perfectly clear why this had been done on such short notice, and why he hadn't been told about the agenda. Dammit—it had all been contrived to force the president into a snap decision to agree to a summit, and for the State Department to gain control of the situation leading up to it.

There was to be no staffing, no discussion papers, none of the deliberations necessary to ensure that all points of view—not just State's—would be included.

Waterman knew from his experience on Capitol Hill that the two critical aspects of summits were timing and agenda. For this one, it looked as though Moscow would determine the timing. And with the State Depart-

ment in charge, he thought grimly, the Kremlin would probably control
the agenda as well.

No wonder Bennet was smiling. He had it wired. Before this meeting
ended, the decision would be made to send some State Department official
off to Moscow to "negotiate" with Novikov's people. The agenda would be
settled, and the summit die would be cast.

Like his boss, James Ryder, Waterman believed that a summit any time
soon was dangerous for the interests of the United States. Of course Novikov wanted one. Not long in office, he needed a public-relations triumph
to demonstrate he was firmly in control of the Soviet state.

As a young staffer on the Senate Armed Services Committee on his first
visit to Moscow, Waterman had seen a group of boys bathing in a stagnant
pool along the road from Moscow Airport. And despite Novikov's reforms—despite *perestroika* and *glasnost,* despite what Waterman perceived
as a deeply rooted hunger on the part of the Soviet people, indeed, of all
those in the Eastern bloc, for their government to move, ultimately, toward
some form of democracy—a stagnant pool was still an apt image of that
unhappy place. Now, the secretary of state was on the verge of maneuvering the president into a summit that was bound to undermine the policies
for which Ryder—and Waterman—had worked so hard.

Waterman knew that in the best of circumstances it wouldn't be easy to
argue against a summit meeting. Americans believe it is always better to
talk. Even that ultimate Cold Warrior Winston Churchill had rumbled,
"Jaw, jaw, is better than war, war." Indeed, Waterman knew that sooner
or later, every president—usually prodded by the secretary of state—comes
to believe that if only he could sit down with the Soviet leader and explain
American policy in an intimate, one-on-one meeting, this alone would
allay Moscow's groundless fears and produce a breakthrough in East-West
relations. But State Department optimism had little to do with any deliberate strategy for advancing toward peace. Rather, it was driven by an
unseemly desire to clamber onto the world's center stage with a spectacu-
lar diplomatic initiative.

But strategically it was far too early for a summit with Novikov. This
was, after all, a Soviet leader in power for less than a year and about whom
no one knew very much—a leader who seemed constantly to be shifting
allegiances, backing the reformers one day, the antireformers the next.

For all its technical wizardry and high-flying spy satellites, the CIA knew
precious little about Viktor Petrovich Novikov. He had been handpicked by
Brezhnev to run the Central Committee's policy group at an unprecedented
early age. But no one really knew which side he was on or what to make

of his talk of reform, which he called *perestroika,* or whether his talk of openness, which he called *glasnost,* was more than a tactical maneuver.

Now, Waterman understood why the secretary of defense hadn't been told about the meeting or its agenda until the very last minute. Winthrop and Bennet knew that to make the case against a summit—overcoming the president's instinctive inclination for such a meeting—would require planning. Moreover, it required getting allies close to the president on board. But thanks to Winthrop and Bennet's strategy, Ryder and Waterman had been caught short, with no opportunity to prepare their own strategy.

Bennet picked up the security phone outside the Sitroom.

"Bennet and Waterman," he said, and waited for the click that would unlock the door. He might just as well have announced "Abercrombie and Fitch," or "Barnum and Bailey," Waterman thought, for, once you got inside the West Wing itself, the White House's vaunted security became remarkably lax.

The electronic lock clicked, and they walked through a small anteroom containing two chairs and an industrial-strength Xerox machine. The Situation Room itself lay behind yet another door just to the left. Waterman let Bennet precede him through, then moved to his right and sat behind the chair allotted to the secretary of defense. A rectangular polished walnut table surrounded by ten upholstered tilt-back chairs filled most of the small, windowless room. On the wall to the left of the entrance, behind a drawn curtain, was a reverse-projection screen for briefing slides. At the opposite end was a door leading to a room full of computers and communications equipment. Along the north and south walls was a row of chairs for staff aides.

The Situation Room was nothing at all like Hollywood renditions. There were no flashing lights, wall-sized maps, or computer-generated displays. Once, during a crisis in Lebanon, when the National Security Council staff had unwisely inserted itself into day-to-day military operations, an army field telephone had been brought in. It sat for months on a chair by the door, gathering dust. One could just imagine Mitchell Wallace on it, barking targeting orders to a battleship outside Beirut Harbor.

In ordinary times the most exotic pieces of equipment in the White House Situation Room were a Princess telephone in a drawer at the end of the conference table where the president sat, and a television, hidden in a cabinet behind the paneled wall, that could display four channels simultaneously on a single screen. When the news was bad, you could get it on all four networks at once.

Bennet took his place behind the empty chair reserved for the secretary of state. The director of central intelligence was huddled with his aide, listening intently and making notes on a yellow legal pad. Bob Reed, two other National Security Council aides, and a staffer from the Vice President's Office, occupied the remaining chairs along the walls.

Gary Burner, the White House chief of staff, who never missed a trick—or a meeting at which the president was present—nonchalantly browsed the pages of *The Wall Street Journal* from his place at the middle of the table. Burner was the object of grudging deference. Had he not been the president's oldest and most intimate friend, no one would have paid the slightest attention to this short, rotund little man with a disproportionately large mustache, whose great distinction was an uncanny ability to remember a mountain of political, professional, and personal trivia about town clerks, aldermen, party chairmen and fund-raisers, heads of women's volunteer groups, student caucuses, conservative clubs and associations, telephone-bank operators, direct-mail houses—in short, everyone who mattered, and their children, when it came to nominating a Republican presidential candidate.

Burner sat in the Sitroom, and the Cabinet officers treated him with respect because *he* had elected the president. It was as simple as that. He had developed the strategy, organized the troops, and orchestrated the most stunning upset in recent political history, defeating a rival who had begun the campaign $14 million and 27 points ahead. Four years later he'd done it again. When he spoke, he spoke for the president. And people listened.

Waterman heard voices outside. He put a legal pad on his lap and patted his pocket, which held a smaller notepad on which he could write quick, private messages to the secretary. Then the door opened, and the president, chatting amiably, entered with Mitchell Wallace and the secretaries of state and defense. Winthrop, an elfin figure in a diplomatic pinstriped suit, was buoyant, even elated. Ryder's face looked as pulpy as if he'd been beaten with a length of two-by-four.

Everyone rose. Smiling, the president waved the aides back into their seats before taking his own place at the end of the table closest to the door.

He looked around the table. "Good morning, all," he said.

"Good morning, Mr. President."

"Well, it's nice to know you could all make the time to be here on such short notice," he observed affably. The president rested his arms on the table, his hands interlocked, index fingers forming a steeple. He sat back in the leather chair and cued the national security adviser with a nod of his head. Then he closed his eyes, as if meditating.

Abruptly, General Wallace began: "I want to apologize for calling this meeting so hurriedly. But we've had an unusually sensitive message from the Soviet leadership, and the president wanted to meet now, before he leaves for California, to consider how we ought to respond."

Smart, Waterman conceded silently. By springing the issue as the president was departing for California and keeping Ryder in the dark, Winthrop had landed a huge preemptive strike. And to Waterman's dismay, the NSC adviser was clearly in on the secret. Defense could expect no help from General Wallace. The NSPG had been called to confirm a done deal. With the president presiding. Except he was not presiding: Wallace and Winthrop were in charge.

The NSC adviser looked around the room. "The message didn't come through normal diplomatic channels, but it was delivered to the secretary of state. There's no doubt about its authenticity. The secretary will give us the background."

Anthony Winthrop leaned forward in his chair. "Several years ago," he began slowly, "after Yuri Marensky completed his tour as ambassador here and returned to Moscow, we began to get occasional messages from him. They were always sent outside normal diplomatic channels.

"When the Kremlin wanted to trade a jailed dissident for a Soviet agent held by the South Koreans, it was Marensky who first contacted us. When they had the accident at the Shagan River nuclear test site, Marensky let us know the fallout would drift into the North American weather pattern. There were other instances as well in which he passed on information useful to us.

"Marensky communicates through a professor at Stanford, Andrew Weston, who worked for several years for the Senate Foreign Relations Committee. Weston is fluent in Russian and travels frequently to Moscow, where he's in charge of the Stanford University–Moscow University Political Analysis Center."

Waterman sat up as if he'd been slapped. Weston was also a Soviet apologist who wrote op-ed articles criticizing the administration, and scholarly papers aimed at showing that the United States was largely responsible for the Cold War. Whenever there was a crisis in United States–Soviet relations, Weston would rush into print defending the Soviet line.

Winthrop continued, "Marensky began to use Weston as a diplomatic backchannel five years ago. The relationship was remarkably successful. So successful, in fact, that these backchannel communications have never leaked out.

"After Marensky became deputy foreign minister, the contact ceased for almost two years. Last year, when Novikov became general secretary,

Marensky's influence increased enormously. In fact, the intelligence community"—Winthrop inclined his head toward McCandless—"believes that Marensky is now the principal figure behind Novikov himself."

Winthrop went on, "After his promotion, Marensky resumed contact with Weston. By the way, before I go any further, I should say that we have always kept Weston's role as a backchannel strictly confidential. As I said earlier, in the time he has been reporting, there has never been a leak."

The president's eyes came open with a start, and his palm slapped the table. "Let me underline what Tony has just said. We've had altogether too many leaks on sensitive matters. I want everyone here to do everything he can to get these leaks under control. That means limiting the information we've just heard to the people in this room. I don't want this all over the government, or it will be in *The Washington Post* tomorrow."

"Mr. President, I appreciate your saying that," Winthrop said as if by rote. "I know how concerned you've been that we treat these matters in confidence. It can't be said too often."

"I'd like to add my strong endorsement to what's been said," Ryder added without much enthusiasm. "As you know, Mr. President, we've been trying by every possible means to get a handle on this situation. I've done everything the law allows within the Department of Defense. And you know about the problem we're having with the Hill."

The president's fingers drummed the table impatiently. "I was just thinking about that. Gary, where are we on the polygraph legislation?"

Waterman looked at Ryder, whose eyes widened noticeably. It was amazing that even here, in a meeting about his first summit, the president would digress from the matter at hand to make time for his favorite irritant. The chief of staff, caught off-guard, blinked. "We still can't get it out of the Senate Judiciary Committee, Mr. President. We thought we had an understanding with Senator Shelton that he'd let it come to a vote in the committee, in which case we have a narrow margin for a watered-down version. But Shelton's insisting on a circuit-court seat for his law-school professor, who's his closest friend and a flaming liberal. So everything's on hold."

"Then what are our options?" the president asked.

"Our best shot is to move after the next really serious leak, the kind that does damage even the Congress can't stomach. Then we'd have a chance at an amendment. We'd have to win a point of order if Shelton insists on referring the amendment to the Judiciary Committee. But if passions are running high, we might make it."

"Well, keep on top of it, Gary. I know there are a lot of bleeding hearts who object to lie detectors. But I'll tell you something—when they wire 'em up to that box, they get a lot of confessions." The president paused and looked around the table. "I mean it," he said. "I do. I've had it up to my keister with all these leaks."

Then he settled back in the chair again, resumed his clasped-hands position, and closed his eyes.

There were some seconds of what seemed to Waterman astonished silence. Then the secretary of state struggled to regain his momentum.

"Weston returned last week from Moscow, where he'd gone to coordinate a series of Soviet-American town meetings sponsored by Stanford and PBS. He told us that over the course of a week's stay he had several conversations with Marensky, the last of which took place the day before he was due to return. Marensky suggested that they go for a walk on the Kremlin grounds. Once there, Marensky got quickly to the point: Novikov wants a summit.

"Mr. President," Winthrop continued earnestly, "I believe that we should take full advantage of this opening. Your policy of restoring our military strength has paid off. Novikov is proposing to come to us. We have a full agenda in mind: human rights; regional issues like Soviet subversion in Nicaragua, the war in Afghanistan; bilateral issues like the dispute over their bugging our Moscow embassy, our desire to pursue a new cultural-exchange agreement, and so on." The secretary of state paused, looked across the table at Ryder, then added, "And, of course, there's arms control."

Winthrop's voice took on an urgent tone. "We've made an immense investment in strengthening our military forces, and it's worked—it brought the Soviets to the negotiating table. But the current arms-control talks remain hopelessly deadlocked. Even our chief negotiator is convinced that it's fruitless to continue."

His gaze swept over his assembled colleagues, lingering on the immobile president. "The only way we're going to move things along is with a summit. It's a summit we'll attend in a position of great strength. It can't have been easy for Novikov to have made this proposal. We must give a positive response to Marensky's proposal and send someone to Moscow without delay."

Waterman took the small notepad from his pocket and hastily scrawled a note. He tore it from the pad, folded it in half, wrote *SECDEF* on the outside, and slid the paper onto the table in front of Ryder. Waterman always addressed his notes, ever since one he'd simply handed forward had been picked up—and read—by the secretary of energy.

Uncomfortable at being seen prompting the secretary of defense, Waterman pushed the paper forward as inconspicuously as possible. Nevertheless, it seemed to him that every eye in the room followed the yellow paper as Ryder unfolded it, slipped a pair of glasses out of his breast pocket, and read.

> *State's trying to rush P's decision. . . . This will mean a policy review, new concessions to the Sovs, and probably a new policy directive. We mustn't pull punches on tech transfer, East-West trade, human rights, arms control, etc. But that's sure to happen if State controls review process. Wallace? No help—State's won NSC over, altho McCandless is our ally. Delay's our best option. Can we get interagency study to stall Winthrop?*

Ryder didn't need a note from Waterman to understand that the president would agree to go ahead with a summit. That had been evident an hour ago upstairs in the Cabinet Room, when Ryder had appeared at the weekly congressional leadership meeting to pitch the administration's defense-budget request; afterward the president had taken him aside to whisper proudly that he'd received "some good news from Moscow."

So there was no point in trying to turn the decision around. The president had made it clear he would not make the first move; but from the beginning he had insisted that if Novikov came to him, he would agree to meet.

Ryder nodded his head almost imperceptibly. Waterman leaned back, anticipating that his concerns were about to be raised.

"Mr. President," Ryder began, "we should begin at once. I recommend we ask an interagency group to prepare an options paper on a summit strategy. This could be completed—or at least be well along—by the time you return from California.

"With such a paper as a basis for discussion, we could recommend an approach to Novikov. The crucial thing is to shape the agenda so our issues, not theirs, are up front. The Soviets are always after the same thing: pressure on our strategic modernization program, especially SDI. We have a much broader agenda, but much of it is less dramatic than treaties affecting nuclear weapons."

"How quickly can we get this under way?" asked the president, turning toward Wallace.

"Mr. President, we've already drawn up a work plan. It should be possible to have something ready by the time you return to Washington."

"Who should we send to meet with the Soviets?" the president asked.

Before Winthrop could speak, Ryder interjected: "That should be one of the issues worked by the interagency group."

"All right, then," the president said.

From the end of the table McCandless leaned forward. "Mr. President, you should understand clearly why the Soviets want a summit meeting. They're feeling the pressure of their own failures and your successes."

"Yes, but—" Winthrop interrupted.

The jowly DCI overrode the secretary of state. "For years—despite a succession of 'peace' initiatives—they've mounted a furious propaganda campaign aimed at deflecting you from the policy of rebuilding our military power. They now accept they failed to do so." William McCandless was a crusty New York trial attorney, a Cold Warrior who had begun his intelligence career as a Jedburgh infiltrator behind Nazi lines in France, when he was a junior officer in the OSS under the legacy of William Donovan. His friendship with the president was decades old, which gave him more power and access to the Oval Office than most DCIs had ever enjoyed. Despite his rough appearance, McCandless was an inveterate scholar who dispensed his history lessons in a heavy Brooklyn accent often underscored with the salty language of a longshoreman. Lately, Waterman noticed, McCandless had been given to mumbling. Now, however, he slapped a palm on the table and spoke clearly.

"If I might add a point, Mr. President, we don't know a lot about Mr. Novikov. He's very private. But we may have gotten some insight from a defector we've been debriefing—he served as a translator for Novikov during the Chinese leadership visit to Moscow last year. He says that just before the Chinese were ushered into Novikov's office, he turned facedown on his desk a framed quotation from Sun Tzu, the Chinese philosopher and strategist who wrote *The Art of War* twenty-five hundred years ago. It was inscribed 'To my good friend and comrade from Dimitri Zalinsky, Chief of the General Staff of the USSR.' Novikov didn't want anyone to see it. Why? Maybe because it would have provided too great a window into his mind. The defector gave us the gist of the quote, and I had it researched. Just listen to this . . ." The DCI read from a sheet of paper:

" 'When able to attack, seem unable; when active, seem inactive; when near, make the enemy believe you are far; when far away, make him believe you are near; when organized, feign disorder; if weak, pretend to be strong and so cause the enemy to avoid you; when strong, pretend to be weak, so that the enemy may grow arrogant.' " McCandless stopped reading.

"What does that prove?" Winthrop asked skeptically.

"Prove? It proves nothing," said McCandless. "But if someone I didn't know and with whom I was about to do business had it sitting on the desk in his office, I'd be careful as hell when I met with him."

"I have no illusions about Mr. Novikov," Winthrop said. "He does not mean us well. But I do believe we ought to explore any possibly fruitful avenue that might mitigate the tension between us. We won't give if they don't give. To plan, to prepare, costs us nothing. *Costs us nothing,*" he repeated. "If Novikov has nothing to offer us when we meet, then we'll have nothing to offer him."

Waterman's annoyance grew. Winthrop was deliberately obscuring the implications of the decision to hold a summit meeting—implications this president, who had the good sense not to be too interested in the workings of the bureaucracy, might fail to comprehend.

Waterman knew the decision to agree to a summit would turn the switch on the vast governmental machine that ground out policy like sausage, a machine that worked according to its own design, a machine that whirred continuously from one administration to the next, independent of philosophy and vision, public-opinion polls and elections. It was a vast, complicated apparatus, far beyond the control of Anthony Winthrop, James Ryder, William McCandless—indeed beyond the control of the president himself. It was a machine manned by an army of civil servants who had no use for the president and his hard-line policies and who could be counted upon to promote a new détente with Moscow because that was what gave *them* the most satisfaction.

But there was nothing anyone could do. There was no way to stay the hand that was poised before the switch; it all sounded so reasonable to just, in Winthrop's word, "to explore."

How had the secretary of state phrased it? "We won't give if they don't give. To plan, to prepare, costs us nothing." Nothing? It could cost *everything,* Waterman thought with agitation. It could bring the rebuilding of American defenses to a screeching halt. But resistance now, when the president had clearly decided to go forward, would be fruitless.

Except for his comments on polygraph legislation, Gary Burner had sat silent through the meeting, brushing at his mustache with a forefinger and reading occasionally from a file of press clippings. The chief of staff never showed much interest in matters of foreign or defense policy except when the popularity of the president might be affected. The president's standing in the polls was Burner's exclusive interest and concern.

So as Ryder, Winthrop, and McCandless argued over the president's policy toward U.S.-Soviet affairs, their words slipped like so much wind by the chief of staff. To Burner, they were bureaucratic white noise. What interested him most about the possibility of a summit was the image forming in his head of Dan Rather, Tom Brokaw, Peter Jennings, and Bernard Shaw anchoring the evening news from platforms overlooking a brightly lit, photogenic summit site. It didn't matter what the networks said, Burner knew—just so long as the pictures they broadcast were awesome.

Burner might have been reluctant to intervene in a foreign-policy discussion, but in his view what was really being debated was an event, a huge photo opportunity that, properly staged, had the potential to boost the president's popularity. To Gary Burner, all the successful arms-limitation treaties ever signed could not equal the significance of a 75 percent approval rating in a Harris Poll.

The chief of staff swiveled to face his boss. "Mr. President," he said, "I think we should all be immensely pleased by this development. A summit with Novikov's a real coup for the administration. It comes at a time when no one knows what we should expect of him. But organizing a summit's a major project. It's not too soon to begin preparations for the political side of this event: the media coverage, the congressional consultations, some lead-in speeches, the tie-in to your travel schedule in the coming weeks, and so forth. This is a great opportunity, and we want to make the most of it. I'll organize a small group to work that side of things, if you approve."

"Well, yes, of course, Gary." The president nodded.

"Mr. President," Wallace said, "that concludes our agenda, unless someone wishes to comment further." Without waiting for any response, he continued, "I'd appreciate it if Dan Bennet and the other agency representatives would be good enough to remain here so that they can go over the IG work program."

Cued properly, the president rose, Burner at his sleeve, and let himself be guided out the door. The DCI took Ryder's arm, and the pair of them left the room, heads inclined in whispered conversation. The secretary of state paused to hand a single sheet of paper to Bennet, then turned and left without another word.

Okay, Waterman thought, now the work, the real work, begins.

CHAPTER TWO

The White House, September 16, 11:45 A.M.

Assistant secretaries are the departmental watchdogs. They guard the home turf.

This means, among other things, never allowing any diminution of the authority of one's department—no matter how slight or how temporary, and no matter what public interest might be served thereby. Anyone who has served in government, even briefly, knows this and treats the guardianship of the assistant secretaries with the respect one accords properties on which large, aggressive Dobermans roam.

Assistant secretaries control a precious commodity that Cabinet secretaries, whether at State, Treasury, Commerce, Education, or Defense, need constantly: answers. Reactions for the press. Clarifications for Congress. Interpretations for their colleagues. Explanations for the president. Assistant secretaries supply Cabinet officers with endless factoids and info-bits. With the help of briefing papers, memos, handwritten notes, three-by-five index cards, messages scrawled on damp cocktail napkins, and occasional whispered prompting, assistant secretaries keep their principals, as the bosses are called, up-to-date and, more important, unembarrassed.

What also makes assistant secretaries so pivotal is that they oversee the work of the senior bureaucrats who are the government's institutional memory, those who are intimately familiar with the histories, cases, procedures, and regulations—in short, the bureaucratic universe—in which policy is shaped and implemented.

The permanent government establishment of senior civil-service and military officials may be paid with public funds requested by the president and approved by Congress. But they work for assistant secretaries, for whom they gather the statistics and legal opinions; prepare the flowcharts and program outlines; and draft the point papers and memoranda that are the sinews of what is called the "policy process."

Every administration approaches the task of staffing differently, but in recent history, when making major decisions, all have depended largely on assistant secretaries.

Now, in the Situation Room, sitting opposite each other at the polished walnut table, the two assistant secretaries Waterman and Bennet were poised to square off as they had so many times in the days since they entered the administration together. Here, however, the battleground was slightly uneven in Waterman's favor. When he had to operate without specific instructions from Ryder, Waterman reacted on instinct, reflecting the views he knew Ryder held. Over the past five years they had been through many battles together, and they thought alike. But more important, Waterman had the authority to speak for his boss. Waterman—with Ryder's consent—carried the imprimatur of the secretary of defense.

So while Bennet had enjoyed the tactical superiority of knowing from the beginning what was going to happen in the NSPG, his advantage ended the moment the initial meeting was over. When the give-and-take began, it was Waterman who knew, with a confidence Bennet seldom enjoyed, that whatever position he took, the secretary of defense would back him up. Bennet had no such certainty about his boss. More than once he had agreed to something only to have Winthrop ignominiously pull the rug from under him.

For his part, Waterman knew what he said now would be crucial. If he failed to protect DOD's turf, if he did not ensure Defense's full participation in the summit preparations before the meeting was over, Bennet would freeze him out. His mind raced as challenges flashed before him: how to shape the papers that would be prepared, how to influence the selection of someone to go to Moscow for the meeting with Marensky, how to firm up the American position on the summit agenda.

He had not always been so zealous or so tough. The only jewel in the crown of a Los Angeles kosher butcher named Sam and his wife,

Esther, Michael Waterman was born in 1943 and grew up in a two-bedroom, one-bath stucco bungalow on Hayworth Street in the Fairfax section of Los Angeles, equidistant from his father's shop and the storefront temple where Sam went to pray. A slight, precocious child, Michael suffered heavily at the hands of his schoolmates. When most boys his age spent their free time playing baseball, football, or tennis, Michael's parents insisted, with the best of intentions, on giving him cello lessons four days a week. So during the fifth through eighth grades—crucial years for youngsters—Michael Waterman didn't carry a fielder's mitt or shoulder pads to school, but a heavy black leather instrument case. Instead of weekends at the beach, he spent his time indoors practicing scales. He was small and perpetually pale and thin and wore orthodontic braces. He was . . . different. And so his classmates picked on him in the instinctive, impersonal cruel way of preadolescents, and Waterman withdrew like a turtle inside an emotional shell.

He was, as a result, an indifferent scholar and a social hermit. His natural intelligence, however, brought him good grades in high school, though he seldom worked for them. He preferred to spend weekday afternoons and evenings reading alone in the large and mostly empty music room at the Fairfax Public Library, and weekends at an endless series of movie theaters up on Hollywood Boulevard, where he'd go for the dollar matinee and stay to see films two, three, or four times before catching the bus back home.

Unlike Bennet, whose family enjoyed a winter home in Palm Beach and a summer cottage on Martha's Vineyard, Waterman spent his vacations working in his father's store, watching as the elder Waterman carved and chopped and boned and filleted. He listened as Sam spoke to customers, telling each new face with what he thought of as high humor, "I'm Sam Waterman—not from the pen family, either, and more's the pity," and vowed silently he'd escape his father's fate and rituals.

Although Sam's butcher shop fell on hard times in the late sixties, Michael's parents encouraged him to apply to private colleges. Later, Waterman would realize they believed he'd be safer in a costly private school—they'd seen all the newscasts about the Free Speech Movement at Berkeley and the student uprisings at UCLA, and worried that the spirit of anarchy would infect their only child. So it was actually with a sense of relief that they greeted Michael's acceptance by Tufts University and sent him East with a suitcase of suits and ties.

Once there, he began to blossom both intellectually and socially. The suits and ties were exchanged for jeans and plaid shirts; the sensible black oxfords for sneakers. He let his hair grow long. He drank cheap Algerian wine and ate foods he'd never been allowed at home: bacon and eggs; ham sandwiches; lobster.

At Tufts he also discovered his natural talent as a debater, the result of a seminar in modern European history his sophomore year. The professor, an Oxford-educated Nationalist Chinese diplomat's son named Hsi Fiu Leong, insisted on inculcating students in the Socratic method. The reclusive Waterman, forced to defend himself out loud, took almost three weeks before he first dared speak in class. Then, under gentle encouragement from his teacher, who saw in the shy youth a spark that needed fanning, he began to open up. Within three months Leong couldn't shut him up, and Waterman found public speaking so enjoyable he joined the debate club. He learned to stand straight, look his opponents in the eye, and beat the intellectual bejesus out of them—and he did it with zeal. His junior year he switched majors from English literature to history, writing his senior honors thesis on the Treaty of Ghent—his parents had the front page with its bold red A+ framed—and he graduated summa cum laude.

From then on Waterman's climb was steady and astronomical. He won a teaching fellowship in international relations at Princeton. He was well on his way to a Ph.D. when he became a casualty of academic burnout and the frustration that comes from daily dealing with academic bureaucracy.

Waterman's deepest dissatisfaction was with what he perceived as the political overlay to all graduate-level education at the university. As a Jew brought up on horror stories of the Holocaust, he was sensitive to the menace of totalitarianism. As a scholar whose specialty was Europe between the wars, he had come to appreciate the dangers of appeasement. The faculty at Princeton, he discovered much to his regret, seemed not to have learned the truth about either.

Disenchanted, Waterman dropped out of Princeton. He bought a backpack and a sturdy pair of hiking shoes and traveled through Western Europe for sixteen months. Fluent in French and German, naturally inquisitive, he conversed with people who picked him up hitchhiking, with students he met in hostels, with waiters in restaurants. His modest budget forced him to eschew the big cities and instead concentrate on small towns in France, West Germany, Austria, and Italy. He came back to the United States with a better understanding of how Europeans regarded America, and what they wanted from their relations with the United States. He also returned deeply in love with an American coed he'd met in a youth hostel in France, Laura Williamson, whom he would marry within the year.

Soon after he returned to the States, he applied, on the spur of the moment, for a job on Capitol Hill. He had the good fortune to find temporary employment (it would be "temporary" for eleven years) on the staff of Senator Arthur Winter, a conservative of the new school (or liberal of the old school, as Waterman preferred to regard his mentor) who saw in Waterman a potential for fire and passion he'd never observed in an aide before.

Winter nurtured the young Californian, honing his instinctual talents for organization and staff work. The senator taught not by dictum but by example. Under Winter's tutelage, Waterman soaked up this education. He studied the art of getting the senator's—and his—way with other staffers or other senators when everyone thought it was impossible. He perfected the techniques of drafting legislation, speeches, and hard-hitting questions that were sure to get his boss onto the front page and into the evening newscasts.

He learned the fine points of committee hearings. One day, for example, Senator Winter took him aside just before the secretary of state was to appear before the Armed Services Committee to testify on arms control. "He knows nothing about arms control—and we're gonna prove it in front of the committee," Winter told his young aide.

He instructed Waterman to rearrange the chairs in the hearing room just minutes before the hearing was set to begin. It was, Waterman saw at once, a devastatingly effective tactic. Normally, a row of aides would sit two feet behind Cabinet-level witnesses, close enough to whisper in their ear or slip notes in case some senator raised an arcane fine point about which the secretary had not been briefed. For this session, Waterman moved the front row of chairs six feet behind the witness chair. No one noticed the shift—until the secretary's testimony was well under way.

The secretary's discomfort at his isolation was evident as he struggled to give complex, technical answers for issues about which he knew nothing. Finally, he was reduced to asking Winter contritely to relocate his advisers so they could help him answer the questions with more precision, and the senator achieved his goal—demonstrating in public the secretary's shallow grasp of the issues.

So, with Arthur Winter's help, Michael Waterman mastered the rules of Senate-league hardball—knowing when to hit and run, when to bunt or sacrifice, and when to go for it—to slam one out of the park. He learned how to draft expansive amendments that could be readily reduced to more modest proportions when it became necessary to gain cosponsors, how to offer up sacrificial amendments to pave the way for real ones, how to structure legislation so senators could vote twice, once on each side of an issue. He learned how to use a Senate hearing to pressure the bureaucracy, how to use congressional purse strings to influence policy that had nothing to do with the budget, how to kick off a debate with a leaked trip report or by putting a reporter in touch with a dissident bureaucrat. By the time he left—at the senator's urging—to work for Secretary of Defense James Ryder, he had served an incomparable apprenticeship. And it was at times like this, when Dan Bennet was about to try something especially egregious, that the lessons Waterman had learned from the Winter years were most valuable.

General Wallace called the meeting to order. "Thanks for staying, gentlemen. We've got a lot of work to do in the next several days. It'll take the cooperation of everyone here—State, Defense, CIA, the Arms Control and Disarmament Agency, and the Joint Chiefs of Staff. I've drawn up a work plan. We can talk about it now, but you may prefer to think about it overnight, so I'm open to a meeting tomorrow. But the president wants to move quickly, so I want to put everything to bed by C-O-B tomorrow. If we can get consensus by phone, we can avoid a meeting. If not, we'll meet here again at seventeen-thirty."

The NSC adviser nodded to his assistant, Bob Reed, who passed photocopies of a two-page outline around the table. Waterman scanned the list of topics and agency assignments. He looked over at Bennet, who scrutinized the pages as if seeing them for the first time. Waterman shook his head. He was sure Bennet had created the document. In all likelihood it had been drafted by State's Soviet Desk, then massaged by Bennet and passed on to Reed, who laid it on his boss's desk without any clear provenance. And General Wallace wasn't the type to make changes on his own.

The more closely Waterman read the list of papers to be prepared and the assignments to each agency, the more he became convinced the work had indeed been done at State, not the NSC. The outline lacked the NSC's distinctive "signature"—a mix of global politics and defense and intelligence perspectives knit together by the small, expert NSC staff. Instead, it contained every one of the Soviet Desk's habitual preoccupations: a new consulate in Kiev; an expansion of cultural exchanges; collaboration on the Middle East; a slew of bilateral agreements covering science and technology, space exploration, medicine, transportation, oceanography, fusion energy, construction, and the like. Even settlement, by conceding the Soviet position, of an obscure dispute over American title to Wrangel Island, a small island in the Aleutian chain to which the Soviets laid a claim the United States had always rejected, was included in the laundry list.

Having learned nothing from the Nixon days, when the U.S. sought to moderate Soviet behavior by engaging Brezhnev in a multitude of coopera-

RICHARD PERLE ─────────────────────────────── 24

tive ventures, only to be rewarded with a vast increase in Moscow's military might, State had for years been champing at the bit for another run at a full-scale détente. There was no issue, Waterman thought, that State was not prepared to open up to new negotiations and compromise.

With Novikov now in power, Bennet had taken the lead in promoting the idea of this new détente, not only because doing such things was the nominal responsibility of the assistant secretary for European and Canadian affairs, but because a victory here would catapult his career to heights otherwise unattainable. Successfully achieved détente meant star status for the diplomat who crafted it and an acceptance by the Foreign Service establishment that was otherwise bound to elude him, as it had his predecessors who were not drawn from the mafia of career Foreign Service officers.

But to pull this off and to veer the great lumbering ship of state toward a policy the president had opposed since taking office would require a sea change in the presidential mind. And *that* could be fulfilled only if Bennet was able to put a fresh palette of colorful options on the desk in the Oval Office. Bennet knew his problem was not just to engineer a from-the-ground-up review of U.S.-Soviet issues, but to do it in such a way that the president would grab at it as at a brass ring. He had been pressing for such a review for weeks, probing constantly within the interagency groups he and Waterman chaired together, for openings to pursue.

But there was little interest outside State for any action, and Waterman, dead set against any reevaluation, found it easy to abort Bennet's attempted launches. Frustrated, Bennet concluded that without some major precipitating event there would be no new thinking. A summit was the perfect solution, and now, as if by magic, he had one.

Scanning the outline his Soviet Desk had, in fact, drafted, Daniel Bennet basked silently in his success. Like a phoenix, he had risen from the ashes of his previous failed attempts: the leaks to the press, the clandestine maneuvers with liberal members of Congress, the backchannel collaboration with officials in the foreign ministries of America's allies. Whatever else happened, the administration was about to conduct a wholesale review of its policy toward the Soviet Union. And the State Department would dominate this summit. It would set the president's agenda and keep him to it. Moreover, the professionals—those same career diplomats who privately derided Bennet and sneered behind his back—would, in this endeavor, support him to the hilt.

It is said that generals are made by wars; and it is certainly true that few great military careers are made in peacetime. Nor has the State Department flourished in periods when the president is indifferent to the talents of the diplomatic profession. No great diplomatic careers are likely to be made in a period when diplomacy is going nowhere.

Inextricably, then, careers and fortunes became bound up with the substance of U.S.-Soviet relations. Ambassadors at their posts, assistant secretaries at their desks in Washington, the secretary of state himself, all came to believe what was in *their* bureaucratic, professional, and—although it went unspoken—personal, interest, i.e., an active, energetic diplomatic relationship with the Soviets, was nothing less than the national interest as well. Oh, Waterman knew all the rationalizations—the concepts that masked, even from itself, the State Department's faith in diplomacy and compromise, when what was really needed was to rally the Western democracies in a great ideological confrontation. The president understood the need to assail the legitimacy of the Communist system. In speech after speech, he characterized the Soviet empire as evil. State wanted to stay mum and negotiate. Now, the whole weight of State's often recalcitrant machinery was acting in well-oiled syncopation at Bennet's command.

Indeed, as Waterman looked over the outline, it became clear State had assigned itself the lead for all the most sensitive papers: the Summary and Overview, the only document the president was likely to read, as well as sections on arms-control objectives, on "regional" issues (Afghanistan, Central America, the Middle East, etc.), on human rights, and on bilateral matters.

To Waterman's dismay, the Department of Defense was reduced to the role of editorial researcher. According to the outline, DOD's only function in preparation for the summit would be to supply statistical information on U.S. and Soviet military forces—the sort of order-of-battle data that a halfway competent editorial assistant could extract from official reports—and to supply a paper on the verification process for arms-control treaties.

The one paper of real importance, an analysis and estimate of future Soviet military forces with and without an arms-control treaty, was shrewdly assigned to the CIA and the Office of the Joint Chiefs of Staff (OJCS), a moribund bureaucracy in which, as Waterman was fond of saying, all the military services had to agree before its staff officers are permitted to sneeze in a sandstorm. The assignment guaranteed a vacuous assessment. But it also, Waterman realized, bypassed the Office of the Secretary of Defense—which in essence removed Ryder (and Waterman) from having any input in the most crucial evaluation the president would be taking to the summit.

"This looks okay to me," Bennet said blandly.

Waterman wagged a finger toward the NSC adviser. He would be direct. "Well, I have problems with it. For one thing, I object to having the Department of Defense, which has an obvious interest in the military balance with the Soviet Union, relegated to the role of a research assistant for the Department of State."

"That's ridiculous," Bennet said, his voice betraying condescension for Waterman's evident discomfort. Before he could say more, Waterman continued, "Second, the whole thrust of this outline is to reopen every conceivable issue in U.S.-Soviet relations at once. This makes no sense . . . you can't expect a sweeping analysis to be completed in less than a week. Even if a decision is made to hold a summit, there's no reason why we have to dispose now of everything that might conceivably come up. We should narrow the scope to address only what's necessary to decide how"—he glared at Bennet—"to respond to Marensky's proposal.

"Believe me," Waterman asserted, looking back at Wallace, "anything else is bound to be hopelessly superficial. State may have nothing better to do than write papers on twenty or thirty topics overnight, but we have a defense establishment to run."

"Hold on, Michael," said Wallace. "No one said this is meant to produce a definitive approach to the summit. This is a first cut, something we can have for the president to review when he returns from the West Coast."

"So this"—Waterman held up the pages between thumb and forefinger as if they were week-old fish—"is not what we'll use to produce the president's summit briefing book?"

Wallace looked at Dan Bennet, who shook his head. "No," Bennet said with a sigh. "This is simply intended to scope out the work program for the president. The briefing books will follow. Don't be so paranoid, Michael."

"Paranoid? Why should I be paranoid? General Wallace passes out a draft work plan as though it had been prepared by the NSC. Now, it's clear from the way he's turned to you to explain it that it must have been done at State. And you tell me not to be paranoid?

"I distinctly heard the president agree to SECDEF's proposal that the question of how to respond to Novikov would be addressed in the work to be presented to him when he returns to Washington." Waterman looked over at the NSC adviser. "Did I misunderstand, or what?"

"No," Wallace replied, "you didn't."

Waterman rapped the table aggressively. "So?"

"Okay," Wallace said. "State will take the lead on a paper defining issues to be resolved before we respond to Novikov. Defense will participate, and anyone is free to propose an option."

"Or options, plural," Waterman added emphatically.

"Or options," Wallace agreed. "*Op-shuns,* plural."

"May I continue?" Waterman asked. "I was about to make a third point."

"Carry on," Wallace whined weakly.

"Third, the last time I looked, we still believed in civilian control of the military. I really object to work programs that task the Office of the Joint Chiefs without some prior consultation with the Office of the Secretary of Defense. I can't stop you from going to them informally, but on interagency studies like this, the proper procedure is to inform the secretary before making any assignments that affect the military side of DOD."

Waterman was pleased to note a pained expression on Bennet's face. "Finally, I really must insist that Defense participate fully in drafting any paper dealing with the future of our strategic and intermediate nuclear forces. Or any other military forces, for that matter. This is not an unreasonable request. After all, I serve as cochairman of the interagency groups dealing with intermediate and strategic nuclear forces. The fact that there's a need for new papers in the context of planning for a summit should not alter the roles of various agencies in the process."

Listening to Waterman, Wallace could imagine him back at the Pentagon briefing the secretary of defense with much the same argument. Worse, he could see a confidential memorandum from Ryder to the president taking shape. And Wallace knew that no matter what he or anyone else did, he could not stop such a message from landing on the president's desk. The Old Man and Ryder had known each other too long. Wallace knew the president saw him and Anthony Winthrop, for all their expertise and power, as subordinates. But he saw Ryder as an equal. So there was no point in denying the inevitable. It was never a good idea to be reversed by the president, which was the certain outcome if Ryder went to him with a personal appeal, as he surely would.

"Michael makes a good point," Wallace said. "The work on arms control should be done by a subgroup of the interagency group, chaired by State and Defense. But this has to be done on a very close-hold basis. We need a new compartment for this work with its own code word and strictly limited access. Only people specially cleared should be authorized to know what is going on. The interagency group has too many participants."

Recalling the president's earlier remarks, Wallace added, "And let's lessen the likelihood of leaks. We should do a paper on how we might respond *if* the Soviets were to propose a summit. We've got to protect the fact they've already asked for one."

Bennet may not have liked the alacrity with which Wallace acceded to Waterman's points, but he was not about to complain over what was, in light of the NSPG meeting, merely a consolation prize. Deciding to throw

Waterman a bone himself, Bennet smiled ingratiatingly across the table and nodded at the national security adviser. "I agree we need a new compartment," Bennet said, "with access limited to principals plus one person from each agency. I suggest we call it 'Dartmouth.' Okay with you, Michael?"

Waterman shrugged. "I don't see why not, so long as the access is kept even."

"Any other objections?" Wallace looked around the table. "Okay, it's agreed. If anyone wishes to propose any other changes in the work plan, let Bob Reed know by the close of business today, and we'll fax a revised plan around tomorrow. I don't think a further meeting will be needed unless we run into problems."

Bennet's irony in using "Dartmouth" as a code word to compartmentalize highly sensitive information originating with an interagency group on arms control was not lost on Waterman. For years an annual Dartmouth conference of Soviet and American personalities had been held with a view to restarting the détente of the early 1970s.

"For the record, I want to be clear," Waterman said. "I have to review this work plan with my staff and the secretary of defense before I can agree to it. I'll present it to the secretary as modified just now. I'll need to tell him something about the schedule. I have an all-day meeting the day after tomorrow, and the secretary has a NATO ministerial on his schedule in which I'm involved. He's going to want to know what sort of deadlines we're working toward. When do we contemplate a summit taking place?"

"Certainly not for several weeks at the earliest," Wallace said. "We do need to get a first cut to the president when he returns from California, but that's just so we structure the main effort, which will follow, according to his wishes."

Waterman leaned back in the sedan and picked up his telephone. He thought about calling home to tell his wife he'd probably miss dinner tonight. His absence at dinner was something she was getting used to. But instead of dialing his house, he reflexively punched his office number. "I'm on my way, Maggie," he said as his secretary answered. "There's lots going on. I'm just crossing Memorial Bridge now. I'll need fifteen minutes of the secretary's time as soon as I arrive." He paused. He knew enough not to say anything sensitive on a car phone that was probably being monitored by half the intelligence services in Washington.

He cradled the phone and watched the stream of joggers making their way across Memorial Bridge and down along the jogging path that paralleled the road to the Pentagon. It was just a short jog, he thought, between the Pentagon, the State Department, and the White House; a serious runner could make it there and back in less than half an hour. To make the same trip, Waterman reflected with a sigh, ideas took much, much longer—if they made it at all.

CHAPTER THREE

The Pentagon, September 16, 1:30 P.M.

When Waterman reached the anteroom of his office suite on the fourth floor of the Pentagon, he found it abuzz. In the reception area the military assistant to the assistant secretary of defense for intelligence sat at attention on a chair by the door, holding an envelope containing a document to be signed. And Øve Anders, a bespectacled, bearded Norwegian journalist visiting from Oslo, had turned up for an appointment made weeks earlier. Slouched on a couch in the corner, a dead pipe clenched between his teeth, Anders was reading a day-old *Wall Street Journal.*

Maggie was on the phone and had two calls on hold while she kept a watchful eye on a technical sergeant crouched in front of the large gray crypto box connected to the secure telephone, a sure sign it was down again. The printer attached to a word processor clattered its way through a lengthy memo. Through the open door to the military assistant's office, simultaneous proceedings from the House and Senate broadcast on C-Span's two cable channels added to the din.

Waterman came through his own front door and surveyed the chaos. "Ah, home sweet home," he said to his secretary. Most assistant secretaries' offices had private entrances; Waterman's did not. It was an inconvenience he tolerated in order to occupy a suite just down the hall and up a floor from the secretary's own on the Pentagon's outer E ring. Waterman had rejected out of hand the option of a larger office with a bathroom and shower on the viewless D-ring. Two rooms on Fifth Avenue had it all over a mansion in the Bronx. So there was no avoiding the assembled mob. He peered across his reception area to where the Norwegian journalist sat. Anders had come the longest distance, and it was an hour past his designated appointment: Maggie's last-minute call to reschedule had come too late.

"Øve," he called from the doorway, "I'm terribly sorry. I got called to the White House unexpectedly. How the hell are you?"

"I'm very fine." The slight, intense journalist wiped wire-rim glasses with a burgundy handkerchief. "I was actually a little late, so I'm rather relieved you weren't waiting for me."

"Come on in," Waterman said, waving Anders toward the door.

Maggie cupped her hand over the mouthpiece of her telephone and pointed toward Waterman's office. "There's someone waiting for you."

"Hang on a minute, Øve." Waterman shrugged apologetically. "Let me check this out first."

He walked into his office to find a naval officer in what had once been a white uniform tunic cursing in Italian at an espresso machine.

"That's what thievery gets you," Waterman said.

The officer turned. "Goddammit, Michael, can't you remember to clean this thing out once in a while? Just look at me."

Waterman had to smile. His longtime friend and onetime Princeton student, Commander Jay Parisi, now a naval intelligence officer assigned to the Pentagon, stood on Waterman's Oriental carpet, his beribboned chest covered with coffee grounds. The machine, a sienna-and-chrome Olympia that occupied a place of honor on its own table, surrounded by espresso cups Waterman and Parisi had liberated from restaurants all over Europe, was furiously spewing steam, hissing, and gurgling.

Waterman strode to the machine, turned it off, then looked at what Parisi had wrought. He had to shake his head. Jay Parisi might have been a first-rate intelligence officer and a communications genius as well as a world-class scavenger—there was nothing the man couldn't lay his hands on given a couple of hours and a long-distance telephone—but when it came to things mechanical, the commander was a complete incompetent.

"It helps to put the coffee holder on right," said Waterman dryly. "When you put it on wrong, all you get is steam, noise, and a mess all over your nice starched uniform."

"This never happened in Naples," Parisi said.

"Yeah, and there'll still be four tires on your car when you leave tonight. *That* never happens in Naples, either." He surveyed his former student.

"For chrissakes, Jay, you're Italian—these things aren't supposed to happen to you: Espresso's in your blood."

Parisi pointed at his short-cropped blond hair. "Maybe I was only raised Italian. Maybe I'm a Finnish orphan."

"Fat chance. I've seen your baby pictures."

"True," said Parisi. "Sadly true. I'm an ethnic—just like you, Mr. Assistant Secretary. By the way, I see we're running low on coffee. One of my tech guys—Mercaldi—is passing through Rome next week. He'll be under orders to replenish our supply."

"*Our* supply?"

"Okay, *your* supply."

"*Grazie,*" said Waterman.

Brushing coffee grounds from his uniform into a wastebasket, Parisi added, "What's going on, by the way? Your front office is a madhouse."

"Can you say 'summit'?" Waterman asked.

Parisi gasped.

"Get yourself cleaned up and be back in twenty minutes. And what I just said is top secret. Eyes only. Not a word."

Parisi actually saluted. "Aye, aye, sir."

Waterman followed Parisi to the door and motioned Øve Anders into the large office. The Norwegian looked and whistled. The view was impressive: Three huge windows overlooked the Tidal Basin, the Jefferson Memorial, and, in the distance, the White House. Anders's eyes widened as he scanned the mountain of paper. Waterman laughed: "I imagine this is as crowded as the *Aftenposten* city room."

"Actually, it reminds me of my first apartment in Moscow—although this place is huge by comparison. I had so many papers the KGB could never photograph them all. The thought of them trying to copy every sheet still makes me laugh."

Anders, now in his early sixties, had served in Moscow twice. His first assignment was a nine-year stint between 1956 and 1965. He'd had a unique perspective on U.S.-Soviet relations during the early sixties, when Nikita Khrushchev brutalized John Kennedy in Vienna; the Soviets breached the moratorium on nuclear testing and almost went to war over the Cuban Missile Crisis. In 1968, Anders went back to the USSR for nearly two years, during which time he often acted as an unofficial interpreter for Aleksandr Solzhenitsyn. When Solzhenitsyn received the Nobel Prize in 1970 and the Nobel Committee had to communicate with him, Anders became their go-between. For this service to literature he had been expelled from the Soviet Union.

Waterman had met the Norwegian a decade before, when Anders had come to Washington in the early 1970s as the one-man *Aftenposten* bureau. Waterman had called Anders to congratulate the journalist on a two-part profile of Senator Winter that, in translation, ran in *The Christian Science Monitor*. The two shared a long lunch, during which they realized that they had a lot in common. Foremost was their shared interest in Soviet matters. Though Anders was officially persona non grata in Moscow, he still had sources there.

On a number of occasions he'd managed to scoop the Moscow press corps *from Washington* on Soviet stories. He had broken the story when the Soviets uncovered a tunnel from which the CIA was monitoring Soviet military communications in East Germany. He scooped the world when a Soviet space mission went wrong and a Soviet cosmonaut crew was killed on reentry.

No one was quite sure how he managed to come up with his exclusives, although there was speculation that his close personal friendship with Alexi Marensky, son of the Soviet ambassador to Washington at the time, had something to do with Anders's journalistic coups. Only after Novikov came to power did Anders again get his visa applications approved, which just reinforced his colleagues' speculation. Marensky, after all, was one of Novikov's chosen few—a privileged position from which Øve Anders (and *Aftenposten*) benefited greatly.

Waterman's time was precious today. So while he always looked forward to the Norwegian's visits, the American knew that this one would have to be truncated.

On the other hand, Anders could tell him things about the Soviet state of mind he probably couldn't discover anywhere else. But he knew he'd have to be careful. Øve Anders was sharp—if Waterman said the wrong thing, he'd sense immediately that something was in the wind.

"Øve," Waterman said, spreading his hands in a gesture of helplessness, "there's a bit of a crisis taking shape—just a sudden staffing dispute. I'm afraid I've only got a few minutes. I feel especially bad because I know you've got to ration your time on these visits, and I'm afraid I've wasted too much of it already."

"Oh, don't worry, I understand," the journalist replied immediately. "When you meet a deadline every day, you become accustomed to crises."

"We're off the record, Øve, right?" Waterman had learned from painful experience to set conditions for talking with all reporters—even old friends—right from the very start.

The Norwegian nodded. "Off the record."

"By the way, where are you coming from?"

"From Bonn, last night."

"Then how's the European pillar of the Alliance?" Waterman asked, mocking the language of NATO communiqués.

"The Federal Republic? In its usual disarray, of course. The Germans can't decide what they want."

Anders's family had been active in the Resistance; Waterman saw his opening.

"Ah, but consider the alternative. When has the world benefited from Germans who knew what they wanted?"

"Never—when they were outside their borders." The Norwegian smiled.

"And the Soviets? What should I be thinking? Where do you come out on Novikov?"

The Norwegian took a yellow plastic pouch out of his jacket, tamped fresh shag tobacco into his pipe, returned the pouch, and pulled a box of wooden matches out of his trousers. He lit one, held it in front of his eyes until it had burned down the proper amount, then applied it to the pipe. A wreath of blue smoke escaped as he drew deeply. "If I'm slow to respond, it's because there's such uncertainty about where Novikov is headed. There's no doubt he's seized with the importance of restructuring the economy. But they're all uncertain of the solution, including Novikov himself. So they grope. One day they move left, the next day they move right. About the only thing they seem to know for sure is that it's danger-ous to do too much too quickly. The economy's getting worse. Novikov's already started to slow things down."

"How should we be responding to Novikov?"

"Like porcupines make love, Michael. Carefully. Very carefully—if you're going to respond at all. Trouble is, people over there are getting impatient. They want to see results. I don't know where it will end. If I had to guess, I would predict Novikov will fail. The rot is too deep, the system too far gone. They've spent decades creating a new Soviet man marching under the banner of 'Bread and Freedom.' Now that they've got him, he can't produce either."

Waterman grunted in agreement.

"But that can't last," Anders said. "The military budget is the only place to turn for relief from the economic stagnation that's brought them to the verge of bankruptcy. By the way, Michael, do you believe the official estimates of the percentage of GNP they're putting into the military?"

"Nope. The CIA says thirteen to fifteen percent—up from the eleven to thirteen they used to quote. I think it's closer to twenty-five percent."

"Or more," Anders said. "It surprises me that your intelligence people have no idea how impoverished the Soviet Union really is."

Waterman gave a dry chuckle. "Tell me about it."

"I wouldn't be surprised if thirty percent of their GNP is going into the military and related programs. Imagine. No wonder the poor bastards are staggering under the weight of failure and repression. Novikov has his work cut out for him, all right."

Waterman nodded. "But suppose Novikov turns out to be a real bastard? He says all the right things for a Western audience. But the KGB's never had a freer hand. Christ, they've been practically walking up to our people in the streets and asking them if they want to earn a few bucks spying for Russia. I'll tell you, I'm worried."

"What's the worst case," Anders asked, "as you see it?"

Waterman was about to answer when the intercom sounded. It was Maggie, sounding harassed. "We're getting stacked up out here four and five deep."

"Two minutes, Maggie. Øve and I are just finishing up."

He replaced the receiver. Øve had already stood up. "I'd better let you get back to work."

"When will you be back?"

"Not before mid-November, when I'm scheduled to go up to a conference in New Haven. Next week I'll be back in Moscow. But I'll be covering the NATO summit in Scotland next month. I assume you'll be there."

"I expect so," Waterman said. "Let's try to get together. I'd really like to continue. I'd also like to hear what you think of developments in Moscow." Waterman put his hand on the door. But he didn't open it. "By the way, you know Marensky?"

"Pretty well. But I know his son even better. Alexi and I did our share of hanging out together when I was posted here."

Waterman cracked a smile. "Did you now? Rumor always had it he was one of your best sources, Øve."

"Rumors are just rumors. But we did spend a lot of time together. We used to have all-night discussions—political, philosophical, everything. It's amazing, Michael, the depth with which he detested the Communist party—even though he's benefited enormously from being the son of a senior Communist official."

Waterman was skeptical. "Sounds as if he was going through some sort of adolescent stage—"

"You're wrong," Anders interrupted. "Believe me, Michael, the things he told me were enough to get him sent to the gulag. He's become a passionate democrat, young Alexi Marensky has. Today, that may be almost fashionable. But I always marveled that his behavior didn't affect his father's career."

"Well, Marensky's always been a survivor," Waterman noted. "He knew whose footsteps to travel in."

"True," said Anders. "Khrushchev's, Brezhnev's, then Andropov's—and now Novikov's."

"We know he's become one of Novikov's inner circle, Øve. The question is, just how close is he?"

"There are those in Moscow who say that Marensky actually *is* Viktor Novikov," Anders said. "But I think that's jealousy on their part. Still, there's no question Novikov pays close attention to what he says."

Waterman nodded. He took the Norwegian's hand. "Øve—"

"I know, Michael. The schedule."

"See you in Scotland."

Waterman opened his outer door and nudged the reporter through it. "We'll talk there. Over dinner. A long one—I promise."

As Anders left, Waterman mulled over the reporter's question. "What's the worst case?" he had asked. The worst case, Waterman thought, was an unjustified retreat from the policy of pressing the Soviets on all fronts—militarily, ideologically, politically—in the hope that Novikov would turn out to be a social democrat in full control of a transition to democratic pluralism. Waterman was convinced that only a hard line would produce a Western victory in the Cold War—and victory, not mere accommodation, had been, until now at least, the president's policy. Maggie came in with a red-tabbed envelope. Waterman tore it open. He peered at the document, a memo going to SECDEF from the assistant secretary for intelligence, Harry Adams. Because it dealt with an intelligence-cooperation program with Italy, Waterman was given an opportunity to concur, by initialing the page containing the recommendation from the assistant secretary for intelligence, or "non-concur"—in the language of the Pentagon.

This arrangement was intended to make sure the left hand knew what the right hand was doing. It wouldn't do to have the assistant secretary for intelligence authorize a cooperative program with Italy at just the moment when, say, the assistant secretary for international security policy was at a critical stage in a delicate negotiation with the Italians on some other matter. Coordination was important for the effectiveness of the Department of Defense, and the system of concurrences was how it was achieved. It also was meant to assure that all the assistant secretaries with an interest in an issue would have a say over how it was handled.

When operating properly, the system protected against ill-considered actions. It could also—and often did—prevent *any* action at all. Sometimes half a dozen or more concurrences would be required before an issue went to the secretary of defense for decision. Weeks could pass while differences that might lead to a divided opinion were negotiated among the various assistant secretaries. When Congress or the press complained about "bureaucratic delay" in the Pentagon, Waterman realized it was this elaborate system of checks and balances they often had in mind.

This particular paper was a routine matter of no great importance. He initialed his concurrence on the appropriate line, and Maggie snatched it away to hand it over to Adams's military assistant, who waited, sitting stiffly at attention, in the reception room.

She was barely out the door when Waterman's assistant, Scott Bracken, followed by a clean Jay Parisi, came through the door. Waterman joined them in a corner of the room furnished with a government-issue faux-leather sofa, three matching armchairs, and a Chippendale-reproduction coffee table, arranged atop a colorful Turkish carpet Waterman had brought back from a visit to Kars, a small town on the Soviet-Turkish border and the site of three Soviet invasions of Turkey.

"What happened at the NSPG?" Bracken asked.

"Oh, nothing of importance," Waterman replied. "Just a decision to hold a summit meeting."

"You're shitting me!" Bracken exclaimed.

"Hold on a second," Waterman said. He took the draft outline from his briefcase and handed it to Bracken. "Make two copies."

In a minute Bracken was back. He handed the original to Waterman, a copy to Parisi. Waterman watched while his aides read the paper he had brought back from the NSPG. Their angry expressions reflected a natural reaction to what they were reading.

Bracken was a kid, really—not yet thirty. He still dressed in the blue button-downs (tie askew), chinos, web belts, and Bass Weejuns popular in think tanks but considered far too casual for DOD. He was awfully young to do such sensitive work, but he was also aggressive and totally committed to Ryder and Waterman and their policies.

Indeed, like Waterman, Bracken came from the Hill: a younger version of Waterman himself, which is probably why he'd hired him in the first place. If he was the department's watchdog, Bracken was *his* watchdog—loyal, smart, energetic, effective . . . and single. Unlike Waterman, whose family life was dominated by his brutal work schedule, Bracken had no responsibilities other than his work. And Waterman worked him hard.

Parisi was different. Waterman had known Parisi since Princeton. A whiz-kid—a bright, first-generation American from Brooklyn's tough Bensonhurst neighborhood—Parisi had used the navy as a way out of the blue-collar ghetto and had managed to overlay his street cool with a veneer of sophistication that seemed almost aristocratic. He'd enlisted as Giovanni Parisi, a seventeen-year-old radio operator, served one hitch, gone on to Princeton on a full scholarship, then reenlisted and been accepted at Officer Candidate School. Now a lieutenant commander with an Americanized name, he hung out with Italian royalty, sang arias from Verdi as well as Neapolitan songs and a rendition of "Danny Boy" that brought tears to the eyes of his superior officer, Captain Sean Muldoon, and had managed to get himself admitted to the Army & Navy Club. Waterman appreciated his former student as a gifted intelligence officer. But best of all he was an old friend, someone whom Waterman had known and trusted for almost two decades. Waterman knew all too well that bureaucratic limits on hiring, combined with the rigid military caste system, made it virtually impossible for an assistant secretary of defense to hire an old friend as a key assistant. So he considered Parisi's assignment to him a gift from God.

"So what the hell happened?"

"Actually, there were two meetings," Waterman replied. He gave a short account of the NSPG and the meeting of agency representatives that followed. He saw them nod and their faces harden as he made it clear he was prepared to fight to the last against the abandonment of a policy that had been working, a policy that had restored confidence in the United States around the world and put the Soviets on the defensive, where they belonged. He related Winthrop's account of the Weston channel (never, of course, using the professor's name) and the argument the secretary of state had made for going forward with a summit.

"How did SECDEF respond?"

"He made it clear he was Not Pleased."

"But did he make the case?" Bracken wanted to know.

"It was clear he knew the president had made the decision to go ahead before the meeting got under way. He realized it would be pointless to object, so he tried to improve our prospects for influencing the preparations. State has finally geared up for the sweeping review of East-West policy they've wanted to do for so long. The summit's given them the opportunity, and they'll make the most of it."

Waterman looked at his assistants. "Our assignment, should we choose to accept it," he said, "is to prevent them from giving away the store."

He paused. "Of course, should we fail, the secretary will disavow any knowledge of our activities, and we'll be the subject of an elaborate *Washington Post* story about how demands for our resignations are growing."

Bracken and Parisi nodded grimly. They knew Waterman wasn't kidding. "So what's the drill?" Bracken asked.

"Seizing back as much of the lead as we can get on the issues of greatest importance," he said, pointing at Bracken with his pen. "Your issues, Scott, are obviously the most critical. We've agreed to set up a special compartment for work on the arms-control review. I'm going to insist you're read in, but you won't be able to discuss it with anyone else."

"Wellll, excuuuuse me," Bracken interrupted. "You mean I have to do a full-blown arms-control review in some code-word compartment without help? You know damn well, Michael, State will authorize access for a dozen of their guys. The last time we got into a situation like this, I was outnumbered six or seven to one. And they didn't give a shit about the access restrictions, while we played by the rules. There's no way I can keep up under those circumstances. I'm willing to die for my country, but not be buried under an avalanche of goddam State Department paper."

"Slow down a minute," Waterman said. "I was about to explain— there's a cover story. You can say we're doing some contingency planning in case the Soviets should alter their present positions. How would we respond—that sort of thing. That's the official story, and it has to be maintained—absolutely—within the building here. You can put a team of people together; you just can't tell them the real purpose.

"Now, here's what we have to do," Waterman said as his left index finger started tapping off the agenda on the upturned palm of his right hand. It was a technique he had begun in the Tufts debate club and perfected in the years since.

Tap. "I need you two to revise this so-called work plan. I want us to propose Defense as author of *all* the critical papers so we can bargain with State over who gets what."

Tap. "I also need a memo for the secretary outlining our strategy. Two essential points have to be made. We must have an understanding with the Joint Chiefs of Staff that we'll coordinate fully on all interagency preparations. The memo should impress on the secretary the importance of his taking this up directly with the chairman. If the JCS go their separate way, Bennet will twist them around his little finger, and we'll become irrelevant to the whole process. And we've got to make the case against slipping back into another mindless détente. You know: how we showered Brezhnev with concessions and how little we got in return, et cetera. We've got to get Defense and Ryder engaged on more than the narrow military and arms-control issues. If we don't, State will be the only voice on regional issues, human rights, trade, exchange programs, and all the rest."

Tap. "We've got to speed up the work on the report on Soviet treaty violations. Bennet will try to slow it down so it can't appear before the summit; we have to make sure it does."

"Now it all falls into place," Bracken mused. "Three times in the last two weeks Bennet has canceled working-group meetings on Soviet treaty violations. And the goddam State Department reps have been sounding like lawyers for the Soviets."

"You know," Parisi added, "the same thing has been happening in the Afghanistan working group. I thought we were getting close to a consensus that the Soviets were supplying the Kabul government with chemical weapons, and then, all of a sudden, State started to back off."

"If you knew a summit was coming, would you be rushing for an indictment against your summit partner?" Waterman asked rhetorically.

"But we have a lot of support, especially on the use of chemicals in Afghanistan. The working group is just about to meet with a defector who was involved with a Soviet chemical-weapons training unit. It took us six months to arrange it—with State and CIA fighting us every inch of the way."

"Get it in the memo to the secretary," Waterman said. "Point out that we fear State may seek to slow ongoing work on crucial issues like Soviet compliance with existing treaties. I want him to be aware of this when he sees the president next. Who's the defector?"

"A psychiatrist who was sent to Afghanistan to advise on how to treat Mujahidin guerrillas traumatized by the grotesque effects of the chemicals they were using. They were using one chemical in particular that came in binary form. A chopper would overfly a village and drop a heavier-than-air gas, which would seep into houses and the tunnel networks the Mujahidin use. Then, after enough time for it to be inhaled had passed, another chopper would drop a second gas, a chemical igniter. Any living thing— men, women, children, livestock, cats, dogs—that had inhaled the first gas would explode internally. Gruesome.

"So this major was sent to help the soldiers get over what they had seen. As part of his job, he went to see it himself. And he freaked out worse than his patients. He walked across the border to Pakistan, and the Paks let us have him."

"Is Bennet aware of this?" Waterman asked Bracken.

"Shit, yes. Wellbeck told me Bennet was going to get the defector's debriefs compartmented."

"Okay, Jay—do a separate memo just on that for the secretary. He'll put it to good use with the president."

Parisi stopped taking notes and looked at Bracken. "Scott," he said, "this is as good a time as any to tell Michael about the JCS paper on SDI. It's bound to figure in all this."

Bracken cleared his throat. "The Joint Chiefs have finished a perfectly half-assed study of the Strategic Defense Initiative that triples the secretary's cost estimates and contradicts what he's been saying in half a dozen ways. It was put together largely by their arms-control staff, led by some asshole colonel who just came back to the Pentagon after a year as a Council on Foreign Relations fellow in New York. He was probably brainwashed by the liberals up there. Most of his assumptions are transparently absurd. I could go on about it—but how much do you want to know now?"

"Goddammit!" Waterman exploded. "With everything else we've got to worry about, here's the JCS wandering off the reservation again. I don't have time now. Just get me a summary of the key points."

"Done," Bracken said.

Waterman got to his feet. He ambled toward his triple window that overlooked the Tidal Basin. "There's a reason for our crashing on this," he said. "You guys should know anything can happen at a summit. You know how the gantry holding the space shuttle is moved back just before the launch? It's like that. The whole restraining process just falls away.

"We won't be able to fight once the summit gets under way. We may not even be there. That's why the battle is now."

He stared toward the White House. "If we do our job, the president will do his."

He turned on the Olympia espresso machine. "Anyone want coffee?" he asked. No one answered. "I'm tied up in an all-day meeting the day after tomorrow. So you've got two whole days to get this stuff to me." Unrepentant at the sound of his aides' groans, he said, "So don't work too hard."

Alone, Waterman filled a metal cup with finely ground black coffee that exuded the aroma of Rome itself, tamped it down firmly and affixed it to the bottom of the machine, pressed the button, and waited for the chamber to fill with enough steam to produce a small pot of thick, rich espresso.

The Olympia began to sputter and hiss gratifyingly. Oh, damn, Waterman cursed silently as he suddenly remembered—he hadn't called his wife.

CHAPTER FOUR

The State Department, September 16, 1:30 P.M.

Without so much as a "Good afternoon" Dan Bennet walked briskly past his secretary into the large sixth-floor wood-paneled office suite assigned to the assistant secretary of state for European and Canadian affairs. Closing the door behind him, he sat down at his large walnut General Services Administration standard-issue (Executive/Group One) desk and removed a manila folder from the top drawer.

It was strictly against security regulations to store classified material outside a container approved for classified storage—a rating that did not include desks. Yet Bennet made a habit of putting some of his most sensitive papers in his desk drawer, beneath a pile of newspaper and magazine articles that had appeared under his name.

He opened the folder and marveled at the secret papers as if they were rare art. To Bennet, that's exactly what they were: the memoranda that, he believed, would someday constitute his historical legacy, crucial communications that shaped American foreign policy in the last decade of the twentieth century. In time they would serve as his portfolio, to be displayed at critical junctures in his career like relics brought out of a crypt on holy days.

But for now, these memos, cables, position papers, and options were private trophies, privileged evidence of victories in the battle to shape the foreign policy of the United States. They were the final versions of documents that had been properly logged and recorded and stamped with an appropriate security classification—*Secret-Sensitive* in most cases—but all had been copied before the classification stamp had been added. To anyone who came upon them, they would appear to be unclassified, and therefore entirely appropriate for storage in the top drawer of an unlocked desk.

The document in which he was most interested lay atop the folder. He had last read it two days ago. But now, after returning from the NSPG at which a decision had been taken to proceed to a summit between the United States and the Soviet Union—the first such meeting with the new Soviet leader—the memo that had made it all happen was a joy to read once again:

Memorandum: Department of State

TO: The Secretary
FROM: EUR/Daniel I. Bennet
DATE: August 20
SUBJECT: Managing the U.S.-U.S.S.R. Relationship in the Second Term

NEXT STEPS IN U.S.-SOVIET RELATIONS

We are getting nowhere with our various approaches toward improving the US-Soviet relationship. Your missionary work with the Germans has had encouraging results: They're trying to sell Moscow on improving the relationship with us, but we are still getting beaten up daily in the Soviet press, there is no movement in the Geneva talks, the president continues to deliver hard-line speeches Novikov bitterly resents, and our allies, especially the Germans, are scornful of our management of East-West relations.

Last week Embassy Bonn reported a Foreign Ministry paper that calls our handling of the Soviets "inept and amateurish." We are told the paper was ordered by Foreign Minister Genscher after the president's speech.

No event on the horizon offers much of an opportunity for changing the present relationship.

There is one idea we might try. Stanford professor Andrew Weston has for many years enjoyed a close personal relationship with Deputy Foreign Minister Marensky.

Weston sees himself as a quasi-diplomat (indeed, he has repeatedly hinted that he would be quick to accept an ambassadorship if it were offered). As you know, we have used him as a diplomatic backchannel successfully in the past. Now, I have learned Weston is going to Moscow tomorrow night. He will be gone for ten days. Twice, the president has said privately he is willing to meet Novikov, but he will not initiate the contact. He says Novikov should come to him.

We could ask Weston to tell Marensky, in strictest confidence, that the president would like a meeting with Novikov but is unable to initiate the contact for political reasons. The president would, however, respond positively to a suggestion to meet—*if* it appeared to originate with Novikov.

Weston could say that if Marensky authorized him to pass word to the president that Novikov also thinks a meeting would be beneficial, he believes a summit could be arranged through diplomatic channels.

Marensky is bound to assume that Weston's message, while informal, has official status. That is okay. Because if he responds as I believe he will and sets in motion the planning for a summit, *it will have been official all along.* If Marensky chooses not to respond, no harm is done. Either way we can't lose.

If Weston comes back with indications they're ready for a summit, we will at least get a crack at reviewing the policies with which we were frozen during the president's first term. If you agree, I'll start work on a very close-hold basis now so that we have some real momentum if this goes forward.

I am not sending this through the Secretariat because of its obvious sensitivity. Renalda has promised you will receive it in the sealed envelope in which I will give it to her. I apologize for this irregular procedure, but Weston's imminent departure makes it essential to get this to you at once. If you approve, Renalda will return this memo to me.

Approve: _____
Other: _____

Finished reading, Daniel Bennet thought gleefully, Bennet, you are fucking incredible to have pulled this off. He knew that at thirty-six he was remarkably young to have become an assistant secretary of state. Still, his work was the best element of his life. His marriage had ended in a bitter divorce; a succession of failed affairs left him distant and wary. Only his job gave him pleasure.

Bennet reached for the telephone on the desk and buzzed his secretary.

"Alice, tell Phil Lanier and Bob Wellbeck I'd like to see them now."

The morning after he had been confirmed by the Senate, Bennet had descended on the European bureau like a Mongolian horde, flinging personnel he perceived as ineffective or potentially dangerous to the far reaches of the empire—the Foreign Service Institute for midcareer training or minor embassies abroad—while retaining and recruiting a circle of tough, ambitious, pragmatic men like himself. Lanier and Wellbeck were two of the survivors. Both were Foreign Service officers who could have been expected to resent an outsider brought in to a post normally reserved for an FSO.

But both were quick to recognize that, outsider or not, Bennet was a man who was going places, a savvy hard-charger who would make his way to the top and carry with him those who were smart enough to get on board early.

So Lanier and Wellbeck jumped aboard. And they were not disappointed. They had moved rapidly in the hierarchy, well up on the ladder toward the ultimate Foreign Service rung, an ambassadorship.

The rung Lanier occupied at the moment was head of the Soviet Affairs Division in EUR. As a Soviet affairs specialist fluent in the language and steeped in the culture, it was the logical post for him. And while he was impatient to advance to deputy assistant secretary—DAS in bureaucratspeak—he was confident it would be his eventual reward for loyal service to Dan Bennet.

As the DAS responsible for European political affairs, Wellbeck was already a rung higher. He was also Lanier's immediate boss.

Bennet deployed his subordinates like a company commander instructing platoon leaders. "Get out there and take that paragraph!" was the sort of order one imagined him urging on his troops as they deployed to seize control of the third subheading in the second option of the first draft of some interagency position paper.

Alike in their seemingly limitless capacity to absorb the most withering criticism from Bennet, Lanier and Wellbeck were in other respects strikingly different. Wellbeck was tall, thin, thin-lipped, thin-skinned, and volatile, given to outbursts of anger. As a junior consular officer on his first tour at the American embassy in Rabat, he had been severely reprimanded for venting his rage on the locals—called Foreign Service nationals—unlucky enough to be assigned to him. But because he subsequently worked hard to keep his anger under control, and because he was unquestionably talented, he had managed to make his way upward in the Foreign Service.

Lanier was slight, short, dark, and good-natured. He sported a Fu Manchu mustache and wore boldly striped shirts, a combination that gave him the appearance of a carnival barker. Incongruously, he also spoke flawless Russian.

Walking into Bennet's office, Wellbeck and Lanier found the assistant secretary leaning back in the swivel chair behind the desk, grinning broadly, his tie loosened, his feet resting on an open desk drawer—the bureaucrat's equivalent of a hunter resting his foot on the neck of a slain lion. Except the lion in question here was back at his office at the Pentagon.

There was something strangely impersonal about Bennet's office, which gave no sense of its occupant. The large American flag on a stanchion that stood behind his desk, as well as the pedestrian collection of pictures on the walls—travel posters from Swissair showing the Grande Place in Brussels, the Trevi Fountain in Rome, and the Jet d'Eau in Geneva—had been there when Bennet arrived. The only evidence that the office belonged to Dan Bennet was the framed presidential order appointing him an assistant secretary of state.

"I take it we won," Wellbeck said.

"Can't you ever think of anything but winning?" Bennet asked in a stern mock-parental tone. "It's not whether you've won or lost, it's how you've played the game."

Wellbeck and Lanier laughed. Then Bennet, too, broke out in a nasal guffaw. If there was anyone alive who cared less about *how* he won or more about *whether* he won than Bennet, neither Lanier nor Wellbeck had ever met him. For Dan Bennet, as for Vince Lombardi, winning was the *only* thing.

Bennet continued, "The secretary was superb: In the NSPG he was cool, calm, steady—fully in command. In the car coming back to the department he told me it had been pretty acrimonious in the pre-meeting he had with the president, Ryder, and Wallace."

Bennet's ice-blue eyes gleamed with satisfaction. "That pre-meeting was the key. Without it I'm not certain we could have pulled it off. Winthrop told me the president balked at first; he was worried he'd find it difficult to explain an apparent shift away from what he's been saying without some move from the Soviets that would justify a change. Ryder was on the way to convincing him he'd destroy his credibility if he met with Novikov."

"So what brought him around?" Lanier asked.

"Winthrop convinced the Old Man that Novikov's asking for a summit could be explained as a victory for the president's tough rhetoric and hard-line policies. Winthrop knew he'd never go for a summit unless it could be explained as a vindication of his policies—and that's exactly how he played it."

"I'll bet Ryder was shitting in his pants," Wellbeck said with relish.

"You could say he was not pleased." Bennet grinned. "He kept repeating that catchphrase of his—you know, 'If I say any more, I would only be repeating myself.' " Bennet brought his feet down onto the floor with a thump. "Unfortunately, he managed to throw up a bit of a roadblock to my being designated to go to Moscow for the planning talks. The question of who goes is now to be considered along with the papers that'll go to the president when he gets back from vacation. Mitchell's on our side, but we'll need a paper he can use to get a sign-off from the president."

"We'll be lucky if we don't get saddled with an interagency delegation. Defense is sure to press for a gang-bang," Wellbeck said.

"So what else is new?" Bennet snapped. "Of course that's what they'll want. It's up to us to argue effectively against sending a group. Fortunately, the Russians have helped my case by specifically inviting an individual, not a delegation. . . ."

Bennet stopped and stared out the window at nothing in particular. His expression became distant, reflective. There was a silence while the others waited to see what more he would say.

"Look," he continued, "let's outline the paper we need right now. First, we should argue that there's no point in getting into an immediate disagreement with the Soviets over a trivial procedural point. Second, Novikov has gone out on a limb in proposing a summit; we don't want to put him in an awkward position by opening the proposal up to a lot of bureaucratic second-guessing."

His quintessentially WASP features complacent, Bennet added, "We should emphasize that we ought to be helping Novikov, encouraging him along a reformist line. There's bound to be a struggle under way over what direction they'll take. We should try to strengthen the hand of the moderates."

"Hey," Lanier interjected, "we should be able to get Hal Engel to produce a paper supporting that view. It's a natural position for the CIA to take. At least it's the way they've argued in the past."

"Good," Bennet said. "That's point three. Point four is this: I want a paper making these points before you guys go home today so I can run a draft by Wallace tonight. We're both going to the Kennedy Center to see the new Andrew Lloyd Webber musical. We've got the presidential box."

Wellbeck nodded vigorously. "Wallace is the key. He's the last guy to see the president at the end of the day and the first guy to brief him in the morning."

Bennet frowned. Wellbeck hadn't been as impressed as he should have been. A small black mark went up next to his name on the tote board nestled in Dan Bennet's cerebral cortex.

Unaware of his gaffe, Wellbeck continued unabated, "Trouble is, he's dumb. It's all those years standing too close to hundred-fifty-five-millimeter howitzers."

"Who said life was easy?" Bennet replied. "Wallace may be dumb, but he's *our* dumb. Find me a smart guy who'll work our side of the street, get him appointed national security adviser by this president, get him to support our positions at the NSC, then we'll get along without Wallace. Until then we'll send him our drafts. We'll listen politely and attentively to his windy views. We'll make the revisions he wishes." Bennet paused for effect. "And we'll pretend not to notice if he catches his necktie in his clipboard."

He scrunched close to his desk. "Next, we've got our work cut out for us on the summit work program. Waterman raised hell about the arms-control paper, and Wallace backed down. That paper's going to be done in the interagency group that Waterman cochairs. That's bad news because—"

"Just a minute," Wellbeck interrupted. "You mean the arms-control work's gonna be done in an IG cochaired by Waterman and Judy Shannon?"

"That's precisely what I mean," Bennet replied with another frown for the interruption. Two black marks now for Wellbeck. "When Waterman pounded the table and demanded to do the work in the arms-control IG, I was hardly in a position to object, because the department is already represented. My sister in Christ, ambassador extraordinaire and plenipotentiary, Judith Shannon—*Mizz* Judith Shannon to you male-chauvinist swine—distinguished officer of the Foreign Service of the United States, cochairs the arms-control IG."

"But," Wellbeck protested, "there's no way we can count on Shannon. She doesn't know shit about arms control. She's only chaired the IG for a month."

"I know." Bennet looked pained. "Believe me, if I could have turned it around, I would have. But it was clear that Waterman was going to get Ryder to make a federal case out of it, and Wallace knew he'd lose if Ryder went to the president."

"So what do we do?" Lanier asked. "The arms-control issues are the key. That's all the Soviets are really interested in."

"The first thing we do," Bennet replied, "is make sure that participation in the IG is limited to two people from State, two from Defense, and one each from JCS, CIA, NSC, and ACDA. That'll take a little maneuvering, because at the meeting this morning we agreed on only one participant from each agency. But I'm sure I can get Mitchell to expand it to two each from State and Defense.

"Then we designate Wellbeck as the second State person. With just you and Shannon," he said, looking meaningfully at Wellbeck, "I'm confident that you'll wind up in control—or don't bother to come home."

"But she'll want her own guy," Lanier protested.

"Ah, Bob, you underestimate me. I engineered the setting-up of a new compartment to control access to the interagency group—it'll be very closely held. *Very* closely held. I'll get word to the secretary this afternoon that the EUR bureau has to be represented, especially since *I've* got the working relationship with Wallace. Shannon doesn't get along with Wallace because he's not a fucking FSO. I'm not worried about getting you designated as the second State person on the IG."

"What's this new compartment?" Wellbeck asked.

"Just what you'd expect. To get access to the papers prepared by a specially designated group made up of members of the arms-control IG, you have to be cleared for a new code word. It'll be called 'Dartmouth.' The group will have a cover assignment: 'What new proposals might Novikov make, and how would we respond to them?' No one is to acknowledge anywhere—including the department—that this work is being done in preparation for a summit. And access is to be limited to members of the group.

"Of course," Bennet continued with a sardonic chuckle, "in the real world it'll be all over the building in no time. We might as well put up a notice in the cafeteria."

"Dan, you're gonna have a problem with that approach," said Lanier. "Okay, so Shannon's a bitch. Okay, so she's an asshole. But she's also an assistant secretary—just like you. And you know she'll be out to screw you every chance she gets if she's not taken out properly."

"And what do you suggest?" Bennet asked archly.

"Judith Shannon's a bureaucrat at heart. She's an old-time FSO. So neutralize her with a piece of paper."

"Such as?" Bennet's eyebrows rose. The kid was all right.

Lanier cracked his knuckles, making Wellbeck wince. "A memo from the secretary to the Executive Secretariat."

"Not a bad idea," Bennet replied. He turned to Wellbeck: "Bob, draft a memo for Winthrop's signature to the Secretariat indicating that he wants *both* Politico-military Affairs *and* EUR represented in the 'Dartmouth' channel, therefore he's designating Shannon and you to represent the department. Get it to Phil before four—that's when I see the secretary.

"Phil, as soon as you've got Bob's draft, have Alice type it up on the secretary's letterhead so I can get a signature before I leave the room. It's safer that way."

"Shannon's gonna be pissing mad when she gets hit with a memo she didn't have a chance to coordinate on," Wellbeck said. "Wouldn't it be better to try to work it out with her—you know, schmooze a little?"

"No way," Bennet said. "Phil's right: She'll want that little asshole who works the arms-control issues for her to have the second slot. She's got no incentive to let you in. She's pissed enough already at having been kept out of the NSPG this morning."

He slipped his feet back onto his desk drawer. "By the way, either of you guys know what Waterman's doing in some all-day meeting the day after tomorrow that he says is more important than the summit work program? We ought to know what he's up to."

"It's some meeting about technical transfers—you know, high-tech stuff going to the Eastern bloc," Wellbeck said. "COCOM—the coordinating committee with our allies that meets in Paris and decides on what we will and won't sell to the Warsaw Pact—"

"I know what COCOM is," Bennet interrupted huffily. "What I want to know is what Waterman's doing."

"All I know is Defense has been pushing some initiative with COCOM. It's being handled by the Econ Bureau."

"I want to know *exactly* what he's up to," Bennet insisted, tapping his desk with one foot for emphasis. "Get a detailed report on Waterman's activities, what he's saying, who he's seeing. And let me know what instructions have already gone out."

"I'll get someone on it right away," Wellbeck said.

Bennet made his way up the stairs at the end of the hall and, pausing long enough to punch in the five-digit code, opened the cipher-locked door to the hallway leading to the secretary's suite. The secretary's office was down the hall and recessed through an inner corridor. Beyond his main office was a small, intimate private office filled, like many of the State Department's most important rooms, with American antiques coaxed over the years from the collections of wealthy contributors to the State Department's antique furnishing fund.

"You can go on in, Mr. Bennet. The secretary's expecting you," said Renalda Astrich, Winthrop's tall, thin, red-headed secretary for more than twenty years.

Bennet entered Winthrop's small inner office. A fire burned in the fire-place; the smoky scent of burning maple filled the room. In addition to the early-American furniture, two cabinet chairs from Winthrop's earlier service in previous administrations sat facing his small desk. Both were adorned with brass plates commemorating his years of service.

The secretary of state was seated in a wingback chair facing the door; his feet, which otherwise would have been left dangling, rested on a Louis XIII ottoman covered in a Gobelin remnant. He had exchanged his suit jacket for a worn rust-colored cardigan. A stack of papers, many of them bearing the distinctive red-tabbed cover sheet used for Top Secret documents, sat on the end table by his side. He motioned Bennet to take a seat in a matching chair opposite his own. Bennet did so, comfortably. He was at home in surroundings such as these. Indeed, Daniel Isherwood Bennet of Chestnut Hill and Palm Beach enjoyed the perquisites of birth: His ancestors had come to America before the Revolutionary War. His trust fund was sufficient to allow him the freedom to work at what he wanted, as opposed to what was necessary to earn a living. His education came at Exeter and Dartmouth, where he majored in political science and minored in skiing and tennis. Afterward, he had selected journalism as his trade, becoming a low-paid staffer for *The New Republic.* There in the cramped offices in downtown Washington, he developed a worldview that was vaguely centrist but he wrote and argued in traditional, fashionable liberal prose.

Bennet's career at State traced back to a free-lance speech-writing assignment he'd undertaken for Anthony Winthrop eight years before, when Winthrop, then the CEO of a Chicago-based holding company, had been invited to take part in a Washington forum on international monetary policy. Winthrop's talk was to focus on whether or not a humanistic approach toward economics was possible, and Bennet's speech, larded with esoteric references to Jeremy Bentham, William Godwin, Thomas Paine, and Malthus, was literary, witty—and largely borrowed from an obscure French work, *The Growth of Philosophic Radicalism.* It was a great success.

After his appointment as secretary of state, Winthrop remembered the earnest young man in the polka-dot bow tie whose words had made his appearance the lead paragraph of the next day's article in *The Wall Street Journal.* Bennet was summoned to Foggy Bottom, where he was offered a job as a special assistant. Much to Winthrop's surprise, he turned the position down but offered himself up as a candidate for another, more visible job. After a week of quiet negotiation Bennet—to the dismay of the State Department's Foreign Service professionals—was announced as Winthrop's choice to be assistant secretary of state for European and Canadian affairs.

"Well, Dan," Winthrop began, "we're off and running. It's taken a long time, but we're finally out of the blocks. You deserve a lot of the credit. You should be pleased."

"There's a great deal yet ahead of us, sir," said Bennet, pulling a memo out of the folder he'd tucked under his arm and handing it across to Winthrop. "This is the next step. I hate to trouble you with these trivial procedural issues, Mr. Secretary, but unless you act right away, I'm afraid we'll lose a week arguing over who will represent the department in the special IG that's being set up to prepare arms-control papers.

"I suggest Judith Shannon, who cochairs the IG with Michael Waterman, and Bob Wellbeck should be our two representatives. I really need Wellbeck there to deal with Waterman. You know Judy—she's tough as nails. But she's not really up on the substance—and it can get awfully technical, as you know. Wellbeck is solid on the substance, and he's a pit bull on these interagency matters."

Bennet put on his most disarming Boy Scout expression—and continued, "There's another reason for having Wellbeck there, too. You know how important our quiet collaboration with Wallace has been in all this. We'd never have got where we are without him. Wallace trusts me. But he's made it pretty plain he has doubts about Judy. And Judy doesn't like him. I worry about not having someone from my shop there to make sure that Wallace is with us."

Winthrop waved Bennet off. "I believe you, Dan. You've made your point." He looked at his aide. "Now, who's going to complain if I sign this? It really should go through the full coordination process, you know."

"Frankly, that's just what I want to avoid. All it would do is alert half a dozen people to the fact that there's a new compartment they're not cleared for. It drives people crazy around here to be cut out of anything, especially some super-secret interagency operation. They all hold the same view: If *anyone* at the Pentagon is cleared, *everyone* at the State Department should be cleared, right down to the garage attendant at the C Street entrance."

Winthrop nodded. "You're right about that, Dan. Okay—I'll designate Shannon and Wellbeck." Taking a pen from his pocket, he signed the memo and handed it back to Bennet.

"I really appreciate this, sir."

"You just make sure that Wellbeck finds a way to get along with Judy. She's sometimes . . . well . . . let's say she's highly protective of her . . . her domain."

"That may be the kindest description ever of Shannon's territorial drive," Bennet said. He saw the secretary's eyes flicker and he decided to drop the subject.

After more than five years of working for him, Bennet had learned about the care and handling of Anthony Winthrop. You didn't make wisecracks. You didn't denigrate. You never used profanity, and you always looked presentable. Winthrop was old-fashioned in a courtly sort of way. He was, Bennet supposed, the sort of man who, as a British diplomat in the mid-nineteenth century, would have always worn thick black worsted, except in the hottest of the tropics, where he would have worn thick white flannel.

"Mr. Secretary," he said, "can you say something more about the pre-meeting? You said as the NSPG was ending that you'd fill me in more thoroughly later. It would be helpful for me to know how Ryder reacted and how he argued. After all, I'm certain to get the same arguments from Waterman."

In fact, what Bennet really wanted was the most inside characterization he could get of the conversation among the president, the secretaries of state and defense, and the national security adviser. He couldn't have cared less about the arguments Ryder had used. But knowing what the president said in a small, elite gathering, Bennet could use it to impress his own staff with his proximity to power, to demonstrate to the press that he was well within the inner circle, to intimidate others in the State Department and in other government departments by suggesting that he knew better—and earlier—those preferences of the president that would ultimately become national policy. It was easy to gain the rapt attention of a Washington dinner party if you had good stuff out of the White House to share.

Winthrop was happy enough to share the conversation with Bennet. "I think I already indicated," he began, "that the way the president raised it didn't leave a lot of room for Ryder to protest. He simply said he'd had a backchannel message from Novikov, that Novikov wanted a summit, and he'd decided this was the right time to collect on our investment."

"He actually used the phrase 'collect on our investment'?"

"Yes. Said it twice. He seemed to like the sound of it. I expected him to repeat it during the NSPG. You know how when he gets attached to a phrase he tends to use it over and over again."

Bennet nodded agreement. "Perhaps we ought to reinforce the investment idea—'it's the strength of our position that has brought Novikov to the table'—that sort of thing?"

"It's our most effective strategy. Where a lot of people in this administration go wrong is to think the way to sway the president is to tell him that what he's doing—which is consistent with everything he's ever stood for all his life—is wrong."

Winthrop smiled complacently. "The previous secretary of state used to go into those meetings—the president told me this, Dan—and say things like 'You can't do that, Mr. President.' Let me tell you, Dan, say *that* to this president—or any other president—and you can forget it. You've already lost."

Bennet nodded. "And Ryder?"

"Oh," Winthrop said, "he's much too smart to tell the president he's wrong. Besides, he's known him a long time. Much longer than I have. I think he's afraid the president's thinking may be changing. He watches the president's reactions. Now he's not so sure about Novikov. None of us are, really. He keeps saying to McCandless, 'Get us more on Novikov. More on Novikov.' "

"What do you think, sir?" Bennet asked almost too deferentially.

But the secretary, eager to expound, didn't pick it up.

"I think we'll never know until we meet Novikov face-to-face. And I'm not sure it matters. We've got to deal with whoever they put up. When you have two countries with the power to destroy each other—and the rest of the world—you've got to find a way to settle differences. There's no other way."

"Could I come back to the pre-meeting for a moment?" Bennet asked with studied casualness. "Was there anything there that would suggest what Ryder's going to do? For example, will he acquiesce and cooperate, or will he try to undermine the summit? I know Waterman will do everything he can to derail us. And he's going to be important, because so much of the work's going to take place in the IG. Is he on firm ground with Ryder? What's your sense of where we're headed?"

"I imagine that Ryder will go all out. He'll fight us every inch of the way. He'll portray Novikov in the worst possible light. He'll produce statistics on their tank production, the massive military investment they seem unable to turn off. It all feeds into his view, which is that we must oppose them with armed strength."

Winthrop leaned forward in his chair and retrieved the fireplace poker from its brass stand. He pushed the burning logs around, releasing a shower of sparks. The fire, which had been slowly dying, came back to life. "I think we've got to be strong. If it were up to me, I'd increase the defense budget and lay on additional taxes to pay for it. It's this crazy opposition, from guys like Burner, to any tax increase that's depressing the defense budget, after all.

"But being strong doesn't mean giving the Soviets the back of our hand at every opportunity. This summit is an open door—and we at State have been the ones to pry it open."

The secretary examined the backs of his hands. "And gotten our fair share of bruised knuckles in the process, eh, Dan?"

Bennet nodded. "That's diplomatically put, sir."

Winthrop smiled. "Well, I'll be damned if I'm going to let Jim Ryder slam that door shut again."

Bennet looked at Winthrop appreciatively. "I thought that's what you'd say. And I want you to know we'll win this one." He stood up to leave. "Thanks for finding time to see me," he said. "I'll leave the memo designating Shannon and Wellbeck with Renalda."

Back in his office, Bennet found an envelope marked with a red tab on his desk. He tore it open at once and read intently.

Memorandum: Department of State
SECRET-SENSITIVE

TO: EUR/Assistant Secretary Bennet
FROM: EUR/Bob Wellbeck
DATE: September 16
SUBJECT: Waterman on the Loose at COCOM

Waterman's up to no good at COCOM. I know you think COCOM's a backwater bureaucracy, but if Waterman has his way, it could become a summit-buster. I've checked with Econ Bureau, Shannon's office, and our rep at COCOM, Andrew Miskell, who's in town for Waterman's meeting. Here's the picture:

1. Waterman is set to present a U.S. proposal at a COCOM Plenary the day after tomorrow. It could lead to DOD gaining effective control of COCOM and a nasty confrontation with Moscow.

2. DOD got the lead on this months ago after Econ Bureau cut a deal with Waterman. The deal: Waterman wants to set up a group of Defense advisers to COCOM to do technical and intelligence assessments of Soviet strategy for stealing Western technology. He got the NSC on board after Econ signed off—largely, I gather, because it had no support in Paris, and they were sure it would fail.

3. Now the bad news: Miskell says several delegations have softened their opposition. The French are actually backing it and have been actively lobbying the Brits and Germans. Because they were adamantly opposed earlier, the French turnaround could have a big impact.

4. Miskell will phone me as soon as he gets more on Waterman's game plan—I'll report to you immediately. In the meantime I've got calls in to the French and Brits to see what they can tell us.

5. The bottom line: By day after tomorrow Waterman will probably get an agreement to set up a COCOM group reporting to Ministries of Defense. We'll surely lose control of COCOM activities.

Moreover, we'll start to see lurid press stories on Soviet intelligence operations to steal our technology—the sort of spy stuff the media loves. It all adds up to bad news on the eve of a summit. We should do whatever we can to stop it.

. . .

    As he read, Bennet understood at once the trouble that was brewing. No one had ever heard of COCOM, partly because it was a State Department responsibility and was run discreetly. With Defense controlling a major COCOM activity, it would be hustled from obscurity—just in time to poison the atmosphere before the summit. Waterman was fishing in troubled waters, all right.

    Bennet finished reading, snatched the phone, and pounded the intercom button with his knuckle. "Get me the assistant secretary of state for economic and business affairs on the line—*now!*" he ordered brusquely.

CHAPTER FIVE

Washington, September 17, 4:45 P.M.

Waterman sat in the backseat reading through his black loose-leaf briefing book as the car inched from the Pentagon through the dense Washington rush-hour traffic. The meeting, for which he was hurriedly making last-minute changes to his talking points, had suddenly, in light of the forthcoming summit, taken on new significance. He looked at his watch: Delegates from COCOM's fifteen member nations would be arriving by now at the diplomatic entrance to the State Department on C Street. This was only a reception. The real work would take place tomorrow, when the business meeting got under way. Tonight it was drinks and small talk with the delegates, followed by a private dinner with François Arnaudet, Waterman's counterpart at the French Ministry of Defense. Waterman looked forward to the dinner, but he loathed the small talk among the milling bureaucrats, forced exchanges with Greeks and Belgians, Germans and Brits, few of whom he could identify but all of whom, it seemed, identified him and expected him to know them. When Laura was there it wasn't so bad. She had an uncanny ability to associate names and faces. And she had learned long ago to step forward and introduce herself before it became apparent that Michael hadn't a clue who stood before him. The reception was duty; dinner with Arnaudet would be a pleasure.

On Waterman's last visit to Paris, François had taken him to Restaurant

Taillevent, where they had dined superbly on a seafood sausage studded with truffles, followed by grilled duck liver, and washed down with Montrachet and Chambertin. Tonight, Waterman would reciprocate by cooking at home. Waterman was a good cook, but this was hardly a fair exchange. The best thing about COCOM, he thought as he fought to concentrate on a boring account of its last meeting, was that it was based in Paris.

COCOM's mission was to maintain an embargo that would keep sensitive Western technology out of Soviet hands. To accomplish this, it brought together, at its dingy headquarters, the representatives of the member countries to negotiate lists of those technologies that would not be sold to the Soviet Union and its allies.

For years the Department of Defense had been trying to get COCOM member nations to do a better job of enforcing the embargo. But there was lethargy in Paris and indifference elsewhere. Soviet agents roamed freely everywhere, buying the technology they needed for military programs. Western governments would turn a blind eye to the purchases, often made through dummy corporations. And when the Soviets could not purchase what they wanted, they simply stole it.

Then, in the early 1980s, the Directorate for Surveillance of the Territory, or DST, the branch of French intelligence responsible for countering espionage and terrorism, recruited an agent in Moscow. The agent, codenamed "Ciao," was a senior official of the KGB's Directorate T, the bureau in charge of stealing advanced technology from Western nations.

Ciao reported that more than five thousand Soviet military programs used stolen Western technology. He also identified the Soviet organization put together specifically for the purpose of stealing it, the GKNT. Not as well known as the KGB, the GKNT consisted of twenty thousand professionals, including intelligence agents, whose full-time job was to acquire the West's best technology. Ciao provided the French—and through them the United States—with thousands of pages of staff papers prepared at GKNT headquarters. There were status reports and requests for money to pull off operations in Germany, France, Japan, and the United States. Ciao even delivered the names of specific engineering groups and individual technicians within Western companies targeted by the GKNT.

When the head of French intelligence, Alain Marron, was taken into a room where the files had been laid out for his inspection, he gasped. Not in thirty years on the job had he ever seen such a haul.

The documents read like a mail-order catalog. They listed the names and numbers of military projects, who was assigned to carry them out—the KGB, GRU, Moscow University, the U.S.-U.S.S.R. Trade and Economic

Council, etc.—the budget in rubles and hard currency, the nomenclature and part numbers for the Western equipment, the dates by which they were required, even substitutes, should the object of choice prove unattainable, rank ordered by cost-effectiveness.

CIA Director McCandless and DST Chief Marron told the president about Ciao at a dramatic briefing inside a special facility at CIA headquarters known to be absolutely secure. The president was taken aback. Shocked by the scope and success of the Soviet operation, he immediately ordered a major effort to strengthen the COCOM embargo. Millions of dollars were transferred from the Defense budget to the Customs Service so a new corps of specially trained agents could be put in the field to track down Soviet techno-bandits.

Waterman had been delighted with the apparent new resolve. But no embargo could be effective without the cooperation of all the countries capable of supplying militarily sensitive technology to the Soviets. The support of one or two—or even a majority—wouldn't do it. Only a comprehensive program could work, and *only* if a way could be found around the tired, trade-promoting diplo-bureaucrats who ran COCOM largely to promote commercial interests and with little regard for security. So Waterman had spent two years shuttling back and forth to Paris, pressing for consultations aimed at bringing the Allies together in support of a tightened embargo, and trying to set up a military subcommittee at COCOM to light a fire under it.

He was tireless. The argument for a military subcommittee was worked into the secretary's talking points on every occasion when he met with defense ministers from COCOM member countries. It was written into Ryder's speeches; it was a prominent feature in Waterman's backgrounders for the press. When a cache of embargoed American high-performance computers was intercepted en route from Sweden to Moscow, Waterman saw to it that *The Washington Post* got the lurid details. He raised the subcommittee idea at every opportunity. When Allied officials came to him for help, they heard about COCOM. When they came to complain, they had to sit through a lecture about COCOM before they could get their complaint on the table.

Eventually, Waterman succeeded in getting his Pentagon colleagues to go along with the idea of granting requests coming from COCOM members only if they would support the military subcommittee. The Allies complained loudly, especially to the State Department, but little by little they began to give ground. Finally, the battles were cut short when Ciao delivered twelve thousand pages of secret documents, and the French discovered that nearly fifty Soviet agents in France were stealing French technology. The French position toward COCOM generally—and the military subcommittee especially—changed dramatically. Then Ciao was caught and secretly executed.

Waterman moved immediately to get the French to go public with Ciao's material. After some months of resistance, he got them to agree. Moreover, he managed to do it through François Arnaudet without State ever getting wind of it. Now he was on his way to launch the next step in the campaign to breathe life into COCOM, armed, for the first time, with real ammunition.

His first task was to brief Andrew Miskell, the newly appointed U.S. delegate to COCOM, on his plan to use the Ciao material at tomorrow's meeting to shock COCOM into action, just as the president had been shocked earlier.

Miskell was new to COCOM. He had been on post only six months now. It had taken a month to find a suitable—and affordable—apartment, buy a car, and handle the kilos of official paperwork the French bureaucracy piled on all resident diplomats. So he was still coming up to speed, still learning his way around the peculiarities of the various national delegations—not to mention trying to duck whenever the departments of State, Defense, and Commerce blasted one another over how COCOM issues ought to be handled. He was also too new to be adamantly opposed to strengthening the embargo—or so Waterman hoped.

There were no surprises in the briefing book, which he snapped shut just as the car pulled up at the State Department.

Miskell was waiting at the entrance, shaking hands and welcoming his colleagues from Paris as the convoy of limousines disgorged them through the glass doors of the State Department diplomatic entrance.

"Welcome to Washington," said Waterman, stretching out his hand. "I'm sorry about this morning. I got tied up with the secretary," he lied graciously. He took the diplomat aside. "Andy, I've got something important to discuss before the meeting. Can you take a few minutes now? Maybe we could use an empty office."

"Sure, there's one in the Econ Bureau; they keep it for visiting firemen like me."

The two men made their way to a fifth-floor suite of offices occupied by the Bureau of Economic and Business Affairs, the State Department office responsible for COCOM.

"In here," Miskell said, ushering Waterman into the office near the door.

"Andy," Waterman began, "you know we've been looking for a way to shake our COCOM partners from their lethargy. I don't need to tell you how we've been hemorrhaging. When we talked in Paris, I was aware how bad the situation was. Now it's gone from bad to worse. Besides, you weren't cleared for some 'Blue Border' material that had a string of code words as long as your arm. I couldn't tell you what we knew. But now, the president's decided to share the information. We got it some time ago, through a Soviet agent recruited by French intelligence. He was caught and executed recently. The French have agreed to let us widen the circle of people who know some of what we learned from him. In fact, for reasons of their own, they wish to create the impression that Ciao—that's the agent's name—was under American control. So we're to give no indication this was a French operation."

"I had an idea this was coming," Miskell said. "There have been rumors about an agent ever since I got to Paris."

Still, Miskell's eyes widened as Waterman described the cache of documents Ciao had delivered, the amazing breadth and depth of the Soviet effort to obtain Western technology. As he went through the list of weapons systems that had utilized American, Japanese, French, German, and British technology, it sounded to Miskell like an inventory of Warsaw Pact military forces. He thought back to the hours spent in dreary meetings. Suddenly, everything came to life.

"The French," said Waterman, "have given me approval to discuss the Ciao material in detail. They've gotten behind our package of measures to strengthen COCOM, including the proposal to establish a committee of military experts to supplement the diplomatic discussions in regular COCOM meetings."

Miskell rapped the table with his knuckles. "So that explains it," he said. "I'd noticed a change. But I didn't know how, or why. It's having its effect on the Germans and Brits, too. For the first time since I arrived in Paris, they've stopped openly bad-mouthing your proposals."

"I'm sure of it. The hard part was gaining French cooperation, first to support our initiatives, then to get approval for the use of the Ciao material. The rest won't be easy, but it's doable."

Listening, Miskell got swept up in Waterman's sense of mission. He became surprisingly enthusiastic about the prospects for rousing COCOM and exhilarated that he would have a major role in it. His State Department colleagues would think he'd gone over to the other side. But, dammit, he thought, Waterman's got a point.

"Are you going to the reception?" Miskell asked.

"Just for a few minutes," Waterman replied. "I'm cooking dinner tonight for François Arnaudet."

"Who's that?"

"My counterpart at the French Defense Ministry. Actually, he's a French Foreign Service officer assigned to the Defense Ministry. Without François the French position would be as bad as the German. He's been an enormous help."

"Maybe he could use his contacts at the Foreign Ministry to push the State Department a little," Miskell said helpfully.

"Not a bad idea," Waterman replied. "I'll raise it over dinner."

Waterman could hear his wife in the shower as he made his way straight for the upstairs bedroom to change out of the dark gray worsted he was wearing into a pair of casual slacks and a navy blazer. The bed was piled high with sweaters—Laura was obviously bringing woolens out of summer storage and reorganizing the walk-in closet they shared in a way she insisted was fair: 80 percent for her, everything else for him. He changed quickly and opened the door to the large, skylit, steam-filled bathroom.

"I'm home," he shouted over the sound of the water and the Beethoven string quartet that was playing on the waterproof radio in the shower.

"I'll be out in a minute," Laura said. Waterman could see her through the glass shower door, her long black hair thick with shampoo, her smooth dark skin reddened by the water she always kept as hot as possible and far hotter than he could stand. Her face was turned toward the opening at the top of the glass door, eyes closed. She called out without ever opening them, "The salad greens are mostly washed, the eggs for the soufflé have been separated, and the potatoes are peeled but not sliced. You had two messages. They're both on your desk. And François called to say he'd be a little late, half an hour or so. Oh, and the table's set. I used the good china. And Jason's got a sleepover at Michael Pietrowski's."

"Great! I'll be in the kitchen," he shouted back.

Waterman came round the corner into the kitchen–dining area and saw the table. It was beautifully done with Laura's sensuous eye: rose-colored linen, rose-and-cream Limoges china, gleaming Baccarat crystal, a floral arrangement of roses and wildflowers.

There was only one thing wrong: The table had been set for three. She'd obviously misunderstood. She was to help get dinner ready and then disappear. This was no social occasion—it was business.

Waterman knew that with Laura present, François would shy away from discussing the issue at hand. While the Frenchman liked Laura, he was bound to be reserved in discussing sensitive matters in her presence. In any case, Laura's good humor just wasn't the right backdrop for strategizing about COCOM. So Laura was not included. But she had assumed otherwise, forcing Waterman to disinvite her. Damn. It wasn't going to be pleasant.

Waterman continued into the kitchen. The separated eggs and some grated lemon peel sat in glass bowls alongside the mixer that would be used to beat the egg whites for the soufflé. The salad greens sat on the counter in three neat bunches. Three cloves of garlic, which he'd need for the salad dressing, sat on a small piece of wax paper near the electric chopper. When Laura was involved, everything was in perfect order. Indeed, their time in the kitchen was a yin-yang struggle between order and disorder.

This was the pattern of their relationship—the tension between his easy and disorganized manner and her disciplined, meticulous management of every detail. That and the prominence of kitchens. They'd met by chance in the greasy kitchen of a youth hostel in Chartres, in the ninth month of Waterman's sixteen-month European walkabout. He was twenty-five and a Princeton ABD; she was twenty, a transplanted North Carolinian about to enter her senior year as an art major at American University in Washington, D.C., and the most beautiful, lank-hipped creature Waterman had ever laid eyes on. So beautiful, in fact, that the prizewinning debater was struck dumb and did not dare to make conversation.

She had scrutinized Waterman through long lashes unsullied by mascara, marveling at what he could do with chicken, butter, fresh herbs, vegetables, a bottle of *vin ordinaire*, and a beat-up sauté pan, on the hostel's one burner. He, of course, had seen her stare and found his tongue long enough to stammer impulsively an invitation to dinner. She'd accepted. And after the simple but good food and nearly two bottles of wine, they'd ended up talking all night in the optimistic tones of innocents abroad, about themselves, their dreams, their hopes. For Waterman, who had never opened himself up like this to anyone in his life, it had been an emotional epiphany.

It was one of those relationships that happens so easily overseas to young Americans who have never before traveled alone in a foreign country: an instantaneous bonding of heart, soul, and mind that comes like a flash. And so, even before they shared *café au lait* and *petits pains* at dawn the next day, their hands shyly entwined as they walked to the café; before they had ever kissed, or held each other in their arms, they were, they knew, deeply, absolutely, and completely in love.

It was a relationship that lasted the remainder of Waterman's European odyssey and Laura's senior year, buttressed by scores of letters and cards and phone calls that wreaked havoc on both their budgets. It was a relationship kept intense even at long distance until Waterman came back to the United States and flew to Washington, arriving unannounced on a rainy, cold February evening. She'd opened the door to her off-campus apartment to see him standing there dripping, a carry-on bag draped over his shoulder, a half-frozen bunch of flowers clutched in his hand, a dumb, lovesick smile on his face. They were married by a justice of the peace three months later—before she'd even graduated, much to her parents' dismay.

But things had worked out. Waterman found his calling on the staff of Arthur Winter. Laura, degree in hand, found a place as a graphic designer at a small, successful ad agency in Rosslyn. They enjoyed the perfect two-income, upwardly mobile life. They had their friends, their causes, and they had time for each other.

He cooked up a storm in the narrow galley kitchen of their rented Capitol Hill town house—a dinner party a week in the best of times. They spent their vacations in Paris and London, Vienna and Siena, sharing the world and its pleasures without a care. He was written up in *The Washington Post* as one of the area's undiscovered amateur chefs—the article tickled him so much he had it framed and hung it in the kitchen. Then, five years ago, Waterman had gone to DOD, and they'd had Jason—and their lives had changed forever.

They'd tried to have a child for three years, and they joyfully bought the house in Chevy Chase as a present to themselves—and their unborn offspring—the week they discovered Laura was pregnant. Six months later, Waterman was hired by Ryder, an unexpected job offer for which he had not campaigned but by which he was thrilled and excited, and even before his Senate confirmation—a breeze—his fifty-hour workweek had doubled.

In the ensuing five years he had made 72 overseas trips, nearly 100 domestic ones, worked 204 weekends, and made it home for dinner 139 times—less than two nights in seven. The situation was not good. He'd become a virtual stranger in his own house.

Three weeks earlier he had been in London on Laura's birthday. He'd called from the embassy on Grosvenor Square to say that he was catching a special military flight to Andrews Air Force Base, just outside Washington, and—despite the time change—he'd be home in plenty of time to cook her a lavish dinner and share a bottle of champagne. He didn't mention the sterling Georgian serving forks he had found for her in the London Silver Vaults on Chancery Lane.

But his flight was delayed ten hours. He'd snuck through the front door at two in the morning to discover Laura had turned down his side of the bed, placed a mint on his pillow, and left a note. It read, *There will be no more room service.*

The toughest challenge they'd faced since Waterman had gone to the Pentagon and become submerged in a bone-crushing schedule was not parenthood. It was the loss of Laura's personal and professional identity. She'd enjoyed a certain growing reputation as a designer. Clients had sought out the agency because of her originality and ability to make something special out of the mundane. Her acrylic canvases, done in a greenhouse studio, were sold by a small but fashionable gallery on P Street.

Then, when Waterman went to work for Jim Ryder, her world changed. She decided to stay home and raise Jason, believing it was more important to be with her son than it was to work—which she still held to be true. But as an assistant secretary, Waterman had social responsibilities he'd never had to assume on the Hill. When he had worked for Arthur Winter, he'd not been called upon to represent the United States government at social functions. Now, it was a vital part of his job description. The upshot of all their newfound socializing was that Laura discovered, much to her consternation, that wives of government officials were treated as nonpersons.

Previously, when the Watermans, he of the Senate Armed Services Committee and she of the Satyaloka Advertising Agency, had gone to a dinner, they had been introduced as "Michael, who works on the Hill, and Laura, who's an up-and-coming artist." Now they were announced as "Secretary Waterman and Mrs. Waterman."

For Laura, official occasions became a form of protracted torture, from which she always felt unable to escape. Her schedule was now filled with an unending stream of meaningless events, teas, and small talk. She hated protocol—and let Waterman know it. He protested there was nothing he could do.

She refused to accompany him on official visits anymore. The final straw had been a NATO trip to Holland earlier in the year. It had begun with a motorcade in which, through a series of bureaucratic errors, Laura was assigned to the staff bus, while Waterman was whisked away in the secretary of defense's limo. Then the luggage van broke down, so the staff bus was delayed nearly an hour at the airport while the luggage was transferred to it. Waterman, meanwhile, was relaxing in a hot bath in their hotel room. When she arrived, fuming, he announced that she had only twenty-five minutes to prepare for the official reception–cocktail party and reminded her that she had to do duty on the receiving line. She told him what he could do with his reception in words Waterman had previously believed she had not known.

The next morning, while Waterman accompanied Ryder—whose wife had mercifully not made the trip—to a series of meetings indoors, Laura, not in the best of moods, was taken—inexplicably, and in the midst of a cold February downpour—to visit a tulip farm on a godforsaken island fifty-six kilometers from The Hague. It was a two-hour round trip in a Dutch Army car built, she and her aching back came fervently to believe, without a suspension system. And there had been no tulips. There had been only endless fields of mud. She ruined her best shoes and came down with a bad cold—and Waterman had borne the brunt of both her illness and her ill temper. He had no excuses to offer. She was right. Official visits were the pits.

Waterman decided to go back upstairs to tell her she wasn't included in the dinner before she got dressed. Always immaculately groomed and fashionably attired, she would have selected with care what she'd be wearing for the dinner she now wasn't going to attend. Better to catch her first.

Laura was standing in front of the bedroom mirror, a hair dryer in her hand, when Waterman walked in. The dress, shoes, and jewelry she had selected were laid out on the bed. As soon as Waterman walked into the room, she sensed that something was wrong.

"Everything okay?" she asked. "Do you like the table?"

"The table's perfect. But . . . look . . . er, this dinner's stag," he stammered.

"What?"

"Sweetie, it's a business dinner. I'd have taken François out, but I've been promising to cook him a meal for months. I thought you knew that."

"How the hell would I know?" she shot back. "You never told me. Parisi never said anything. Maggie called to check that there was no conflict when the date was made. How the hell did you expect me to know?"

"Darling, I'm sorry," he said lamely. "I screwed up. I should have checked. But it never occurred to me—"

"Of course it didn't occur to you. *I* almost never *occur* to you anymore. Next time I'm the *sous chef* but uninvited to dinner, have your goddam staff send me a memo." She pointed the hair dryer at Waterman. "Now get the hell out of here before I lose my temper."

Waterman was bent over peering into the refrigerator when he heard the sound of the ignition in Laura's car. He walked to the front of the house and looked out the window.

He was just in time to see the maroon Fiat disappear down the street.

CHAPTER SIX

Chevy Chase, September 17, 8:55 P.M.

François Arnaudet was the enfant terrible of the French Foreign
Service: bright, tough, ambitious, and five years younger than
anyone so knowledgeable and well connected had any right to be.
Finishing first at the École Superiore d'Administration in Paris, he'd been
given his choice of ministry from which to launch what was certain to be
a distinguished career in the upper reaches of the French civil service.
Much to the surprise of his classmates, who'd assumed he would choose
the Finance Ministry, François entered the Ministry of Foreign Affairs.
After publishing a long article outlining the history and principles of
French nuclear strategy, he became the chief political adviser to the minister of defense.

He and Waterman had hit it off from their first meeting. Arnaudet was
clearheaded and outspoken about the Soviets. He shared Waterman's
apprehensions as he watched the energy behind their buildup of strategic
weapons. He wrote fiery speeches for the minister extolling the virtues of
French-American cooperation, a position considered much too forthcoming by most senior French officials, who resented American leadership in
Europe and sought constantly to diminish it.

Now, he stood on the covered porch chez Waterman with a plastic
shopping bag, holding a bottle of wine in one hand and a Quai d'Orsai
briefcase in the other. The briefcase, with the initials *RF*, for *République*

Française, stamped in gold on the flap, was standard issue; the wine, a 1969 Clos de Vougeot from the small vineyards of Jean Grivot, was anything but.

Waterman put down the watercress he was rinsing, dried his hands with a kitchen towel, turned on the hall lights, and went to the front door to admit his French colleague. "François, welcome," he said. "It's a pleasure to see you. Hope you didn't have any trouble finding the house."

"None at all," said the French diplomat, peering out from behind steel-rimmed glasses as he extended his hand. "My driver knew the street. It turns out one of our attachés rented a house down the block for years."

Inside, with a look that bordered on reverence, he took in the huge, ornate Victorian mantel over the fireplace that dominated the living-room wall. "I wouldn't live anywhere but Paris," he said. "But unless you're very rich, it means apartment living. Your fireplace is the size of my kitchen."

The Waterman home was not a showcase house—one of those places lavishly described in local magazines. Nor was it distinctive from the outside—just another Chevy Chase center-hall Colonial, on a cul-de-sac called Keokuk, off River Road two tenths of a mile beyond the District line. But since the Watermans had moved into it six years previously, all their spare time and effort had gone into making it their true haven.

Rooms had been gutted and floors stripped. Walls had been moved and ceilings raised. A 26-by-20 addition in the rear had added a restaurant-size country kitchen for Waterman to cook in. Below it was a wine cellar and tasting room, which adjoined a basement office where he could work and not disturb the rest of the family. Behind the kitchen, a glassed-in greenhouse held a studio for Laura's painting.

If the kitchen reflected his interests, the rest of the house was evocative of Laura's artistic love of colors, shapes, and textures. One foyer wall was finished with hand-painted trompe l'oeil marble; in the living room, another looked as if a Renaissance fresco were in the process of restoration. The furnishings were a loving mélange of antique and modern pieces that had come as souvenirs of trips abroad, foraging expeditions to flea markets, and just the plain luck of being in the right place at the right time.

In the living room off the hall a large Russian samovar sat on an elaborately carved antique mahogany corner table, miniature paintings on bone and ivory from Esfahan flanked a lithograph in a gilt frame, of a dark and brooding Rimbaud, and a large red-and-blue Turkish rug on the dark hardwood floor picked up the colors of the Provençal fabrics that covered the chairs and sofa.

Waterman led Arnaudet past the living room into the kitchen at the back of the house. It was here, in the huge terra-cotta-tile-floored and oak-countered kitchen, that Waterman sought refuge from the share of the world's ills that touched him. Unlike practically everything else he did, cooking promised instant gratification. No long-term projects, no protracted wars, no slowly evolving plans. In the space of a few hours a dinner could be conceived, cooked, and consumed. It was amazing how slicing, chopping, grating, and mixing, the least intellectual of activities, could force from one's mind the most intrusive concerns.

"Formidable!" Arnaudet exclaimed. He peered at the professional kitchen, replete with indoor charcoal grill, restaurant stove, sixty linear feet of counter space, and a *batterie de cuisine* worthy of a good-size restaurant. Recessed halogen lights played on a huge collection of brightly polished copper pots hanging from a large oval oak rack suspended from the ceiling. A copper marmite gurgled on the stove, the white porcelain tureen into which its contents would be placed by its side.

"It keeps me sane," Waterman replied. "The last complete diversion."

"Well, this has certainly found the right home," Arnaudet said. He reached into the plastic bag and withdrew the bottle of burgundy.

"Whew," Waterman whistled as he read the label. "Serious stuff." He set it gently on the kitchen counter and stepped back to admire it. Once, on a wine-tasting trip through Burgundy, he had stopped at La Domaine de Romanée-Conti to sample the new La Tâche, still in the oak casks in the cellar. He had tried to buy a bottle of the dark, rich, impeccably balanced king of the burgundies. But he'd made the mistake of answering that he was American when asked his nationality. *"Je suis desolé, monsieur,"* the *patron* had said. *"Il existe un quota pour les Américains mais il est fini pour cette année."*

Waterman peered critically at the label. "We won't be able to drink this tonight," he said.

"Of course not," said Arnaudet, "I've brought it for your cellar, Michael. No—it's been bruised by its journey. It'll take at least a week of peace and quiet. But I thought you and Laura might enjoy it on a quiet night."

"Believe me, François, there are too few of those." Waterman cradled the bottle. "Excuse me for a sec—I'm going to take this downstairs."

He left the Frenchman fiddling with his briefcase and descended the circular wrought-iron staircase that led from the kitchen to his wine cellar, then reappeared momentarily, bottle in hand. He set it on the sideboard. "Perhaps we should decant it now—give it a chance to breathe."

Arnaudet was searching for the corkscrew before he looked properly at the bottle. "But we shouldn't drink this just yet," he repeated. "It hasn't had a chance to rest."

"Yes it has," Waterman answered, smiling broadly. "It's been standing upright all day in the cellar. I found two bottles of Grivot' Clos de Vougeot '71 in Paris last year. You know the little wineshop on the Place de la Madeleine?"

Arnaudet nodded.

Waterman handed him the corkscrew. "Well, let's see if they stored it well."

The Frenchman carefully removed the cork, then sniffed. "It's perfect, a true masterpiece; there's nothing to compare with it. And," he added, "it will go well with this." He extracted a large piece of perfectly ripened Vacherin and a smaller goat cheese, St. Marcellin, from the plastic bag. "What else are we having?" he asked.

"Well," Waterman replied, "it's not Taillevent. But I've made a *soupe de moules* using the Paul Bocuse recipe. Then I thought we'd grill some steaks, accompanied by a *gratin dauphinois*. There's a salad of mache, radicchio, and watercress, all grown by my neighbor across the street. For dessert there's a lemon soufflé—my specialty." Waterman knew that his guest would get a better meal than at most restaurants in Washington. In Waterman's view there was really only one great restaurant in Washington, Jean Louis, and the last time he had drawn "representation funds" from the Pentagon entertainment budget to cover dinner there with an Italian official, the disbursing administrative officer had photocopied the $270 dinner check and sent it to half a dozen Pentagon offices as an example of unacceptable profligacy. After that he began to take visiting foreign officials to one of the better Tex-Mex restaurants, where comparisons with classical French cuisine were unlikely and the novelty stood a decent chance of pleasing his guests.

Waterman moved purposefully around the kitchen, stirring the mussel soup, seasoning the steaks, lighting the grill, and checking on the *gratin* bubbling in the oven. Arnaudet watched with admiration.

"Have a look at these," said Waterman, handing Arnaudet his talking points for tomorrow's meeting. "Here's how I propose to raise the military subcommittee after I break the Ciao material. I know it looks long, but I can say it all in less than thirty minutes."

Arnaudet was still seated at the kitchen table reading when the phone rang. Waterman lowered the flame under the soup and picked up the phone. "It's for you," he said, handing the receiver to Arnaudet. "If you prefer, you can take it in the study, through the door on the left." The Frenchman nodded, rose, and walked toward the extension. In less than two minutes he was back, looking grim.

"François, not bad news I hope?" Waterman said.

"I'm afraid it is."

"Anything you can talk about?"

"Something we must talk about," Arnaudet said formally, resuming his seat. "The call was from the *chef de cabinet* of the minister of foreign affairs. I didn't say anything earlier about this—I was hoping things would sort themselves out. But they haven't. Bad news, Michael. You are being denied permission to use the Ciao materials at the meeting tomorrow."

Waterman was stunned. "But it is all worked out. Everything is agreed."

"*Was* agreed," Arnaudet said wistfully. "Let me tell you what I know. But don't shoot the messenger. At seven tonight I got a call from the chief of staff at the Ministry of Defense. He warned me there's been some reconsideration about using the Ciao materials. He didn't know why, he simply wanted me to know something was up. When I tried to pry the reason out of him, he said, 'François, it's above my pay grade.' Then he said that the Quai was involved."

"The Quai?" Waterman frowned. "The Quai's been kept out of this— just like the State Department. We compartmented everything to do with Ciao, François. How could this have happened?"

"I have no idea," the Frenchman said regretfully. "But it has. And the coup de grace was just delivered by phone. I was told that your own Anthony Winthrop concurs in the new French position of denying the Ciao materials to you tomorrow."

Waterman was speechless. He found his tongue. "Impossible. Winthrop actually said that to someone?"

"Not in so many words," Arnaudet said, "but it was implied."

"God*dam*." Waterman's palm struck the tile counter. "Is there nothing we can do?"

"Nothing but wait. As the man said, it's above our pay grade—at least it's above mine."

"I could call the secretary of defense—"

"It wouldn't do any good, Michael. This is a fait accompli. We can only wait. Perhaps Ciao can be retrieved another time. But as far as tomorrow goes, the Ciao materials are a dead issue."

"The I'm out of business," Waterman said. "Without Ciao, it's goodbye." Waterman laughed at himself, a strained, pained laugh. He shook his head. What the hell could have happened?

Arnaudet looked grim. "At least you've kept your sense of humor."

"*Merde!*" was all Waterman could bring himself to say.

PART TWO

CHAPTER SEVEN

The State Department, September 26, 11:30 A.M.

When he was angry, Dan Bennet's loud, gravelly rasp could be heard in the next corridor through the State Department's thin Sheetrock partition walls. His secretary was accustomed to buffeting audial shock waves two or three times a day radiating from the assistant secretarial epicenter that sat less than fifteen feet away. Once she made a point of sitting at her desk wearing the bulky earmuff-like hearing protectors that her husband, a D.C. policeman, wore on the firing range. Bennet hadn't noticed.

She could hear him quite plainly now, holding the phone receiver upside down and shouting into the mouthpiece as though it were a microphone. It was an act, of course, a carefully orchestrated performance intended to pummel adversaries and subordinates into submission. The key thing was not only to be heard by one's interlocutor-victim, but to be seen by others so the word would spread. Much of the time his secretary was the hapless audience. So it gave her quiet satisfaction to understand—from his side of the conversation, at least—that Bennet wasn't getting results. He was pouring it on, but Michael Waterman wasn't being blown away.

"Don't give me that shit—just send someone. What the hell are deputies for? I'm not stopping the world just because you insist on going to every goddam meeting yourself. What the hell are you, anyway? The world doesn't move unless you're there? I know what you're doing . . . you're stalling.''

Two and a half miles away as the crow flies, the object of Bennet's tirade held the phone in a raised-arm salute, so Jay Parisi, who sat across the room, could hear the shouting. Waterman made a face at his military aide, returned the receiver to his ear, waited for Bennet to draw breath, then rushed in edgewise. "Dan," he protested blandly, "I'm not stalling. If I were stalling, I'd be demanding a month, not two days. I can't see over the stack of papers on my desk. This meeting's about the most important decision this administration's likely to make, and I want to make damn sure we get it right. We're simply not ready for an interagency group meeting—not on something as important as intermediate nuclear forces.''

Despite his seeming cool, Waterman was angry. First Bennet had sabotaged his COCOM initiative. Months of effort and long hours of negotiation with the French about the release of the Ciao materials were down the drain. He pushed the mute button on the phone console, which allowed him to speak without being overheard. "You know what really pisses me off?'' he asked Parisi.

"What?''

"The prick should be drinking champagne with his orange juice after what he did to me at COCOM—but noooo, he's celebrating by screaming at me as if I were one of his staff flunkies.''

"So scream back.''

Waterman shook his head no. The way to deal with angry fulmination was to stay calm, to portray an imperturbable tranquillty—no matter what. That's baloney, he thought, but babble on, Dan. Bust a gut. He could see Bennet behind his desk clutching the phone with both hands.

Waterman released the mute button. "Believe me, Dan, there are a million things I'd rather be doing than sitting in an IG. Ordinarily, I'd say go ahead even though I can't be there. But I've got to come to this one because the position the president takes now will shape the way the INF thing comes out later—and it's just too damn important to be left to subordinates.''

Bennet was having none of it. "Goddammit, this is the second time in two weeks we've had to postpone a meeting because of you, and I won't tolerate—''

"And it won't be the last," Waterman interrupted, a steely reserve creeping into his voice despite himself. He caught his change in tone and stopped, hoping Bennet hadn't sensed anything. "Look, whatever time we lose now we'll make up later.''

"You're doing everything you can to see that this negotiation doesn't get off the ground," Bennet accused, his voice rising. "I . . . will . . . not . . . tolerate it. I'm calling the IG into session this afternoon, whether you're there or not."

Waterman had had enough. "Now just hang on, Dan," he said icily. "The last time I looked, I was still the cochairman of this interagency group. Cochairman, Dan. Equal. I don't work for you." Bennet began to reply, but Waterman cut him off. "Let me set the record straight. For more than four years I've let you chair the meetings—all of them, I might add. I let you hold them at State, which is an inconvenience for me and my people. Most of the time I even let you decide the agenda. I've given you a freer hand than you had any right to expect. But if you insist on calling a meeting today, I'll simply order my people not to go. Without Defense there, you can't do a damn thing, no matter how many people you get around the table. If we don't show, there ain't no meeting. So what's the point of these threats?"

Waterman heard Bennet's receiver slam down. A dial tone burred annoyingly in his ear. He slapped his own receiver onto the cradle with a curse.

"What's eating him this morning?" Parisi asked.

"Insubordination. Mine. Contempt. Mine again. He really doesn't have any choice about the IG, and it drives him nuts. After the way he screwed us, I'm enjoying making him crazy."

"You're sure it was Bennet who screwed us?" Parisi asked.

"I'm *positive.*"

"How so?"

Waterman held a note up for Parisi to examine. "Maggie took this message from Miskell," Waterman said. "He didn't use his name—he wouldn't—but it couldn't have been anyone else."

"Hmm." Parisi squinted and read, his nose wrinkling in distaste as he did so. "Says here it was the secretary of state himself who convinced the French about not using Ciao." He scratched his chin. "You're right—it had to be fucking Bennet. No one else could have gotten to Winthrop so fast."

"Or persuaded him to torpedo an initiative so clearly in the U.S. interest," Waterman said. "I can't begin to imagine the argument he used to persuade him."

Parisi handed the note back to Waterman, who removed a thick, legal-size manila folder marked *BCN* from his bottom desk drawer and added the note to it. The folder slipped from his grasp, hit the floor, and spewed paper all over the carpet. Waterman dropped to his knees and began picking up the scattered papers. Parisi did the same. He glanced at the collection of cables, memos, press clippings, message sheets, and handwritten notes as he handed them to Waterman.

"Material for a memoir?" Parisi asked. "Or maybe you're planning to write an obituary some day?" He sounded hopeful.

"Just a private archive," Waterman said. "No memoirs."

"What does 'BCN' stand for?" Parisi asked.

"Bennet Coffin Nails." Waterman laughed.

Parisi rolled his eyes. "I should have known."

"What makes it bearable—just—is that Bennet may have won on COCOM, but eventually I'll get my way." Waterman struggled to his feet, took the file from Parisi, and returned it to his desk. "He can mobilize the secretary once, maybe twice. But he can't keep going back to him over and over. I'll get Ciao on the COCOM agenda . . . it'll just take a while longer. Next time he won't be able to scotch it. He can't win every time."

"What about the IG?"

"That's one we've got to steal." Waterman knew it would be an uphill battle. He was widely regarded by State generally, and Bennet specifically, as an opponent of *any* arms-control agreement with the Soviets, and ready, therefore, to use any pretext to slow the negotiations. So even when he had good reason—Waterman really wasn't ready for an IG meeting, having failed to prepare a negotiating position—it was bound to look like a dilatory tactic.

"Should I call Bennet back?" Waterman asked.

"Let him stew for a while," Parisi said. "He hung up on you. He's probably sitting there waiting for the phone to ring. Let him wait. Let him think you've gone to SECDEF to complain. Let him worry that you're doing an end run at the White House. He's sitting there right now wondering."

"Sounds good," Waterman said. "And in the meantime we can get some work done; we can clear out some of these actions."

So he and Parisi killed two hours going through his In-basket. Parisi pulled action files from the pile and explained what was needed. Waterman signed them out or penned notations on the cover sheets for further work or sent them back to be redone. When the In-basket got filled up, as it often did when Waterman was away on a trip, the mere thought of having to wade through it would make him yawn. A week's backlog was likely to mean a dozen personnel actions—merit pay approvals, transfer requests, efficiency reports, applications for educational leave, secondments to other departments, and the like; half a dozen administrative budget matters; a score of travel approvals; two or three reports to Congress, artfully worded to dampen controversy, to be reviewed and signed out; a slew of memos to the secretary to be approved for his signature, or initialed in the case of those that would go out from another office; requests for briefings and interviews with the press; trip proposals and itineraries; scores of letters . . . the range and number of items was endless. By one-thirty the stack of papers had been largely shifted from In to Out.

Waterman looked at the big wall clock. "What do you think?"

"Yeah—do it."

Waterman picked up his desk phone and had Maggie put him through to Bennet. Parisi picked up the extension on the conference table and readied a notepad.

"Look, Dan," Waterman said as if there had been only a momentary interruption, "there was no need to hang up on me. I was about to say I'd manage to get to an IG this afternoon—*if* we can agree it's premature to discuss options for the negotiations."

"So why the hell meet?"

"We have to clear the papers we're taking to the Allies, remember?"

"That can be done without a meeting. Frankly, Michael, I think you're stalling because you don't have an option to discuss and you're afraid of ours."

Waterman looked over at Parisi and clutched his chest. Bull's-eye. He hoped his voice didn't betray him. "Think what you want—I'm only trying to be helpful. I can rearrange my schedule to meet late this afternoon. We can clear the papers for the NATO meeting at Gleneagles. We can *discuss* the arms negotiations in Geneva. But we're not ready to propose options for the Geneva talks. It's too early for that."

There was a long pause. "Okay, okay," Bennet groused. "We won't discuss options." Then his voice modulated into a more amiable tone. "But we've got to send a position on intermediate missiles to the president by next week. There's no time to screw around. Dammit, Michael, the Geneva talks start in days. Not weeks, not months—*days.* You can't argue that."

"No, Dan, I can't. For once I agree with you." Waterman's jaw tightened. He was on his way to a meeting on medium-range missiles, and the Defense Department didn't have a position. "Make it five o'clock," he said. "I'll be there." He hung up.

Parisi put down the extension phone gently. "What are you gonna do?"

Waterman shrugged. "The only thing I can do—filibuster. Jay," he continued, "we'll limit the damage with a little, uh, structural work before the meeting. Get hold of the guy from the Department of Energy who comes to the IG. He's an engineer from Los Alamos. Name's Doug something-or-other. Tell him we don't want to discuss options on medium missiles, and if he'll back us on this, we'll oppose discussing State's options for limits on nuclear testing. The only thing DOE cares about is nuclear testing. Tell him the missile issue is as important to me as nuclear testing is to him.

"Then call the Arms Control Agency. Make sure they know that Bennet's pushing us to take a position on medium missiles before ACDA finishes its paper on verification—which will make the ACDA paper an irrelevant waste of time. It's the only important piece of work they've been given, and it'll make 'em mad as hell if it's marginalized. Tell 'em we don't see how any option can be seriously studied before their paper is finished."

"Nice touch," Parisi said. "Anything else?"

"Not now."

Parisi wheeled to leave. He had his hand on the door when he turned, a sly look on his face. "Michael, when I call over to Energy, what about inviting Doug what's-his-name to come with us to Brussels for the next High Level Group meeting?" Parisi grinned broadly. "Nobody's ever asked him before. It'll be like an invitation to the prom."

"Bingo," Waterman said. "Brilliant. And you know what I like best about it?"

"Tell me."

"He'll be so flattered, he's bound to back us in the IG. Of course, we'll be stuck with him in Brussels. But at least we'll get something for it. The best part is that Bennet will have to invite him to *his* Brussels meeting or he'll drive him crazy. So when you invite him, tell him we're asking Bennet to include him in State's Brussels delegation also. We'll get credit for both invitations."

"Double bingo."

It was hot and crowded in the State Department conference room where the Interagency Group on Intermediate Nuclear Forces was meeting. A narrow, windowless room off an interior corridor, poorly served by an underpowered air-conditioning system, it was never comfortable. But today it was worse than usual. The No Smoking signs were contradicted by the half-dozen ashtrays spread across the table, and the haze of gray smoke hung suspended just below the low ceiling.

There were better conference rooms in the State Department, but none was as close to the office of the assistant secretary for European and Canadian affairs. Dan Bennet preferred to meet in his large private office. If the meeting was too large and that became impossible, he held meetings as close to it as possible—and comfort be damned.

So thirty people were crowded into the conference room just down the hall from Bennet's suite. It was, of course, far too large a group for its intended purpose: to hammer out a set of recommendations that would go to the National Security Council, then form the basis for a Cabinet discussion, out of which would come—eventually—a policy for the conduct of negotiations with the Russians over intermediate-range nuclear weapons of a type the Russians had long deployed in great numbers and the United States was now preparing to deploy in five European countries.

Every agency with an interest in the matter was represented. There were representatives from the Joint Chiefs of Staff, the Arms Control and Disarmament Agency, the Department of Energy, the Central Intelligence Agency, the National Security Council, and the Office of the Vice President. In addition, the INF negotiating team, made up of representatives of the same agencies, attended IG meetings when they were not in Geneva.

The State Department, Waterman noted from his seat at one end of the table, always had more representatives than anyone else. In this they were indulged by other agencies, whose members understood that the infighting among parts of the State Department was such that several bureaus had always to be represented. It was an annoyance—and it swelled the size of the meetings—but it had some benefits, too. There was no point eliciting agreement from a State Department representative only to learn later that he was not the *right* State Department representative. Furthermore, the opportunity to split the State Department into opposing factions or, to put it more precisely, to enlarge the split that invariably existed, appealed to some others, to Waterman especially. He took particular pleasure in deepening the differences that invariably existed between Dan Bennet and Bennet's rival, Judith Shannon.

When it came to policy concerning American and Soviet missiles in Europe, the State Department was deeply divided between Dan Bennet's Bureau of European and Canadian Affairs, on the one hand, and Judith Shannon's Bureau of Politico-military Affairs, on the other. It would be difficult to identify a philosophical difference between the two bureaus. Their battle was, pure and simple, one of turf.

The fact that no matter of substance underlay the differences between them in no way moderated the ferocity of their rivalry. They quarreled over which bureau had responsibility for this paper or that, who would call in the French or German ambassador for consultations or represent the department at a conference or in interagency deliberations. Their frequent disagreements were savored in the department cafeteria lines and corridors. Shannon had once sent her deputy to London to meet with a Foreign Office official without first getting Bennet's approval. Bennet retaliated: He had arranged, at exactly the same time, an urgent meeting in Brussels of a NATO committee he chaired. The British official, who headed the United Kingdom delegation to the committee, was forced to choose. Eighty-seven officials from fifteen countries had gathered in Brussels on short notice so Bennet could trump Shannon.

This meeting, which Bennet had insisted on convening, was known, was under instructions to develop the position the United States would table when the stalled negotiations with the Soviets resumed in Geneva in two weeks. Painstaking preparatory work had gone on for months— endless analyses had been prepared; the political and military implications of various positions had been scrutinized; the intelligence community had issued lengthy and indecipherable reports on probable Soviet approaches to the negotiation; endless consultations had been held with the European allies.

At the insistence of the Defense Department, a detailed assessment of the military threat to NATO of Soviet medium-range missiles had been pre- pared by a NATO committee that Waterman chaired. The State Depart- ment, led by Dan Bennet, had opposed even the idea of Waterman's NATO paper.

Bennet's opposition to Waterman's NATO study was hardly surprising: It became the focal point of the Alliance's preparation for the negotiations. As a result, much of the work had wound up in the hands of the High Level Group (HLG)—as the NATO committee Waterman chaired modestly called itself—not at State, where Bennet believed it should reside. Moreover, as chairman of the group drafting what became the principal Allied paper on medium-range missiles, Waterman had assumed a central role in a matter that State had always considered its sacred ground. Bennet was out to get even.

The group that filled the State Department conference room knew that the discord that had been building for weeks between State and Defense— between Bennet and Waterman—was likely to erupt with fury before the question got resolved of what proposal to make to the Soviets. Indeed, they were there, many of them, to witness the event. Like spectators at a prizefight, they had come to see blood.

Trailed by two anonymous, striped-suit note-takers, Dan Bennet slid into the chair at the end of the long table opposite Waterman, nodded perfunc- torily at him, opened his folder, and rapped a pen on the table to get the room's attention. "We have a larger-than-usual group. There are some people in the room I don't recognize. I'm going to ask everyone to sign in on the yellow pad that comes around."

He handed a yellow pad to the person on his right and adjusted his tie. "We have two major topics on the agenda. The IG has spent several months looking at various aspects of the INF issue. We're nearing the point at which some proposals have to go to the NSC. Looking at the time necessary to formulate negotiating instructions and working back to where we are now, I think it's clear that this meeting should give final approval to the High Level Group paper on a threat assessment and NATO's requirements so that Michael Waterman"—he nodded in Waterman's direction—"can gain final approval from the HLG. That shouldn't take long, because the working group has already reviewed it, and as I understand it, there are no significant problems. Then we have to get on with formulating some options for the NSC.

"Today, I want to get an idea where the agencies stand on the negotiating proposals for Geneva."

Waterman was furious. Bennet was breaking his word. He'd promised not to bring up the Geneva negotiating positions. He interrupted. "Dan—"

Bennet never broke stride. "In a minute, Michael," he said patronizingly. His eyes swept the room. "We've begun to work on a paper laying out the issues. The section of the paper that has specific proposals won't be drafted, of course, until the IG has had a chance to develop them. But I didn't think it was necessary to delay any further the drafting of sections of the paper that give the necessary background. If we leave that to the last minute, we'll never make our deadlines.

"Is there any comment?" Bennet paused, scanning the table and the row of chairs beyond, along the wall.

A drawl from way below the salt interrupted Bennet's momentum.

"We have some specific comments on the threat-assessment paper. Should we make those now?"

Bennet's eyebrows went up. He squinted down the table and saw the upraised hand of the Department of Energy representative, a longtime bureaucrat in the DOE's international-affairs section whose name he couldn't recall. The man was a literal-minded engineer who had worked on nuclear tests at the Nevada test range for twenty years before coming to Washington. Like many DOE personnel from the New Mexico labs, he wore a bolo, or string tie—a leather shoelace hung around the neck and held in place by a huge chunk of turquoise mounted on a clasp of Indian silver.

"You'll have a chance in a moment," Bennet said curtly, giving String Tie short shrift. "For now, all I want to know is whether the agenda and plan for the meeting are acceptable to everyone."

Waterman spoke up through clenched teeth. "I certainly agree we ought to clear the papers for the HLG. The working group has done a good job, and I believe we have agreement."

He consulted his notes. "As you know, we'll be making a major presentation to the NATO defense ministers at the Nuclear Planning Group next month. I want to be certain everyone's happy with the result. Obviously, we need clearance from the IG.

"But I'm a little unclear as to what you mean, Dan, when you say you want to 'get an idea of where agencies stand on the negotiating proposals.' What proposals? What do you have in mind?"

It was a bogus request for clarification: Waterman understood all too well the purpose behind Bennet's question. He was on a fishing expedition—looking for intelligence about the Defense Department position. Moreover, he surely knew that no position had been worked out between the secretary of defense and the Joint Chiefs of Staff, between the civilian and military authorities in the Pentagon. By pressing now for a discussion, Bennet could hope to identify differences that might be exploited. In any case he would be able to characterize Waterman as laggard, thus adding to his image as an opponent of arms control. This would end up diminishing the weight of Waterman's position when it was eventually put forward. Waterman had been pursuing a deliberate policy of saying little about a negotiating position until one could be formulated internally and sold to the Joint Chiefs of Staff. If the JCS opposed the secretary of defense, the Pentagon would be neutralized—and State would end up writing the proposal by itself. Bennet's query was intended to draw people out prematurely. It was Waterman's responsibility not to let that happen.

Bennet clasped his fingers together and made a steeple out of his hands. "I mean simply that we need some indication of where agencies stand, Michael," he said smoothly, "so we can begin to rough out the decision paper that will eventually go to the NSC. I'm not asking for detailed positions."

"I really don't see what good it does to speculate," Waterman countered. "The logical order of things would be to get the HLG paper approved by NATO ministers—or at least by the HLG—and to get ACDA's verification paper agreed on first. Then we can develop negotiating options that reflect those papers. We're certainly in no position to comment, since we haven't formulated any position yet."

"Goddammit," Bennet exploded, "this is just obstructionism! You know damn well it's impossible to draft a decision paper without some idea of the range of possible options."

"I don't recall ever agreeing that work should begin on a decision paper," Waterman said obstinately. "And I'm certainly not prepared to turn over the task of drafting a paper that represents the culmination of months of work and the start of a crucial negotiation to one agency. As for your wanting to know the 'range of possible options,' the HLG and ACDA papers certainly give enough of an idea, and the DOE representative was ready to offer some comment a moment ago."

Waterman looked around the table at the crowd that had been watching them volley back and forth as in a tennis match. He knew the lesser agencies—Energy and Arms Control—chafed under State's high-handed management of the IG process. He hoped one of them would intervene, both to break the pattern of exchanges between himself and Bennet and to support the position he'd outlined. He turned toward the man from DOE, as if to cue him.

There was an awful moment of silence. Then, slowly, hesitantly, DOE's representative spoke up from behind his string tie: "DOE would certainly welcome an opportunity to help outline any decision paper. After all, we do make and test the warheads that go on these missiles."

Bennet's eyes narrowed. He stared at String Tie as if to say, "Who let this guy in here?" But before he could say anything further, he saw in his peripheral vision the Arms Control and Disarmament Agency representative, a gaunt woman with flaming red hair, throw back her head and open her mouth with the obvious intention of making an Important Statement. Bennet gave her a drop-dead glare of such velocity and mass that her words, whatever they were, emerged as a wheezy squeak, barely audible and wholly unintelligible.

But she managed to recover her composure enough to stammer, "We agree with the DOE."

Others joined in. It was obvious that Bennet's effort to gather intelligence on the views of the various agencies was collapsing. And, to make matters worse, his plan to turn over to his subordinates at State the task of drafting the IG paper for the NSC was fast going down the drain. Other agencies were asking to get in on the drafting. Retreat was in order. But before Bennet could mount a retreat, the air-force major-general representing the Joint Chiefs of Staff raised his hand to indicate he wished to say something.

"I don't wish to comment on how the first draft of the IG paper gets accomplished. JCS would be quite content to review a draft prepared by State if that's what the IG wants. But I do want to explain why we're unable to express any opinion about what our negotiating position ought to be. That is a matter to be worked out between the chiefs and the secretary, and I wasn't given any guidance that would permit me to say anything. So I'll just have to pass on that agenda item."

"All right, then," Bennet snapped. "We'll piss on the negotiating-positions agenda item . . . I mean—" His face reddened as the room full of bureaucrats erupted with laughter. "I mean of course we'll *pass* on the negotiating positions. . . ." Then Bennet, too, began to laugh. "Okay," he said as the laughter subsided, "let's tûrn to the HLG papers."

The meeting ended an hour later without further acrimony, the HLG paper approved. An exhausted Waterman packed his document case and trudged toward the bank of elevators. He hoped his car was waiting. He had just pressed the down button when the JCS representative, whose uniform bore the name IRVING on its breast, emerged from the men's room across the hallway and walked toward the elevators.

Waterman nodded in the general's direction. "Long session."

General Irving nodded in agreement. "You can say that again."

The doors opened, and the two men walked inside the empty elevator, Waterman turning right, General Irving turning left. They stood with their backs to the paneled wood and stared at the numbers above them. Finally, Waterman spoke. "We've got to move quickly to get a position on intermediate arms we can offer and defend in the IG," he said. "You can only get away for so long saying that the chiefs are still looking at it."

"Roger that," the air-force officer said.

"I sure as hell hope we'll be together on it, General."

"So do I," Irving said. "Question is, how far along are you? We can't write the review until we see the play."

"I don't have anything in hand yet," Waterman said candidly. "It's a real problem. I've got to come up with something that will give us some relief from the demonstrations, the protests, the pressures to abandon the deployment altogether—something that appeals to the imagination, puts the Soviets on the defensive, and turns out to be in our interest if they should agree."

"That's a tall order," the officer said as the elevator doors opened and they went their separate ways. "When you've got something," he said over his shoulder, "just give us a call. We'll be waiting."

Of course they'll be waiting, Waterman thought. They sure as hell won't take the lead. During the ride back to the Pentagon, Waterman decided he had damned well better have something by Monday morning. He didn't like the idea of spending the weekend in the office, but to take home the highly sensitive papers he required was unthinkable.

The worst of it would be breaking the news to Laura.

CHAPTER EIGHT

The Pentagon, September 27, 11:00 A.M.

At eleven Saturday morning, the Pentagon was like a morgue.
Waterman looked up from the pile of documents on his desk. All
around him, in bookcases along the walls, in mounds on the floor,
and atop virtually every other available surface, were strewn books, papers, congressional testimony, and back issues of scholarly journals. There
were stacks of manila folders containing God-knows-what, correspondence files, portfolios of clippings, notes of long-forgotten meetings, dog-
eared conference agendas—in essence, the sort of detritus from which
needed items can almost never be retrieved but that nevertheless imparts
a certain solace to people who cannot bring themselves to throw anything
away.

Waterman groaned audibly. From somewhere, he thought, there's got
to be an unassailable proposal we can put to the Soviets. The whole matter
of medium-range missiles had been trouble from day one. The decision to
deploy American medium-range Pershing II and cruise missiles in Europe
had been painfully and reluctantly reached by the previous administration
under pressure from the European allies. It had come after the Soviet Union
rejected all Western pleas to halt the deployment of its new, highly mobile,
three-warhead exceptionally accurate missile, the SS-20.

That decision, a watershed, had been adopted formally at a combined
meeting of NATO foreign and defense ministers in Brussels that was in-

tended to stress the political, as well as the military, Western response to SS-20 deployment.

The NATO decision was followed immediately by massive protests, which Moscow actively supported. The so-called peace movement in Europe was, Waterman knew, largely financed from Soviet funds. And as the protests widened, spilling into the streets of West Germany, Holland, Italy, Belgium—even Thatcher's Britain—Waterman watched as the very parties that had voted in favor of the U.S. position to deploy now demanded a unilateral halt to American weapons. Deployment of Pershing and cruise missiles became symbols of the president's policy of rebuilding American military strength. As such, it set the stage for a test of wills of fundamental importance to the postwar structure of Western security and the integrity of the NATO Alliance.

The Novikov regime intensified the pressure on European governments to abandon the NATO deployment scheme—even though the Soviets continued to deploy SS-20 missiles of their own. The Western strategy was teetering on the verge of collapse. The opening of negotiations could lead to a reprieve. Waterman was determined to make the most of it.

Finding a negotiating position that could sustain support for deployment while bargaining about it would not be easy. It was made more difficult still by circumstances favoring the Soviets: They were putting SS-20 missiles into the field every week. The United States had not yet begun its own deployment. Moreover, NATO had agreed to deploy only 572 warheads on new missiles, no more. The Soviets could go on deploying with impunity, placing many more in service if they wished. All the leverage was on the Soviet side.

For Waterman, negotiation was a fine art, a highly complex competition in which a vast array of elements combined to produce victories and defeats. To him, victory meant coming away from the bargaining table with more than one's position implied; defeat was leaving with less. One could win with a weak position, but only by gaining more than that weak position ought to have allowed. Similarly, one could lose with a strong position by failing to get from the other side all that one's strength entitled.

For as far back as he could remember, Waterman had been intrigued by the art of negotiation. It was such a rich mélange of the classical elements of statecraft and power—military, economic, political, psychological—all brought to bear, under battlefield conditions of uncertainty and imperfect information, against skilled adversaries. It was, he believed, the ultimate game—a game that was often played badly. But it could be played well.

As an undergraduate, Waterman had done his honors thesis on the negotiations at Ghent, in Belgium, that ended the war between Britain and

America in 1814. The American negotiating team had been headed by John Quincy Adams, a man of great learning, a classicist who would later become president. It included no less a figure than Albert Gallatin, America's first treasury secretary. The British, who had sacked Washington and in a military sense won the war, made the fatal mistake of underestimating the American negotiating team. They sent to head their delegation a recently retired admiral, well connected at court, whose principal claim to fame was the shelling of Copenhagen during the war against Napoleon.

The British were no match for the Americans. On issue after issue they were outnegotiated. The Americans' brilliantly conducted negotiations succeeded in reversing the spoils of war. They had, in effect, won the peace.

To the Department of State, Waterman believed the purpose of negotiation was not to win—but simply to *get an agreement.* The reward was not the satisfaction of having made the most of one's hand, even if one had to leave the table without an agreement, but simply a signature on a piece of paper.

He thought he had a president—and he knew he had a secretary of defense—who shared this view. But he also knew if he did not come up with a negotiating proposal that would win the peace, there were plenty of diplomats in Foggy Bottom who would come up with something—anything—just to get those signatures.

So Waterman sipped thick black coffee as he read and reread the mountain of papers—military assessments, political analyses, estimates of Soviet positions and tactics, and intelligence reports topped with a string of code words a mile long. None of them shed much light on what a well-crafted proposal would look like.

By three in the afternoon, Waterman was exhausted. One last paper, he thought, as he came upon, in the midst of a dusty pile of rejected analyses, a short paper with the intriguing title "Warsaw Pact Coverage of NATO Targets."

It argued that NATO had, in reality, only 150 truly important facilities—nuclear-weapons storage sites, main airfields, naval bases, and operational headquarters. The Soviets, the analysis continued, could strike 150 targets with a mere fifty SS-20 missiles, as each missile held three warheads. So, unless the United States could obtain a reduction of the Soviet missile force to fewer than fifty, the Soviets' ability to attack and destroy all the critical facilities on which the defense of Europe depended would be unaffected—no matter how many missiles they agreed to dismantle.

Waterman called the authors of the analysis at home and summoned them to his office for a detailed briefing. They were grumpy about having their weekend ruined, but they made their case convincingly. Their numbers checked out. They *had* identified all critical NATO installations. They had painstakingly calculated the effectiveness of SS-20 warheads against those targets.

Their theory point was valid: To be militarily useful, any agreement would have to hold the Soviets to a very small number of missiles.

After they left, Waterman wandered down into the bowels of the Pentagon to the gym. There, he took a long shower, shaved, then sat in a sauna, perspiring in the dry heat for almost half an hour. The problem with diplomatic formulas, Waterman thought as he adjusted himself on the cedar boards, was that they spoke to no one. What did a diplomatic formula and its mealymouthed language say to Dutch antinuclear protesters, or German parliamentarians, or Italian journalists, or to the housewives, bus conductors, farmers, grocers, and university professors all over Europe who had to live with the decisions made by remote bureaucrats?

That, Waterman decided, was wrong. My father, he thought, Sam Waterman—God rest his soul—would be able to understand the U.S. position in the blink of an eye. It wouldn't have to be explained by an anchorman— or a political analyst, or rocket engineer or scientist or anybody. What the hell would my father care about "throw weight" or "circular errors probable" or "miss distances" or "warhead loadings"? What my father cared about was being safe. What we all care about is being safe.

It's like television, he thought. My father didn't care how telecommunications technology worked—he didn't give a damn about megahertz and spectrum allotment and UHF and VHF and high-end frequencies and fiber optics. All he had wanted to know was that when he pressed a button he would get *The Tonight Show* or *Wheel of Fortune.*

What were the opposing philosophical views, anyway? He scrubbed himself with a towel and tried to list them all. The Russians argued that the Americans were upsetting the balance of power in Europe by deploying missiles that could start a war and turn Europe into a nuclear battlefield. It was effective propaganda because Europe had been a battlefield twice in this century, and Europeans were afraid of having it happen again. A cartoon from a German newspaper Waterman had come across during the night summed up the Soviet campaign. It depicted the president, a ghoulish smile on his face, pushing buttons frantically while London, Paris, Lisbon, Rome, Vienna, Bonn, Frankfurt, Amsterdam, Brussels, and Oslo were shown ruined and in flames, nuclear mushrooms rising above them. The caption read, "I'll fight to the last European."

How the hell could you fight propaganda with press releases that read, "The United States is prepared to achieve stability in the balance of medium-range missiles at the lowest level acceptable to the Soviet Union"?

That was Bennet's solution, the State Department's preferred formulation. Waterman knew it wouldn't work.

When it finally came, the idea for which he had been searching, it came so quickly it literally took his breath away. He dressed rapidly and, taking the steps two at a time, ran up to his office, pausing as he turned on his computer, cranking up the strength to let it fill his mind once again, half afraid that when he thought it a second time, it would appear with some disfiguring flaw that he had missed the first time around. Or vanish entirely.

Zero. That was it. Zero. Zero for both sides.

Get rid of all of them—SS-20s, Pershing IIs, ground-launched cruise missiles, the whole lot.

We will abandon our deployment if the Soviets give up theirs. Oh, it was perfect. It was fair. Balanced. Simple. Elegant. Obvious. Clean. Tidy. Neatly wrapped.

How could they say no? How could *anyone* fail to say yes? Who would criticize it—and how? With what argument? The simple flawlessness of it. It was exquisite. It was fastidious. It was sublime. It was . . . *inevitable.*

His fingers flew like Bach's at the harpsichord. The words were music to his ears.

Memorandum: Department of Defense
SECRET-SENSITIVE

TO: The Secretary
FROM: ISP/Michael Waterman
DATE: September 27
SUBJECT: Intermediate Nuclear Forces Proposal

I have been working to come up with an INF proposal we could table in the opening round that meets five critical tests:

1. Puts the Soviets on the defensive and relieves the pressure on U.S. deployment plans;

2. Launches the talks with a proposal that has staying power;

3. Is simple, clear, and dramatic, readily understood as fair and equitable, and easy to explain in plain language;

4. Enhances our security if agreed to; and

5. Minimizes our exposure to Soviet cheating.

I believe that a proposal to *eliminate all intermediate nuclear missiles on both sides, those now deployed and those planned for deployment,* meets these five tests.

This Zero Option has the potential to reverse quickly the deterioration of the American political position in Europe, by demonstrating that it is the Soviet Union, and not the United States, which is responsible for the existence of intermediate nuclear missiles in Europe.

Because the Zero Option will come as a complete surprise, it will have a dramatic impact and catch the Soviets and our critics in Europe off guard.

To be most effective, we should propose to eliminate all SS-20s, SS-12s, SS-22s, SS-23s, SS-4s, and SS-5s on the Soviet side; and all Pershing II and ground-launched cruise missiles on the American side. The independent deterrent forces of Britain and France would not be included.

There could be a schedule of reductions in stages until the last missiles were destroyed. The United States would pledge to halt its deployment plans as soon as agreement is achieved.

Now, the arguments in detail.

PUTTING THE SOVIETS ON THE DEFENSIVE

Soviet propaganda says deployment will alter the existing, stable balance of power in Europe with new missiles that can reach Soviet territory in a matter of minutes. We need to find a way to call attention to *their* missiles, which can reach targets in Europe in a matter of minutes and which are *already* deployed.

What better way to turn public attention on the Soviet missiles than to propose that there will be no American missiles if the Soviets simply remove theirs?

Surely, this proposal would place the Soviets on the defensive. Even Soviet apologists will have a tough time with this one.

The left in Europe—the source of much of our political problem with respect to keeping the deployment plans on track—would be compelled to embrace the Zero Option. It is, after all, *what they have been asking for.*

A PROPOSAL WITH STAYING POWER

Where does one go from Zero? One of the great advantages of Zero is that there is no way to improve it. It is difficult to imagine Soviet proposals that would have broad appeal, since any counteroffer is bound to permit them to keep at least some missiles.

Once presented, who would urge us to compromise the Zero Option? Certainly not the peace movement, since any compromise would mean the Soviets could keep some of their SS-20s. Not the supporters of our deployment, who will surely understand that a move such as this is necessary to sustain support for our deployment.

In short, no one has an incentive to move off Zero. It thus has a durability that has seldom been found in American negotiating positions. There is no doubt that the president will come under pressure to compromise. Zero is likely to be far more resistant to pressure than any other proposal we can imagine. It has the potential to gain adherents, a constituency that identifies not simply with the idea of a negotiated settlement but with *this* negotiated settlement. That is a significant anchor that other proposals lack.

It Is Simple, Clear, Dramatic

Most recent American arms-control proposals have been complex— sometimes to the point that only an expert can evaluate them. The president can explain Zero Option in a single, simple sentence: "Today, I propose to Mr. Novikov that the United States and the Soviet Union eliminate the entire class of intermediate nuclear missiles." That is something that everyone can understand.

Zero is dramatic because, ironically, Soviet propaganda has conditioned opinion in Europe to expect an aggressive, defiant American position that appears aimed exclusively at allowing American missiles on European territory. Drama lies, in this case at least, in the abrupt transformation of expectations.

We cannot be certain, but it appears likely State will propose something along the lines of reductions "to the lowest level agreeable to the Soviet side." This strikes me as a typical diplomat's formulation: perfectly sensible, staid, sober—and utterly lacking in popular appeal. Pizzazz sells cereal, automobiles, and air tickets. Why not an arms-control package? After all, we are seeking to communicate not with diplomats, but with mass opinion in a number of countries whose cooperation is crucial if we are ultimately to deploy.

Will It Enhance Our Security?

It is unlikely the Soviets will agree to give up their SS-20s and other missiles that would come under the definition we propose. But if we stand with the Zero Option, for however long it takes, and if we can sustain momentum behind our deployment, there is a chance that the Soviets will come around. So the question must be asked of this—or any other—proposal: Would our security be enhanced by an agreement that eliminated all intermediate nuclear missiles?

There are some who believe the United States ought to have missiles that are capable of reaching deep into Soviet territory deployed *in Europe*. They would not give up an American deployment even if the Soviets removed their SS-20s. They would argue that acceptance of the Zero Option would weaken, not enhance, American and Allied security.

Those who hold this view believe the key to peace in Europe is the possession by the United States of a credible nuclear deterrent that would be used against the Soviet Union in the event of an attack on Western Europe. I disagree. My staff has done a study on the NATO installations that might be attacked by Soviet SS-20s. There are approximately 150 of them. Just fifty SS-20 missiles, each with three warheads, would be sufficient to attack and destroy nearly all of those crucial installations. Thus, in order to achieve a militarily significant result at the negotiating table (i.e., in order to enhance our security with a treaty), we would have to limit the Soviet SS-20 force to well below fifty missiles. If we can demand they reduce that far, why not go all the way and demand zero?

But there is another reason for believing that the elimination of the entire class of weapons would enhance our security. The argument that the new missiles are needed to deter assumes they are capable of surviving attack. After all, a missile that can be destroyed before the war begins, or that is destroyed in the first salvo, is hardly an effective deterrent. Yet Pershing II and cruise missiles are dangerously vulnerable. And, needless to say, they would be the highest-priority Soviet targets in the event of war.

They are highly vulnerable because to survive they must be moved to field locations, away from their bases, at the earliest sign that an attack may be coming. If they are still on their bases when the attack arrives, they will surely be destroyed. The shelters in which they are kept are vulnerable, even to conventional bombs.

Yet there is no reason to believe that they would be dispersed in a timely manner. Most of the governments will not allow us to disperse them in peacetime. And if war appears to be looming, the last thing we will wish to do is exacerbate the situation by moving nuclear missiles around. That has been our past experience. We have actually moved our forces less in periods of tension and crisis out of a concern that troop movements could worsen things.

Well aware of their vulnerability, the Soviets practice attacking them. They have actually built a mock Pershing base near Kishinev, where they can be observed using special forces, *Spetznaz*, to destroy them. Literally thousands of troops have trained to attack missile bases whose locations are well known.

The bottom line is this: We are not giving up very much in readying ourselves to scrap the plans for Pershing II. By contrast, the Soviets give up a formidable force that is not vulnerable to our forces. It is a good deal for us.

WHAT ABOUT CHEATING?

One of the great advantages of the Zero Option is that it is by far the easiest arrangement to verify, although it will not be easy to achieve high confidence of compliance.

If neither side is permitted any intermediate-range missiles, then it follows that neither side would be allowed to train troops on medium missiles, to maintain production, maintenance, and repair facilities for them, or test them. Our ability to monitor Soviet compliance with these restrictions is much greater than our ability to count the number of missiles they have if they are allowed any. Moreover, if none are allowed, then the detection of *even a single missile* is a violation, and a rather clear one at that.

If you agree that the Zero Option is an appropriate position for the Department of Defense, we will have to map out a strategy for selling it to the president.

Approve _____

Approve in principle _____

See me _____

SECRET-SENSITIVE

CHAPTER NINE

Potomac, Maryland, September 28, 2:00 P.M.

Waterman could make out Laura's bright red down parka at the far end of the playing field as he maneuvered his car into the most remote parking space on the furrowed suburban meadow that served, every fall, as a parking lot for the Montgomery County Junior Soccer League. In the distance he could discern the erratic movements of the teams as they followed the ball, but he couldn't spot Jason among the knot of running five-year-olds in their Domino's Pizza red-and-gold jerseys.

He was bleary-eyed from eighteen straight hours at the word processor and jumpy from the caffeine overdose brought on by half a dozen espressos. Yet he was also exhilarated by having written what he considered a terrific arms-proposal memo—just in time to reverse DOD's sinking fortunes. He had left it less than an hour before in a sealed envelope with the cables clerk, who would hand it to the secretary of defense the moment he arrived at the Pentagon Monday morning.

Then he had rushed home, doused himself under the hottest shower he could stand for five minutes, shaved, climbed into a pair of old chinos, ragged tennis shoes, and a flannel shirt so old it felt like silk, and raced out River Road, north to the Potomac playing field where Jason's Domino's Dynamos were slugging it out with the Montague Academy Misfits. He knew Jason would be pleased that he'd managed to arrive in time to see most of the second half. It would be the first time he'd seen his son play all year.

Waterman had never been much of an athlete. An occasional game of tennis, a morning's excursion on well-marked paths in Switzerland or Colorado, an hour or so of snorkeling in the Caribbean—those were the outer limits of his athletic endeavors. Laura, on the other hand, was a tournament-level tennis player, a natural and graceful skier, and an inveterate jogger. So it hadn't been hard for her to convince herself that young Jason was his mother's son in the exercise department, with the result that the youngster had been enrolled, much to his delight, in half-pint soccer, kid tennis, junior basketball, pre–Little League baseball, kinder-karate, and horseback riding.

He trudged the length of the field, looking blankly at the faces of the other parents as they watched the game's progress, chatting easily with one another or laughing at their kids' antics. He knew no one—unhappy evidence of the degree to which he had absented himself from his role as parent, chauffeur, and cheerleader.

It was not by his choosing, of course, or so he said. Yet, when parental push came to parental shove, it was Laura who did all of the work. His habitual truancy was a source of friction between them. She understood intellectually that Waterman's work was important to him—and to the country. But she had never been able to accept it emotionally. To Laura, whose childhood had been spent in the bosom of a large, close-knit Southern family replete with dozens of cousins, aunts, and uncles, all within walking distance of her parents' house, the thought that a father would put his work ahead of his child was apostasy pure and simple.

Waterman, on the other hand, had grown up in a home where he remained at the dinner table until every detested vegetable had been consumed. His work, whether it was a school assignment, cello practice, or religious-school lessons, came before everything else, including television, movies, even pleasure reading. That was how his father, Sam, had been brought up, and young Michael Waterman's inculcation was no different. As a Capitol Hill staffer, he had gained a reputation as single-minded, persistent, and tenacious, even though he habitually put things off until the last minute. As an assistant secretary of defense, he'd brought those qualities to the Pentagon, where he defended his turf, and Ryder's, with a dogged ferocity.

But he'd done it by working eighty-plus-hour weeks at the expense of his family—a fact Laura made abundantly clear to him at every opportunity. So he was happy when, instead of upbraiding him for being late, Laura put an arm around his waist and said, "I'm really glad you made it. Jason must've asked a dozen times whether you'd be coming."

"I hope you didn't promise I'd be here. That's just asking for trouble."

"It's been years since I've promised to deliver you anywhere, Michael—least of all to expendable events like your only child's soccer games." She waited for him to say something. Wisely, he remained silent. "Well," she finally asked, "did you get it done?"

"Yup—gave it to cables at one. You know," he burbled, still running on adrenaline, "it's incredible—I knew it would take an all-nighter to get it done the way it had to get done . . . that's the only way I can really concentrate. But, boy, this time I really left things for the brink. I was really on the edge of the envelope this time—I won't do that again soon."

"*This time!* Give me a break. For God's sake, Michael, you're always leaving things until the last possible moment. You've been doing it for years. I can live with the fact that you neglect us. I can deal with the fact that you're married to your job." She withdrew her arm and took a step backward. "But don't try to justify your chronic procrastination by telling me it has some purpose, like enabling you to concentrate."

She was being prickly, and right or wrong, Waterman began to resent it. "Hey, c'mon, sweetie—cut me some slack, will you? I've been up all night. And then I raced like hell to get here so I could watch a bunch of five-year-olds stumble around as if *they'd* been slaving over a hot word processor for the past eighteen hours, and all you can do is pick a fight."

She looked at him and shook her head, then she smiled. "You're right, of course. Why would I ever think you'd change?"

"I'm too old to change, sweetie."

"Not too old, Michael—too lazy. Like an old dog—set in your ways. But you know what?"

"What?"

"We love you anyway. Even though you're not perfect."

"What?"

"You're not perfect."

"Surely, you jest. I'm perfection personified. I have it in writing."

"From who? *Good Housekeeping?*"

"Better—Senator Arthur Winter himself. Remember the joint resolution he sent me when I went to the Pentagon—the one that's framed on my office wall?"

She laughed. "The joint House-Senate resolution declaring you a national treasure?"

"Yup."

"I stand corrected. And it doesn't even matter that he had it printed as a joke, right?"

"A resolution is a resolution—even though it never made it onto the floor." He swept her back into his arms and kissed her on the lips. "A perfect kiss for a perfect wife."

She kissed him back. "On that, I agree a hundred percent."

They stood for a moment watching the kids move awkwardly across the field in pursuit of the ball. "Hey," he asked, suddenly remembering why he'd shown up, "what's the score?"

"We're down two goals. Thank God Jason was too far away from the action to be responsible for either. You know how he hates to lose. I wonder where he gets that?"

"Maybe you'd prefer a kid who *likes* losing?"

"About as much as a husband who does."

He grinned. "Aren't you going to ask me what I came up with?"

"You took the words right out of my mouth. What did you come up with?"

"Zero."

"Zero?"

"Yup. Zero. Zilch. *Rien. Nada.*"

"So why are you smiling?"

"Because," Waterman said, "Zero is the perfect answer to our problem."

Laura looked at him strangely. "Maybe you better run that by me again."

"It's simple. I'm proposing we eliminate all medium-range missiles on both sides—zero. Double zero. It'll knock their socks off."

"Frankly, it doesn't sound like something Ryder would jump at," she said, still looking somewhat confused. "In fact, it sounds rather like something George McGovern might propose."

"That's why it's perfect," Waterman replied. "And I think Ryder will jump at it—when he reads my memo."

"Well, I'm just glad it's finished. Perfection notwithstanding, Michael, you've been beastly to live with lately. First you were down about what happened at COCOM. And with all the work you've been doing on the summit, you've been uptight and cranky. Frankly, I've felt frozen out. That's the thing, Michael—you never let me in anymore. You're carrying around all this weight—but you won't share the burden with anybody."

"It isn't easy, sweetie. I—"

"Of course it isn't easy, Michael. I just want to help, that's all."

"I appreciate that."

She pulled away. "See—that's what I mean. You 'appreciate that.' It sounds like you're writing me a memo. For God's sake, Michael—talk to me. Don't cut me off."

He nodded. "Okay—I'll try."

"Will you promise?"

He held up three fingers like a Boy Scout. "On my honor."

She smiled. He loved it when she smiled. "Tell you what—let's celebrate Zero. We can take next weekend off. I'll arrange a sleepover for Jason on Saturday night. His friend Jacob's family spends weekends at a cabin in the Shenandoah. We'll go out to dinner, just the two of us. Then we'll come home and make love nonstop until Jason gets back Sunday night. It'll be like Italy. Don't stop to think—say yes."

A knot formed in Waterman's stomach. "I—I can't," he stammered. "Sweetheart, I should've told you before now—I've known for two days, but I've been so damn preoccupied—I've got to go to Paris Thursday for three days."

"Paris? Why?"

"Christine Caronne wants to interview me."

"Jesus, Michael—"

"Look, the piece will run a full page in *Figaro*. It's a terrific chance to make the American case for midrange-missile deployment."

"I thought you said you'd just come up with a plan to eliminate medium-range missiles."

"I did."

"Then why the hell do you have to do an interview promoting deployment?"

"That's complicated—and I really don't want to talk about it now."

"I'll bet."

"Look, Laura, we can't go into the details standing on a soccer field in public. All I know is I've been given a terrific opportunity to make the American case. Ryder's keen for me to do it. And besides, everyone reads her pieces. It'll be an important interview."

"That's because she asks questions like whether or not you sleep in the nude. She's not serious, Michael."

"Of course she's serious. She's interviewed everyone from Qaddafi to Novikov himself. Believe me, this is a coup for us—for DOD's position." He crossed his arms defensively. "It's a must-do."

Laura looked as if she'd been mugged. "Okay," she sighed. "I can understand you going to Paris. If Jim Ryder wants you to do this, then who am I to object? But can't you come back right after the interview? Do we have to lose the whole weekend?"

"I go out Thursday night. The interview's on Friday. It gets transcribed overnight, she goes over it Saturday morning, then we tape another session to fill in the blanks. Then there's a working dinner Saturday night."

"That's the pits."

"What can I do?"

"Well, if she wants to interview you so badly, you could use some of your allegedly world-famous negotiating skills to get her to agree to finish with you by noon Saturday. There's an afternoon plane from Paris that would get you back here in time for dinner. And we could still have all of Sunday together."

"You're forgetting the working dinner Saturday night."

"Screw the dinner, Michael. It can't be that important."

"Yes it is," he insisted. "It's with all the top *Figaro* editors, and it's being held in my honor at the paper's town house."

The look she gave him indicated that she wasn't buying a word of it.

"Okay, okay," he said after a long pause. "I'll have Parisi call first thing Monday and see if the schedule can be changed. But I'm not optimistic . . . this thing is set in stone."

The Pentagon, October 3, 5:00 P.M.

The intercom on Jay Parisi's desk buzzed, and Maggie's voice paged him brusquely. "Laura for you. She doesn't sound happy."

Parisi plucked the phone from its cradle. "Hi, Laura, what's up?" He liked Laura Waterman—as much as he liked any VIP's wife. She was less demanding than most, and she didn't treat him like a servant.

"What's up is my temperature. Michael's in Paris for what he assures me is the interview of the century, and the phone number I've got for him is wrong."

"Wrong?"

"Wrong. I just phoned the Inter-Continental, and they said he's not registered." Her voice became plaintive. "Jay, I've got to reach him. Jason's locked himself in the wine cellar and won't come out because I took away his Nintendo. I took away his Nintendo because he wouldn't get out of the car at the dentist's. He gets uncontrollable because Michael's away so much. Normally, I can deal with it. But now he's been in the wine cellar for three hours. *Three hours!* And there's no sign he's weakening."

Parisi frowned. "Maybe if I talked to him?"

"That might work if there were some way you could do it. But there's no phone."

"Oh."

"I can't break the door down. There's a spare key, Jay—do you know where Michael keeps it?"

He sighed. "Sorry, Laura, I don't."

She sounded desperate. "Well, Michael knows where the spare key is—I've just got to get hold of him."

"Of course you do." Parisi slid his file drawer open and riffled through it, coming up empty. "But he's not at the Inter-Continental, Laura."

"But on the itinerary he left for me—"

"They were full. *Figaro* found him a room at the Meurice."

"Do you have the number there?"

"I've been looking for it while we've been talking. I guess Maggie has it. Tell you what—turn on the fax, and we'll send you the whole trip book. That's got his schedule right down to the minute they put the mints on his pillow. That way, even if you don't reach him at the Meurice, you'll have all the other numbers."

"God bless you, Jay. I'll run downstairs right now."

Six minutes later, he took a second call from Laura.

"Don't say a word, Jay. No comments, no interruptions. Just take notes. And please listen carefully, because I'm only going to say this once. Are we clear?"

Parisi grabbed for a notepad and pencil. He'd never heard a woman so furious. "We're clear—but, Laura, what's—"

"I said no interruptions, Jay. On the second page of Christine Caronne's letter to my husband the assistant secretary of defense—a letter that was faxed to me just minutes ago—the following passage appears. Quote: 'We'll be finished by eleven on Saturday. We can easily get you to De Gaulle in time for TWA's nonstop to Dulles, which leaves at one P.M., or Air France's flight at three.

" 'But, if you could spare the time in your busy schedule, I would be delighted to host a small dinner party for you with some of *Figaro*'s editors, as well as one or two officials who work on defense matters, and we'll also invite Robert Mitchum and Victoria Tennant, old friends of mine, who are in Paris to film scenes for a World War II movie. I guarantee that if you are able to stay, I'll make it a pleasant evening.' End of quote."

"Yes? So?" Parisi was confused. What was her point?

"This, Jay, is the same dinner that my husband the assistant secretary assured me was so important, so crucial to the vital national interests of the United States, that he had to cancel a weekend with me to attend it.

The first weekend we would have had alone together in more than a year. Correct me if I am mistaken, Jay, but the tone of this message seems to indicate that the dinner in question was what you military types might designate an optional event."

He blinked. He understood. "Laura—"

"Shut up, Jay." Laura's voice was like ice. "Remember—I said no interruptions. Just take notes. First, I have broken into the wine cellar with a sledgehammer to retrieve my son. A few of the assistant secretary's bottles of wine were destroyed in the process—irreplaceable bottles, if you must know, but there's no crying over spilt wine, right? Second, I do not wish to waste any of my own money on a phone call to Paris. So please use tax dollars to inform the assistant secretary that if he doesn't have his house keys with him as he arrives home from the indispensable, critical, momentous dinner party he chose to attend instead of spending the weekend with me, he'd better call a locksmith from the airport. Because I will not be there when he gets home."

CHAPTER TEN

Andrews Air Force Base, October 8, 7:30 P.M.

Standing at the cabin door of the Special Air Mission C-135 with UNITED STATES OF AMERICA written across the fuselage, Waterman craned his neck to watch as the last of the footlockers inched up the conveyor belt into the hold. It was the treasure chest—the protocol trunk—filled with gifts and mementos, to be presented by the secretary of defense, or in his name. For ministers there was engraved Steuben glass in the shape of an American eagle. For the British security details, ballpoint pens imprinted with the seal of the Department of Defense and the secretary's signature, and for those in between, gold-plated cuff links, tie clips, pins, and pendants, all emblazoned with a rampant American eagle clutching arrows in its talons.

As Waterman watched, the crew closed the cargo door. In the distance he could see the flashing red lights of Ryder's limousine and chase car winding their way past the chain-link security fence beyond the VIP lounge. Already, the plane's scratchy P.A. system was playing Willie Nelson's "On the Road Again," selected by SECDEF's military assistant, Bill Collins, as the "wheels up" theme for all foreign trips.

The limo pulled up alongside the forward door. Ryder scampered up the steps, a leather portfolio clutched like a football under his left arm, and went directly to his private compartment. Immediately, the plane taxied onto Andrews' main runway. From his seat, Waterman could see the dim outlines of F-15 Eagle fighter aircraft in the distance. He saw the lights move faster and faster until, with a surge of power, the C-135 rose into the night sky.

He settled back into his seat, lost in thought. His return from Paris had been dismal. He arrived at De Gaulle to find his plane overbooked. So, instead of getting upgraded, he'd been placed on standby. When he finally received his seat, moments before takeoff, he discovered he'd been plunked in a middle seat, flanked by a teenage mother clutching a bawling, colicky infant, and an old man who snored like a locomotive from the moment the plane took off until it landed eight hours later.

Moreover, the trip had been a complete bust. Christine Caronne was less than he'd imagined, a weary, distracted, neurotic egocentric who knew a good deal less about arms control than Laura did. Her interview was ordinary, neither probing nor particularly insightful. It had run in Monday's *Figaro*—a third of a page buried in the midst of half a dozen stories about antinuclear protests in various European capitals.

Waterman's much-anticipated weekend with the Paris glitterati turned out to be pedestrian in all respects, too. The conversation was boring, the company banal, the food lukewarm and badly catered, the wine pretentious but mediocre. The Hollywood stars failed to show up, pleading jet lag. The next morning he read on the way to the airport that they'd been seen in a chic three-star restaurant in the Place de la Madeleine.

Arriving home to an empty house was even worse. He tried calling North Carolina—a dozen times in the first hour—but she wouldn't take his calls, so he wandered through the silent rooms like a sleepwalker, picking up articles of clothing that had been left behind and straightening pictures on the walls. He cracked the door of Jason's room and was almost brought to tears when he saw his son's empty, unmade bed. He descended to look at the ruins of his wine-cellar door and the shards of glass that had once been Chablis, Châteauneuf-du-Pape, and, worse, La Tâche. Both precious bottles. The first night, he made a berm of pillows on Laura's side of the bed and rolled up against them for the worst night he'd had in his adult life. He was, to put it succinctly, miserable.

There had been arguments before, sometimes heated. And occasionally she'd left the house, slamming the door behind her and driving off—God knows where—for two or three hours. But never before had she, well, abandoned him. Never before had she taken Jason out of kindergarten and driven back to her parents' home in North Carolina. Waterman tried obsessively to call her long after it was obvious she wouldn't take his calls.

Now, he was on an airplane, anxious and depressed over Laura's departure, worried about the resilience of his marriage, facing a sleepless night that would be followed by an eighteen-hour day at a NATO ministerial meeting. He crossed his arms and tried to get comfortable in the lumpy seat. It was crazy to fly all night and work all day. It was crazy for Laura to have left him. It was all just plain crazy.

His mind abruptly switched gears. There was his Zero memo, to which he had had no response. He knew the secretary had read it, but Waterman had absolutely no idea whether Ryder liked it or not, and if he did approve of Waterman's idea, how he would get Zero onto the president's desk.

As the plane leveled off, the secretary appeared in the entrance of the forward cabin, where Waterman and the rest of the senior aides sat two abreast. He caught Waterman's eye, motioned him forward, and turned on his heel without a word. Waterman fumbled under the seat for his attaché case and followed.

Ryder's airborne office contained a well-worn leather judge's high-backed chair, which faced an L-shaped banquette. Between the two sat an imitation leather–covered trapezoid-shaped coffee table, which could be raised or lowered by manipulating a lever on one of its chrome legs. The secretary's plane had once been the *Air Force One* craft used by Lyndon Johnson. Waterman could imagine the lanky president raising the table to accommodate his knees and holding court before a gaggle of staffers arrayed along the banquette.

Ryder plunked himself into the judge's chair. Reaching into a pocket, the secretary withdrew a pair of tortoiseshell half-glasses and placed them partway up his high forehead. Then he nodded, barely—just enough to indicate to Waterman that he expected him to sit at the L of the banquette closest to him.

James Ryder, longtime friend and confidant of the president, had been the president's first Cabinet appointment. In the five years he had been secretary of defense he had enjoyed the president's support on every matter of controversy that was important to him. His legal training, followed by a successful business career and two decades of government service, had honed his powers of advocacy. Those qualities, together with his long and intimate association with the president, made Ryder the most powerful secretary of defense since Robert Lovett served Harry Truman.

Ryder believed that power and influence increased by being used, and he used his liberally. He had clashed with the secretary of commerce over restricting the sale of advanced technology to the Soviet bloc; with the director of the Office of Management and Budget over the size of the defense budget; and with the secretary of the treasury over both issues. The Congress considered him rigid and uncompromising because he steadfastly refused to say where the Defense Department budget could be cut without jeopardizing national security, leaving members to defend their actions when they imposed cuts.

Ryder hated to lose. He had hated to lose in the Lions' Club high school oratorical contest back in Appleton, Wisconsin—and so he practiced until he won. He had hated to lose as a starter on Harvard's wrestling team—and so he did what he had to do to win. The same behavior was true in moot-court competition at Harvard Law, in corporate litigation in New York, and later in life during the perpetual competition for the president's mind in the White House's Cabinet and Situation rooms and the Oval Office. But as a man of the highest moral and ethical principles, he believed the end did not justify the means. Ryder played political hardball—major-league political hardball. But he played the game fair.

As a Senate staffer, Waterman had observed Ryder during a decade of appearances on the Hill as a member of half a dozen presidential boards, delegations, and special oversight commissions. He admired the man's toughness, his ability to confront detractors head-on, his commitment to American strength, and, above all, his mistrust of the Soviets—and had repeatedly made his sentiments known to Arthur Winter. So, when the senator called Ryder the week after his confirmation and suggested he appoint Waterman an assistant secretary, he knew he was brokering a marriage made in heaven.

It had turned out that way, too. Ryder was quick to see Waterman's strengths and employ them effectively. He was also quick to forgive the younger man's flaws and, through effective management, temper his weaknesses. After their half-decade together they could start and finish each other's sentences like a couple of old-time radio broadcasters—without a hint of dead air.

It was a relationship that many in Washington found remarkable. Few Cabinet officers ever entrusted to their inferiors the powers Ryder gave to Waterman. But, then, he was more than an aide—he was treated warmly by the crusty secretary of defense, if not like a son, then like a favorite nephew. In fact, they were even on a first-name basis. Ryder called him "Michael," and he called Ryder "sir."

"I thought we might go over the briefing book now," Ryder said. He squinted at Waterman. "You know," he said, "you've been looking most dispirited for the past few days, Michael."

"It's nothing, sir, really."

Ryder crossed his arms. "Don't give me that. You've been moping like a sad puppy. What's the problem?"

Waterman sighed audibly.

Ryder shook a finger at him. "Come on, tell me. It's in my interest to know. I can't operate as well as I might if you're not up to speed—and you're not up to speed."

It all came out in a flood—so fast that Waterman was surprised at himself. "I've got problems at home. The travel's started to wear on Laura. She's been left to cope with Jason pretty much by herself, and it's been a real strain on her. And this last interview I did—the one in Paris with Christine Caronne—I shouldn't have gone. Much less stayed for the dinner on Saturday."

"Oh?"

"Laura had planned a weekend, and she was disappointed when I had to cancel it."

"Well, don't neglect things at home, Michael. Stability. That's what keeps us going. You have to balance things out. We work too hard—and we won't stop. But every second you can spare, you must give to your wife and child. For example, why not call Laura now—use the onboard phone."

"She's not home, sir. That's the thing—she took Jason and drove to her parents' house in North Carolina." Waterman's voice turned desperate. "She won't even take my calls."

"It sounds as if she was a little more than 'disappointed,' Michael. If I'd known, I wouldn't have permitted you on this trip," Ryder said sternly. "Look, first thing after we get home, you take a few days off. You go right down there and patch things up. I have nothing against hard work. But take it from me—your family has got to come first. This job won't last forever. Your wife and your son are your life. So go to her, Michael. Talk to her. Bring her home."

Waterman blinked. Of course—he had to go down to Riverton and see Laura, convince her to come with him. The fact that going to North Carolina had never even occurred to him brought home in a rush the dismal state of his marriage. He responded gratefully, "Thank you, sir. That's exactly what I'll do—the minute we're back."

"Good," Ryder said. "Now"—he leaned forward and indicated Waterman's briefcase—"what's first?"

Waterman unlocked the case and withdrew the briefing books. There was one for the NATO meeting itself, another for the separate bilateral meetings—bilats, as they were known—which would be sandwiched in between plenary sessions. He also took out a yellow legal pad, the most recent cable traffic, and one red and one black soft-tip pen.

If there was one specific duty Waterman liked above all others, it was briefing Ryder. It brought out the best of Waterman's academic qualities, and challenged him intellectually in a way few things around the Pentagon did. The secretary was quick to absorb huge amounts of information, but he also expected—demanded—that Waterman have a command of the material for which he was responsible; and while it was perfectly all right if there was a fact here or there he didn't know—a name that was unfamiliar or a statistic that he hadn't thought to present—it was a good idea to keep those lapses to a minimum. Above all it was unacceptable to pretend to knowledge you didn't have.

For ninety unbroken minutes Waterman forgot his troubles as he ran through the briefing book, making notes in various colors on his legal pad in response to Ryder's questions. On some issues Ryder probed deep, on others he merely nodded, his eyes closed, as Waterman recited a litany of trivia about issues that might be broached by one or another of the ministers gathering at Gleneagles. He finished with a narration of Ryder's schedule, and then read the arrival statement that would be issued in the secretary's name. Ryder penciled some changes and handed the statement back. Waterman took it and closed the briefing book with a slap. "That's it."

"Are you sure?" The secretary's eyes twinkled. "Will there be a test now?"

"Not necessary. I think you've got it down pretty well." Waterman checked his legal pad. "We've covered everything."

"Not quite." Ryder pushed a paper across the table. "I thought we might go over this."

Waterman recognized it immediately—it was his Zero memorandum, now in the form of a Ryder memo to the president. He read it greedily, his eyes moving rapidly across the pages. There were changes here and there, all penned in green and easy to identify. Lines had been crossed out and new wording substituted, sentences inserted and deleted, notes added, some question marks inserted in the margins, and a few passages underlined for emphasis. In two places unwieldy phrases had been simplified and improved. But—oh, God—the proposal for the Zero Option was unaltered, and none of the editorial changes was of great significance.

As he read, the pulse pounding in his head, Waterman recognized the one change of consequence Ryder had made. It was a brilliant stroke: a single short sentence added to the end of a paragraph about the probable international political reaction to Zero. *You would certainly be nominated for, and very likely be awarded, the Nobel Peace Prize if this proposal is accepted.*

Ryder watched Waterman, followed his widening eyes as they came to rest on the handwritten passage about the Nobel Prize. "That will get his attention," Ryder said. "And so it should. He'll need to know something like that when the going gets rough—and it will get rough.

"I'm sending your memo—as amended—overnight from the aircraft.

It'll be in Washington for the president's morning briefing. I've arranged with Gary Burner to hand it to him when he meets with him tomorrow morning. McCandless will be there, too, and he's also been primed. Sad to say, Winthrop won't be around—he's in Brazil." He broke into a broad grin.

"Burner's on our side on this," Ryder continued. "He doesn't understand all the subtleties, of course. But he's shrewd enough to know the proposal will be a public-relations triumph—and that's all he really cares about." Ryder smiled paternally. "I'm hoping the president will decide to go with your proposal before we leave Gleneagles. It's a brilliant proposal and a first-class memo, Michael."

Waterman returned to the forward cabin walking on air. For the moment, at least, the problems he'd left behind in Washington were forgotten. He locked his briefcase and stowed it beneath his seat. Eyes wide open, he scanned the dark skies outside the aircraft window. How the hell would he ever get to sleep tonight?

He awoke with a start, sweaty and wrinkled in his seat, from a dream he couldn't remember, to hear a steward announce they were on final approach. He looked out the window. The plane was descending rapidly over rough terrain, buffeted by crosswinds and bouncing in the wind shear. He had no idea where he was. By the time he realized he was over Scotland, the flaps were down and the pilot was turning into his final approach. It was a struggle to get himself awake enough to disembark.

Immediately after landing, the secretary and senior staff—including Waterman, to his intense relief—climbed into helicopters just a few yards from where the aircraft came to rest. The remaining aides, the security detail, and the press were all loaded into buses for the hour-long drive to Gleneagles.

Waterman peered down at the rolling green Scottish countryside below. He could always count on the logistics at NATO ministerial meetings to be handled with superb attention to detail and a lavish use of resources. Any trip that would take more than twenty minutes by road was likely to be done by helicopter. All the army choppers in Scotland must have been assigned to ferrying defense ministers and their staffs.

Nose to glass, he watched as his chopper dropped onto an emerald-green fairway on the vast hotel grounds. Despite the fact that each national delegation had been assigned an office equipped with secure telephone lines, copy machines, and typewriters, little office work actually took place at NATO ministerial meetings. The agenda always included briefings on the military forces of the Alliance and its enemies, updates on the progress of the major Alliance projects, and a report from the Supreme Allied Commander or the general then serving as chairman of the Military Committee.

The centerpiece of every NATO ministerial meeting was the communiqué, a statement agreed to by all the countries represented and issued at the conclusion of the second day. Because it was a consensus document, it was invariably bland and often convoluted. Terrible battles, in fact, were often fought over whether to say "wishes," "hopes," or "desires" in the third sentence of the ninth paragraph.

Waterman was determined that this meeting's communiqué would not be a source of controversy. With the United States yet to decide on a negotiating strategy for talks with the Soviets, coupled with intense interest around the world about what Washington would do, there was nothing to be gained by an argument among allies that would inevitably become public. But disturbing signs began to surface over dinner.

The dining room was set up for a buffet, and ministers and staffs mixed freely as they piled their plates with smoked salmon, cold roast beef, pork, ham, an array of salads, mousses, and patés, cheeses, vegetables, breads, and those leaden, cloying desserts with which the British have burdened themselves and every corner of the empire over which they once presided. Waterman had arranged to dine with the heads of the British and German delegations to the High Level Group, the committee he chaired. They were soon joined by the Italian delegate.

Waterman lost no time getting down to business as they settled at a corner table. "We just about have a quorum," he said. "Anyone expecting anything more eventful than bagpipes and a stroll around the golf course?"

"Well, there's the haggis tomorrow night," laughed John McBride, Waterman's British counterpart, a dedicated Scotsman and the host-country official responsible for the Gleneagles meeting.

"Whatsa thees 'aggis, John?" Carlo Giannini asked. "Itsa some Scottish custom, no?" Giannini spoke perfect Oxford English but delighted in pouring on a comic-book accent around the subdued, stiffly correct, and sometimes melancholy Scotsman.

"Carlo," Waterman interjected, "seldom in your career will your patriotism be more thoroughly tested than tomorrow night when you dine on the intestine of a sheep that's been stuffed with innards and baked, or boiled—I'm not sure which—for half a day."

"Just a minute," McBride demurred. "I'm quite certain our distinguished chairman has never had a properly prepared haggis. Our Gleneagles haggis will be memorable."

"I hope so," Waterman said. "But before we get to the haggis, we face another unappetizing main course: the communiqué—or at least the initial drafting. What should I be expecting?"

McBride waggled an index finger. "Well, you may have one problem, Michael. The Dutch are circulating a paragraph urging NATO not to deploy medium-range missiles if the Soviets halt deployment of SS-20s at present levels. They call it the Zero Freeze. The Danes, Norwegians, Greeks, and possibly the Belgians will support them." He sniffed disdainfully. "My prime minister is dead set against it, of course. We'll oppose it because there's an agreed Alliance mechanism for developing a negotiating position, and a communiqué isn't it."

Waterman was stunned. The consequence of another Zero Option would be a death blow to his own idea, which had only hours before been sent to the president. Worse, the Dutch plan wasn't a real negotiating position—it was a unilateral act that would kill Allied deployment while allowing the Soviets to keep their already-deployed missiles in place.

Waterman turned to the German delegate. "Hans?"

"We're under a lot of pressure to support the Dutch. The chancellor is worried about local elections next week in Westphalia, where there's been a large number of antinuclear protests lately."

Waterman kept a poker face and turned toward the Italian. "Carlo, what's your government's position on a freeze?"

"I don't know. Defense Minister Sardini meets with his Dutch counterpart at breakfast tomorrow. I know the freeze is on the agenda. It could be tough: The Dutch are about to choose between an Italian gun or a French one for their frigates. The deal's worth two hundred million to us, and there are three hundred jobs at stake in the prime minister's home district. That gives the Dutch a lot of leverage."

Waterman had a sinking feeling as he listened. There was no obvious way to defeat the Dutch initiative without exactly the sort of public fight he was under instructions to avoid. Yet any sign of softness could fuel the antideployment movement's momentum. He knew that with millions of demonstrators in the streets on a daily basis, governments all over Europe were under tremendous pressure to announce they would do something to halt the spread of nuclear weapons—whether or not they believed such a move was strategically correct.

He took a breath. "Let me speak plainly," Waterman said. "We will categorically oppose the Dutch Zero Freeze, or anything like it, in the communiqué. There's no way an American secrctary of defense can agree to language proposing an outcome to negotiations that have not even begun."

The German frowned. "But, Michael, the point is the Dutch have come up with a new idea—something that hasn't been tried before. Look, a freeze may not affect America. But it makes sense to many of those of us who live where your missiles will be based."

"Hans, the Dutch proposal is b.s., pure and simple. Look, if two hundred Russian SS-20s are aimed at Western Europe—as they already are—and we don't deploy our own missiles, where's the equality to the equation? They have two hundred—we have none."

"We all understand that, dear boy," McBride interrupted. "But we're bound to hear the argument that a forward-leaning statement in the communiqué is essential to keep deployment on track."

This was lunacy. "Look," Waterman said, trying to keep his voice even, "shouldn't we find Henk van den Berg and talk him out of it now? We're far better off discussing things privately over dinner than in a big drafting session with fifty people in the room."

"I'll find him," Carlo Giannini said.

Waterman turned to the remaining pair. "I take it the three of us agree, at least, that we won't have any real leverage until we actually have missiles deployed."

"Absolutely," McBride said. "That's my view—" He looked at the German, who nodded. "It's Hans's view, and Carlo's—and I even imagine it's the Dutch view, too."

"We'll find out soon," said the German, pointing across the room with his nose. Waterman looked up to see Carlo approaching the table with Henk van den Berg in tow.

"Welcome to Scotland, Henk," McBride said. "Pull up a chair. Dinner seems to have turned into a sort of rump session to discuss the communiqué. I'm glad we found you."

The Dutchman shook hands all around and grabbed an empty chair from an adjoining table. Tall and thin, with a ruddy complexion and thinning white hair, Van den Berg was within six weeks of his retirement from a job he'd held for thirty years at the Dutch Ministry of Defense. His last assignment was not a happy one: arguing the case for the presence of nuclear weapons on Dutch soil at a time when pacifism and antinuclear sentiment swept The Netherlands like wildfire.

"Henk," Waterman said, "I've been telling our colleagues that we are absolutely opposed to a freeze on intermediate nuclear missiles. We can't agree to anything like that."

"Michael, Michael, it wasn't my eye-dee," the Dutchman said defensively. Henk van den Berg spoke six languages fluently but never managed to pronounce "idea" correctly. "I support it, of course—it's the policy of my government. But I knew it would be unacceptable to you, and I told them so in The Hague."

"So?" Waterman interrupted. "What happened?"

"Our Foreign Ministry," the Dutchman explained, his palms wide. "They led our defense minister to believe you could live with it."

Damn, Waterman thought. The goddamn State Department probably fed it to the Dutch. It was probably Bennet's "eye-dee" all along. He sighed audibly. "So what's the bottom line, Henk?"

"Politics—as usual. My minister believes that by calling for a freeze, we'll be able to keep control of the debate in The Netherlands. Otherwise, he's convinced we'll be overwhelmed by the opposition."

"The Soviets already have more than two hundred missiles in place."

"I know that. We all know that. And if it were up to me, I would withdraw our Zero Freeze eye-dee. But I have no authority to drop language my government supports." He leaned forward conspiratorially. "But, Michael, my minister is a realist. If he cannot gather enough support, he'll fold his tent. This isn't something he'll go to the mat on. And I'll certainly tell him you're strongly opposed."

"Don't say 'strongly,' Henk—say 'unalterably.' "

Waterman had a problem. Mobilizing to fight the Dutch would mean headlines. Allowing the Dutch to win would mean even more headlines: NATO CALLS FOR MISSILE FREEZE—he could see it on the front page of *The Washington Post.* So, directly after dinner he paid a call on Ian Jones, NATO's acerbic, subtle assistant secretary general. If anyone could find a way to scrub the Dutch Zero Freeze, Jones could.

Seated in Jones's suite, a single-malt whisky in a crystal glass in his hand, Waterman decided to be absolutely candid. "Ian," he said, "there's something I need to tell you. But in strictest confidence."

"Speak to me as you would a priest, my boy."

"As you know, the president hasn't decided yet what the American negotiating proposal will be. But Ryder's pressing him to propose the elimination of all intermediate nuclear missiles. We call it the Zero Option—zero intermediates on both sides. But we can't talk about this publicly. The president hasn't made up his mind, and if the NATO communiqué calls for a Dutch Zero Freeze, even though it's different from what Ryder has in mind, it'll look as though he's orchestrated a NATO declaration to pressure the president."

The NATO official cracked a wry smile. "Which means," he said, "that you're forced to oppose anything that looks even vaguely like a Zero Option."

"Exactly. I need all the help I can get."

"Well"—Jones scratched his beard—"I'm not worried about the Dutch; they never push very hard. Oh, they'll try for a while; but they'll back off. No, Michael, it's the bloody Germans you have to worry about." He took a sip of his whisky, savoring it. "Now the best way to deal with them is to bring them inside your little circle."

"How do you mean?"

"Tell them what you just told me." The Scot took another sip of whisky. "Better—*you* shouldn't be the one to tell them. Let me do it. No—let the secretary general do it. He's meeting the German defense minister for breakfast. Once the Germans know that pressing too hard on this communiqué could kill a Zero Option in Washington, he'll have a basis for supporting you and a plausible explanation for the coalition back in Bonn. That's the way to do it."

Waterman broke into a smile. Jones was almost certainly right. He inclined his glass in the Scot's direction. "Ian, you're a gem."

━━━━━━━━━━━━━━━

October 10, 7:58 A.M.

Waterman was awakened from a deep sleep by his phone. He fumbled for the receiver and groaned a hello.

"Good morning, Mr. Secretary," said Øve Anders brightly. "I'll buy you a cup of coffee if you can spare the time."

"Øve—great to hear your voice." Waterman tried to focus. "What time is it?"

"Eight. Shank of the morning."

Waterman sat straight up. He'd overslept. "I think I can meet you—let's say the lobby in forty-five minutes." That would give him time to call Ian Jones and make sure the Dutch Zero Freeze proposal was as dead as boiled haggis.

"Sounds good to me. But you'll have to call security or they won't let me into the building. It's off limits to press."

"It's about time they started discriminating against you guys." Waterman laughed. "Long overdue. I'll call down right now."

Showered, shaved, and reassured that the morning's communiqué would not make any news, a happy Waterman bounded down two flights of stairs to find Anders standing in the lobby, sporting a gray tweed jacket with a tartan woolen scarf and puffing on a half-bent pipe. They shook hands warmly, then headed through the front door down a path leading to the road that paralleled the famous golf course. It was a cool autumn day, unusually clear for Scotland, brisk and breezy. Waterman was glad he'd worn his overcoat.

"You're in the spirit of things," he said, pointing to the scarf. "Anders clan?"

"McAnders, actually." The Norwegian laughed. "You know the Outer Hebrides were once Norwegian. If we'd known about the oil . . ." He trailed off, set the pipe between his teeth, and started out at a good strong pace. "Wonderful weather, Michael. Bracing. Norwegian summer." He looked at the younger man. "It's good to see you. I've been running around trying to get a story out of this meeting."

Waterman pulled on a pair of gloves. "I wish you bad luck. For us the best meetings are the ones not worth writing about."

"That's how this one may wind up," Anders said. "Last night it looked like fireworks, what with the Dutch Zero Freeze and all."

"You know about the Dutch proposal?"

"I was told about it."

"Have you written anything?"

"Not yet."

Thank God, he thought. "Øve—let's go on deep background."

"Agreed."

"The Dutch withdrew the proposal this morning."

"Really? I was told about an hour ago there might be some alternative statement in the communiqué."

"That's not the case anymore," Waterman said, trying to sound definitive. He kicked a pebble and sent it into the ditch at the side of the road. "How in the world did you learn about the Dutch language? They'd agreed not to go public."

"They didn't, Michael. Your people told me."

"My people?" Waterman was incredulous. He turned to face the Norwegian. "Who?"

"Well, the American delegation," Anders replied evasively.

"Who on the American delegation?"

"Now, now. You wouldn't want me to compromise a source, would you?"

"Of course not," Waterman said. "Just give me his name, and I'll do all the compromising." He was livid. He'd find whoever had done the leaking and crucify him.

"He's got to remain unidentified. But I will tell you he works for the State Department."

The goddam State Department again. Waterman made up his mind to have it out with Bennet once and for all, just as soon as he got back to Washington. He'd kill the son of a bitch. "And precisely what was this unidentified source saying?"

"He told me the Dutch came up with a valid position for the Geneva talks—a Zero Freeze that guaranteed NATO wouldn't deploy intermediate missiles if the Soviets froze their SS-20s at current levels. He said the Dutch wanted their idea included in the communiqué, but that Ryder, as always the hard-liner, was trying to kill any possible compromise with the Soviets. The word is there'll be a fight over the communiqué, with Germany and several others lining up behind the Dutch."

"Your source is inaccurate," Waterman said. "The Dutch withdrew their proposed language this morning."

"Then I guess there's no story," Anders said, sucking on his pipe.

"Seems that way to me, too," answered Waterman, much relieved.

They had reached the pub already. The place was picture-postcard perfect, a squat two-story stucco-and-thatch building with small windows and a low, heavy wooden door above which hung an oval hand-painted sign that read THE SWAN, 1758. It was set back from the road behind a small pond on which several ducks paddled about. The sign on the door said CLOSED, a formality required by pub-licensing laws. But it was, of course, open for business, as everyone in Gleneagles, the local constabulary included, well knew. Waterman pushed the door open and was greeted by the pungent smell of a peat fire, which burned smokily in an enormous hearth at one end of the main saloon.

They took a table near the fireplace and ordered two coffees, which the barman supplied with a small earthenware pitcher of thick, sweet cream and a small glass of locally produced single-malt whisky for Anders. Waterman looked longingly at the liquor and ordered his own.

The two men lifted their glasses, touched them briefly, and sipped. Waterman set his glass down. "How's Moscow these days?"

Anders poured a generous dollop of cream into his coffee. "Unsettled. In the early days of *glasnost* it was riveting to watch all the change. The denigration of Stalin beginning to spill over onto Lenin, the rehabilitation of Solzhenitsyn, all those articles critical of the party and the state apparatus, the increased travel abroad. Every day something new would happen. Now, things have changed. Most of our sources have become guarded and cautious. No one knows where things are headed."

"These things take time, especially in a society as slow-moving as Russia."

Anders nodded. "A lot of people are scared. I saw Alexi last week—"

"Marensky?"

"Yes. We spent a whole night drawing up a kind of ledger sheet on Novikov, trying to see how far he's prepared to go. We ran through the whole litany: private property; joint ventures in which foreign capital can be repatriated; a convertible ruble—everything. But in the end we agreed the gut issue is whether he's ready to jettison communism. Flush it down the toilet. Alexi hopes so, but he doesn't know."

Anders puffed on his pipe, wreathing his head in blue smoke. "I used to spend hours in Alexi's apartment listening to him describe the new world Novikov was going to create. He was wildly enthusiastic for *glasnost* and *perestroika*—wouldn't hear any criticism of Novikov. For Alexi, Novikov walked on water. Now, he's not so sure."

"But surely he's able to learn a lot from his father. You couldn't ask for a better inside track. At least that's what our experts say."

"I don't know," Anders said. "This past visit I began to get the sense that Alexi's almost as unsure of his father as he is of Novikov."

"Are they close?" Waterman asked.

"I always thought so. But this time I thought I detected a strain. Not that he said anything specific."

"Maybe it's a generational gap," Waterman suggested. He drained his whisky. "How's Novikov getting along with the military and the KGB?"

"The KGB regards him as one of their own. That's one of the things that makes Alexi uneasy: It was the first thing he put on the dark side of the ledger. The military seems to be happy enough. Nothing Novikov's done should cause them any great concern."

"Well," Waterman said, "that makes sense. He imposed only the slightest cutback in military spending; and given the desperate shape of the economy, the military was lucky to get off so easily."

"I wouldn't call it luck," Anders said. "After all, the military has a lot to say about who runs the place."

Waterman nodded. He finished his coffee. "I've got to be getting back," he said. "I have a pile of work to finish for Ryder before today's session." He also had to get on the secure phone to Parisi and find out what the hell

Bennet had been doing to sabotage Ryder. God damn the man anyway. He looked at Anders and smiled. The journalist had been a help, whether he knew it or not. "The work never stops, does it?"

Anders shook his head. "Deadlines—will we ever be able to live without them?"

"Doubtful," said Waterman. "Besides, what the hell would we ever do for excitement?"

PART THREE

CHAPTER ELEVEN

Carderock, Maryland, October 12, 1:00 P.M.

Dan Bennet was already seated at a corner table near the fireplace in the rustic stone-and-slate roadside inn as Waterman made his way across the room. He looked at Bennet guiltily. He was almost half an hour late. Lost in thought over the condition of his marriage, he'd driven right past the squat, unfamiliar stone inn that sat partially hidden from view on a narrow, winding road that paralleled the C&O canal. He was a good eight miles away when he'd realized his mistake.

Waterman's intentions had been good. He had made plans to show up on Laura's doorstep in North Carolina as soon as he'd returned from Scotland. But events had intervened, and as had so often happened, his personal life took a backseat to his professional one. The result—one with which Waterman was not at all happy—was that instead of trying to work out the knots in his thorny domestic relationship with Laura, he was working out the knots in his thorny professional relationship by having a quiet, off-the-record lunch with his preeminent adversary, in order to clear the air and, perhaps, even improve their working conditions.

"Sorry to be late," Waterman said as he approached the table. "I overshot and had to double back."

Bennet was just draining the last of a Bloody Mary. He half rose in his seat. "Well, I'm just glad you made it," he said. "I was beginning to think I'd been stood up." He turned to the waiter who had preceded Waterman to the table. "I'll have another one," he said. "And bring one for my friend."

Waterman sat down. "I'm glad you suggested this," Bennet said. "It's long overdue." He stirred his drink with a long celery stick.

"That's what I thought, too. I don't expect us to agree on much, Dan, but at least we might understand each other better."

"Nothing would please me more than to narrow our differences," Bennet said formally.

Waterman had decided to be blunt, so he weighed in without hesitation. "There are no differences that couldn't be resolved with a little help from State—getting behind SDI, for example, or pressing the Soviets to agree to zero medium missiles. That's what we need. What we get from State most of the time is zilch. No help with our allies, no help with the Soviets, no help on the Hill. I don't mean to get us off to a bad start, Dan, but there's no point in pulling punches.

"In fact," Waterman continued grimly, "the lack of help is the least of it. We face a massive Soviet military machine with nothing—an arsenal depleted by years of neglect and underinvestment. Finally, we have a president who recognizes the gravity of the situation, and all you guys at State want to do is go out and broker a new détente."

The waiter, who had appeared to take their order, stood back waiting for Waterman to arrive at a natural break. At the word "détente" the man stepped forward, served the Bloody Marys, and handed over two menus in thick leather covers. Falling silent, the two men quickly scanned the menu—the food was hardly worth much deliberation—and ordered. Handing his menu back to the departing waiter, Waterman was about to pick up where he'd left off when Bennet preempted.

"Look, you and I both know we've got different missions. You can't expect us to adopt the Pentagon agenda any more than we expect you to follow ours. But there's no reason why we can't work as a team."

"You mean we work to build up our defenses, and you work at giving them away?" Waterman asked ironically.

Bennet cracked a pained smile. "I mean reasonable collaboration, recognizing our differences. It'll never be all sweetness and light. But it doesn't have to be all-out warfare either." He paused while the waiter served large plates of something that resembled pasta and uncorked a bottle of wine.

"Hold on," Waterman interrupted. "Let's make this a little more concrete. Take the Zero Option. You opposed it. You and Winthrop did everything you could to stop it. The ink is barely dry on the president's decision and you're all over town saying it paints Novikov into a corner."

"Now, just a second," Bennet protested. "It sure as hell didn't take State to persuade the press you were trying to paint Novikov into a corner. A six-year-old could have figured that out."

"You think we want a deadlock?"

"Well?" Bennet said, putting down his fork and shrugging with out-stretched arms. "Can you deny it?"

"I sure as hell do," Waterman replied. He paused to take a sip of his Bloody Mary. "But our motive—the president's, Ryder's, mine—that's not the issue. The decision's been taken. Our position is Zero—not my position, not Ryder's—it's the president who has decided on it. Now it's your job to support him, too—either support him or resign." He swallowed some more Bloody Mary and tapped the glass on the table for emphasis. "What really pisses me off is the way you guys started to chip away at it from the moment it was adopted."

Bennet flushed angrily. "What's that supposed to mean?"

"I mean, despite what the president said in his announcement, you backgrounded reporters that the Zero Option was not a 'take-it-or-leave-it proposition.' Shit, you might just as well have said that if Novikov resists, we'll cave in. There's no other way what you said could be interpreted."

"Easy for you to say," Bennet replied testily. "We had a firestorm of complaints from the Allies. They all demanded we show flexibility—all of them."

"You mean your Foreign Office colleagues."

"That's who I work with."

"Come on. Don't tell me you're just responding to pressure from the Allies. You're as eager for an agreement as they are, maybe more."

Bennet pointed at Waterman with a forkful of pasta. "You know, the more you talk, the more I'm convinced you're only happy when our relations with the Sovs are in the deep freeze."

"That's crap," Waterman snorted.

"Is it? You couldn't contain yourself when the president called the Soviet Union an evil empire. You gave interview after interview—each more provocative than the last—as if you were daring the Sovs to do something about it. Daring someone to fight isn't a good idea, Michael. It makes you sound like a bully."

"Dan, that's—"

"A bully. And you know what happens to bullies—they get theirs, sooner or later. Believe me, a policy of confrontation doesn't work. In the long run it's bound to fail. You always put the State Department down. You should be grateful we're here gathering up what crockery is left before you can break it all. No harm was done by saying we weren't giving Novikov an ultimatum. That statement kept the Allies together. It kept us in the game."

"That's the point—you play a different kind of game. You'll settle for a draw. Dammit, Dan, I want to win." He poured them each a glass of wine.

Bennet spoke softly: "So does Novikov. But you can't have it all any more than he can. Neither side can play hardball all the time." He lifted his fork to his mouth and ate.

Waterman put his own fork down and sipped the wine. "We're never gonna settle this," he said. "So let me change the subject. When are you gonna get behind the Strategic Defense Initiative? The Russians are all over the place denouncing the president's program. Novikov brings it up in every speech. You should be out there defending it. Half our allies know nothing about the Soviet program. It's bigger than ours. They've been working at it for years. And they're breaking the ABM treaty to do it. Can't you use a little of your diplomatic hocus-pocus to get our story across?"

"But you know our view," Bennet said intently. "SDI's a showstopper. In the end we'll have to drop it because Novikov will never agree to missile reductions unless we do. It'll come down to a trade. You'll see." He drained his wineglass and poured himself more.

Waterman nodded. "Okay—I accept that premise. I agree, it may come down to a trade. But isn't that all the more reason for you to get behind SDI? You should want the biggest damn bargaining chip you can get. But if you weaken our position now, we won't have anything to bargain with later."

Bennet took a large sip of wine and shrugged. "Look, bargaining chips cut both ways. If you get too attached to them, you can't let go when the time comes. That's why we're worried about you guys at Defense. You fixate on things and hold on to them, no matter what the consequences. Okay—you say State is wishy-washy. We think Defense is intractable. The trick of the democratic system is striking the right balance between us. I know you don't think we're going about this the right way, but I want you to believe me when I say we're for SDI all the way."

"Or at least until it's time to trade it in," Waterman said cynically.

"Let's just say until it can be used to protect the Republic in whatever way makes sense," Bennet replied, pouring the last of the wine into his glass. He waved the waiter over. "Coffee?"

Waterman smiled. "Espresso, please."

Bennet nodded. "Two." He cracked a smile. "See—we can agree on something, at least."

"Maybe we can reach another agreement, too."

"I'm listening."

Waterman paused. He made a tent with his fingers. "If you'll quit doing Novikov's job by trying to trade SDI away before we have to, if you'll back us on the Hill, if you'll get the Allies to keep their opposition to SDI to themselves—if you'll do that, you'll find the Pentagon a lot easier to deal with. What do you say, Dan?"

"I think I'll just pick up the check instead."

CHAPTER TWELVE

Memorandum: Department of State
SECRET-SENSITIVE

TO: The Secretary
FROM: EUR/Daniel I. Bennet
DATE: October 14

I have managed to lay my hands on a memorandum from the chairman of the Joint Chiefs of Staff to the secretary of defense making it clear SECDEF has been vastly underestimating the cost of the SDI program while overestimating both its near-term feasibility and technical progress. It is a devastating critique of everything Ryder has been saying on the Hill and at NSC meetings. It validates the skepticism you have expressed about SDI and, indirectly at least, supports our view that we should use SDI as leverage in the Geneva negotiations and quit pretending it will ever work.

The JCS memo indicates the cost of a Phase I defense is likely to be nearly *three times* the highest estimate we have ever seen in the SDI semiannual reports to Congress. It also makes the point that the earliest likely deployment opportunity is a full three years *after* Ryder has been predicting. Moreover, it identifies a number of problems in developing low-cost manufacturing technologies—critical to a cost-effective system.

As you know, we have had great difficulty getting the Defense Department to accept the criteria we proposed for deployment of a strategic defense system. Ryder has refused to sign off on our benchmarks of cost-effectiveness and survivability, which we developed to contain the unrealistic optimism about SDI that Ryder has been pushing with the president. So long as he believes SDI is just around the corner, the president will continue to be rigid and inflexible.

This, of course, suits Ryder just fine. Because of his deep opposition to any agreement with the Soviets, inflexibility doesn't trouble him at all. As a matter of fact I believe he deliberately exaggerates the potential of SDI in order to keep the president from moving. That is also, I believe, the reason behind his latest ploy, the so-called Zero Option, which he went behind our backs to lay at the president's feet. He knows it will never work. But he submitted it to keep the president from accepting our more realistic, workable—and diplomatic—solutions.

Ryder enjoys good press on his Zero proposal. Somehow the media never asks the critical questions that would show his positions for what they are. Next Tuesday, however, Ryder testifies before the Senate Foreign Relations Committee. He plans to explain the criteria for SDI deployment. For once, he'd be in the open and vulnerable—if committee members asked the right questions.

I would appreciate five minutes with you late today to discuss this further in private.

Approve: ————————

Other: ————————

SECRET-SENSITIVE

New York Times E-Mail
CONFIDENTIAL

TO: Bill Kantor, Washington Bureau Chief
FROM: Michael Gray, National Security Correspondent
DATE: October 15

I've got a blockbuster! Last evening I was invited to the office of a reliable source at the deputy assistant secretary level. I was permitted to read (but not copy or remove) an official report classified Top Secret.

What I was shown was a memorandum from the chairman of the Joint Chiefs of Staff to Defense Secretary Ryder. In the memo the chairman takes violent exception to the things Ryder has been saying about the strategic defense program.

Bill, it's an explosive memo because it's clear from the chronology

Ryder had it *before* he testified last week before the Armed Services Committee—and he ignored it entirely! I covered that hearing, and there were a number of questions put to him he should have answered differently on the basis of the JCS paper.

The specific points on which the JCS, according to the memo, disagree with the secretary of defense include both the cost and timing of a first phase Star Wars defense, as well as the progress in the development of manufacturing technologies, which would allow low-cost fabrication of components that would be needed in quantity for any "space shield."

I agreed to certain preconditions in order to gain access to the memo. First, I agreed nothing would appear before next Tuesday. Second, I agreed to source the story from Capitol Hill. I tried hard to discourage this, but my source is absolutely convinced a leak will point directly to the State Department. He made it clear he would not share the document unless I agreed to his conditions.

I doubt I'll be able to see the document again, although I can probably confirm it exists. I'll try to get a refutation of its substance from someone in Waterman's office. As an ardent supporter of Star Wars, he may argue against the JCS position and thereby confirm the existence of the memo. But as I actually saw the original document, I don't believe a second source is required.

I'll keep you informed. I hope we can give this some play—Ryder will be testifying before the Foreign Relations Committee on Tuesday. If we lead with this the same day, I can guarantee it will dominate the hearing.

New York Times E-Mail
CONFIDENTIAL

TO: Bill Kantor, Bureau Chief, Washington
FROM: Arnold Goldman, Managing Editor, New York
DATE: October 15

Congratulations on Gray's coup. We'll hit hard with it, which means making it the centerpiece of a three- or four-story package for Tuesday. I'm getting an update piece out of science on the technologies involved in SDI. And we'll roll with something from the Livermore Labs that'll lend real weight to the JCS memo—Livermore, it seems, has become very skeptical about the Star Wars X-ray laser on which it is working.

I'm not worried about pressure over the classification issue. Obviously, we should listen to any government argument and not give the appearance of having our minds made up. But we're sure as hell not obliged to accept their argument, and from what I know already, there isn't a chance in hell that we will. This is one of those leaks that may lead to embarrassment for some people, but it will hardly give aid and comfort to the enemy.

On the Allies: I checked with foreign desk. They'll provide comment from FO sources, etc., in London and Paris. We'll also get background out of Brussels, where a NATO study's under way on the implications for Alliance strategy of the deployment of strategic defenses. But don't expect too much; this isn't a front-burner issue in Europe at the moment. As you know, the Europeans are full tilt on intermediate-missile deployment and on SDI don't really give a damn.

I'm concerned about this breaking somewhere else. Gray should make sure his source understands we buy an embargo only so long as this is our exclusive.

New York Times Interoffice Memorandum

TO: Michael Gray
FROM: Bill Kantor
DATE: October 15

Michael—

Please go back to your source and make sure he's not shopping the story around. You can tell him we're going to play this one big—three or even four tie-ins. But before assigning four bureaus to bust their behinds, we want assurance it's our exclusive.

Telephone Memo: United States Senate
Committee on Foreign Relations

TO: Chris Wentwood
FROM: Susan Kelly
DATE: October 16

You got a call from Michael Gray at *The New York Times*. He said he'd run into a friend of yours at Nora's Restaurant who mentioned she was going with you to Fire Island and you'd be gone through the weekend.

Gray wants you to know the Ryder hearing Tuesday "won't be as routine as you think," whatever that means. He said it could turn out to be "page-one stuff."

I told him you were out but you'd probably check your messages before catching your plane. When's my turn for Fire Island?

New York Times *E-Mail*

TO: Bill Kantor
FROM: Michael Gray
DATE: October 16

You asked for assurances my source at State isn't shopping the JCS memo. When I asked him not to share the memo with anyone, he said he'd put his ass on the line by letting me see it in the first place and had no intention of repeating. He also said no one at State was aware of our meeting. I don't believe him—I've known this guy for three years, and he doesn't make a move, *any* move, without guidance from Dan Bennet.

The White House
Office of the Press Secretary
WASHFAX
CONFIDENTIAL

FROM: The Press Secretary to the President
TO: Assistant Secretary of State, PA
       Assistant Secretary of Defense, PA
       PAO, Joint Chiefs of Staff
       Public Affairs Director, NSC
       White House Chief of Staff
DATE: October 20, 7:30 P.M.

I just received a phone call from Arnold Goldman, managing editor of *The New York Times*, who solicited comment on tomorrow's lead story. From what he had to say, all hell's going to break loose when the *Times* reports on a Top Secret JCS memo to the secretary of defense.

According to Goldman, in the memo, dated September 24, JCS Chairman Sloeman advises Secretary Ryder that deployment of a first phase SDI program will trail Ryder's estimates by at least three to four years and will cost three times as much as he has been saying in public.

Moreover, I am told the story quotes Ryder's testimony to the House Armed Services Committee, in which he used the precise figures the JCS memo disputes. According to the story, the SECDEF gave Congress no indication he had been advised by the chairman that his estimates were absurdly optimistic with respect to cost and timing of SDI deployment.

The story quotes extensively from the JCS memo. And, to make matters worse, it's apparently sourced from the Hill, which means that we'll get a stream of negative comment out of congressional offices.

Needless to say, I declined any comment.

What the hell is going on? It's now 7:30 P.M. By 10:30 the bulldog edition of the *Times* will be on the stands, and my phone will be ringing off the wall. The only guy in this town who is going to feel worse than me is Ben Bradlee.

If I'm not going to look like an idiot at the morning briefing tomorrow, I need talking points.

- Is there such a memo?
- Was it sent?
- Did the SECDEF receive it?
- Was it signed out by the chairman?
- Was it complete or just a draft?
- Are the quotes accurate?
- How should we handle the fact that the *Times* is printing excerpts from a Top Secret document? (Tempting as it may seem to some of you, we can't get by simply saying we don't comment on classified documents.)

State and DOD will get hit, too, as soon as the *Times* is on the streets. Please fax me draft talking points by 9:00 and plan on a meeting in the Sitroom at 10:00 P.M.

I'd like to release a statement by 10:30 that all departments can stand by. I'd also like a copy of the report, assuming that it exists.

I intend to send a note to the president, who has retired to his quarters for the evening, immediately following the 10:00 meeting. If he's still up, he'll see it tonight; otherwise he will have the pleasure of arising to news of another damn leak. Can't you guys keep *anything* secret?

The Assistant Secretary of State for Public Affairs
The Department of State
Washington, D.C. 20520

TO: Alan Kirkwell, the White House
FROM: G. A. Worthington, Deputy Assistant Secretary/PA
DATE: October 20

The assistant secretary is unreachable in the time frame indicated in your Washfax memo (he's playing tennis somewhere, but not, evidently, where his secretary thought he was), so I have taken the liberty of preparing this response as there is obviously some urgency here.

I have checked with the assistant secretary for Politico-military Affairs and with the deputy director of the Policy Planning Staff. Neither has heard of the document reported in the *Times*, and neither felt comfortable commenting.

I also talked with the assistant secretary for European and Canadian Affairs, Dan Bennet. Dan is concerned about the likely impact of the story among our NATO allies, who, with the exception of the British prime minister, have been privately critical of the SDI program. Most of the

European governments are under pressure from their Social Democratic opposition parties to disassociate themselves from "Star Wars."

Dan suggests some draft guidance, which he's already cabled to U.S. embassies in all NATO countries. It would be useful if this paragraph were incorporated in any White House statement as well. It reads as follows:

"As the president has stressed repeatedly, most recently in his speech to the United Nations General Assembly, the United States Strategic Defense Initiative is a research program only, which is being carried out consistent with the ABM Treaty. No decision has been taken to deploy strategic defenses. Before any such decision was taken, the president would have to be convinced that the deployment would be survivable and cost-effective, and he would consult thoroughly with our allies and, as the ABM Treaty provides, with the Soviet Union."

Dan is at a dinner at the Spanish embassy. He asked me to tell you that he'll represent State at the 10:00 P.M. meeting. He hopes you will include this language in a draft statement that could be used by all departments.

Memorandum: Department of Defense

TO: White House/Alan Kirkwell
FROM: ISP/Michael Waterman
DATE: October 20

The secretary has asked me to deal with the leak discussed in your memo to the assistant secretary for public affairs. Until half an hour ago I have never known the secretary to lose his temper or say an unkind word about anybody. All that changed when he got your Washfax memo at 8:15 as he was on his way out the door to a dinner at the Spanish embassy.

The secretary is, of course, familiar with the JCS memorandum. He read it three weeks ago last Wednesday, the day it came in. He thought it was garbage. He has since been reinforced in that view by memos from the undersecretary for procurement and the undersecretary for policy as well as the program manager, General Wilson, all of whom have reviewed the JCSM and disagree with it.

This is not the first time that the JCS has prepared a memorandum with which the secretary disagrees. For your background, perhaps I should say a word about JCS memoranda and the JCS-SECDEF relationship.

JCS memoranda (JCSM) reflect the views of all the service chiefs— army, navy, air force, marines, and the chairman himself. Not a word appears in them that is not agreed on by all five. As they are frequently in disagreement, their memoranda are frequently incoherent, vacuous, or wrong. Sometimes they are all three.

Whatever they purport to be, most JCSMs are really statements about defense-budget priorities and part of a larger struggle over shaping them. So a JCSM attempting to throw cold water on the president's Strategic Defense Initiative really means the air force wants planes, the navy wants ships, and the army wants tanks and choppers.

Anyone who has spent an afternoon in the "tank," the room where the JCS meets (while sipping iced tea and munching on Butterfingers and Mr. Goodbar candy bars), knows that for the last two years each of the chiefs has been maneuvering to get the tab for the SDI picked up by some service other than his own—ideally by some mythical budget account outside the Department of Defense. What is at work here is an effort to slow the SDI program so that it will not claim such a chunk of the defense budget.

There's another thing you ought to know about JCS memoranda. They are drafted by the Joint Staff, a collection of functional illiterates who loathe their assignment and can't wait to be assigned to a job in the service from which they come. When their JCS tour is up, most air force or navy officers will tell you that they are "going back to the air force," or the navy, as the case may be. They consider time on the Joint Staff as a purgatory, during which they are separated from the institution about which they care most, deprived of command responsibilities, and forced to do staff work.

They loathe staff work in general; but their deepest loathing is reserved for the preparation of papers, a task for which they are hopelessly ill suited. I have heard better arguments on *Divorce Court* and seen more astute problem-solving on *Wheel of Fortune.* I have seen better writing from nine-year-olds.

I have sent a courier with a copy of the leaked document. Call me when you make it through the thicket of acronyms, abbreviations, and verbless sentences. It is crap—which is precisely how we ought to describe it.

Now, as to relations between the secretary of defense and the JCS: They are compelled by the nature of the Department of Defense to work together. But the secretary has wearied of their endless bickering and paralytic indecisiveness. He is too much a gentleman to tell them what he thinks, but I have watched him in the tank lately. And when you know him as well as I do, you see it is an ordeal for him to meet with them.

The secretary feels *very strongly* that we should not hedge on this one. He doesn't give a damn if the JCS are offended by a straightforward rejection of the memorandum, which is what he is insisting on.

He asked me to forward this draft guidance, every word of which he dictated to his secretary in my presence:

"The president has seen the document referred to in today's *New York Times* and disagrees with the calculations of cost and schedule that were done by joint staff officers. The secretary of defense has had the document reviewed by senior officials of the Department of Defense who believe that the analysis is deeply flawed in a number of important respects. The Joint Chiefs of Staff, who had forwarded the document to the secretary of defense without a full review, will now undertake a thorough study of the issues raised therein."

Alan, you know very well Jim Ryder is never so peremptory. That he has drafted the enclosed guidance himself and is insisting on it is an indication of how strongly he feels in this case. I'll come to the 10:00, but I'm not going to have much flexibility on this one. If you think we're going to have great difficulty getting a consensus, you'd better expect Jim to go directly to the president.

Memorandum: Office of the Joint Chiefs of Staff
The Pentagon
Washington, D.C. 20301

TO: Mr. Alan Kirkwell, the White House
FROM: Col. A. McNaughton/Director, Public Affairs
DATE: October 20
SUBJECT: Reply to Washfax Memorandum from Mr. Kirkwell

The above-captioned memorandum was received by this office at 2000 ET and presented to the chairman and to each of the service chiefs and/or his designee. We are in a standby mode awaiting their responses.

It has been determined that the document *The New York Times* has drawn its report from is JCSM 1027, which was signed out by the chairman on 24 September at 1445 ET and sent to the secretary of defense the next morning at 0830 hours ET. We have initiated a search of the classified-document transfer log to establish the number of copies circulated and their addressees.

We cannot now determine whether *The New York Times* has had access to the final document or to one of the interim reports that was prepared in connection with JCSM 1027. Nor can we inform you whether the substance of the final version of JCSM 1027 differed from previous interim versions and/or working drafts.

It is highly unusual for a JCSM to reach the media, so we believe the *Times* may be operating off of an early version or working draft.

We are not able at this point in time to propose draft guidance since the chiefs and/or their designees have not yet had a chance to discuss this matter. We shall dispatch a representative to the meeting at 2200 ET who may have instructions by then if the chiefs and/or their designees have been able to come to closure on the draft-guidance issue.

The chairman has ordered a full-security investigation into this incident.

Memorandum: Department of Defense
SECRET

TO: The Secretary
FROM: ISP/Michael Waterman
DATE: October 20

As you know, I attended a meeting chaired by Alan Kirkwell in the White House Situation Room at 10:00 tonight. This is my joint report on the meeting, which will be delivered to you in the early morning courier run—by which time you will doubtless have seen *The New York Times.*

Kirkwell opened the meeting by saying we had only an hour to come up with agreed talking points. He then proceeded to spend the next ten minutes in a rambling, pointless tirade against leaks.

This would have been annoying under any circumstances; but, given the way Kirkwell curries favor with the White House press corps by leaking every rumor, whisper, slander, and innuendo he can dredge from the bottom of the press-office swamp, his display of hypocrisy was especially galling.

Kirkwell views the leaked JCSM more as an embarrassment to the president than a threat to a major part of the president's program, for which he cares little. When I suggested that the JCSM was inadequate and wrong, he said that what mattered most about it was that it was reported in detail on page one of *The New York Times.* He pointed out— and on this he is correct—that the networks will send crews to chase down the chairman in the hope he will stand by the memorandum and prolong the controversy.

In the discussion of press guidance it became clear State wants to use the leak to *increase* its adverse impact on SDI. This was evident in the draft State tabled, which stressed that SDI is a "research program only," which would not be deployed until the president was "convinced that the deployment would be survivable and cost-effective." It went on to promise thorough consultation "with our allies and, as the ABM Treaty provides, with the Soviet Union."

I argued that State's draft was much too defensive and raised new doubt about the administration's commitment to the SDI program. Moreover, I urged, our response to the leak ought to reflect what we think of the substance of the JCSM. The JCS analysis assumes a Soviet threat *almost twice the size the intelligence community projects for the period in question.* It explains this inflated estimate of the number of Soviet missiles by assuming that they will, *without regard to cost,* respond to SDI with a massive increase in their offensive forces. JCS has no evidence to support this assumption because there is none.

I insisted that, as you had dictated it yourself, we work from your draft and not the one sent over by the State Department. This we did, for an hour and a half, with the following agreed text:

"The president has been briefed on the document referred to in today's *New York Times.* **He understands that it has been reviewed by senior officials of the Department of Defense, who believe that critical assumptions upon which the conclusions are based may need revision. He has asked the Joint Chiefs of Staff to review their findings in a careful study that relies on agreed intelligence projections."**

Assuming the president agrees when this is taken to him at his morning briefing with Mitchell Wallace, it would be read by Kirkwell at the noon briefing on an "if asked" basis. State would refer all questions to the White House—indicating it has not seen the JCSM.

The JCS rep said he would report back to the acting chairman, the chief of naval operations. All of this is *ad referendum* to principals, of course, so you could insist on changes if you wish. But I believe we got everything important you wanted.

Your hearing may never get beyond the JCSM. I recommend that you not wait for a question but preemptively raise it in your opening statement and deal with it so definitively that senators are disinclined to dwell on it further.

If you choose to lead your testimony with a refutation of the JCSM, the committee will have to go into closed session since you can't get very far without talking about intelligence estimates. This is actually helpful. You could make a statement indicating you disagree with the JCSM, that it is flawed and invalid, and that you will elaborate in closed session.

The committee won't want to go closed since their whole purpose is to impugn SDI by burdening it with impossible deployment criteria and to do so while grandstanding for the cameras.

Memorandum: United States Senate
Committee on Foreign Relations
SECRET

TO: The Chairman, Senator Albert Martin
FROM: Staff Director, Chris Wentwood
DATE: October 20

Attached is the memorandum I am circulating today to the full committee membership. As it is going to the Republican members, it does not do much more than frame the issue for the hearing.

You should know there is much more to this issue than the memo suggests. Our friends at State have been attempting for months to get Ryder to support the administration position on criteria for the deployment of SDI. Thus far they have failed. Ryder simply refuses to accept the "president's view" that SDI must be survivable and cost-effective.

The issue is important because anyone who gives it a moment's thought would know that SDI will never meet that test. Once that sinks in, it should be possible to move the president off his stubborn support for SDI, the principal consequence of which has been to block any American flexibility at the Geneva negotiations.

Tomorrow's hearing may be a unique opportunity to settle this issue once and for all. Michael Gray, national security correspondent for *The New York Times*, is an old friend of mine. He called me at home to say the *Times* is running a lead story tomorrow on a JCS study that fixes the cost of SDI at three times Ryder's estimate and puts the earliest deployment date off by at least three years.

I have prepared the attached list of pertinent questions for the hearing. They will make great sound-bites for the network news shows. If you indicate the ones you wish to use, I'll see that the others go to senators Grammant, Flagg, and Riskind.

P.S. My relationship with Gray is obviously sensitive.

Memorandum: United States Senate
Committee on Foreign Relations
Office of the Minority Staff

TO: Minority Senators
FROM: Jeff Robbins, Staff Director for the Minority
DATE: October 20

The ranking member, Senator Hardesty, and several other members have asked for staff support for the hearing with Secretary Ryder. I have prepared the attached memorandum for use of the minority. It lays out an analysis of the SDI program I hope proves useful.

Tomorrow's hearing with the secretary of defense is part of the chairman's campaign against SDI. There is no doubt that the chairman and most Democratic members of the committee have joined forces with SDI opponents at the State Department. Together, they wish to kill any serious prospect of a strategic defense by trading it away at the strategic arms negotiations. And they have sought to starve the SDI budget while the negotiations continue, so it does not progress rapidly enough to escape being used as a bargaining chip.

We believe the Democrats will turn out in force tomorrow to press the secretary of defense. Members are urged to participate in this important hearing both to demonstrate support for the administration and to counter the majority attack on the SDI program.

CHAPTER THIRTEEN

Senate Office Building, October 21, 9:00 A.M.

From the moment the early edition of *The New York Times* appeared with the headline JOINT CHIEFS DISPUTE RYDER: SDI TO COST MORE, TAKE LONGER, SECRET MEMO SAYS, every bureau chief in Washington, after kicking himself for missing the story in the first place, planned extra coverage of what would otherwise have been a routine appearance of the secretary of defense before the Committee on Foreign Relations.

By the time Waterman arrived shortly after nine, the hearing room on the fourth floor of the Dirksen Senate Office Building was overflowing with spectators, press, and Senate staff. He walked down the marble hallway, his heels clicking on the stone, past a bank of television control consoles that took up most of the passageway, listening as producers argued with cameramen about which side of the room would produce the best cutaways.

Outside, a crowd of spectators had already formed a queue under the direction of a Capitol police officer. Waterman walked up to her and showed his DOD identification. "I'm with the secretary."

"I know—you're Mr. Waterman. I remember when you worked here—Senator Winter's staff, right?"

Waterman nodded.

The officer opened the door for him. "Too bad about him. It must have been a real loss for you."

"For the country," Waterman said. He meant it. Arthur Winter's fatal heart attack two years before had hit Waterman hard. It meant not ever being able to come back to this building he'd loved so much. Indeed, until Winter's death, Waterman thought of his work at the Pentagon as temporary. He'd always known there was a place for him on the senator's staff. Working there brought with it a special feeling of permanency, of belonging to something familial and close that he'd never enjoyed before—and that would never, he now realized, be repeated.

He surveyed the room with practiced eyes. It was all so familiar. How many hearings had he overseen here in this place? Fifty? A hundred? At the moment the committee members' leather swivel chairs at the elevated semicircular table were vacant. The long table and chair reserved for the witness was empty, as was the row of chairs behind the witness table, where Waterman would be sitting.

Half a dozen staffers busied themselves placing papers in front of the seats assigned to the members for whom they worked, chatting to the reporters, or distributing copies of the opening statements prepared for the members. The committee clerk adjusted name plates as he received word that one senator or another would or would not attend the hearing. A clerk went from place to place tapping the microphones to be certain they were working. At the back of the room cameramen from the three networks, CNN, C-Span, a dozen local stations, plus several foreign news organizations jostled one another as they set up their tripods cheek-to-jowl. Radio reporters, who had their own table, plugged long cords into the "Mult"—the audio feed from the dais and witness table. Print reporters jockeyed for good seats. Spectators shifted around and rustled newspapers as they waited for the action to begin. It all had, Waterman believed, some of the same hurly-burly anticipation and kinetic excitement that precedes a prizefight.

Waterman went around the side of the dais and through the door into the committee offices. He passed through a narrow hall and tapped on Jeff Robbins's door. The prematurely gray, fireplug-shaped minority counsel looked up from a computer screen.

He rose, came around, and grabbed Waterman's hand in his own. "Hi, stranger. Welcome home. I thought you'd be arriving with the secretary."

"I decided to reconnoiter. How goes?"

"I think we'll get five members to show the flag from our side. But it's really been touch and go. You know how it is—the *Times* says Ryder is dead meat, and the members don't want to catch the smell."

Waterman thought the minority counsel looked taut and anxious. "Don't tell me *you've* got doubts, Jeff. We've been over this."

"Not me, Michael. I know he's going to be okay. But convincing some of my people—"

"I know, I know. What's Wentwood got up his sleeve?"

"The distinguished majority staff director plans to make it as rough on Ryder as he can. If I had to guess, I'd say he got hold of the JCS memorandum, or parts of it. I'd expect questions based on specific points in the text."

"Sounds reasonable. We're ready."

"So's Chris. He's been closeted with the chairman for hours, coaching him. That's not easy, either—the good senator's only firing on three cylinders these days."

Waterman laughed. Robbins was right. Senator Albert Martin, who had ruled the Foreign Relations Committee for a decade, was not only old and getting senile, he was a dimwit to boot. Getting him up to speed to do battle with Ryder would have been a formidable task.

Robbins continued, "Tell your boss to watch out—Martin's out for blood today."

Waterman's mouth tightened. "So are we, Jeff."

He returned to the hearing room. The advance agent from the secretary's security detail was already in place, talking into a microphone just inside the right cuff of his tweed jacket. As Waterman had instructed, the secretary's limousine deliberately drove at a crawl during its short ride from the Pentagon, so he would not arrive until the committee chairman had taken his own place. It was a peculiar form of "chicken" that Waterman had learned to play when he worked here. Last one in was the winner.

At ten past the hour the TV lights came on to full brightness. As if on cue, Senator Martin, the gaunt, ruddy senior senator from California—long the darling of the Hollywood left—emerged through the heavy wooden door behind the dais and took his place at the center of the curved table. The photographers in the well clicked furiously. Other senators, eleven in all, were either at their places or milling about behind the horseshoe table. All eight Democrats on the committee had turned up, but only three Republicans sat stiffly and uneasily behind their name plates. Behind Martin, in a baggy gray suit and frayed-collar shirt with a pile of briefing books at his feet, sat the short, shaggy-haired committee staff director, Chris Wentwood.

If Martin triumphed today, Wentwood would be the shadow whose work made it possible; the source of documents that would enable him to prove his case; the architect of coordinated lines of questioning worked out in advance among staffers and senators opposing SDI, the administration generally, Ryder, or all three. Arrayed to Wentwood's right and left, other committee staffers half sat, half crouched in their side chairs, holding sheafs of guidance papers, questions, and prepared statements for their senators.

There was an audible murmur as James Ryder, flanked by his security detail but followed by no aides, strode purposefully into the room, passed the witness table and the well, and went directly to the chairman. They shook hands as the shutters clicked. There was nothing cordial in the act—it was simply a ritual, much the same as the touching of gloves between fighters before a title bout.

Waterman looked around the room. The presence of so many Democrats was a sure sign they expected to draw blood. So was the absence of most of the committee's seven Republicans. The imbalance meant that for much of the hearing, after a round of alternating between Democrats and Republicans, a succession of Democrats would grill the secretary, each taking his allotted ten minutes, without an opportunity for the Republican senators to intervene. Wentwood had certainly been busy.

Martin gaveled the proceedings to order. "This hearing," the thin, balding senator read carefully, "is part of a continuing series with various administration officials about weapons programs that figure importantly in the diplomatic relationship between the United States and the Soviet Union. The most important of these is the Strategic Defense Initiative, or 'Star Wars,' as it is more commonly known.

"As the committee knows, we have been concerned for some time to understand the basis on which the administration wishes to proceed with deployment of an advanced strategic offense"—he corrected himself to titters "—I mean strategic *defense*. We also have sought to encourage the completion of negotiations leading to a treaty with the Soviet Union—a treaty that would limit sharply both offensive and defensive strategic systems. To conclude such a treaty, we believe it will be necessary to accept limitations on SDI."

Martin shifted the sheets in front of him as the junior senator from Wyoming, Robert Becker, made his way from the center doorway behind him and took his place. Becker looked at Waterman and nodded in recognition. Waterman was relieved: another Republican to help even things up—and a bright, articulate one at that.

"The secretary of defense," Martin continued, "is eminently qualified to testify before this committee on both these matters. Especially in light of the forthcoming summit, the views of the secretary are of great importance."

Martin made no reference to the *Times* story or the JCS study, although most of those in the room knew that the JCS study would dominate the hearing, and almost everyone knew that the *Times* story had been timed to shape it.

Martin peered toward Ryder. "Mr. Secretary, I understand that you have a prepared statement. But before you begin, a number of other members of the committee have asked to make opening statements. I'll call on them now, and then we'll hear your prepared statement."

As Waterman listened to the members drone on, each of the Democrats attacking a different facet of SDI and each of the Republicans defending it, he became convinced that Wentwood had indeed been given access to the leaked JCS memorandum. The statements couldn't have been prepared today—they were too well coordinated and too specific.

Forty minutes into the hearing the chairman finally turned to the secretary of defense. "You may proceed," he rasped.

The secretary of defense had sat stonily as committee Democrats attacked SDI. Now, he slipped his glasses on and hunched over the table, his hands holding the statement firmly. "Mr. Chairman, members of the committee, let me begin by thanking you for this opportunity to appear. I would like to dispense with my prepared opening statement, which responds at some length to the two points raised by the chairman. I would request that it be inserted in its entirety in the record."

"Without objection, so ordered," Martin said.

"Let me turn instead," Ryder said, folding the papers and putting them in his jacket pocket, "to a related matter, a draft analysis of SDI, which was prepared by the Joint Staff of the Joint Chiefs of Staff and reported in today's *New York Times*. Several senators have referred to the *Times* story this morning, and I believe that Mr. Gray, who reported at length on this classified document, is sitting at the press table. So I welcome the opportunity to enlighten both the perpetrator of this cruel hoax and several of his remarkably trusting victims."

For the next half hour Ryder conducted a narrative monologue. He spoke without notes and, to Waterman's delight, with such force and attention to detail that no one on the dais attempted to interrupt him. Finally, his monologue finished, the secretary looked up at the members. "Mr. Chairman," he said with exaggerated courtesy, "I am ready for any questions you may have."

The chairman scanned his notes. Chris Wentwood leaned forward and pointed to something on the page. Martin nodded.

"Mr. Secretary, thank you for your statement. I have several questions—but my colleague, Senator Libby, a most conscientious and valuable member of this committee, has indicated he will have to leave early; so I will withhold my own questions in order to give him a chance now."

Score one for the good guys. Waterman's experience on Capitol Hill made him familiar with what had just happened. Ryder's performance had been so strong that Martin had lost confidence in the effectiveness of the questions Wentwood had worked up for him. He needed more time to confer with his aide and put together another list. Had he been ready, he wouldn't have deferred to anybody.

On the other hand, Bill Libby, second-ranking Democrat on the committee, was far more intelligent and knowledgeable than Martin. A former prosecutor and professor of law, he could be a formidable opponent.

"Mr. Secretary," he began, "the president has proposed a strategic defense that has frequently been likened to a shield over America, an invisible, impenetrable shield. The image we see in TV cartoons used by the networks to illustrate what Star Wars is all about usually has Soviet missiles winging their way toward the United States—until they smash into the shield and are stopped from doing any damage." He paused as Ryder, taking notes, looked up.

"Senator?"

"You've seen those portrayals?"

"I have, sir."

"Then perhaps you might tell us, Mr. Secretary, is this also how the Department of Defense conceives of SDI? Are you contemplating a 'Gardol' shield strong enough to make Soviet missiles just bounce off?"

Ryder paused momentarily. Privately, he had spoken out against the cartoons, which he believed gave audiences false expectations about SDI. But that was something he couldn't say in public. He tapped his pen on the legal pad in front of him. "Let me say, Senator, first, I do not agree with those who hold SDI has to be perfect in order to be useful, or even effective. It is true that a defensive shield that allowed some incoming enemy warheads to 'leak' through would fail to prevent massive damage to America's cities. But even a partially effective defense—say, one that intercepted half the warheads headed for the United States—would disrupt an enemy attack aimed at destroying our retaliatory forces. That alone would add immeasurably to the effectiveness of our deterrent."

Waterman bit his lip. It was a perfectly good answer. Except it failed to support the president's policy. He watched as Chris Wentwood rose from his seat behind the chairman and whispered something in Senator Libby's ear.

"Then I take it," the senator said, tightening the screws, "that your vision of SDI is a good deal more modest than that of the president. Would that be a fair characterization?"

The secretary squirmed visibly in his seat. "I would prefer, Senator, not to characterize my statement, which speaks for itself. I believe that a partially effective defense is a great deal better than none at all."

"Do you"—Libby drove the point home—"believe that a perfect defense is feasible?"

"There is, Senator, no such thing as a perfect defense. But neither is there a perfect offense. Let's just leave it at that."

"I thank you for clarifying that." Libby smiled. "I hope the White House reviews the transcript of this hearing." He waited for the laughter to subside, then turned to the chairman. "Mr. Chairman, I have no further questions."

"Thank you, Senator." The chairman peered at Ryder. "Well, I do have some questions," he said pointedly.

He scanned the list in front of him, peered at the language intently, then began to read. "Could you tell the committee whether you share the view we understand to have been adopted by the administration—that in order to justify its deployment, SDI must be cost-effective at the margin?"

"I'd like to make sure I understand the question, Senator," Ryder said evenly.

Martin nodded. "Of course," he said. "Could you tell the committee whether you share the view we understand to have been adopted by the administration—that in order to justify its deployment, SDI must be cost-effective at the margin?" he repeated.

"I wonder if you might define what you mean by 'cost-effective at the margin'?" Ryder asked innocently.

Martin looked around anxiously at the staffers behind him. Wentwood was already scribbling. He ripped a page from his notepad and handed it forward.

"As I understand it," Martin said, reading slowly, "a system is cost-effective at the margin when the cost of an increment of defense is less than the cost of an increment of offense."

He scowled at Ryder. "Using that definition, Mr. Secretary, can you please calculate for us whether SDI will be cost-effective."

"Should I calculate in rubles or dollars?" Ryder asked. "It's important to know which one, because the results are entirely different. Or perhaps you'd like to suggest a conversion formula? I do assume you wish to measure the burden on the Soviet economy of deploying a unit of offense to counter a unit of defense."

Martin blanched. He turned to Wentwood, who again handed him a note. He was about to respond when the buzzer high on the wall above the dais sounded five times. A vote was on. Waterman smiled: saved by the bell.

"I'm afraid, Mr. Secretary, we're being summoned to the floor for a record vote. It shouldn't take more than ten minutes." Martin slammed his gavel down. "The committee will stand in recess, subject to the call of the chair."

The chairman left quickly. Other senators followed. The television lights dimmed. Ryder leaned back in the witness chair, grinned, and gave Waterman a big thumbs-up. An alert photographer caught the moment. Waterman grinned back. He'd enjoy it even more if that was the picture they'd use on the front page of tomorrow's *Washington Post*.

Idly, he looked over at the press table. Michael Gray sat writing furiously in a spiral notebook. He tore out a page and folded it twice. Then he wrote something on the folded paper and waved it in front of him, until he caught the majority staff director's eye. He motioned to a secretary, who walked to the press table and retrieved the note from Gray. Wentwood pored over the message and smiled. His thumb and forefinger made a circle in Gray's direction. Waterman was angered by the blatant collusion between the *Times* reporter and a committee staffer. He wondered whether Wentwood or perhaps another committee staffer or, for that matter, one of the senators had been responsible for leaking the JCS study. Committee staff and members frequently got copies of classified documents, even ones that were supposed to be internal to the DOD. Disgruntled officers who wouldn't dream of leaking a classified document directly to a newspaper or television reporter might well pass sensitive material to a Hill staffer—knowing full well that it was likely to wind up in the press. Waterman tried to recall whether he had ever done that in his days on the Senate staff. He couldn't be sure. Perhaps he had.

The senators began to drift back. Finally, the chairman appeared in the doorway, resumed his place, and took the gavel in his hand. As he did so, Chris Wentwood unfolded the paper Gray had sent him during the recess and placed it in front of the senator. Martin read the note. Then he refolded it and handed it back to Wentwood, shaking his head and whispering something to the young staffer.

He slapped the gavel twice. "The committee will come to order once more," he said. "Mr. Secretary, I apologize for the delay. Can we please continue where we left off?"

"Thank you, Mr. Chairman," Ryder said, "I'd be delighted. We were discussing how one would calculate costs—in dollars or rubles."

"I think the question of how to calculate costs is best left to the experts,"

Martin parried. "But I think the general principle—that it should be cheaper to intercept a missile than add a warhead—is sound. Otherwise the Soviets could respond to SDI simply by deploying more missiles."

Ryder nodded toward the dais. "To be honest, Senator, the issue of cost-effectiveness has been distorted in a most shameful way by critics of the president's program. I welcome this opportunity to set the record straight." Ryder's short, wide hand tugged at his cuff, bringing into view the heavy enameled cuff links bearing the presidential seal.

"First, it is not the president's policy that the actual cost to the United States of a strategic defense must be less than some theoretical cost to the Soviet Union of programs designed to counter it. Remember, as I said earlier to Senator Libby, the defense would be effective even if it intercepted only *some* of the incoming warheads, enough to preclude an attack that would effectively disarm us by destroying our capacity to retaliate."

Ryder's eyes flashed. "But the Soviets must be able to destroy our defense utterly. Utterly," he repeated for emphasis. "It is they, not we, who require perfection. I don't see how they could begin to estimate the cost of a perfect counter-SDI. Nor do I see how they could possibly afford it."

The secretary of defense modulated his voice, causing the senators to have to listen closely. "This brings me to point two: the relative difference in our ability to pay. The Soviets are now spending nearly twenty-five percent of their gross national product on the military. How much more can they devote to the military? So, if you take this 'cost effective at the margin' business literally, we would be comparing our costs with theirs without factoring in the Soviet ability to pay. On the other hand, if you're telling me it would be foolish for us to deploy an expensive defense for which there is a cheap counteroffense, I couldn't agree more."

The senator nodded dumbly. He began to say something, but Ryder cut him off in midbreath. "That, Mr. Chairman, is why I reject totally the conclusions of the JCS memorandum that has been discussed here this morning. The Joint Staff failed to take into account the technical and financial bind in which the Soviets find themselves—the source of the same pressures that led them into the Geneva negotiations in the first place."

Ryder then demolished the JCSM point by point. So deftly, in fact, did he dispose of it that a sense of anticlimax began to sweep over the crowded room. Waterman looked over at the press table. The *Times* correspondent, Michael Gray, who had entered to the whispered congratulations of his colleagues, now looked dispirited. His scoop was fast becoming a one-day bubble.

"I hope, Mr. Chairman," Ryder concluded, "that we have been responsive to your questions. As you know, we have a summit coming up. We need all the help and support we can get. The country is not well served when our policy is encumbered by rigid formulas that the Soviets can count upon to work in their favor."

Ryder leaned back in his chair, smiling broadly. The television cameras were switching off. Even before another question was asked, the news-worthiness of this hearing had ended. Waterman was delighted. He knew the rest of the hearing was going to be child's play. He'd be leaving for Riverton the next morning.

PART FOUR

CHAPTER FOURTEEN

North Carolina, October 22

Waterman wheeled his rented car south off the main road to Laurinburg and onto a winding two-lane blacktop that ran due east from the center of Riverton, North Carolina. He was some forty miles below Grannis Field, Fayetteville's municipal airport, south of the knots of convoys of army trucks and buses destined for Fort Bragg, and west of what remained of the Wilmington beach traffic. He was in what he had always considered the most beautiful part of the Tarheel state: the pine forests close to the South Carolina border—low, rolling hills covered with evergreens, the air giving off their gentle, distinctive scent; the ground permanently crunchy as generation upon generation of old needles decomposed into mulch.

The reason behind his trip lay, officially, in a long-standing invitation to appear at a foreign-policy seminar in Aspen, Colorado. Under normal circumstances Waterman would have declined to go. There was too much happening right now for him to get sidetracked for almost a week with a gaggle of academics. But as much as preparation for the upcoming super-power summit demanded his time and energy, he had a second, even more important, crisis to deal with as well—his domestic one.

Waterman was not a man given to introspection. He was primarily a doer, not a ponderer. His talent lay in his ability to channel energy, to focus on problems until they were solved. Now, he looked at his marriage in much the same critical way he had examined the intermediate-range-missile question. He attacked it with the same kind of intensity with which he did everything else. And he began to see a possible solution.

His marriage, he realized, was not a lost cause. Oh, the sheer quantity and tempo of his work had taken a lot of the life out of his relationship with Laura. He'd forgotten about the domestic niceties, and, he realized when he scrutinized what he'd done, he had been taking his wife for granted. He had accepted the fact that she would always be there for him—be there when he came home, no matter what the hour; be there when he needed help packing for trips, helping him organize his already overorganized life. Be there emotionally, too, when he felt beaten down by the endless work and attention to detail, by the bureaucratic infighting, the inaction and bungling. It was a lot to ask of anyone. He knew that. And he knew he hadn't been as attentive, as caring, as thoughtful, as he once had been.

Waterman asked himself when was the last time he'd bought Laura flowers. He couldn't remember. When had they been to a movie together? It had been more than a year. When had the two of them shared a leisurely candlelight dinner? What was candlelight? The copper fait-touts and sauté pans in his kitchen were gathering dust. He, who had done all the cooking until he'd gone to the Pentagon, never cooked for his family anymore. But—and it was a big "but," he knew—she did still love him. He'd sensed as much when he spoke to Gloria, even though Laura wouldn't come to the phone. And he loved Laura. Utterly and completely. It was just, he realized, that he hadn't told her so very often lately.

It was, he decided, a matter of having enough time together to help repair something that was not fractured, only badly sprained.

So when the decision to go to Aspen came down to the wire, he'd decided in favor of the trip. He had an ulterior—well, not really ulterior—motive. Laura and he had spent wonderful weekends in Aspen when he'd worked on the Hill. She was a skier and reveled in her hours on the slopes. He, who had never been able to understand why people paid to get cold, loved to curl up in front of a fireplace with a good book. Since Aspen held such warm memories for them both, Waterman rationalized that if he could get her there and they could spend time together, he would be able to begin the work of repairing their marriage. And since she would not speak to him directly at the moment, he decided to show up in Riverton unannounced. The last time he'd done that sort of thing, she'd ended up getting married to him. This time perhaps she'd consider staying that way.

He peered through the windshield at the familiar winding road. He loved this part of the country. Laura's mother had grown up here in a tiny community called Riverton. It was no more than a collection of a dozen or so houses—log cabins, many of them, most built by hand and with incredible care, by members of Laura's extended family. Gloria Fay was the sole daughter of Methodist missionaries. She'd been born in China and had spoken fluent Mandarin before she'd learned proper English. When the Japanese went into Manchuria, she was sent home to Riverton, although her parents stayed behind to run their school and mission—only to be executed by the Japanese as spies. Orphaned, Gloria was taken into the bosom of her four aunts and three uncles in this tight-knit Carolina community, where Scotsmen loyal to Bonnie Prince Charlie had once settled.

Gloria; her husband, Charlie; Titus, the black Labrador retriever; and Lao-tse, the cat, all lived in a cabin Charlie had built and Gloria Fay filled with flea-market treasures and the remnants of her parents' Chinese antiques—the ones they'd shipped back with her in 1937. It was a house of good cheer and good memories. It had always been a haven for Laura, who would visit whenever she could, bringing Jason, who loved to ride his grandfather's horses, play in the huge garden, and listen to his grandmother speak in the Chinese she still practiced every night before she went to bed. It was a place that time seemed to have forgotten. Outside, in the root cellar under the shed, country hams better than the best Parma had to offer hung to cure. Down the road the Lumber River flowed, its water so clean you could drink it.

Waterman eased the car onto the narrow driveway that stretched six tenths of a mile from the Riverton road. As he pulled close to the Williamson cabin, he could hear Titus barking. The big black Lab ran to the car, put his paws on the window, and greeted Waterman with a doggy smile as he turned off the ignition. He climbed out of the car, paused momentarily to rub the dog behind the ears, and walked, Titus licking his hand all the while, up to the cabin. He knocked on the screen.

Laura opened the door halfway. She wore a Black Watch plaid flannel shirt, jeans, and Wellington boots. Her hair was pulled back and tied with green wool, and Waterman had never seen a more beautiful woman in his life. He was as smitten at that instant as he had been when he'd seen her for the first time at the hostel in Chartres.

"I love you," he said dumbly, unable to think of anything to say—except the truth.

"Michael." Her eyes went wide. "What are you doing here?"

"I—I—I was in the neighborhood," he stammered.

She stood in the doorway.

"Aren't you going to invite me in?"

"Laura, who's there?" Gloria's drawl came from deep inside the cabin.

"It's Michael, Mama."

A long pause. "Well, don't leave him standing."

Laura opened the door all the way. Waterman walked inside. The cabin was small but efficient. He passed through the galley kitchen with its thirty-year-old electric stove and wonderful cooking smells into the low-ceilinged living room. "Where's Jason?"

"He's out with his grandfather," Laura said. "They're fishing."

Gloria Fay came in from the screen porch, as trim as ever. She and Laura were a matched set, Laura inheriting what Waterman liked to call "designer genes."

"Nice to see you, precious," she said, reaching up to kiss him on each cheek and hug him warmly. "Between meetings?"

"As a matter of fact, Gloria . . ."

"Now don't let me rag you. It is good to see you—I'm glad you're here." She headed toward the kitchen. "I'm going to put on a pot of nice jasmine tea and then leave the two of you alone. I've got work to do in the garden. Now, Michael, don't feel as if I'm abandoning you or anything. I'm fascinated to hear about your life among the rich and famous and all that, but my acorn squash just won't wait, if you know what I mean."

Gloria smiled playfully, and Waterman understood that his mother-in-law wasn't mad at him—just upset. "Your ears must have been burning, Michael; you've been all the topic of conversation in Riverton for more than a week now."

He sank onto the sofa. "I can believe it." He looked at his wife, who shed her boots and settled herself cross-legged in a well-used oversize armchair. He suddenly felt very awkward, the chubby adolescent with his cello case again. "You okay?"

She shrugged. "Surviving. Lonely. You?"

"Surviving. Lonely."

They spoke for perhaps an hour, perhaps more—Waterman never could quite remember—as they sipped the delicately scented tea from hundred-year-old china cups. At first the words were hard to come by, and the air was often filled with silence. But as time progressed, words became easier to find until they poured out from both husband and wife in torrents. Later in the afternoon, they walked the mile and a half down to the riverbank, Waterman feeling somewhat out of place in his dark suit and city shoes crunching across the spongy pine-needle path. They sat on the smooth trunk of a tree, felled by a storm some years before, that formed a natural bench, and talked some more. What they said to each other may not have been profound, but it was heartfelt and honest—spoken in the special, tender shorthand husbands and wives reserve for each other. Waterman realized that afternoon he had come close to losing not only his wife, but his best friend. It was a loss he knew he could not afford.

By early evening they'd wandered back to the house hand in hand, reconciled by Waterman's pledges to move the family up a notch in the competition for time and attention and by Laura's forbearance in accepting that he meant what he promised. The truth was they loved each other; Michael's government service was a trial they were resolved to endure. When they reached the cabin, Jason was at the door with Charlie, proudly waiting to show his father the first three fish he'd ever caught.

He and Laura shared the guest room out behind the house that night. The next day they left together for Aspen.

Aspen, Colorado, October 27

Waterman leaned back in his chair staring idly at the evergreen landscaped courtyard beyond the glass wall of the conference room. Some academic was droning on in highly theoretical terms about policy options that any clerk-typist in the Pentagon would know were wholly unrealistic. The price you paid for an autumn escape to Aspen was having to listen to a bunch of professors spin out theories about a world of which they knew nothing. What made it tolerable was that the seminar met only in the morning; during the afternoons he and Laura were free to enjoy the cool, clear alpine setting.

Their suite had a fireplace, and Waterman splurged on half a case of Krug *première cuvée* champagne, which they kept in the small refrigerator alongside the brie and *chèvre* cheeses he'd found at a gourmet store. The schedule was simple. Mornings, Waterman would attend a seminar. Then he would excuse himself from the group, and sneak off with Laura to share a lunch at one of the town's better restaurants, spend the early afternoon strolling along mountain trails, then repair to the room for champagne and what Waterman liked to call a nap, but which entailed precious little actual sleeping. At dinner they stared into each other's eyes like honeymooners.

It was the morning of the fourth day. Waterman had glanced at his watch for the third time in fifteen minutes when a message, passed hand to hand down his side of the long conference table, was slid in front of him.

He unfolded it. *Call your office ASAP.* Taking care not to scrape his chair against the concrete floor, he got up quietly and, carefully closing the door behind him, went down the stairs to a telephone booth on the floor below the conference room. He waited while Maggie accepted the collect call.

"Sorry to interrupt, but Scott Bracken insisted I track you down."

"What does he want?"

"He's in his office. I'll transfer you." Waterman waited while the phone clicked. Then Bracken's voice came on. He sounded upset.

"Scott? What's wrong?"

"I've got to be a little cryptic on this open line. The negotiation our white-haired friend is involved in—it took an unexpected turn."

White hair—that would be Ambassador Ellis Moore, the administration's chief arms negotiator. "Okay, I know who you're talking about. What happened?"

"Ten days ago he made a proposal of a far-reaching nature without any instructions from Washington. No one knew. Now he's gone to the NSC to get approval to propose it formally. In the meantime he's waiting for an answer from over there."

"He made a substantive proposal entirely on his own?"

"That's right. Just like that."

"What was it?"

"We're on an open line, Michael."

"I know, Scott. But dammit, give me some general background."

"Our white-haired friend just attended two conferences, one in Berlin, the other in Bonn. At both, supporters of our position were disheartened by mounting opposition in the Bundestag—particularly among the foreign minister's party, the Free Democrats."

"Okay, so?"

"So our friend was shaken by the vehemence of the opposition and the ineffectiveness of the government officials supporting deployment. He went back to the INF talks in Geneva overwhelmed with pessimism. He felt something had to be done, but he knows the interagency group in Washington that reads his cables and makes day-to-day decisions on his instructions would almost certainly fail to appreciate the gravity of the situation. So he did what he thought he had to—he drew up a list of issues that divided the two sides and fashioned a compromise."

"Entirely on his own?" Waterman was aghast. Moore had broken all the rules. This was unforgivable.

"If anyone else knew, they're not owning up to it," said Bracken.

"What's the reaction over there?" Waterman ran a hand through his hair in an agitated gesture.

"That's what I can't discuss on an open line. But these are important developments. You really should get back right now, Michael."

"Impossible. I'm committed to be here another two days, and I can't change my plans." Especially, Waterman thought, with the progress he and Laura were making. Not even a monumental screw-up in arms negotiations could haul him back to Washington.

"Then I'll need guidance."

"Let me think a minute." Waterman was confused and angry. With Zero on the table, the administration already had a negotiating position for Geneva—one that he believed would result in a true arms agreement. So what the hell could have possessed Moore to do something like this? It was incredible.

Still, Ellis Moore was no ordinary ambassador. He had served Democrats and Republicans alike in administrations reaching back to FDR. Trim and white-haired, he had the confident bearing of a man who had made a fortune early in life and gone on to a career in public service in senior positions in every important government department. He was a man who moved freely among Wall Street bankers, corporate executives, and members of Congress. He was cold, distant, aloof, and strangely vain. He soaked up flattery like a sponge—but only when he respected the flatterer. Waterman admired him enormously, and enjoyed giving Moore great deference as much as Moore enjoyed receiving it from him.

Moore was also a man of such remarkable intellectual rigor that even those who couldn't follow his sometimes-complicated arguments were habitually prepared to accept that he must be right. He had enormous influence with the press; he was close enough to the highest reaches of the administration so that his views were considered authoritative. At the same time he was independent enough so you got more than the administration line. Indeed, Waterman could spot a blind Moore quote in the newspapers by the second sentence, which typically began, "But other senior administration officials are thought to disagree. They believe . . ."

He had been made arms negotiator by the president just after his seventy-fifth birthday, appointed on the advice of NSC adviser Mitchell, who had been impressed with Moore's opposition to a strategic arms treaty brought home by the previous administration.

The downside to his selection was that Moore was convinced he knew how to handle his assignment better than those—the president included—who gave it to him. Moreover, Waterman knew he was convinced Germany was the key to the success of American policy, and he was sure he understood the Germans better than anyone else arrayed around the table when negotiations were under discussion.

The Germans were critical to the successful completion of an American intermediate-missile deployment because the first missiles were to be deployed on German territory. Without missiles there could be no negotiated settlement—the Kremlin wasn't a charitable institution, and Soviet leaders would not give up any of their missiles unless the United States was certain to get its own missiles deployed.

Waterman had talked to Moore. He knew the ambassador believed the Germans would not support deployment when the chips were down. So he had gone off on his own and done something rash. Goddammit.

Waterman brooded, looking through the glass of the telephone booth into the wood-and-glass lobby of the institute. "Look, I've got an idea," he said. "I'm calling from a phone booth. I don't want to give you the number because they'll just enter it into the computer and pick up our conversation just like they're recording this one. But if you call me from a phone booth, say, in thirty minutes, I'll be waiting at the phone booth next to this one. There's no way they can intercept a call between two phone booths when they don't have either number. Scott, listen carefully. I'm going to give you a number. It's the sum of the telephone number in the booth next to mine and Maggie's ex-husband's home number. It's unlisted. She gave it to me once, and I've still got it on the phone list I keep in my wallet. All you have to do is subtract that number from the total I give you. Then call me in half an hour. Give me a second to do the arithmetic."

Waterman put the phone down and peered into the next phone booth. He wrote down the telephone number and did his addition. "Scott, take this down: one-five-one-eight-six-eight-zero-zero. Ask Maggie to give you the number to subtract, and you've got it. Forget the area codes. I'll be waiting."

"You're a genius," Scott said.

"No. My security violations are just more complicated than yours." They both laughed. Waterman hung up, scribbled *Out of Order* on a sheet of paper, and attached it to the quarter slot on the next phone over with a bent paper clip.

As quietly as he had left, he returned to the seminar and took his place. It would be over soon. He might as well be lost in thought there as somewhere else.

The phone in the booth rang at the precise appointed time. "If you bastards have managed to find Maggie's former husband's unlisted number and reprogram the computers in twenty-eight minutes, you deserve to record this conversation," he said into the receiver. "Carry on, Scott."

"Okay," Bracken said. "Moore proposed a package in which we'd give up our Pershing Two missiles. We could keep some air-breathing cruise missiles, and they could keep some SS-20s. There'd be two hundred twenty-five warheads allowed on each side. There's more to it than that, but that's the key provision."

"So numbers would be equal for both sides?"

"Not exactly. The numbers *in Europe* would be equal, but they'd have the right to keep up to three hundred warheads on one hundred missiles in Asia. We'd have a theoretical right to match them. But Christ, Michael, there's no place in Asia to deploy intermediate missiles. So in practice they'd have roughly twice what we'd have."

"All hell must be breaking loose. How did we learn of this?"

"Moore walked into Mitchell Wallace's office cool as a cucumber and told him. Evidently, Moore proposed it to Rogov on the last day of the round of talks—ten days ago. They'd just finished lunch at some alpine restaurant, and Moore suggested a walk in the woods. After an hour or so they stopped to rest. They sat on a log. Moore pulled out a piece of paper and began to outline an eleven-point package. He told Rogov he was proposing it on his own, and it was all-or-nothing. Take it or leave it all—he wouldn't negotiate further.

"Rogov copied down the eleven points. But he balked at the point about Asia. Moore proposed allowing two hundred twenty-five warheads for each side in Asia. Rogov complained that Moscow already had two hundred seventy. So Moore said okay, he could live with two hundred seventy."

Bracken paused, then gave a wry chuckle. "Then Rogov says he's gotta take the whole package back to Moscow—he'll phone Moore at his vacation home in Maine after he returns to the States for home leave.

"Moore sat by the phone for a week. Rogov never called. Finally, he asked for an appointment with Wallace."

"Where do things stand?" Waterman asked.

"There's a meeting later this afternoon at the NSC to decide what to do. Moore's pressing for authority to make his proposal formal. State's on his side, of course, except Bennet's furious because Moore did something on his own and kept him in the dark. Wallace is annoyed with Moore's free-lancing, but he's not about to take him on. We don't know where the JCS stands—they're preparing a paper."

Waterman frowned. "Look, Scott, what troubles me most is not the substance of the deal. It's the procedure—Moore's end run. It's a lousy way to do business. Moore may have told Rogov it was his own proposal, but they'll never believe it in Moscow. They'll take it as an authorized feeler.

They'll conclude we're ready to abandon parts of our position. The worst thing is that they'll think we're collapsing just before a summit.

"Novikov'll certainly reject it; but our policy will never the be same. Our insistence on the deployment of some Pershings and on global equality—the two elements we've been saying all along we won't negotiate—will have been shown to be negotiable."

"Slower, Michael, I'm trying to take this down."

Waterman caught his breath. "Look—the worst of it is political, not strategic. Suppose the Germans find out we offered to give up our Pershings. The chancellor's out on a limb supporting deployment, while Moore is in Geneva giving it away."

"What do you want me to do?" Bracken asked.

"Get the guys working on a detailed analysis. It should look at the military implications of giving up Pershings while still facing SS-20s. In the meantime give the secretary a note telling him in general terms what I just told you."

"Done."

"Tell him I get back late Sunday afternoon. But I want him to know I'm working on this—I'll have something for him about this whole mess by the time I get back. When I get your analysis, I'll fold it in at the last minute."

"It'll be waiting at the airport—the driver'll have it."

"Good. And if there are any changes, Scott, call me right away. I have to know what's going on. I have to know what the secretary's thinking."

"You got it."

So much for Shangri-La, thought Waterman as he left the phone booth.

━━━━━━━━━━━━━

October 29

Waterman rolled to his right and looked at the digital clock bolted to the night table. Nine-twenty. He was alone in the king-size bed. Laura was already out, running her usual five miles.

He picked up the conference folder that lay on the floor next to the bed, where he'd dropped it the previous evening, and squinted at the agenda. The final morning session—starting in ten minutes—was on arms control and antisubmarine warfare, a complex issue about which almost nothing useful could be said except at very high levels of security classification. The conference was unclassified, and no secret material could be discussed. Most of the participants lacked access to it anyway. He decided to skip the session and begin work on a memorandum for the secretary of defense—a background document on the Moore proposal. On the other hand, they'd had a lot of champagne last night, as well as the one form of exercise Waterman found truly rewarding, and Waterman had awakened with a bit of a hangover. The proper thing to do, he decided, was sharpen up the old brain by giving it some rest. No use trying to write when you're tired. So he rolled over and promptly fell asleep again.

By late morning the sun above the Aspen mountains was burning brightly in the clear sky. At seven thousand feet, in the thin air, the sun touched everything—leaves, ledges, treetops, water—with a wonderful incandescence. There was, Waterman decided (now that he'd had ten and a half hours of sleep), a clarity to the light at this altitude that encouraged the beginning of projects.

He sat on the balcony, a fresh yellow legal pad on the table in front of him. As he saw it, there were two issues to be addressed, one of substance—in other words, the nuts and bolts of what Moore had said—and another of procedure—the way Moore had gone about making his proposal and why he'd done it. With respect to substance, he'd deal with it when he got back to Washington and had Bracken's assessment in hand.

But the procedural issue was absolutely clear to Waterman. He was convinced that by altering American policy without instructions, and hiding the fact that he had done so, Ambassador Moore had chosen to substitute his own judgment for that of the president of the United States.

In so doing, Moore had stolen the president's authority. It was theft, this usurpation. A piece of the president's mandate had been taken from him.

The more Waterman thought about it, the angrier he grew. His hand flew across the page as he wrote.

Memorandum: Department of Defense
SECRET-SENSITIVE

TO: The Secretary
FROM: ISP/Michael Waterman
DATE: October 29
SUBJECT: Rogue Diplomacy

We worked long and hard to persuade the president to propose the Zero Option to the Soviets. Ellis Moore has been an opponent from the very start. The issue was debated—we won a clean victory. And now this single individual, one who has had every opportunity to argue his case within the councils of the administration, has single-handedly reversed the president's decision and abandoned our policy.

In making this totally unauthorized proposal to the official representative of the Soviet Union, Ambassador Moore has betrayed his colleagues, robbing them of their arguments, their reasons, their concerns, and their hopes. After all, interagency groups meet frequently to consider whether to recommend changes to American negotiating positions. Moore was almost always present for those deliberations. And while they were debating the ambassador's view that the American position ought to be changed, the ambassador in effect slipped from the room in the dark of night to go and change it.

On matters of political judgment, I believe that, for all his incontestable brilliance, Moore is superficial and insensitive. He is given to imposing logic on situations that are illogical, order where there is likely to be chaos. It has been evident for some weeks that he has been overreacting to the shrill debate in Germany over the deployment of American missiles. It is true there is a great deal of opposition to deployment. It is true that the German chancellor is in trouble with his own party over the issue, and might not survive long enough to lead the Social Democrats at the next election. But it seems highly unlikely that Germany will back away from a NATO plan to deploy missiles in five countries, a plan approved by all NATO countries and inspired largely by a speech by the German chancellor.

An intellectual himself, Moore makes the mistake of listening to other intellectuals. He does it in Washington, and now he has done it in Europe. Intellectuals have a way of adopting positions with disastrous practical consequences: If German intellectuals, for example, had their way, our missiles would *never* be deployed, although the Russian ones would remain, of course. Moscow's monopoly would be continued, and even legitimized. And the professors and writers and artists would rejoice in the triumph of reason in human affairs.

Moore also habitually gives credence to diplomats. In this he errs. It is foolish to attribute too much weight to Foreign Service officers. It is extraordinary how absorbed in the inconsequential machinations of their colleagues professional diplomats become.

If you listen to diplomats, you are bound to come away with a distorted view of the world. For one thing, they live and breathe international affairs. They can be moved to tears by the sight of a well-crafted demarche, to despair by a clumsy departure from protocol. Because they are involved daily with international affairs, with the positions of governments and parties and factions, with votes in parliaments and changes in ministries, with the drafting of communiqués and official statements, with caucuses and congresses, committees and consultations, they believe—wrongly—that the world turns on a diplomatic axis so exquisitely poised that the slightest perturbation will bring it to a halt.

Thus, a sense of urgency infuses everything they do, and the distance and detachment that are crucial to sound judgment is readily lost. It is my guess that Moore's end run was a reaction to the intellectuals' and diplomats' fears about Germany. He was driven to expect disaster if the Geneva talks failed to produce an agreement. His move was an act of desperation. It stands little chance of success.

But it could have dangerous consequences. Can you see the headline in *Der Spiegel:* U.S. OFFERS TO SCRAP PERSHINGS? The German chancellor would be made to look ridiculous, arguing for deployment while the Americans were secretly preparing to walk away from it.

The argument that deployment of Pershing IIs is essential for Western security would lose all credibility. The whole intricate timetable for the deployment of American missiles in Europe, beginning with Pershing IIs in Germany and eventually including cruise missiles in Britain, Italy, Belgium, and the Netherlands, would unravel.

I can't figure how Moore believes the Soviets would respond positively to any offer a scant five months before the German elections. Clearly, Moscow hopes the peace movement in Germany will exert enough pressure to block any deployment. If the Social Democrats win at the polls, that is the likely outcome. So no proposal short of complete capitulation would appeal now to the Kremlin leaders. Especially with the prospects of the Zero Option staring them in the face. This is—

He heard the door open and looked around. It was Laura, back from her run.

"I thought you were going to the seminar."

"I stayed in—writing a memo for Ryder."

"On what?"

"There's a mess in Washington. Ellis Moore—the arms negotiator—took a walk in the woods with a Russian and he made a proposal he shouldn't have." He explained the problem in detail.

Her face screwed up with concern. "How's it going?"

"Okay, I guess. But I've had enough for now. What about a swim?"

"But what about the seminar? You can't tell them about this. What'll you say about not showing up?"

"Nothing. I'll go to the final lunch—you'll come too—looking as official and secretive as I can manage. Believe me, no one will ask. Someday they'll learn all about it—probably from Moore."

He pulled a pair of trunks from the dresser and put them on. "You know what galls me? Most of them would applaud Moore's position and even his tactics. They don't like my Zero Option idea. They're just like Dan Bennet— convinced it's intended to deadlock the negotiations. And there's nothing these academics dislike more than deadlocked negotiations. We propose something, the Soviets reject it. Half an hour later the same people I'm listening to here are writing papers on how we can advance the negotiations by adopting a new position."

"You don't have to make a case with me to justify a swim, Michael. Come on—we can order coffee by the pool."

CHAPTER FIFTEEN

Washington, November 3, 8:30 A.M.

Waterman arose at what he considered the crack of dawn Monday, and headed toward his E-ring office on the Pentagon's outer corridor at eight-thirty. With traffic he would be in the office by nine. Nine was considered bankers' hours at the Department of Defense, but not for Waterman, who had years ago developed a habit of working late and sleeping late. His was not a schedule common to the Pentagon, and from time to time the secretary of defense would remark on it. Arriving most days at about ten meant Waterman almost always missed the secretary's morning staff meeting, held daily at 8:00 A.M.

In most government departments workdays began with staff meetings presided over by the secretary himself. Considerable prestige attached to those invited to attend—a sign that one had been admitted to the inner circle. And whether at the State Department, Treasury, Agriculture, Commerce, or the National Security Council, nearly all morning meetings were the same, with the faithful gathered around their leader, keen to make their presence known by reporting on their areas of responsibility and receiving instructions.

At the Pentagon, morning meetings took place in the secretary's office, a sprawling room rather like the oversize drawing room of a large country house. Unlike the secretary of state, who had a ceremonial office, an everyday office, and a hideaway office, Ryder had only one. It was huge—

big enough for ceremonial occasions as well as the daily staff meetings. Five floor-to-ceiling windows looked out onto the Tidal Basin and a small boat marina, then across the Potomac to Washington. If you looked behind the sheer curtains, you would see PVC pipes—the kind used by plumbers—placed horizontally across the tops of the windows. They were the only visible part of a system using sophisticated sonic techniques to defeat unfriendly listening devices that work by picking up vibrations off the windows with a laser beam.

A red-and-white-striped sofa flanked by several easy chairs sat at one end of the room in front of a coffee table on which a bullet case, a sword, a belt buckle, and various other bits of Civil War memorabilia were laid out for display as though placed by a butler.

Hand-carved wooden models of eighteenth- and nineteenth-century men-of-war—everything from the *Bonhomme Richard* to the *Monitor* and *Merrimac*, the kind of miniatures Jason could only dream about, sat on small tables in clear plastic cases, one in front of each window.

The walls were covered with military art—which is to say, mediocre paintings of military subjects—ornately framed and scattered among bronze plaques presented by this service unit or that foreign air force. The center of the room was dominated by a massive, ornately carved nineteenth-century mahogany partner's desk on which sat a collection of ... Waterman could not describe them except as "things," which had been presented to the secretary by various foreign dignitaries. The bizarre assortment included a ceramic figure of a gaunt Spanish rider that might have been Don Quixote, a bit of gold filigree looking as if it had been ripped from the altar of a Thai temple, a silver bowl with the insignia of an Italian naval unit, a twenty-millimeter shell casing from the Bundeswehr that had been chrome-plated and fashioned into a vase.

Nowhere in the office of the secretary of defense was there a hint of high technology. Even the telephone console with its thirty-six buttons, a system that could establish instant hot-line connections with telephones on the desks of other Cabinet officers and the heads of the military services, was curiously old-fashioned. Waterman had always thought it resembled a switchboard behind the desk of a 1940s New England hotel.

At morning meetings the secretary and his deputy faced each other in matching easy chairs, flanked by the assistant secretaries and other senior officials seated in a row of straight-backed chairs moved each morning from a dining table at the far end of the cavernous room.

The power of the press hovered over morning meetings like a ghostly presence. It was a rare day when there was not some story damaging to the department featured prominently among the press clippings prepared at 7:00 A.M. by bleary-eyed assistants in the public-affairs department who had been clipping wire copy and photocopying faxes since the middle of the night. These stories invariably provoked extended discussion as the secretary elicited answers to be used in reply.

It was this obsession with reacting to the press and never admitting error that allowed the media to exert such exaggerated influence over high public officials. They could not seem to begin the day's business without first being certain they were girded to deal with yesterday's stories. The offending feature might have taken up one and a half inches on page B-1 1 of the *Des Moines Register,* but artfully arranged among the morning clips, it looked like page one in *The New York Times.*

Then discussion invariably turned to overnight developments in Congress. This allowed the assistant secretary for legislative affairs to demonstrate his detailed knowledge of the progress of countless bills and amendments that, at any moment, were winding their way through the tortuous legislative process.

His less-than-absorbing recitation, which could last as much as fifteen minutes, was of undoubted, albeit passing, interest to the secretary and the assistant secretary for legislative affairs. Everyone else's eyes generally glazed over.

Then, because the general counsel was a regular at morning meetings, the discussion got around to legal issues. Another five or ten minutes shot.

And so it went. Eventually, having disposed of the press, the Congress, and the judiciary, the secretary would go around the room offering anyone who wished to do so an opportunity to raise any issue of interest. This was accomplished by his looking at each official in turn and nodding. A slight motion of the secretary's head was the cue that invited his assembled subordinates to speak up if they had something to say.

On days when the morning meeting dragged on, Ryder's head would move like one of those gear-driven cameras that swivel slowly from left to right to enable a large group of graduating seniors to be captured in a single photograph, scarcely pausing long enough for anyone to respond. One didn't detain the mechanism by raising new issues. At least not without annoying everyone else present.

On the rare occasion when Waterman dragged himself to a morning meeting, the secretary would invariably have a question for him, usually late in the proceedings, when everyone else was anxious to get the hell out of the secretary's office and back to his own. Waterman's answers were always a model of brevity, reflecting his distaste for what he considered a colossal waste both of his time and the secretary's.

At two minutes to nine Waterman strode into his reception area. Maggie looked up from the word processor. "Welcome home, stranger. You didn't by any chance make the secretary's staff meeting, did you?"

"Certainly not," Waterman replied. He removed a pile of papers from his briefcase and grinned as he dumped them on her desk. "That's for you. Souvenirs."

She looked at the paperwork with distaste. "It's *so* nice to have you back, Michael. It was crazy around here. Mr. Moore—he was a naughty boy, wasn't he?"

"Let's say he didn't play by the rules."

"He sure had Scott in a lather. Scott turned the office upside down trying to keep up with the secretary. I tried to discourage him from phoning you in Colorado, but he insisted."

"He did the right thing, Maggie," Waterman assured her. "Did Scott go to the morning meeting?"

She nodded. "He's still there. It should be breaking up any minute."

"Phone his office—let him know I want to see him when he's free."

In his inner office Waterman turned on the espresso machine and was about to grind himself a cup's worth of beans when the hot-line telephone on the conference table rang. The green light flashing indicated it was the military assistant to the secretary, Major General Bill Collins, on the secure line. Terrific, Waterman thought, the meeting must have ended. He snatched the receiver up. "Morning, Bill. How's life among the apparatchiks?"

"That's what I'm calling about. The boss wants you to come and read something. If you were to come now, it would be a good idea. You won't be bored."

Waterman didn't hesitate. "I'm on my way."

He took the corridor at a medium-paced lope, ninety-five feet door-to-door to the secretary's office complex, hoping as he went that the people who had attended the secretary's morning meeting would have departed. It was awkward to run into them immediately following a meeting from which he'd been AWOL; and, as Collins's office was connected to the secretary's, it was hard to avoid it.

As it happened, the morning meeting had dispersed, and Waterman walked into Collins's office without encountering any of his colleagues. He liked the general. Bill Collins was a huge man of remarkable equanimity, an island of tranquillity even when storms raged all around, a man of cool, deliberate judgment, even temperament, and, remarkably enough, good humor.

The general looked up from his paper-laden desk as Waterman walked in. "How good of you to visit us, Mr. Secretary. Will you be staying long in our miserable company?"

"Hey, I take a few days in Colorado, during which abuse and opprobrium are heaped upon me by the combined faculties of Harvard and MIT because I'm associated with this ungrateful department. I have my peace and tranquillity ruined by a rogue ambassador who thought the president was talking directly to him when he called on the private sector to show more initiative. I find myself summoned here at the crack of dawn. And now, just when I deserve a little sympathy, I get flak about my travels."

Waterman picked up a miniature American flag that sat embedded in a paperweight on Collins's desk and began to wave it slowly in the general's face. "I know you think it's a vacation every time I take the red-eye to Brussels, go into meetings on arrival, host a dinner that night, and chair a meeting all the next day. What I can't understand is why American Express hasn't figured out what fun it is and offered a seventy-two-hour European vacation that includes NATO headquarters. What's up?"

"Read these," the general said, snatching back his flag and handing over a manila folder, "and weep."

Sitting on the government-issue imitation-leather sofa, Waterman looked quickly at the contents of the folder. Inside were two papers. One he recognized immediately. It was Bracken's memo. Scrawled across the cover sheet, in a hand unmistakably that of the secretary of defense, were the words *I disagree completely with this!*

Waterman found the exclamation point particularly daunting. James Ryder was a man of letters, a former *Crimson* editor, and without doubt a man who held the exclamation mark in low regard. That he'd resorted to it could mean only one thing—he'd been in a rage when he penned his comments.

Waterman looked at the second document. It was an "Eyes Only" memo to the secretary from the chairman of the Joint Chiefs of Staff. The most significant thing about it was the bold handwriting across the top of the page: *I agree completely with this. This is the policy of the Department of Defense!*

Wide-eyed, Waterman read on. For a JCS product, the chairman's memo was unusually direct: The chiefs were "unalterably opposed" to any deal with the Soviets that allowed them to keep ballistic missiles, like their SS-20s, while the United States was restricted to nonballistic missiles, like cruises. The memo was a three-page frontal assault on the Moore proposal on military grounds. The conclusion was supported by a fair amount of military mumbo-jumbo about target coverage, balance of forces in the theater, operational concerns, and the like, all of which gave an air of authority to the paper.

Waterman looked up. Collins grinned broadly. "You've been outhawked by the chairman." The general laughed. "You want to know what all this means?"

"Do I ever. But speak slowly, Bill. I'm a little shell-shocked. How the hell did the chairman ever get this past that mush-filled Joint Staff?"

Collins chortled. "They never saw it until it was finished. The chairman dictated most of it. All he asked the staff to do was fill in some of the numbers and prepare an appendix."

"But—"

"Look—the secretary went ballistic when he learned about Moore's proposal. You were out of town, so he asked the chairman for a memo outlining his views, and told me to get a memo from Bracken as well. They both went to him in Vermont. As you see, he preferred the chairman's position."

Collins's blue eyes twinkled in his ruddy face. "Since then, Ryder's been in touch with Wallace, who's assured him there's no way Moore's proposal will go forward. No way. It's dead—or it will be dead, as soon as we can kill it without leaving too much of a mess. For one thing, Wallace agrees with the chairman. For another, he's furious at Moore's tactics—he only learned about Moore's little walk in the woods with Rogov when Moore came into the NSC office and demanded to see the president.

"Now, the secretary wants you to write the memo he'll send to the president. But the order's clear: Incorporate the chairman's military arguments as well as your own. And do it quietly. No staff, Michael. No leaks."

Waterman nodded. "Got it. But you should know one thing out front, Bill. You might want to pass it on to the secretary, too."

"Okay—shoot."

"Truth is, I don't think this is such a bad deal for us."

Collins's eyes widened. "Huh?"

Waterman continued quickly. "Oh, not that I think the Soviets would ever go for it—certainly not five months before German elections."

"You can't let that affect the memo," Collins insisted.

"I'll do the best I can to give Jim what he wants. But I've never believed Pershing Twos are as important as the chiefs think they are. Most of their so-called military analysis is rubbish. Deployment is a political issue, not a military one."

Waterman opened the door. "Thanks for the help, Bill." He thought things in Wonderland were getting curiouser and curiouser.

CHAPTER SIXTEEN

Chevy Chase, November 3, 9:00 P.M.

After he and Laura had packed Jason off to bed, Waterman repaired to his basement office, turned on the light over his desk, and unlocked his briefcase. Inside were the analyses done by his staff, a copy of the JCS memo, Bracken's memo, and several papers relating to intermediate-missile systems that might contain useful background. He was struck by the irony of it all. Ryder had assigned him to write the paper disposing of the Moore proposal—and yet he believed Moore's idea contained a tolerable outcome. Still, no matter what he himself thought, the department—or more specifically, the secretary—disapproved. And disapproval is exactly what Waterman wrought as his fingers danced on the computer keyboard.

Draft Memorandum
SECRET-SENSITIVE

TO: The President
FROM: The Secretary

In your NSC memorandum you asked for my opinion of the proposal Ambassador Moore made to his counterpart in Geneva. This memorandum responds to that request. The chairman of the Joint Chiefs of Staff has participated in its preparation and agrees with its conclusions.

In our judgment, Ambassador Moore's proposal is seriously flawed. Any treaty incorporating its central features would, perhaps irreparably, damage our national security and the effectiveness of our nuclear deterrent in Europe. The proposed agreement would greatly favor the Soviets.

Worse, it is likely that NATO would fail to carry out its planned deployment of intermediate-range missiles in the aftermath of a treaty that alters fundamentally—as the Moore proposal does—the current deployment plan for the Alliance.

The problem is that the Moore proposal scraps Pershing IIs intended for deployment in Germany. If they are scrapped, other allies, the Dutch and the Belgians especially, will surely refuse to admit missiles on their territory. Moore's proposal, therefore, could cause the entire deployment plan to unravel.

The chairman and I share the opinion that we should not now offer the Moore proposal. The mere existence of an American proposal so laden with dire political implications, even if not responded to, leaves us in a dangerously vulnerable position. For this reason we believe the proposal should be withdrawn as soon as possible.

The alternative would be to allow the proposal to wither away by refraining from any further comment. This runs the risk that it might leak, with adverse consequences for the German chancellor, who is struggling to retain control of the German Social Democratic party.

Ambassador Moore's Proposal: Military Aspects

Two points of a military nature should be made at once: First, the Moore proposal leaves the Soviets with a total of 495 warheads; the United States would have 300 at most. Second, all the Soviet warheads would be ballistic—capable of striking their assigned targets in a matter of six or eight minutes. Ours would be cruise missiles, which take two hours or more to reach their targets. (As the Soviet SS-20 missiles are highly mobile, we must assume that even the 270 confined to the eastern portions of the Soviet Union could be moved, in a crisis, to within reach of European targets.)

In every important respect ballistic missiles are now, and are likely to remain for the foreseeable future, superior to cruise missiles. Cruise missiles fly within the atmosphere at relatively slow speeds. In principle, conventional air defenses can be deployed against them. The Soviets are at work developing upgraded air defenses against cruises. Within a few years we expect them to be able to intercept current U.S. cruise missiles.

By contrast, there are no defenses against medium-range ballistic missiles. Even under the most optimistic SDI projections, none will be available for the next decade.

Ambassador Moore's Proposal: Political Aspects

The proposal was put forward without guidance from Washington. Indeed, it is inconsistent with guidance previously sent. Moore has, from the outset of the talks, been under instructions to insist on the central features of your "Zero Option"—that is, equal numbers of warheads for each side on a worldwide basis, with freedom for each to choose the proportion of cruise and ballistic missiles.

Moscow could take the Moore proposal as a starting point. It is free to accept the parts it likes and reject those it doesn't like. This tactic of picking the raisins out of the cake is one at which the Soviet negotiators are adept.

We are concerned that the Soviets will claim their larger entitlement (595 warheads in all) proves they are entitled to compensation for the French and British independent deterrent forces, even though Moore's proposal (and your policy) explicitly rejects this claim.

Unfortunately, the argument that the Soviets are not entitled to compensation for British and French forces, while valid, is difficult to make persuasive to the general public, particularly in Germany, the Netherlands, and Scandinavia.

Developing a consensus within the NATO Alliance behind the Zero Option has not been easy. The Germans are chronically overwrought, constantly looking for signs of "flexibility" in the American position. The Dutch have yet to make a firm commitment to deployment. The British are solid, due largely to the prime minister's uniquely strong leadership; and the Italians have been strong and consistent. The Norwegians seem to be suffering the thought of deployment in silence. The Danes, who contribute next to nothing to the Alliance, have taken to expressing their doubts about deployment in footnotes to NATO communiqués.

Thus the political picture is mixed. But despite the misgivings, there is quite remarkable support for eliminating intermediate missiles entirely. Once we agree to allow *some* number, the opponents of U.S. deployments may well stop supporting *any* U.S. deployment, even one to which the Soviets agree.

For this reason we ought not to abandon Zero—a clear, simple, and understandable proposal. It is by far our strongest negotiating position. And, if agreed to, it would serve our security interests by eliminating *all* Soviet SS-20s.

Finally, we are deeply troubled by the manner in which Moore's proposal was offered to the Soviets. There is a well-established interagency procedure for adopting changes to the U.S. position. It includes consultations with our allies, especially the five basing countries. These procedures were circumvented. No consultations were held. Neither you nor your principal advisers were given an opportunity to judge the wisdom of such a proposal at this time. We urge that you take steps to assure that there is no repetition of this departure from established procedures.

The Pentagon, November 4, 8:15 A.M.

The call from Bill Collins indicating the secretary wished to see him came shortly after the daily staff meeting. Waterman made his way into the secretary's suite of offices and waved at Ryder's secretary as he pushed the concealed button in the doorframe, releasing the electronic lock on the heavy door to the secretary's office. The secretary of defense stood midway between his desk and a console on which the telephone was placed. Ryder was on the phone, Ryder's back to the door. He heard Waterman come in and motioned to him to take his accustomed place at a round table next to the big partner's desk.

The call completed, Ryder sat opposite Waterman.

"It was a fine memo," he said, dropping his reading glasses into the breast pocket of a rumpled gray-pinstripe suit jacket. "It was clear at the meeting yesterday that the president had read and absorbed it. You'll be amused to know Winthrop regarded it as effective, too, since he took great but unavailing pains to dispute it. He was incensed that the chairman and I would dare comment on political affairs—which he believes to be the exclusive province of the Department of State. But not to worry, Michael—I don't think there's any doubt we prevailed. Wallace was with us. So were McCandless and the vice president. Burner was angry on procedural grounds, so he didn't give Winthrop the help he might have expected. You should be pleased."

"Did the president say anything?" Waterman asked.

Ryder grinned broadly. "At one point he said something like, 'We can't have this sort of thing going on,' referring to Moore's having operated without instructions. And, you'll be pleased to know, he was quite insistent on the virtues of the Zero Option."

"Terrific."

"NSC was tasked to prepare a draft National Security Decision Directive by next weekend. The president'll take it with him to Camp David then, where he'll work on the final language. There should be something just after that. Then, I gather, the Senior Arms Control Group will draft instructions, based on the NSDD, for the next negotiating round." Ryder stood and rocked back and forth, as if waiting to receive a tennis serve. "You'll need to keep watch on the NSDD—you should see it a week from Monday—and then on the instructions, later next week."

"I take it you and the chairman argued that Moore's proposal should be withdrawn. Is it really dead—or just wounded?" There was a slightly apprehensive note in Waterman's voice. Wounded would not be good enough.

"I think it's dead," Ryder said with conviction. "At worst, Moore will be instructed not to mention it further, in which case the Soviets are likely to regard it as dead."

"It would be better to drive a stake through it—"

"A point I made several times, Michael," Ryder interrupted.

The Pentagon, November 10, 10:15 A.M.

Monday morning Waterman arrived late. As he walked through his front door, Maggie handed him a red-tabbed envelope from the National Security Council. He slit it open and stared incredulously at the words on the page he held in his hand, stunned. It was like the Dow going up eighty points, then looking up *your* stock to find it dropped six dollars a share. He read the page again.

National Security Decision Directive Number 116:
National Security Council
Washington, D.C. 20002
TOP SECRET
SYSTEM II

The president has reviewed the U.S. negotiating position in light of the proposal made by Ambassador Moore to the Soviet side last month.

The president has determined that while not all the elements of the Moore proposal would be in the U.S. security interest, further negotiation to determine Soviet attitudes would advance the American purpose in the negotiations.

The Senior Arms Control Policy Group (SACPG) should develop instructions for the next round as it has done previously. No reference should be made in these instructions to the Moore proposal.

However, the principal members of the Senior Arms Control Policy

Group shall also consider which elements of the Moore proposal are consistent with U.S. interests, with a view to guiding further negotiation should the Soviet side respond with interest to the Moore proposal.

In order to facilitate this possible further negotiation, a special group, to be composed of principals only of the SACPG, will be established to follow developments and make recommendations to the National Security Council, as appropriate.

A special code-word compartment shall be established for all communications and papers sent to or from the special group.

The president has asked me to reiterate the importance he attaches to utmost confidentiality concerning this matter.

> FOR THE PRESIDENT, Mitchell Wallace
> Assistant to the President for National Security

Paper in hand, Waterman buzzed Maggie on the intercom. "Mag," he said, "see if you can get hold of Bob Reed at the NSC on the secure line. It's urgent."

It was only a moment before the secure phone gave out its familiar buzz. Waterman picked up the receiver. He did not say hello.

"Bob, I'm standing here with a draft NSDD in my hand. It's Monday morning. The secretary of defense is in San Francisco on his way to South Korea.

"We're supposed to get six inches of snow this evening, a freak storm for this time of year. The heating system in the world's largest office building never works right on Mondays, and hence I'm freezing my ass off. And you guys have nothing better to do than send over mock NSDDs to test my sense of humor."

"How long have you had it?"

"About two minutes."

"Shit, that'll cost me five bucks."

"What are you talking about?"

"I bet Kramer you'd be on the phone within ninety seconds."

"You failed to allow for momentary paralysis brought on by disbelief and a sudden, sharp loss of comprehension."

"You were surprised?"

"Why would I be surprised? The SECDEF returns from a meeting at the White House and tells me we've won a richly deserved victory—in a battle which, in any even halfway organized administration, would never have been fought in the first place. The only issue, I'm given to understand, is the extent of the victory. All that remains is for a draft NSDD to be circulated, killing the Moore proposal either by benign neglect or—as I suggested—by administering a stake through the heart.

"And what happens?" He shook the NSDD at the phone receiver. *"This* happens, Bob. This happens. And you ask if I'm surprised? No, I'm not surprised. I'll tell you why. Because this goddam government, which used to be incompetent but at least predictable, has now become incompetent *and unpredictable.*"

"Well, you *should* be surprised. *I* was surprised, and I wrote the sucker."

"How the hell—"

"Before you ask me how it happened, lemme tell you I don't know how it happened. I watched the chopper lift off the South Lawn for Camp David last Friday. I know what was in the briefcase that went with the president. And what you got is what came back."

"Did anyone visit Camp David? Who was with the president?"

"It was just the two of them—the Old Man and Wallace."

"How much margin do we have for change?"

Reed gave a hollow laugh. "You might consider the adjectives. The nouns are in stone."

"What the hell is going on?"

"Hey, don't yell at me—I just work here. Look, I'm sending a paper for you to sign. It gets you into the special compartment, which we're calling 'Prince.' "

"What the hell do I need that for?"

"So when we write the paper—"

"Paper? Another goddam paper?" Waterman was really steamed now. "The last paper did a lot of good!"

"Look," said Reed, "maybe the president really bought your argument. Maybe he wants the Russians to deep-six the Moore proposal, so when it finally leaks, they'll be the ones shown to be unaccommodating."

Waterman snorted. "You're an optimist."

"You have to be—working here." Reed rang off. Waterman put down the phone, angry and dispirited. Nothing ever got settled. Nothing was ever clear. You fought the same battles over and over again. To the outside world there might appear to be some strong and consistent line. But to anyone inside there was only a constant struggle, one skirmish after another.

The president was growing increasingly indecisive. When he made the original decision to go for the Zero Option, over the violent objections of the secretary of state, he had resisted all pressures to blur and fudge despite State's unrelenting campaign to get him to do so. But recently things that should have been clear were coming back murky, decisions that ought to have been final were tentative. There were fewer yes's and no's—and a lot more maybes.

The Pentagon, November 14, 5:00 P.M.

Waterman was already in his car when Maggie came screaming through the mall entrance doors and pounded on the window.

"Bob Reed said he had—had—*had* to talk to you," she wheezed breathlessly. "He's in a phone booth at National Airport on his way out of town."

Waterman took his time getting back to his office and was surprised to find Reed waiting patiently on the line.

"You caught me performing a duty vital to my own national security," he said.

"What's that?"

"I was on the way to my son's soccer game."

"That's different—since when did you believe in a domestic life?"

"I'm planning to be the first assistant secretary for international security policy in three administrations who isn't going to be divorced when I leave this job," Waterman said. He meant it, too.

"Well, not to interrupt your paternal-bliss insurance, but like I told Maggie, this is important," Reed said. "There's a message in the 'Prince' compartment. State's got it—they've had it for two whole fucking days. I had to pry it out of them. Now that I've seen it, you shouldn't have any trouble getting it."

"What does it say?"

"We're on an open line."

"Sorry. Forgot. How did they explain holding it two days?"

"Oh, they blew smoke about cabling some questions to Moore and waiting for a response. Bullshit from Bennet, of course."

"I'll call right now, Bob. Thanks."

Waterman put down the phone, then pushed General Collins's hot line. He got a busy signal. "Damn," he said, and turned to Maggie. "I'm late for Jason's game—and I promised him I'd be there. Keep trying General Collins. When you get him, say there's a message in the 'Prince' compartment that we haven't got yet. Ask him to get it from State. I've got to see it when I get back."

. . .

Of course they'd keep it for two days, Waterman thought later as he snatched the cable off his desk. God knows what desperate maneuvers they had tried in order to salvage the Moore proposal before they had to admit defeat. He began to read intently:

Secret-Sensitive-Prince

I met this morning with Ambassador Rogov. I began to make the points laid out in special group guidance, specifically indicating that we were prepared to continue to discuss the idea I had put forth during our walk in the woods.

Before I could work through the talking points, Rogov interrupted me. "You don't need to go on," he said. "I was shot down in Moscow. The idea is dead. I have no authority whatsoever to discuss it any further."

Moore

Secret-Sensitive-Prince

" 'Good night, sweet Prince.' " Waterman dropped the message into his shredder and watched as it was ground into confetti.

CHAPTER SEVENTEEN

Moscow, November 20, 8:00 A.M.

Breakfast at the Intourist Hotel in Moscow was drab, the service slow and surly. But the tea was excellent, and the yogurt surprisingly good. Waterman, Bennet, and Ellis Moore shared a corner table for six in the cavernous second-floor dining room. One empty chair was piled high with the briefcases and briefing books that the delegation would need for the meeting scheduled to take place at a Foreign Ministry dacha outside Moscow. Another held a pile of overcoats.

The visit was being downplayed at home. The summit, Waterman knew, was where the chief of staff wanted all the attention. So their departure had been simply that: a departure. As anonymous as any business travelers, they'd flown economy to London, where they were met by an air-force Gulfstream for the three-and-a-half-hour flight to Moscow. There, they were met by embassy officials and unceremoniously whisked into the city to register at the Intourist.

All anonymity, however, was blown during the next morning's forty-five-kilometer drive from Moscow to the Foreign Ministry's dacha. They were picked up by a convoy of Chrysler K-Cars from the U.S. embassy, led by a Zil from the Soviet Foreign Ministry, and driven along broad avenues heading westward out of Moscow. Waterman, in the last car, noticed a green Mercedes following the minimotorcade. He turned to the embassy interpreter sitting alongside him.

"Who's that—KGB?"

The interpreter peered out the rear window. "No," he said, squinting to see who was in the green car that was now edging closer. "I think it's CBS."

Indeed, once the motorcade hit the road west out of Moscow and began to pick up speed, a thin, ruddy cameraman with a drooping red mustache and wearing a green knitted cap appeared through the sunroof. The Mercedes began to thread its way in and out of the gaps in the motorcade, the cameraman swiveling as the Mercedes slalomed between the official cars, recording the delegation's trek to the negotiating site.

It was, Waterman thought, precisely the sort of imbecilic coverage network producers thought necessary in order to avoid the most dreaded of all TV images, the "talking head." Network anchors made millions reading the news. But the nightly news producers still crammed each story full of visual wallpaper so viewers wouldn't get bored watching those high-priced kissers.

The pursuit didn't end when the motorcade arrived at the site. The Mercedes, which had followed closely all along the route, passed with the rest of the motorcade through the gates of a palatial Russo-Georgian estate, the big house looming in the distance down a long gravel driveway that ran between poorly tended formal gardens more Italian than Slav. Waterman looked back to see the uniformed guard at the gate salute the cameraman—who saluted back.

The meeting took place not in the main building but in a rustic, ivy-covered wood-and-fieldstone building, converted from what had probably been servant quarters.

The Americans ran the video gauntlet—only after they'd got pictures was the crew hustled away by Soviet guards, leading Waterman to believe that perhaps they'd tipped the network off in the first place—then crunched across pea gravel to the steps of the dacha. There, waiting, were their Soviet counterparts, Kalinin, Kulikov, and Kagarovich (Waterman thought of them as the KKK), arrayed in ascending order of protocol.

Aleksandr Kagarovich, resplendent in a lieutenant general's uniform heavy with ribbons, stood on the bottom step; dour Vladimir Kulikov, a veteran Foreign Ministry apparatchik, was in the middle. At the top stood Andrei Gromyko's best protégé, Viktor Kalinin, flaunting a Khrushchev-era gray suit and a carnivorous grin that flashed the poor quality of his dentures. The three men reminded Waterman of the May Day lineup atop Lenin's tomb.

The Americans, ascending in descending order of protocol, stopped to shake hands as they climbed the steps. Moore went first, followed by Bennet, then Waterman, then the note-taker from the embassy, then the interpreter and the embassy security officer who would watch the Americans' briefcases when they left the room to caucus or go to lunch.

Inside, Waterman looked around the large main room of the dacha. Its walls were covered with modern imitation-wood paneling; crystal chandeliers of Venetian glass hung between exposed ceiling beams of unfinished pine. The stuffed head of a wild boar looked out from one wall, a set of elk antlers hung on another. The Russians motioned the Americans to their assigned places on the far side of a table covered in green felt and laden with heavy glasses and bottles of sulfurous mineral water, labels peeling away from the bottles. Pads of rough notepaper were set out in front of each chair.

There was a fair amount of shuffling as both sides arranged their papers and notebooks atop the conference table. When each had finished, there was a moment of silence.

"Now," Kalinin said, adjusting the collar of his gray shirt, "we can begin."

Protocol called for the Soviets to offer the Americans the chance to speak first, and Ellis Moore, his glasses on, had his notes out in front of him. He took a breath and opened his mouth. But before anything came out, Kalinin interrupted.

"Ambassador Moore, welcome to this place. It was once the estate of a rich landowner. It now belongs to the Ministry of Foreign Affairs for meetings with distinguished foreign guests. You are here—we are here— for an important purpose."

Kalinin leaned back in his chair and displayed his dentures. "In a very short time our two leaders will meet for their first summit. This will be a crucial meeting, not only for the United States and the Soviet Union, but for the whole world. The world wants peace. The world waits anxiously. For many months now we have been deadlocked. That is not the fault of the Soviet side, which has always been ready, and remains ready now, to move great mountains in the service of peace." The Russian broke into a Cheshire-cat smile. "So I and my colleagues invite you, Ambassador Moore, to tell us what you have brought."

Waterman was outraged. In the crudest possible way Kalinin was demanding shifts in the American position, new concessions.

"Well, Viktor," Moore finally said, "I trust you won't be disappointed when I say we think this is not the time for new ideas, but an occasion to clarify where things stand between us, so that when our leaders get to Helsinki, they'll understand clearly what divides us, and why."

Moore's index finger tapped the green felt tablecloth for emphasis. "I want to emphasize that word—*why.* We know your positions, on medium-range missiles, for example. You want to eliminate all of ours and keep some of yours. We know your opposition to our SDI research program. We know you believe we should halt all nuclear testing, and dismantle all our military bases overseas."

Moore paused. "What we don't know is *why* you take these absurdly one-sided positions. Oh, we know what you say. I can't turn the television on these days in Washington without seeing you or one of your colleagues stating the Soviet position. *Nightline, Meet the Press, Face the Nation,* Brinkley. Next thing I know you'll be on Johnny Carson. You're all over American television, Viktor—do you ever appear on Russian television?"

Kalinin stiffened. He forced a smile. "Only sometimes."

"Well, that may be because they don't appreciate you as much here. But let me tell you, Viktor—you're very popular in the United States." Moore opened a bottle of mineral water and poured himself a glass. "The problem is, popularity doesn't help us understand."

Moore inclined his head toward Waterman. "My young colleague, Mr. Waterman, for example, is especially puzzled about your opposition to SDI. He recalls it was not so many years ago that the Soviet Union was a great proponent of strategic defenses. I must also tell you that we cannot accept your suggestion that the United States is responsible for the current impasse in our negotiations. To be frank, the reason we find ourselves at an impasse right now is that no one knows where Mr. Novikov stands on these matters."

Kalinin looked uncomfortable. Kulikov scowled and puffed determinedly on a Marlboro. Kagarovich sat stiff and expressionless, rolling a Mont Blanc pen the size of a good cigar between the palms of his hands. The Soviets' behavior was to be expected. What was not, Waterman saw, was the performance Dan Bennet was putting on. He pouted. He pursed his lips. He rolled his eyes ceilingward in obvious exasperation at Moore's aggressiveness.

Moore paused and took a long drink of the bottled water. His expression indicated what he thought of it, which was not much. He replaced the glass and went on, seemingly oblivious to Bennet's discomfort, pounding Kalinin on nuclear testing and SDI. When he finished, he turned to Waterman.

Now, Waterman began, his eyes fixed on General Kagarovich. "I always understood it to be the Soviet view that defense of the homeland is a sacred duty. Indeed, as General Kagarovich knows well, the military writings of the Soviet Armed Forces are full of references about the necessity of defending Mother Russia." He watched as the general nodded in agreement.

"But now," said Waterman, "the Soviet Union rejects the counsel of its own history and tradition. Why? If you are justified in protecting your territory against aircraft, why should we not protect ours against missiles? If it makes sense to both of us to hide, move, and fortify our missiles against attack, why does it not make sense to protect them with strategic defenses?"

"I have listened carefully," the general began, "to what Mr. Waterman and Ambassador Moore have had to say. As a military man, I must agree with much of what Mr. Waterman says about the history of weapons development and the historical emphasis on the defense of the homeland. But these are abstractions." He paused, reached down the table past Kalinin for Kulikov's hardpack of Marlboros, took one, and lit it with a gold Dupont lighter that he kept in the breast pocket of his tunic. "Mr. Waterman"—he exhaled forcefully—"has tried to show we have somehow accepted the principle of strategic defense.

"You are asking us to accept limits on our offensive forces while you go about developing a Star Wars defense that would tilt the balance against us."

"But why should that be the case?" Waterman asked. "Why should we consider that your massive air defense is legitimate, while our research on missile defense is menacing?"

"Because your Star Wars will extend the arms race into space," Kalinin said.

"That's a slogan," Waterman snapped. "We'll never come to terms if you retreat behind slogans."

"You're not talking to schoolboys," Kalinin shot back angrily, his voice rising. "You think you can use technology to inflict a competition on us that we can't afford. But I assure you that we will do whatever is necessary—"

"To protect the homeland?" Waterman interjected.

"To . . . protect . . . our . . . security," Kalinin bellowed, pounding the table with his fist.

Moore rapped the bottle of mineral water with his gold pen. The sound brought the shouting to a stop. "Viktor," he said softly, "this is not a point of contention. We take it as given that each of us will act to protect our country. We're here to see whether we can manage that task in a more cooperative, less confrontational way. I hope we can agree on that."

Bennet used the moment of silence that followed to jump in. "We've learned in the past we can find a practical basis for agreement without having to agree on doctrine or philosophy," he drawled congenially. "I don't think it's useful to get into a philosophical dispute," he said, looking directly at Waterman. "What we must do is sort out the practical issues between us."

"I agree," Kalinin said. "We need to find practical solutions."

"We've come to Moscow to search for common ground," Bennet said. "Obviously, that requires practical proposals. My colleague"—he nodded toward Waterman—"is interested in philosophical exposition, which would be fine and perhaps even useful—if we had the time. But, gentlemen, time is flying. We have a summit to prepare."

Bennet looked around the table, watching in satisfaction as both sides nodded in agreement. He smiled graciously at the Soviets. "Perhaps it would help if Ambassador Kalinin tells us what limitations on SDI would allow us to go forward. That would be a practical step."

Waterman stared at Bennet, his eyes wide with disbelief. Moore, too, was stunned. He shot a long, intense, menacing look at Bennet.

The Soviets, obviously delighted at the opening that had been handed to them, were about to take up Bennet's invitation to outline restrictions on SDI when Moore proposed a short recess.

Protocol required the American delegation to remain in the meeting room. So they waited in silence as the Soviets gathered their notes and withdrew to a room across the hall. Alone at last, Moore lost no time upbraiding Bennet in caustic language for what he regarded as a wholly unjustified and embarrassing episode of free-lance diplomacy.

Finally, Waterman broke into Moore's monologue. "We spent hours going over our approach to this meeting. I thought we were all agreed," he commented.

"We did agree, Michael," Moore said. "But I think Dan's right in one respect: Their side won't be drawn out. It's time for something new."

"But Dan practically told them we'd accept limitations on SDI," he said.

"Do you want to screw around for the next two days or do you want to get something done?" Bennet asked.

"Dammit, whose side are you on?" Waterman said, his fists clenched. "You sound just like Kalinin."

"And you sound just like Curtis LeMay," Bennet shot back. "We're here to negotiate, not just posture."

"Don't kid yourself," Waterman said. "Even if they didn't hear every word said in this room, they'd know from what was just said across the table that we're ready to abandon the line we agreed on yesterday. They're not going to give us a damn thing. If you want to take two days to find that out, that's okay with me. But I'll be damned if I'll encourage them to believe we're ready to abandon SDI or the Zero Option."

The Soviets returned, and after four hours' argument without the slightest hint of movement from either side, they broke for lunch. As they sat down at the long table, the U.S. and Soviet positions were precisely where they'd been left in Geneva. The morning session, Waterman knew, had been a total loss.

Moscow, November 20, 3:15 P.M.

There was a half-hour break after lunch and before the afternoon session was slated to begin. As they passed through the grand foyer outside the mansion's dining room, Waterman took Bennet aside. "Let's go for a walk," he said. "We need to talk."

"What about Moore?"

"He's drafting something. He wants to be alone."

They passed through tall carved-wood doors and paused on the front portico. "Sure. Just give me a minute to go back to the meeting room; I ran out of cigarettes, and I'd like to get an overcoat."

"I'll wait for you down there." Waterman, who was layered up in a down parka over his three-piece suit, pointed at an iron bench that sat just in front of a magnificent stand of birch and pine trees.

The autumn leaves had long since fallen. Bare maples and golden elm could be seen among the green pine and fir that crowded the path. In the distance someone was burning leaves, and the sweet-smelling smoke drifted over the dacha's richly wooded grounds.

He reached the Victorian bench and sat down, closing his eyes and turning his face to the warming sun. Then he looked around for some carelessly telltale wire that would reveal the existence of a hidden microphone. It was nowhere to be found. He pulled off one glove and ran his hand on the underside of the slats of the bench. Nothing there, either.

How often, he wondered, had an unsuspecting foreign delegation gone outside the conference room at the Foreign Ministry's dacha in the belief that once outside they could confer among themselves in private? Waterman knew, of course, the KGB planted eavesdropping devices outside as well as inside. There were microphones everywhere: Gardens, paths, and driveways were bugged along with the dining rooms, lobbies, corridors, and toilets.

Toilets were a particularly productive source for intelligence. During breaks in tense negotiations there would be a rush to the toilets. How easy it was to comment carelessly, sometimes tellingly, on what had been going on. It was a mark of Soviet society that the plumbing was rotten but the electronic systems that accompanied it were first-rate.

Waterman looked up to see Bennet approach. He pushed himself to his feet and joined Bennet on the path, falling into stride.

"Look," Waterman said, as they strolled toward the woods, "we're getting nowhere. If the afternoon's anything like this morning, we'll leave with no results."

"You could hardly expect it to be different, considering you won't give an inch on anything," Bennet said.

"Not anything," Waterman protested, annoyed. "Just *some* things. Essentials, Dan. Besides, there's not much point in our signaling flexibility when the other side's rigid and unyielding."

"But it's perfectly clear they're not going to agree to anything unless we accept at least some limitations on SDI. If we go on stonewalling, so will they."

"Dan, you were there. They didn't say a damn thing all morning—they ignored our arguments completely."

"Screw the arguments. This has nothing to do with arguments. Michael, look—this isn't your collegiate debating society. It's a negotiation, and those guys have their instructions—"

"And those instructions," Waterman shot back, "are to kill SDI one way or another without even acknowledging they have a comparable program. What kind of deal is that?"

"You don't need to tell *me* what's wrong with the Soviet position, Michael," Bennet said huffily.

"It didn't look that way in the morning session."

"What the hell do you mean by that?" Bennet demanded.

"For God's sake, Dan, the way you sat there during Moore's opening, rolling your eyes, pursing your lips—broadcasting your dissatisfaction with our position to those guys across the table—"

"You're getting paranoid."

"There's body language and there's body language," said Waterman, "and yours was giving them the message loud and clear. You told 'em, 'Don't pay any attention to this guy.' "

"Bullshit."

Waterman stopped and turned to face Bennet. He jabbed an index finger in the taller man's sternum. "I'll tell you what bullshit is, Dan. Bullshit is abandoning the president's policy because *you* don't like it.

"I happen to agree with him on SDI," Waterman continued, "but suppose I didn't. I'd still be obliged to fight for his position. He's the one who got elected. He's the one who has to answer for failure. The mandate's his—not yours or mine."

Bennet brushed away Waterman's hand and started down the path again.

"Cut the crap, Michael. It's just posturing to say, 'I'm obliged to represent the president.' Take that line and what do you do when he comes up with some half-assed idea that can't possibly work?"

"You talk it over with him," Waterman said. "But if it reaches the point where you can't support his policies, you quit. You don't undermine the president while serving as his representative."

"Get off it, Michael, you're not talking to a fourth-grade civics class. When was the last time you talked anything over with the president? You're lucky when they let you warm a back-row seat at an NSC meeting."

Waterman's face grew warm. Bennet was right. The idea that he could go in and see the president to discuss policy differences was silly. Still, he thought, the principle was right.

"Besides," Bennet went on, "the word 'undermine' is invidious; it tilts the argument. Let's use a neutral term like 'change,' or 'alter,' or 'influence.' Why is quitting morally superior to *influencing* the president? Quitting's a cop-out—it may make you feel better, it may do something for your personal sense of honor or integrity, but where does it leave the country, the public interest?"

"I'm not arguing against trying to influence the president. We all do that," Waterman conceded. "But there's a line to be drawn between influence and manipulation. And it has to do with whether you engage in argument or deception. You guys at State have been working overtime to maneuver the president into a new détente. You've been selling Novikov as Western-style liberal—without serious evidence to back it up. You cooked up intelligence estimates to show that because Novikov's trying to reform the economy, he's ready to abandon Communism and Soviet global influence. *He* keeps repeating that he's a Communist—and you keep editing that out of the papers going to the Old Man."

Waterman stopped in his tracks. The sun shone brightly through the silver birches, refracting off the leaves. The smell of smoke was growing stronger, richer.

"Dammit, Dan, you've read the same intelligence I have. You know, despite all the rhetoric, Novikov's refused to cut back on military production. Moscow produced more tanks last year than in any year of the Brezhnev regime."

"Hold on, Michael," Bennet said. "Novikov withdrew fifty thousand troops from Eastern Europe and demobilized half a million more. You never give him credit for what he's doing, or trying to do."

"That's just not so," Waterman replied. "We've bent over backward to analyze fairly what Novikov's doing. What's so striking is what he *isn't* doing. He isn't reducing Soviet military power. He's consolidating it. Even the troop reductions were perfectly consistent with rationalizing and modernizing the Soviet Armed Forces, replacing a bloated army with a smaller, better-armed one. And he's never cut the military budget."

"We're getting off the point," Bennet said. He bent down and picked up a pinecone and threw it at a squirrel scampering along a section of dilapidated fence. "We were talking about SDI. And the undeniable fact is Novikov fears it enough to block any movement toward an arms-control agreement as long as we insist on the unencumbered right to go ahead with strategic defenses. If we're ever gonna get an agreement, we've got to move—now."

"But," Waterman said, "the point is not to get *any* agreement, it's to get a good one."

Bennet picked up another pinecone and hurled it into the distance. "Damn," he said. He stopped short and turned to face Waterman. "Let's cut the bull. You don't want any agreement. Not a bad agreement. Not an indifferent agreement. Not a good agreement. You don't want any fucking agreement, period."

Bennet's voice began to rise. "Everyone knows the Zero Option is a sham, a device for preventing any serious negotiation. You knew the Soviets would reject it. And that's precisely why you wanted it.

"For years you've believed that any serious arms-control agreement would lead to psychological disarmament in the West. You think any agreement's bound to be a soporific. Why don't you just come out and admit it instead of pretending you're simply interested in improving the terms?"

"I could turn that around," Waterman said, "and say you've been ready for any damn agreement the Soviets would sign up to, no matter how disadvantageous to us. In fact, I could go further. You guys never pay more than lip service to ideas about what constitutes a good agreement. You think all that's involved is politics and diplomacy. You don't give a shit about the military consequences. You're after a piece of paper. And to make matters worse, you're in a damn hurry. You're racing to push this along so there's something to sign at the summit."

"But that's the point, Michael—to get going on a path to peace."

"Come on, Dan. The issue isn't who's for peace. We're all for peace. At least I am. I don't doubt you're for peace, too. I'm not callous about human life, or indifferent to the horror of a nuclear war. Jim Ryder doesn't rub his hands at the prospect of war. McCandless isn't spoiling for a fight.

"The issue is how to achieve peace. Or, to put it differently, how to avoid a war without sacrificing our beliefs or abandoning our friends. If we sacrifice our values and leave our friends to the mercy of the Soviets, we'll end up having the war we're all trying to avoid."

Waterman angled his head toward Bennet. "For me personally, I couldn't care less about the garbage you've leaked to the press. What gets me—"

"What!" Bennet exploded. "I don't leak, goddammit."

"Oh, come off it, Dan. Of course you leak. Some of the stories I've read in the *Times* recently sound just like your IG memos—right down to your little nuances of language. But even your behavior's beside the point. You want the press to think of me as the guy in the black hat. Okay, so what? The black hat doesn't bother me. After more than fifteen years in government I've got skin like the bark on that tree. What bothers me is the malicious way you've transformed our debate into a contest between good and decent proponents of peace and negotiation on one side, and dark, malevolent warmongers on the other.

"I know damn well what's coming." He put his gloved palm on Bennet's chest and gave it a slight push. "We're gonna leave this miserable place tomorrow"—he pushed again—"and the next day I'll be reading in *The Washington Post* how the Defense Department's chief black hat"—he pushed again—"sat in a dacha outside Moscow and blocked any progress toward an agreement that could save the world from a nuclear holocaust."

Waterman backed Bennet up against a maple sapling and stood close to him, crowding, jabbing the tall diplomat's cashmere-covered chest with each syllable. "And the only reason it'll bother me so much is because it's a damn lie."

"If you're through with your sermon," Bennet said, abruptly shoving Waterman out of his way, "let me get to the bottom line: You're losing it with the president. There was a time when he'd have agreed with you. But now he's facing a summit, and he wants to be damn sure it doesn't fail. I've been watching him. He used to sound like you. But that's changed. Every meeting, every paper, moves him further."

Bennet's patrician profile looked smug. "You may not have noticed, but the president actually *believes* in disarmament, Michael. He wants to get rid of nukes. And the Department of State is gonna help him achieve his policy. Either we get a deal here, or we'll get one in Helsinki."

Waterman kicked at a pile of leaves. The painful truth was that Bennet was probably right. For weeks the State Department had been working on the president, bombarding him with briefing papers, memos, background documents. State had even prepared a videotape on Novikov in which what was known as fact and what was mere speculation—all of it benign—were skillfully commingled. The overall impression was of a new leader who was ready to end the adversarial relationship with the United States and play by American rules.

"You may be right—for the moment," Waterman said. "But if anyone's going to give away the store, it's not going to be me."

"What it comes down to in the end," Bennet said, "is a question of judgment about Novikov. You're so damned sure you understand him, so sure you know what he'll do. I doubt Novikov himself knows where he's headed—he's groping, trying to find a way. I've no doubt there are people around him who prefer the old hard line, but—"

"That's just it," Waterman interjected. "He's being pushed on all sides. How we handle him—how we stand up to him—is crucial. Give him what his hard-liners are demanding, and we'll be putting *them* in charge. Stand up now, and there's hope we can shape his policies. It's precisely because he's being pushed on all sides, as you put it, that we have to be clear about which side *we're* pushing. The least we can do is push *with* the reformers, not against them. Which side are you on, Dan?"

Without waiting for a reply from an openmouthed Bennet, he turned on his heel and stalked off toward the dacha.

Moscow, November 22, 4:00 P.M.

By Moscow standards, the deputy chief of mission's apartment was gigantic. To Americans, it was a modest-size, dingy apartment in a dilapidated building that also housed the American embassy. After the fruitless three days of pre-summit sessions, it seemed only fitting that the delegation's trip would end here, over instant coffee served by an elderly butler who was probably the oldest KGB agent on the books.

The delegation—Moore, Waterman, and Bennet—and the DCM,

McLaughlin Poolsby, Jr., known to everyone as Pool, sat glumly around the dining table at one end of the combination living room–dining room that faced the Pushkin Street side of the embassy compound. Irina, the housekeeper, poured Maxwell House into Washington Redskins mugs. Waterman, who alone among them had an unfailing appetite, munched on slices of Russian black bread spread thick with Finnish butter.

"The bread's terrific," Waterman said. "But otherwise Russian cuisine's the pits."

"Don't forget the caviar," Pool said. "The caviar's top drawer."

"But not so easy to come by," Waterman said. "I tried to get some through my usual sources at the embassy snack bar, but the clerk told me he's been ordered to stop supplying it. It's a shame—I used to be one of his better customers." He nudged Moore. "I suppose we should take this stamping out of the entrepreneurial spirit as a sign they're cracking down under Novikov."

"It wasn't Novikov," Pool said. "It was us. The ambassador got nervous when Novikov came in. You knew it was illegal, didn't you?"

Waterman shook his head. "Sure. But it went on for years. The KGB had to know all about it."

"Of course they knew. And for a long time they turned a blind eye. But you could never tell when the authorities would choose to enforce the laws against private trade in caviar, and the ambassador didn't want to find out. Still, Michael, you should've told me you wanted caviar. There are other sources. . . ." He sipped his coffee. "You won't believe this, but it's actually easier to get caviar than the lemon to squeeze on it."

Waterman polished off his third slice of bread. "I should have come to you earlier. As it is, I'm leaving with four kilos of black bread and a wooden model of St. Basil's."

"Terrific. You can report that to the NSC when we get back," Bennet said coldly. "They'll be pleased to know we didn't leave Moscow empty-handed."

"Jesus, Dan, lighten up. It's true we're not taking anything back—but we didn't leave anything behind, either. On the whole I'd say it was a success."

The telephone at the far end of the room rang. Pool dashed for it and picked up the receiver. He spoke in Russian, then put his hand over the mouthpiece. "We may be delayed." After a brief conversation he hung up the phone. "That was the Foreign Ministry. They wanted to know how long we'd be here. I said we were about to leave for the airport, and they asked if we could wait just long enough for a package to be delivered.

Traffic should be light—I told 'em we could wait. If I had to guess, I'd say there's caviar on its way for you all."

"I wondered what had happened to the traditional departure gift," Moore said, settling himself in the room's sole overstuffed armchair. He held out his Redskins mug. "Pool, what about another cup of coffee?"

In a quarter of an hour the apartment's intercom buzzed loudly. "The package," Poolsby said. "Okay—let's leave for the airport." Poolsby went to the door while the delegation wrapped themselves in coats and scarves.

In a moment Poolsby returned to the living room, where Moore, Bennet, and Waterman were gathering up their bags and briefcases. Looking sheepish, he handed Waterman a shopping bag. "It's addressed to you," he said. "From General Kagarovich, with best wishes."

Waterman looked inside and tried to suppress a smile. There, under the general's engraved card, were four half-kilo tins of fresh Beluga Malossol caviar.

CHAPTER EIGHTEEN

Washington, November 25

Waterman let Moore and Bennet precede him back to Washington, while he spent two days closeted at a British facility outside London playing the president of the United States in a NATO war game that went right to the brink of a nuclear exchange. It was a mistake in timing. The same day the delegation left Moscow, news stories out of New Orleans began to report on the bungled handling of a Soviet defector by U.S. officials. By the time Waterman arrived at Dulles, the situation had grown into a full-blown administration crisis that was worse by the hour.

His driver handed him a briefcase full of papers and had the key in the ignition before Waterman could say hello. Taped to the outside of the briefcase was a note from Parisi:

> *You're going straight to the Sitroom for a meeting on the crisis. Inside is a memo and news clips. SECDEF will be attending, but he asked that you make every effort to get there. You're to go in even if the meeting is in progress. Welcome home. Jay.*

On the way downtown Waterman quickly skimmed the newspapers in the briefcase. His political instincts led him to believe that whatever the NSPG did now, it could only cut the president's losses; and damage control, as his Capitol Hill mentor, Senator Arthur Winter, had always said, was among the toughest tasks of and rarest skills in politics and government. Winter's rules were simple and effective: If you've done your homework and if you know your stuff and if you've got a first-rate staff minding the store, you'll be able to manage crises.

The administration for which he worked, Waterman knew, habitually broke all Winter's rules. The president didn't give a damn about staff work. Homework was seldom done. The White House chief of staff was a man of little talent, so he was surrounded by mediocre people in the White House itself.

One of the last to arrive at the White House Situation Room, Waterman took his seat behind Jim Ryder and looked around. With the exception of the vice president, who was representing the United States at a UN conference in Nigeria, virtually the whole National Security Council was there. There was one unexpected face: the attorney general, a beefy Omaha lawyer who'd been selected for his job by virtue of his thirty-five-year friendship with the president.

He looked around the room for a friendly face and discovered one in the CIA director. He nodded at McCandless, who shook his jowls in Waterman's direction by way of greeting.

Then the president came through the door looking unusually grim, accompanied by Mitchell Wallace and Gary Burner. Wallace, his face puffy from lack of sleep, had developed nasty red splotches on his forehead and neck. The normally jocund Burner sat down without so much as a word to anyone. He had reason: The administration was taking a pounding in the polls; the president's approval rating had plummeted eleven points in the past forty-eight hours.

General Wallace spent no time on amenities. "On Monday night," the NSC adviser read from notes, "a seventeen-year-old Soviet seaman from"—he looked carefully at the pad in front of him—"Zhovthevoye, named Mykola Kostiv, jumped from the deck of the *Sevastopol,* a Soviet grain carrier, into the Mississippi estuary eleven miles north of New Orleans. He was found, shivering and exhausted, by a couple—Luther and Amy Watkins—whose small shrimp boat was moored at a wooden pier a few yards from where Kostiv came ashore. They took him aboard and gave him blankets and hot coffee. They spoke no Russian, and Kostiv spoke no English—except the words 'be free,' which he repeated over and over to them."

The NSC adviser turned a page. "While Amy stayed with Kostiv, Luther went to call the police. When the sailor saw Luther dropping change into the pay phone on the pier, he became frantic. Then he bolted, running into a maze of sheds and warehouses on the riverfront.

"The police arrived on the scene almost immediately, followed, a few minutes later, by two agents from the Immigration and Naturalization Service. Together, they searched and found Kostiv hiding in the corner of an empty garage.

"The cops regarded the affair as an INS matter. They were only too happy to leave."

Ryder interrupted. "So it wasn't the police who took the boy back to his ship?"

"No. The INS did that."

"Inconceivable," said Ryder. "Why? Why would they do that?"

"That's still unclear," said Wallace. "It seems the INS agents spoke Spanish, but no Russian—"

"Typical," harrumphed McCandless under his breath.

Wallace shot the DCI a nasty look. "They attempted to interrogate Kostiv, first in the garage where they found him, then in the cabin of the Watkinses' boat. They got nowhere. Finally, unable to figure out what to do, they called the INS regional director at home.

"On instructions from him, one of the agents phoned headquarters here, where they found a duty officer who said he'd arrange to have a Russian interpreter call back. That took about an hour. When the call came in, it turned out all the INS could find on such short notice was a young woman who spoke Polish and a word or two of Russian. Still, the conversation lasted almost an hour, Kostiv's voice rising from time to time and, as the agents said, repeating certain phrases over and over again."

"Certain phrases?" Ryder looked quizzically at Wallace.

"As I was saying," Wallace said, peering over his glasses accusingly at the attorney general, whose purview included the INS, "the interpreter spoke almost no Russian."

"That obviously couldn't be helped, given the circumstances," the AG said petulantly.

"But Kostiv's Ukrainian—he doesn't speak Polish," Wallace explained. "In fact, his Russian's not very good. I debriefed the interpreter myself. She says it's her impression Kostiv was seeking political asylum. She says that's what she told the INS agents on-site. But she also says they told her she had to be absolutely positive, and the language problem left her a little uncertain."

"A little uncertain," McCandless muttered to himself, shaking his head. Waterman looked at the faces around the table. They were expressionless: imperturbable masks. Wallace continued in his monotone. "The agents called the regional director again. Somehow—and no one I've talked to is willing to take the responsibility for it—a patrol boat was ordered up.

Kostiv must have understood he was about to be returned to the *Sevastopol* because, before they could hustle him onto the craft, he jumped and scrambled up the embankment. The INS agents caught up with him, put him in handcuffs, and headed toward the *Sevastopol*."

"Oh, hell." Ryder's tone was filled with disgust.

"Wait," said Wallace. "It gets worse. When they pulled alongside the *Sevastopol*, a gangway was lowered, and the Soviet captain came aboard the INS craft, very friendly and low-key. He spoke English pretty well and told the INS agents Kostiv had suffered a mental collapse while en route to New Orleans, that he had been confined to quarters, and that when he was discovered missing, it was assumed he'd jumped ship to escape the disciplinary action awaiting him in Odessa. With that, the INS agents placed Kostiv between them, boarded the *Sevastopol*, took off the handcuffs, and handed the sailor over to the Soviets. The captain thanked them profusely, apologized for any problems this mentally deranged sailor might have caused, and told 'em he'd be well looked after."

"I'm sure they meant well," said the attorney general. "How were they to know what the kid wanted? I mean—he couldn't speak English."

"He could!" McCandless exploded. "He knew two words—'be free.' And your people screwed it up!"

"Enough, Bill," said Wallace, cutting off the DCI. "There's more than enough blame to go around."

He checked the notes in front of him. "All this happened on Saturday night. But the wire services got hold of the story because they monitor police radio frequencies, and the cops who showed up told their dispatcher about a Russian trying to defect. By Sunday morning the story had moved on the wires. By Sunday night the TV networks were in a feeding frenzy."

"It must have been madness," Ryder said.

"It was," Wallace answered dryly.

Winthrop sat at the walnut table examining his manicured nails and saying nothing. He tried not to look smug. Still, it was hard to contain his self-satisfaction. State, he knew, had performed admirably. Even if he hadn't been able to keep Kostiv in the country, he'd made the appearance of trying hard. State would come out of this mess looking good. That was because he'd been decisive from the very start.

His first exposure to the problem had come Sunday morning as he stood in a Ralph Lauren bathrobe in the kitchen of his Foxhall mansion, pouring himself a cup of decaffeinated coffee from a silver pot and listening to the voice of Amy Watkins on an all-news radio station: "That poor boy was no older'n my own son Jesse. He was pale and half-drowned an' frightened, an' the State Department jes' plain abandoned him to the commonists."

The secretary's anger had risen with each succeeding minute. He'd realized the problem as soon as he'd heard Amy's accusation: While the INS may in fact have been a bunch of screw-ups who couldn't handle a simple defection, it was the State Department getting all the blame. What the hell did anybody out there beyond the Potomac know about bureaucratic responsibility?

White with rage, Winthrop had picked up the phone and called Dan Bennet. "Get the Soviet embassy. Get on top of this immediately," he'd demanded. "Get that guy back or tell me why we can't."

Now, Wallace was summing up. He turned to Winthrop. "Mr. Secretary, is there anything you'd like to add?"

Winthrop nodded, paused, then began in a quiet tone, "It might be useful if I bring us up-to-date. A lot has happened. When the courier arrived at my home Sunday morning, I read the report prepared by the watch team at the operations center. Despite its absence of detail, the outline of the situation was clear enough. I instructed Dan Bennet to inform the chargé at the Soviet embassy that the *Sevastopol* would not be permitted to leave port until Kostiv was interviewed, so U.S. authorities could judge for themselves whether or not he'd been seeking political asylum.

"By eleven the Soviet chargé received Bennet's demarche. Dan told me he felt the Soviets had spoken with the *Sevastopol*'s captain, as the embassy officer gave Dan a letter-perfect recitation of the captain's comments to the INS agents the previous night. Kostiv was unstable; he'd attacked another crewman; he'd been confined to quarters. There was no issue of defection or political asylum—this was a case of shipboard discipline, and so on, as you can imagine." Winthrop paused. His expression left no doubt he didn't believe a word of it.

"Dan insisted he was acting under my direct instructions and told the chargé that *Sevastopol* would not be permitted to sail until Kostiv was interviewed. The Soviet agreed to seek instructions from Moscow, while still protesting vociferously that the United States was detaining the ship illegally and without cause. He and Dan finally reached an agreement Kostiv would be briefly interviewed at the INS office in New Orleans."

Winthrop looked up and down the table. "I must emphasize," he said, "that if we'd been contacted in the first place, none of this would have happened. We are the department most capable of dealing with issues of defection and asylum."

Winthrop continued his narrative. At first, he said, Bennet insisted that Kostiv be unaccompanied during the interview. But the Vienna Conventions clearly provided for the presence of a consular official; and while there had been several instances when Americans detained in the Soviet Union had been deprived of the presence of an American consular official, Soviet authorities had always contrived some excuse; they had never actually denied a request. In the end, therefore, Winthrop said, Bennet conceded the point, and a Soviet consular official named Oleg Bassov was allowed to travel from Washington to New Orleans to visit the *Sevastopol* and be present during Kostiv's interview. And to ensure that everything went according to the letter of the law, Winthrop added, he'd gone to the extraordinary step of having the entire session videotaped.

"Play the tape," he commanded. At the far end of the room, Bob Wellbeck switched on a VCR and a television set that was positioned near the president's chair. "This was taped," Winthrop explained, "in the INS regional director's conference room in New Orleans."

The Situation Room fell silent as the camera panned from one side of the green-walled room with its framed posters to the other. The people there sat stiffly, clearly uncomfortable under the lens's scrutiny. Arrayed on one side of the long Formica table were two Russian-speaking State Department officers, one of whom was clearly in charge; the INS regional director; a note-taker; and two Justice Department attorneys. A State Department interpreter, fluent in Ukrainian, Russian, Uzbek, and Georgian—Bennet had been ordered to take no chances—had been hurriedly flown in from the Foreign Service Institute in Washington. He sat at the far end of the table.

The boy—Kostiv—in a set of blue coveralls, his hair unkempt, was slumped in his chair. His skin was translucently white—even in the videotape the veins on his arms could be seen. His face was blank, expressionless—and, Waterman thought, childlike and vulnerable. The Ukrainian's eyes wandered absently around the room, focusing, Waterman realized, only where there were no people to look back at him. Opposite the sailor sat a large, black-haired man in a dark, fashionable double-breasted Italian-cut suit whose attaché case glistened on the table.

"The big guy across the table from Kostiv is Oleg Bassov, the Soviet vice consul," Winthrop explained.

A sandy-haired State Department official introduced himself and began to speak in Ukrainian. The interpreter translated, phrase by phrase, for the benefit of the others in the room. "Is your name Mykola Kostiv?"

"Yes."

"Did you jump from the *Sevastopol* on Saturday?"

"No."

"If you didn't jump, how did you leave the ship?"

"I fell."

"Fell?"

"I was drinking."

The American nodded solemnly. "Do you wish to remain in the United States?"

"I wish to return home."

"You wish to return to the Soviet Union?"

"Yes."

"Has Mr. Bassov, or anyone else, told you how to answer my questions?"

"No."

"Did anyone say anything to you?"

"I was told I have the right to return home. I was told I will not be punished for the trouble I have caused."

"Did you tell the woman interpreter you wished to remain in the United States?"

Kostiv, whose answers had come close to preceding the questions, now hesitated.

"I told the interpreter . . ." Then he paused. The sailor peered around the room. He looked tired, confused, fearful. His head snapped back. "She didn't understand me," he said. "She didn't . . . I didn't understand her language."

The Justice Department attorney spoke up from the end of the table. "Mr. Kostiv, you have the right to remain in the United States. You can be given political asylum. No one can take that right away from you. If you say you wish to remain here, it will be arranged. You will not have to return to the *Sevastopol.* The crew will return to the ship. Mr. Bassov will go back to Washington. And you can remain here. All you need to do is tell us you wish to seek political asylum in the United States."

The camera caught Bassov glaring at the Justice lawyer. Kostiv listened carefully, but he was having obvious trouble concentrating.

"I fell overboard," he said. "I was drinking. I wish to return to the Soviet Union."

The lawyer from the Justice Department sighed audibly and pushed his chair away from the table as if to leave. His action said it was all over. But the second State Department official decided to try again.

The American looked at the sailor with obvious compassion, then spoke. "I'm saying this slowly," the interpreter began, "to make absolutely sure that you understand each and every word I'm about to say.

"Do you understand me, Mr. Kostiv?"

"Yes, sir."

"Good." The American rose. He walked to the end of the room, where a large American flag stood in its stanchion. "This is our flag," he said, taking the gold fringe in his hand and shaking it softly in Kostiv's direction. "This is not the Soviet Union. Do you understand that?"

The sailor shook his head up and down. *Yes.* He listened while the interpreter translated back into English.

"Good," said the man from State. He let go of the flag. "Mr. Kostiv, no one can tell you what to do or say. Many Americans are aware of your plight. You would be very welcome here. If you say you have been threatened in any way, or told what to say, we will make a strong protest to your government."

The State Department official was now standing directly behind Bassov, so that he looked down into Kostiv's waxy face. He spoke slowly and deliberately, waiting patiently as the interpreter, using similar intonation, did the translation back into English for the rest of the room.

"Mr. Kostiv, when you were pulled out of the river, you said two words to Luther and Amy Watkins. Those words were 'be free.' You can be free, Mr. Kostiv, if you want to be. So I will ask you one more time: Do you wish to remain in the United States? Do you want to be free?"

Waterman watched intently as the drama played out before his eyes. He heard the president say the first words he'd uttered since entering the room. "Say yes," the president exhorted the screen under his breath. "Oh, say yes, boy."

Waterman watched as Kostiv struggled to understand. It seemed to him the American's words were suspended within the boy's reach, floating for him like a life preserver or up in the air like a brass ring. But then—you could see it—Kostiv's eyes clouded over. He looked up into the compassionate face of the State Department official. And he looked across the table at Oleg Bassov. He said, "I want to go home."

The video ran out. The lights were turned up. The president was daubing at his eyes with a handkerchief.

Winthrop sighed. "Mr. President," he said, "there is one more thing. Shortly before this meeting, we received, through the privacy channel, a message from General Secretary Novikov. He protested the detention of the *Sevastopol* and hinted—although by no means actually said—that it could cause a hitch in the summit."

"Exactly how did Novikov put it?" Gary Burner rapped the table with his knuckles.

"By saying if the ship is not permitted to sail, he will be forced to draw—and I'm quoting his message directly here—'appropriate conclusions.'"

"Mr. President," the secretary of state continued, "everyone around this table sympathizes with Kostiv. We all want him to remain in the United States. But, owing to the most incredible mismanagement by the INS, a difficult but straightforward matter has become hopelessly complicated. Now, we can't turn back the clock; we can't undo what has already been done. Kostiv is aboard the *Sevastopol*. As Mitch Wallace knows, I immediately ordered that he be interviewed when I learned what had happened. We pressured the Soviets into that interview—they didn't have to agree to it." Winthrop paused. "In fact, we owe Dan Bennet a debt for getting them to agree—he'd be here for this meeting, except that he's trying to tie up all the loose ends." He smiled in the president's direction. "So," he continued, "Kostiv's been interviewed by a team from State, INS, and Justice. You saw it just as it happened.

"Kostiv was undoubtedly under great pressure. I think he was probably drugged when he said he wanted to go back. But he said it three times—he wants to go home."

Winthrop opened a brown leather folder in front of him and removed a thin document, closed the folder, and placed the document on top of it. "I asked the State Department legal adviser to prepare a memorandum on the international legal aspects of this case. I'm afraid it's clear that we have no basis for detaining the *Sevastopol*."

Winthrop sighed regretfully. "Mr. President," he said, "I believe we have no choice but to permit the *Sevastopol* to return to the Soviet Union. I wish we had another option. We don't."

He leaned back slightly in his chair, folding his rather small hands and placing them on top of the papers in front of him.

Ryder looked at his notes, then removed his half-glasses before beginning to speak. That was the protocol at NSPGs. The NSC adviser led the discussion, State responded first, then Defense, then everyone else piled on. "As you know, Mitch," Ryder said, addressing the NSC adviser, "I wanted this meeting to take place earlier. In cases like this, the sooner we act, the greater the range of options available to us. But we've made our decision. Let's try to make the best of it. I can add a few things to what Tony Winthrop's said. We know for certain Kostiv was drugged; we know what they said to Washington. We know Bassov is not a vice consul but a KGB officer. I believe you've all seen the NSA transcript of the phone call—it was absolutely frantic—from the captain of the *Sevastopol* to the Soviet embassy here. Let me quote for you: 'Do not allow any access to Kostiv until an embassy officer has arrived on board the ship with help and instructions.'

"You all know as well as I do what that meant: Some KGB thug would arrive on board with a supply of chlorpromazine and God knows what else. By the time Dan Bennet got the Soviets to agree to the interview, Kostiv had been pumped full of chemicals."

Ryder turned to the president. "You saw the tape, Mr. President. The boy was drugged. It was obvious. Statements made under those conditions are not legally valid. The secretary of state has made a great deal of the legal aspects of the case. I agree. But I believe that legally, Kostiv's statement is worthless. At the very least we have the right—and so long as we can prevent the *Sevastopol* from sailing we can insist on that right—to conduct another interview. But this time, we should take a sample of Kostiv's blood and determine whether drugs are present."

Ryder looked at the chief of staff. "Gary, so far, congressional reaction has been uniformly critical. I even saw the minority leader—*our* minority leader—on TV. So far, he's only been critical of INS, but that won't last long. A broader attack on the administration is coming. It's much too easy to suggest we can make this thing go away by giving in to Novikov."

There was a silence. Then McCandless harrumphed twice. "Mr. President," he began, "I myself haven't the slightest doubt Kostiv was drugged. We also know Bassov—like Jim says, he's KGB, and an expert in the subtle arts of persuasion. Now, as to whether Kostiv wanted to defect," he continued. "I had my people go over the police and INS reports. Kostiv had a packet of papers with him when he jumped, sealed in a plastic case, waterproof. He had his seaman's papers, family photographs, and two hundred rubles. Now what sailor walks around on deck carrying his seaman's papers in a waterproof case?

"We know that every working-class Russian Jew who emigrates to Israel carries work papers—their license to drive a bus or operate a tractor or work in a medical lab or teach piano. The papers are worthless, but they don't know that. They all bring 'em out. And then there's the pathetic matter of his English. 'Be free.' He can't manage more than two words, but it's clear he went out of his way to have 'em ready, like a passport."

The DCI slammed his palm on the table. "The poor kid had his goddam passport with him, and we wouldn't recognize it.

"Most often the Russians are able to play the Congress against us, but not this time. I had breakfast today with several members of the House Intelligence Committee. They're with us. They're mad as hell at the INS, but they're not mad at us—yet. When they're prepared to back us, we should make the most of it."

Winthrop shook his head. "We cannot jeopardize the agenda of a summit for which all of us have worked so hard and so long. I don't want to sound callous, but is one Ukrainian sailor worth giving up a summit that could make this world a safer place? I say, cut our losses, face the reality of the predicament we're in, and let the ship sail."

Ryder chose to ignore Winthrop's rhetoric. "What harm would come from another interview?"

"It will only prolong the agony," Winthrop said.

"But at least it will clarify the situation."

"I doubt it," Winthrop snapped. "Kostiv is likely to say he wants to go home again. It will look as though we're deliberately pumping up a crisis."

"It's *their* crisis, not ours," Ryder said.

"It may look that way today," Winthrop said, "but in three days it will be our crisis, too."

"Mr. President," Ryder said brusquely, "we shouldn't give in on this. If I were to say any more, I would only be repeating myself."

"I want to talk to Gary about this," the president said. "It's important that, whatever we do, we not leave anyone in doubt as to what has taken place. The Soviets deserve a black eye, and I want to be sure they get it."

He rose. "Mitch," he said, "let's do what we can to find out what's going on aboard that ship."

Everyone remained seated as the president headed toward the door. In the doorway he turned and addressed the room. "You know, there's all this talk about things changing in Russia. Well, there's a story about an American in Moscow trying to explain our system to his Intourist guide. 'In America,' he says, 'we have complete freedom. Why, I can stand in front of the White House and shout, "To hell with the president of the United States," and nothing will happen to me.'

" 'It's the same here,' the guide said. 'I can stand in front of the Kremlin and shout, "To hell with the president of the United States," and nothing will happen to me, either.' "

They all laughed politely as the president turned and walked back to his office a flight above the Situation Room.

The room emptied quickly. Wallace went directly to his office. Winthrop, McCandless, Ryder, and the attorney general, followed by their assistants, went through the hall past the White House mess, turned at the guard's desk, and went through the double doors to East Executive Drive, where their cars were waiting.

On the way out the attorney general took Ryder aside. "I would have intervened to support you," he said, "but I had my staff review international law and—unfortunately—Winthrop's right."

"Thanks anyway," Ryder said, his voice ironic as he strode briskly to his limousine, ignoring the shouted questions from the press corps gathered fifty feet away. Outside, the day reflected the NSPG: gray, bleak, cold, and overcast—without a hint of sun.

Memorandum: Office of the Assistant Secretary European and Canadian Affairs

DATE: November 25, 8:10 P.M.

Dan, I'm leaving this note taped to your chair to be sure you get it. I'll be at the German embassy for dinner if you need me (phone number 555-4026).

I attended the NSPG this afternoon. The NSDD will be issued later this evening. The president obviously is torn about what to do.

We've got a problem. I watched the president when he saw the videotape of the interview. He was practically in tears. I'm worried the tape might get out. It's dynamite. If it winds up with the networks, you can forget the summit.

That's the bad news. The good news is I have the only copy.

Please advise. Wellbeck.

The Assistant Secretary of State The Department of State, Washington, D.C.

DATE: November 25, 11:45 P.M.

Bob, got your note when I got back to the office at 11:00 P.M. With respect to the home movie: Lose it. Dan.

National Security Decision Directive Number 121 National Security Council Washington, D.C. 20002
SECRET-SENSITIVE
SYSTEM II

TO: The Secretary of State
         The Secretary of Defense
         Director of Central Intelligence
         Attorney General
         Director/INS
         White House Chief of Staff
DATE: November 26

Following Tuesday's meeting of the National Security Planning Group the president has decided that:

1. Navy shall continue to block *Sevastopol's* departure from New Orleans until instructed otherwise by the secretary of defense. Navy should continue to monitor all communications to and from the ship on a priority basis.

2. SECSTATE shall arrange an interview with Kostiv as soon as possible, to be conducted by Department of State officers together with regional director, Immigration and Naturalization Service.

3. A Department of State physician should be included in the interviewing party. He should attempt to secure a blood sample from Kostiv and to make any other observations that would be helpful in determining whether Kostiv has been drugged. He should report his findings as soon as possible.

4. White House Press Office and State Department spokesmen shall prepare releases for use at noon briefings, to be followed by press backgrounders. No mention should be made of the request for a blood sample, the presence of a physician in the interviewing party, or the possibility that Kostiv might have been drugged.

5. White House and State Department offices of legislative affairs should work with the congressional leadership to discourage any sense-of-the-Congress resolution that would limit the president's options in handling the Kostiv matter.

> For the President:
> Mitchell Wallace
> Assistant to the President for National Security

SECRET-SENSITIVE

Memorandum: Department of State
SECRET-SENSITIVE

TO: The Secretary
FROM: EUR/Daniel I. Bennet
DATE: November 27

Following your instructions, I met with the chargé at the Soviet embassy, once yesterday and twice today. I informed him the president has decided the *Sevastopol* will not be permitted to depart New Orleans until we conduct a further interview with Kostiv. He was furious and, egged on by Deputy Consul Bassov, staged a tantrum worthy of the ambassador himself. The chargé accused us of creating a crisis with a view to casting the Soviet Union in a bad light and sabotaging the summit.

This morning, while still refusing our request, he began to probe about the conditions under which an interview might take place. He demanded assurances that if Kostiv repeated his desire to return home, we would permit the *Sevastopol* to sail immediately. Since it is obvious we will not be able to hold the ship after a second interview in which Kostiv tells us he wants to go home, I agreed to his condition.

Then, saying that he was only speaking unofficially and hypothetically, he said he was certain that if Moscow agreed, they would insist that the only question to be put to Kostiv was whether he wished to remain in the United States. He went on to say there could be no press present to observe the interview, or the circumstances under which it was conducted.

He concluded by telling me he was sure Moscow would insist that an embassy officer, probably Bassov, be present. As these conditions seemed consistent with our plans, I said I thought we would be able to agree.

This afternoon the chargé told me he had received instructions. Moscow, he said, wanted to defuse the situation. "If there is to be a crisis," he said, "we want to make it plain that it's of your making. So we will agree to the interview provided that it takes place aboard the ship and there are no more than two Americans present."

I told him we could agree to conduct the interview on board the *Sevastopol*, but we would have to have three Americans. As far as I was concerned, they could send their entire embassy staff to New Orleans— but we could not accept fewer than three on our side. After nearly an hour he agreed. He concluded by saying we could not have any press present as the interviewing party left for, or returned from, the ship.

I told him we didn't control our press the way they control theirs, and I couldn't guarantee that the arrangements would not leak out. He was blunt in saying that if there were any press present as the party left by launch, they could cancel the interview.

With your approval I have decided to head the team myself. If we send a lower-level officer, it will suggest we are not in fact serious, giving weight to their claim that we are looking for an argument. With an interpreter and a physician, we will have used our three places, so we will be unable to take someone from the INS. Having got us into this mess, they don't deserve to go anyway. But the NSDD specifies that the INS be included.

I called Wallace to explain the situation, and we agreed to ask the INS to supply the physician. I plan, however, to wait until tomorrow morning to do so. If they cannot get us an M.D. on short notice, too bad. I plan to have Bob Manning of our drug-interdiction staff standing by. He's a qualified physician and will know whether Kostiv is under the influence.

Wellbeck and I have reviewed in great detail the transcript of the interview with Kostiv, which was done by Gralnik and Josephson of Consular Affairs. We are familiar with the way the questions were originally put to him, and we will make sure they are more diplomatically phrased this time around.

The NSDD puts you in charge. I suggest you inform Wallace of these plans on a close-hold basis. There's no need to consult Ryder. The NSDD doesn't suggest that we do so, and he will only interfere. This is messy enough without a lot of second-guessing from the Pentagon.

Approve _____
Other _____

SECRET-SENSITIVE

CHAPTER NINETEEN

Memorandum: Department of State

TO: The Secretary
FROM: EUR/Daniel I. Bennet
DATE: November 29

The interview with Kostiv went as we expected it would. We were taken to a small wardroom where Kostiv, Bassov, the ship's captain, and an interpreter were waiting. The Russians were unusually efficient. Tea was poured as we sat down. We decided to wait until the interview was completed before asking for a blood sample. Of course, they refused—as I expected they would. But Manning had a good opportunity to observe Kostiv, and it is his opinion that while Kostiv was understandably nervous, there were no signs that he was drugged.

He was obviously tired, but his eyes were clear, he spoke fluently, seemed responsive and in full possession of his faculties. I asked him several times whether he had intended to jump overboard for the purpose of remaining in the United States. He was emphatic that he had not jumped and that he wished to return to the Soviet Union. He said he had a family in Kirovograd and was engaged to be married. He volunteered he was content with his life at sea and in the Soviet Union, that he made good money, and that he only wished the whole incident could be brought to a close.

Neither I nor Manning nor the interpreter sensed he was lying. What-ever he had in mind last week, it is clear that he now wishes to go home. There were no signs of physical abuse. Neither Bassov nor the captain made any effort to interfere with our questioning. The mood was formal but not hostile—although Bassov could make a wedding seem like a funeral.

Life on a Soviet ship must be even worse than I had imagined. Kostiv looked a good deal older than he really is; the quarters on board (judging by the officers' wardroom) are abysmal.

We rented a small launch to avoid bringing the navy or coast guard into the picture and to be certain that there was no leak about our visit to the *Sevastopol*. Bassov returned to New Orleans with us and pestered me the whole way about releasing the ship. I told him that the order would have to come from the president.

I recommend the ship be released. Manning's report should be helpful in settling the drug issue—if it gets out—although diehards like McCand-less, Ryder, and Waterman will complain about our not actually being able to get a blood sample.

Washington, December 5, 10:30 A.M.

The armed CIA courier who brought Ryder the Top Secret mes-sage waited in the outer office in case there was to be a reply. He had delivered the double envelope (one sealed envelope inside another sealed envelope) addressed EYES ONLY—THE SECRETARY OF DEFENSE directly into the secretary's hands as he had been instructed. The secretary took a letter knife from his desk and slit open one envelope, then the other. He read quickly.

The hot line in Waterman's office buzzed. He picked it up immediately. "Michael, I'd like you in my office ASAP."

Waterman dropped what he was doing and half ran into the secretary's suite, opening the secure door for himself by pressing the hidden release button.

Ryder was standing framed by one of his windows. His face was ashen. He looked distraught. He held a single sheet of paper at his side. "Read it," he said in a choked voice.

Waterman squinted at the sloppy penmanship.

I received a call over a secure line early this morning from Alain Marron, the head of French intelligence. They have an agent in the Kremlin who reports regularly and reliably. He's absolutely trustworthy.

He quotes his Kremlin source as follows:

"They're laughing their heads off at Dzherzhinsky Square. The man the American State Department officials interviewed on the Sevastopol was not Kostiv. Another seaman was substituted, and the Americans never suspected a thing."

Marron's source says that on the voyage back to Odessa Kostiv was locked in a storeroom below decks. He was kept under constant surveillance. But a day out of New Orleans the ship's doctor who was drugging him evidently left an empty vial in the room where Kostiv was being held—or he stole it, they don't know for sure. He broke the glass and cut his veins. They found him when blood seeped under the locked door.

We've been had. The worst part of it all is that Bennet evidently never watched the video. We know that because the Russians talked among themselves after Sevastopol sailed. Marron's source says they knew about the videotape and were scared shitless Bennet would realize they were using an imposter.

This is best kept between us. The president would be miserable if he knew, and there's nothing he can do about it now. Marron will protect the information; he won't jeopardize his source. If you will return this note via the courier who brought it, I'll see it's destroyed.

He was just a kid, and he deserved to live. He deserved his chance to be free.

McC

Waterman handed the page back. The secretary of defense folded the message carefully and replaced it in its envelope. He walked slowly to his communications console and pressed the intercom button. "Sandra, you can tell the CIA messenger there's no need to wait."

Ryder slipped McCandless's envelope into his suit-coat pocket.

PART FIVE

CHAPTER TWENTY

The Pentagon, December 8, 9:30 A.M.

James Ryder looked across his desk at Waterman. "Michael," he began, "the president's decided you should represent the Department of Defense in Helsinki."

Waterman's eyes opened wide. "My God." He could hear his pulse rushing.

Ryder continued, oblivious to Waterman's obvious shock and amazement. "I can't think of anyone who's better equipped. You know the issues as well as—no, better, much better—than anyone else who'll be there. And I know you'll give the president all the help and support he'll need. It's a heavy responsibility."

Waterman started to answer Ryder, but all he could summon was a mangled croak. "I—"

"Take your time."

He cleared his throat. "I'll do everything I can, Mr. Secretary. But I'd be a lot more comfortable if you were there."

Ryder nodded sadly. "To be honest, so would I. But that's impossible. The president's decided."

Immediately, Waterman's mind shifted from euphoric to strategic. He was being asked to hold the line against the State Department and the White House entourage, dozens in all. "Will I be on my own, or will I have some help?"

"That's still undecided," Ryder said. "I've talked with Gary Burner. There'll be battalions of State Department people, of course. I've insisted that you be allowed to take at least one person with you—I imagine you'll want Scott Bracken."

"Yes."

"I've also asked General Collins to be in touch with the Defense attaché in Helsinki through our own backchannel. He'll give you logistic and communications support—I don't want to depend on embassy communications, because anything you say will get copied all over the place. I've arranged for a secure phone you can keep in your room."

Waterman nodded. "DCI McCandless told me he has ways of keeping secure lines, too. Should we ask him for help?"

Ryder thought for a minute. "Sure. He's a friend. The important thing, Michael, is that I be kept up-to-date on what's happening. I'll be reachable around the clock. I may not be able to do much about it, but I can't do anything unless you keep me informed. The president knows I may want to talk to him while he's in Helsinki—he said this morning he'd welcome it. So I may get a shot yet."

"I hope so. He values your advice."

"That's why I wish I were going. You'll do a superb job—I trust you— but I'm his friend . . . we go back a long time."

There was an awkward silence. Then Waterman spoke. "When will we know about Bracken, Mr. Secretary?"

Ryder's tone was back-to-business normal. "I expect to hear later today. There's tremendous pressure for places."

"I can imagine," Waterman said.

"Get Laura on the phone for me, Maggie," Waterman said as he ran through his reception room into his office.

In a moment Maggie buzzed. He launched himself at the phone.

He found it impossible to stop the pounding in his chest. "Summit. Helsinki. Me. Alone."

"What?"

He took a deep breath. "I'm the Defense Department's sole representative at the summit."

The shock in Laura's voice was evident. "You mean Ryder's not going?"

"No. I mean, yes—yes, he's not going."

"Michael—what happened?"

"Winthrop maneuvered him out."

His intercom light buzzed. "I gotta go, darling. See you later."

Waterman hit the intercom button with his left hand and started making notes with his right. The list forming in his mind was long. He'd need reference materials—once in Helsinki it would be too late to get any files that might be necessary. They'd have to assemble specialists to stand by in case questions requiring urgent answers should come up. They'd have to arrange for someone to be on duty around the clock for incoming messages and to coordinate any outgoing traffic. He'd need to requisition a secure laptop computer, approved by the National Security Agency, for his classified material. And a cache of food—the sort of munchies that sustained assistant secretaries out to save the Free World: kosher salami, cheese, crackers, and chocolate brownies from Suzanne's on Connecticut Avenue.

There was so much to do. "Maggie, brace yourself. I'm going to the summit." He heard her gasp but didn't wait for a response. "Better get Bracken up here right away. And beep Parisi." He paused. "And see if McCandless can see me this afternoon. Tell his office it's urgent, but I can be in and out in ten minutes."

Waterman pressed the button on his flashing private line.

"If you're inviting me for an espresso to celebrate your trip to Helsinki, I accept." Jay Parisi's voice was ebullient.

"Word travels fast."

"I got good sources."

"Get up here fast, Jay, we gotta talk." Waterman hung up the receiver, turned on the Olympia, and ground a batch of fresh coffee, a scheme hatching in his mind. Parisi would be perfect. Instinctively, Waterman realized he'd need a friend in Helsinki—and Parisi was about to be drafted. He was watching the coffee gurgle into two cups when Parisi came through the door.

Parisi dropped onto the sofa and slapped his feet onto the coffee table.

"How'd you like to go to Helsinki?" Waterman asked, handing him a cup of espresso.

Parisi blinked twice. "You mean the bleak, frozen outpost of Western civilization across from Leningrad? The land of summer sun, winter darkness, velvet vodka, succulent crayfish—and tall blondes?"

"Always at a loss for words, I see."

Parisi didn't miss a beat. "I assume you're planning on, say, late June?"

"Actually, late next week's what I had in mind."

"Next week. What a coincidence—did you know the president'll be in Helsinki next week?"

"Nooooo," said Waterman. "Well, fancy that." He took a sip of coffee and grew serious. "Jay—do you have a passport?"

"Sure—an official passport."

"No good. You'll have to go as a tourist."

"Come on, Michael, what the hell is going on?"

Waterman continued, lost in thought, "There's no way I can get you on the official delegation, but if you just happened to be on leave visiting Helsinki as a tourist during the summit, there's not much anyone could do about that."

Parisi's face grew serious.

"Jay," Waterman said, "I'm going to need help. A summit's like a three-ring circus, and I need to cover all of 'em. I can sign travel orders to get you there on a commercial flight. But it'll be unofficial. Can do?"

"When do I go?"

"The weekend. I want you there before the official delegation leaves Washington."

"Hell, yes." He waggled his eyebrows in a full Groucho. "And do we get to screw the exalted Department of State?"

"Whenever possible."

"Then it's irresistible."

"Good," Waterman put down his cup. "I'm working on a plan now. Let's talk in about two hours—in the meanwhile, get yourself an ordinary passport."

Alone, Waterman went back to his list. Then inspiration hit again. He picked up the phone. "Mag, see if you can get hold of Øve Anders in Oslo." He glanced at the digital clock on his wall. "He should still be in his office."

In a moment Anders came on the line.

"Øve, I'm glad I caught you in. I've got a huge favor to ask. I assume you're going to the summit?"

"Of course."

"Me, too."

"You're going?" The Norwegian's voice took an upswing. "That's terrific, Michael."

"I'm representing Defense."

"Ahh—so Winthrop finally froze Ryder out. We'd been wondering. The Soviets have been putting a lot of pressure on from the European side—lots of anti-Pentagon editorials in newspapers here, including my own, I'm sad to say."

"Øve—"

"Yes?"

"I need a favor. Do you know where you're staying?"

"Not yet. We've put in a request, but we're still waiting to hear from the Finns."

"You must have friends in Helsinki?"

"Oh, yes."

"I'm in a real squeeze here. I need a room in Helsinki during the summit."

"For you?"

"No—I'll be with the delegation. For a friend of mine."

"I'll give it a try."

"Great. I may not be able to get my friend on the official list, in which case the Finns won't make a hotel room available. If that happens, he'll need a place to stay."

"When do you need to know?" Anders asked.

"Tomorrow. If you can't manage, I'll have to try something else."

"Look," Anders said. "I'm leading the *Aftenposten* group—there'll be three of us. I could put in a request for a fourth room—just in case your friend can't find something."

"Fantastic. If it works, it would probably be even better than a private home."

"Okay, Michael. I'll give you a call as soon as I can."

"Øve, thanks a million. Take care."

He hung up the receiver and went back to list-making. He looked at the ever-lengthening column. The thing he needed most for this summit he couldn't put on the list. It was a president willing to hear what he had to say, and a gap in the State Department encirclement that would give him a chance to break through and say it.

He was busy making out the list when Scott Bracken came through the door grinning broadly.

"So you're going!" he exclaimed. "Great news. In the interagency group this morning Wellbeck hinted Ryder was out. I had a sinking feeling we'd been aced out altogether. But if you're along, we're in much better shape."

"Well," Waterman said, "let's just say we're in—how much remains to be seen. I'll feel a lot better if Burner gives you a thumbs-up."

"Me? You mean I may be going, too?"

"I sure as hell hope so. Can you imagine what it would be like to be there alone?"

"Yeah." Bracken laughed. "Lion in the Daniel's den." He dropped onto Waterman's couch. "What's my chances, Michael?"

"To be honest, not very good. As far as Burner's concerned, a summit's merely the world's greatest photo op. Anything of substance is purely incidental."

"The thought that that asshole will decide whether I go or stay is almost certain proof there is no God," Bracken said. "The final proof would be if the decision were left to State."

Waterman grimaced. "Ugh."

"I know. Think about it—Bennet getting to make the decision about whether we go or not." He stood up. "Well, there are things you'll need, and I guess I should start assembling them. No use sitting on my . . . tenterhooks. When will we know about me?"

"Ryder's waiting to hear now. I hope we'll know soon."

Memorandum: Department of State
SECRET-SENSITIVE

TO: The Secretary
FROM: EUR/Daniel I. Bennet
DATE: December 8
SUBJECT: Summit Participation

I received a call from Gary Burner this morning after he'd been called by the secretary of defense. SECDEF asked for an additional slot on the summit delegation for Waterman's deputy, Scott Bracken. Ryder even called a second time to press for Bracken; Burner wanted our view before approving it.

Burner told me there was only one slot left. He said he didn't think he could say no to Ryder without a solid explanation. Then he asked whether we had any requirements of our own beyond those already approved. I thought it best to block Bracken if we possibly could. Waterman will be a problem as it is. But if he's there alone, there isn't much he can do. Besides, Bracken's a tough infighter who would push his way into any working groups.

I told Burner you wanted to bring along a consultant who has especially good contacts in the Kremlin and who knows Marensky well.

He said he could add this consultant to the manifest and tell Ryder there were no spaces left. I gave him Andrew Weston's name.

If you agree this is the best way to proceed, we'll need to go through the formality of making Weston a consultant to the department. This can be done by the end of the week.

I knew you hadn't yet responded to my suggestion that we invite Weston as a reward for his vital role. But I had to act immediately to block Bracken and thought you wouldn't mind, under the circumstances, if we went ahead with Weston.

If this poses a problem, I can go back to Burner and tell him we've decided not to take Weston. But I would urge you to approve his going both because he deserves it and because we just may need a go-between at a critical juncture.

Agree: ————
Other: ————

SECRET-SENSITIVE

The Pentagon, December 9, 2:30 P.M.

Parisi was sitting at Waterman's desk sipping coffee as Waterman came through the door. The navy officer looked up. "It's about time you got here," he said. "I've been protecting this parking spot for the last twenty minutes."

"Sorry," Waterman said. "I was late getting back from the CIA."

"McCandless?"

"Exactly." He nudged Parisi out of his chair. "How are things coming?"

Parisi waved a blue passport at Waterman. "So far, so good."

"Listen, Jay, I called an old friend of mine at *Aftenposten* in Oslo who's covering the summit, to see if he could help find you a place to stay. He thought he had something, but it fell through. Then he said he'd share his room at the Pasila Hotel. It's near the center of town."

"Sounds good to me. What's his name? Does he snore?"

"Øve Anders. And you'll tell me in a week."

Waterman went to his closet and pulled out an attaché case. He handed it to Parisi. "The secretary arranged for this secure fax communications link. You'll hook it up in your hotel room—you're the one getting messages to him. I'll have to stick close to the meetings—if I'm lucky, I'll be able to get away for a few minutes during breaks. But we'll have to work some way for you to get hold of my notes so you can boil 'em down and send 'em on."

Parisi opened the case and shook his head approvingly. "Nice stuff. Efficient, too. What about a secure cellular phone?"

"Would you believe there are none available?"

"Makes you think about what would happen in a war."

"Makes me wonder who borrowed them for the wife and kids."

Parisi scratched his chin. "My beeper—will it work over there?"

"Maybe. You'll need to check. We'll also need a way for you to get incoming messages to me. You just can't hand them over—access to the site will be tight, and you won't have credentials." Waterman scratched his head. "Jay, you're the intelligence guy. You work out the logistics. But I need results—no excuses allowed."

"Aye, aye, sir."

"There's another problem. The crypto system operates off the telephone lines. It's neat technology—but when the phone circuits are busy, you can't get through. So McCandless is helping out. As soon as you get to Helsinki, you call the station chief. He'll put together backchannel communications for us."

"Thank God for McCandless. Did you get Bracken cleared for the official delegation?"

"No. Burner called the secretary and told him there were no places left."

"So it's just us."

Waterman nodded.

Parisi drew a small notebook from his tunic. "Let's talk intelligence," he said. "What do you have in the way of the schedule—meeting places, briefing sessions, things like that?"

"Zilch," Waterman said. "I tried to get some info from the advance team, but they wouldn't tell me a thing."

"I'll call around. There are ways to get these things."

"What time's your flight?" Waterman asked.

"I leave National tomorrow at three-thirty and make a connection in New York. I'll be in Helsinki in time for brunch Friday. That'll give me time to meet the station chief, make sure the communications are in place, and scope the situation." Parisi rapped the secure telephone that sat on Waterman's desk with his knuckles. "I'll call you here Friday, noon your time, and we'll work out the rest then."

"Goodness, Jay," Waterman said, embracing Parisi. "You seem to have thought of everything."

"Goodness had nothing to do with it," Parisi said with a flourish of eyebrows. "See you in Helsinki Monday night."

━━━━━━━━━━

Chevy Chase, December 9, 9:15 P.M.

"I'm home," Waterman shouted. He pulled the door closed behind him. And then, hearing nothing: "Where is everybody?"

"We're in Jason's room," Laura shouted from upstairs.

"I'll be right up." Waterman took the stairs two at a time. He opened the door. Jason sat on the lower red metal bunk bed surrounded by a zoo of stuffed animals; Laura sat on the floor reading him a story. It was the end of the nightly bedtime ritual.

He dropped his briefcase on the rug and went to embrace his son. "I wanted to get home in time for dinner with you," he said. "At least I got here before lights-out."

"Just before," Laura said. "We're on our third story."

Waterman crawled into the bunk bed next to his son, who wore his version of pajamas: a pair of Jams and a Redskins T-shirt. He pulled Jason onto his lap and hugged him tightly. "I'm gonna miss you, goose," he said. "But I'll have lots of stories to tell you when I get back. War stories. Not exactly G.I. Joe, but war stories all the same."

"When're you going, Daddy?"

"Sunday," Waterman said. "I'll be able to make it to the soccer game Saturday."

"There won't be a game—we lost in the semifinals when you were in Moscow."

Waterman looked in time to catch Laura's bemused glance.

"Well, we'll get a chance to play Saturday. Besides—this'll be a four-day trip for me, which means it's probably, oh, a two-present trip for you."

Jason brightened. "Okay!"

Laura spoke. "From the looks of that briefcase this is going to be an all-nighter, right?"

"God, I hope not. I've got a dozen, maybe fifteen, actions to go over and sign out. I want to get a decent night's sleep."

"Well, if Jason's going to get a decent night's sleep, we'd better say good-night."

Waterman lifted Jason onto the upper bunk and pulled the covers up over him. He leaned over and gave him a long kiss. "Good night, goose. I love you."

"Daddy, leave the light on in the closet." He and Laura closed the door behind them and headed downstairs for the kitchen.

"How does it look?" she asked.

"Could be worse. I got a hot schedule this afternoon from Jay Parisi. They've got me on *Air Force One*—then I can keep an eye on things. And I'm scheduled to be in most of the substantive meetings. At least I think I am. There are several meetings shown on the schedule as 'operations meetings.' There's one every morning. I'm not listed for any of those."

He wondered if Dan Bennet was.

Washington, December 14, 5:45 A.M.

The Defense Department sedan was already in front of the house, the engine idling to keep the heater going, when Waterman's alarm went off. He dressed quickly and went downstairs, pausing just long enough for a last kiss for Jason. Shortly after six he put his bags with their rectangular red, white, and blue laminated staff tags in the trunk of the sedan and slid into the backseat.

As the car made its way through the empty streets toward Andrews Air Force Base, Waterman turned on the reading light and perused the thick blue-covered pocket-size trip book that bore the seal of the president on the cover and the title *Trip of the President to Helsinki, Finland.* Issued by the Presidential Advance Office, it was a detailed, minute-by-minute plan for the movement of the president, from the early morning pickup by *Marine One* on the South Lawn of the White House until his return after the summit. The schedule, which was known as the "bible," would be handed out after *Air Force One* took off. Parisi, however, had managed to get him a copy late on Wednesday.

Waterman squinted at the small type. The summit events were outlined down to the most infinitesimal detail; diagrams showed where the president would stand during the various ceremonies, which way he would turn to face the cameras or his interlocutors, where the press risers would be located, how and where the limos would line up, and who was assigned to each numbered car.

For each venue where meetings or other activities would take place, there was a floor plan showing the location of staff holding rooms, interpreters' booths, communications facilities, designated places at conference tables, and lists of participants. Times were given to the minute:

21:35 (local time): *Air Force One* arrives Helsinki-Vantaa Airport. Live coverage.

21:42 (local time): The president and first lady, accompanied by U.S. ambassador, deplane and turn to left before proceeding past honor cordon to podium for brief remarks. President stands at lectern. Others stand at indication marks. Live coverage (150′ throw from press platforms).

21:50 (local time): President concludes remarks, and accompanied by first lady, proceeds to motorcade for boarding. (See diagrams 3 and 4.)

21:54 (local time): President and first lady depart Helsinki-Vantaa Airport by motorcade en route American embassy. (Accompanied by press pool 1-A.)

21:57 (local time): Secretary of state motorcade departs airport en route Inter-Continental Hotel.

22:24 (local time) Press buses depart Helsinki-Vantaa Airport for press hotels 1, 2, 3, 4. (See attached press accommodation sheet for room assignments.)

As the car pulled up outside the VIP lounge at Andrews, an air-force sergeant removed Waterman's bags, checked off his name on a list, and carried the baggage into the terminal to be X-rayed and loaded. "You'll have to carry anything you'll be needing on the flight topside," he said cheerfully. "Everything else'll be delivered to your room at the Inter-Continental." He saluted. "There's coffee inside, sir."

Waterman joined the White House staffers, Secret Service agents, technical personnel, and communications specialists manifested on *Air Force One* and *2800*, the backup aircraft, who were milling about in the lounge. The press planes had already departed: By the time the delegation touched down in Helsinki, they would be in position to cover the arrival ceremony. Taking a cup of coffee from a barlike counter, he found an empty seat in a corner and scanned a wrinkled *New York Times.*

The lead story, written by Michael Gray, outlined dissension between the departments of State and Defense on handling significant summit issues. Nothing surprising there, although Waterman thought the unnamed "high government official" who said, "The Soviets realize 'SDI' rhymes with 'pie in the sky,' " sounded curiously like Dan Bennet's smarmy deputy Bob Wellbeck.

As if to confirm his suspicion, Waterman looked up to discover Dan Bennet and Bob Wellbeck—who was manifested on *2800*—across the VIP lounge in deep conversation with Gray. The *Times* reporter, it seemed, would be traveling to Helsinki on *Air Force One* as part of the press pool. Mitchell Wallace stood off to one side of the room clutching a gray Samsonite attaché case, looking like an accountant waiting for a commuter train. It was indicative, Waterman thought, that he hadn't been included on *Marine One*, which would be bringing the president, Winthrop, and Gary Burner straight from the White House.

Exactly at the time noted in the bible, an air-force officer announced that *Marine One* had departed the South Lawn. "Ladies and gentlemen, please get on the bus to board *Air Force One* now," he ordered. Waterman joined the crowd as it moved onto the blue air-force school bus for the two-hundred-yard trip to the tarmac. He looked up at the huge silver, blue, and white aircraft, the presidential seal eight feet across and just forward of the main hatch. The fuselage bore the legend UNITED STATES OF AMERICA in letters four feet high. Once at the aircraft, everyone boarded rapidly. The president would arrive in less than seven minutes and pause only for a brief photo opportunity as he ascended the stairs of the 707. From his seat in the second cabin, Waterman watched the Old Man come aboard, waving to the cameras. No more than ninety seconds after the president had strapped himself into one of the leather chairs in his private quarters in the 707's forward compartment, the aircraft started to roll smoothly down the taxiway toward the main runway.

Shortly after *Air Force One* lifted off, an assistant from the State Department Secretariat distributed copies of the detailed schedule and, for those cleared to see it, the president's briefing book. Waterman opened the bible to see whether there had been any changes since he got his bootleg copy from Parisi. One modification of great importance caught his eye: Unlike his version, the final schedule listed the participants in morning and evening "operational" meetings—meetings Waterman had assumed would be about mechanics rather than substance. His mouth went dry when he saw the list: the president, the secretary of state, Mr. Burner, General Wallace, Mr. Kirkwell, Ambassador Bellmeyer, Mr. Bennet, Mr. Wellbeck.

The only missing name was his.

They were barely airborne, and the battle had begun: He'd be absent for crucial policy-making sessions each morning and evening. The substantive sessions in which he had been included—two on the first day of the summit and one on the second—were sandwiched between meetings with Novikov. They were bound to be hurried. And, he knew from experience, such meetings could end abruptly if the president decided he needed the time for some other purpose.

He put the schedule aside and turned to his copy of the master briefing book, a fat three-ring binder with talking points on every subject that might possibly come up in the meetings with Novikov. It was the product of countless wars and innumerable skirmishes in the interagency theater. Every paragraph, every sentence, every word, every comma, had been extracted like moisture from a dry sponge, by endless squeezing.

As he turned the pages, he was stunned by what he saw: On virtually every key point there were marked differences from the versions he had seen and labored over. Material deleted long ago in interagency meetings was back; material that had been inserted at DOD's insistence was gone. Every hard edge had been filed down. Every shot between the eyes had been reduced to a cream pie—at best. Punches were pulled everywhere— on human rights, on strategic defenses, on medium-range missiles, on regional issues.

Waterman's face went white with rage. If the president followed these talking points, nothing he'd say to Novikov would be clear or decisive. But there it was—page after page after page of diplo-mush.

It seemed hopeless. "Goddammit," he muttered, unbuckling his seat belt. He walked forward three rows to where Bennet sat next to the tall pin-striped stranger from the VIP lounge, engrossed in *The Washington Post.*

Waterman shook the briefing book in Bennet's face. "I can't believe these talking points."

"Don't complain to me," Bennet said coyly. "I told you in Moscow the president was changing. Take your complaint to the NSC—they did the final version."

"Are you saying you're surprised by what's in here?"

"I'm saying the NSC did the final version. I think they worked all night. As to whether I was surprised, I saw it coming. I tried to tell you."

"I'm going to insist that we go back over the main talking points," Waterman said.

"Fine with me. In the end the Old Man'll use three-by-fives anyway," Bennet replied.

"Then we'll have that much less to do." Waterman turned and walked back to his seat. He took an *Air Force One* notepad from the seat pocket and began to write feverishly.

FROM: Michael Waterman
TO: General Wallace:

A number of the president's talking points, which I have just seen for the first time, entail significant departures from interagency agreed language. I would appreciate an opportunity to discuss them further before they are approved. We could speak on board, if you agree.

He called a steward and sent the note forward. He had just ordered a cup of tea when Wallace appeared at his seat. "I was just going through the book myself," he said. "I rather thought I might be hearing from you. I agree—the changes go pretty far. Farther than I'd fully appreciated." His watery eyes turned up in a half-smile. "The last revisions were done in a great rush."

"Then they're not final?"

"Not *final* final," Wallace said. "Hey, I'm willing to go back over them. How about doing it in Helsinki?"

"I think we'd better do it now," Waterman said. "If we wait until Helsinki, the president may have already read it."

"Right now he's reviewing other papers. But you're right—I can't guarantee he won't leaf through the book during the flight. But I wouldn't be too concerned, Michael. You know how he reacts to thick briefing books— he'll probably ignore it until the last minute. I promise you'll have a chance to make your case—but let's wait until Helsinki."

Waterman was adamant. "Helsinki's too late. And besides, neither of us can be sure we'll have the time in Helsinki. If there's a coup attempt in Tanzania or a hijacking out of Athens or a hostage gets taken in Lebanon, the time to work talking points would evaporate, and there'd be no chance to sort things out. Let's do it now, Mitch, now."

"All right," Wallace said resignedly. "Give me an hour up front with the boss."

"I'll use the hour to take a rough cut at the draft. You tell Bennet."

"Agreed." Shoulders hunched as if fighting a great wind, Wallace made his way up the aisle, pausing momentarily at Bennet's seat. Waterman smiled to think of Bennet's reaction.

Wallace, Bennet, and Waterman sat cheek-by-jowl for three and a half hours in the nose of the plane, poring over talking points. They added, shaded, deleted, until, at the end, Waterman was content. He was exhausted, but he'd managed to regain two thirds of the lost ground. It wasn't everything; but it was a hell of a lot better over the mid-Atlantic than when the seat belt signs had come off. He sank into his seat, declined lunch, and slept the sleep of the innocent.

Helsinki, December 14, 10:35 P.M.

The arrival ceremony went by the script. It had been snowing all day. There was fresh snow on the ground when they landed, at least fifteen inches of it, and it was bitter cold. No one lingered after the president finished his few words. Within minutes his motorcade was on its way to the American embassy compound, the chained tires on his limo throwing up huge white clods as it disappeared into the driving snow.

The secretary of state's motorcade, in which Waterman was assigned to car number three, pulled up at the Helsinki Inter-Continental at number 46 Mannerheimintie just as the little blue book said it would, at 10:20 P.M. Neither snow nor sleet nor dark of night, Waterman thought, as he looked admiringly at the motorcycle outriders who, caked with ice, gunned their engines.

He was just beginning to unpack when the phone rang.

"Welcome to Helsinki," Parisi said. "I just happened to be in town for a few days of vacation when I heard you might be coming with the president. Let's get together." He laughed heartily.

"Come on over," Waterman said, echoing Parisi's laughter. "I'll buy you a nightcap."

"On my way."

"How long will you be?"

"About forty-five seconds."

"Where the hell are you?"

"In the lobby."

Waterman called room service. He hadn't finished hanging his suits when Parisi rapped on his door. "Not bad," he said, looking around the suite. "Who sent the flowers?"

"Finnish Foreign Ministry."

"They'll do for a wedding."

"Or a funeral." Waterman slid his suitcase into the closet. "I ordered drinks—some liqueur made from arctic bramble on the rocks. It's all the rage here."

He looked at Parisi, resplendent in a heavy Donegal tweed suit and Wellington boots, carrying a bulky khaki GoreTex down-filled L. L. Bean parka, which he hung up. "So, Jay, what's going on?"

"These are for you," Parisi said, throwing down a thick envelope. "Soviet press releases, compliments of Øve Anders. He says to tell you he knows how much you love reading fiction."

"I'll use them instead of Sominex," Waterman said. "How're you finding things at the embassy?"

"The military attaché is bloody useless. The station chief's another matter. Couldn't have been more accommodating. We're to call any time—day or night—and he's got a great communications setup." Parisi's eyebrows waggled playfully. "We can reach out and touch *anybody*."

"Can he send secure fax, too?"

"Absolutely."

"Terrific. Then the first thing he can do is send these to Ryder," Waterman said, taking the newly revised talking points from his briefcase.

Parisi scanned the papers with a critical eye. "How was your flight over—I mean, apart from having to fight for these?"

"I'll tell you," Waterman said. "It'll be tough to go back to waiting at airports after flying *Air Force One*."

Parisi didn't wait to be asked. "*My* flight was super, too. Got upgraded to first. They served Dom Pérignon and a splendid Pauillac, and the stewardess was a knockout."

"Jay—"

"Don't worry, Michael—I've been an absolute monk since I arrived. Spent all my time securing your little communications network. Your friend Anders couldn't be nicer, by the way."

"He's a terrific guy," Waterman agreed.

"And a hell of a journalist."

Waterman nodded. "That's what makes him so special. He's tough and fair and has the kind of institutional memory that makes people like you and me weep. I wish the American reporters covering this thing knew as much as Øve. If they did, I wouldn't be so worried about what's going to appear in the papers."

"And on the nets. There are more TV people here than diplomats. If Øve hadn't taken me in, I'd be sleeping in the streets." Parisi shuddered at the thought. "As it is, we're sharing a huge room, and he's discreet enough not to ask what I'm doing, even though he knows that I know that he probably knows anyway. He's even invited me to dinner the day after tomorrow— wants me to meet this friend of his, Alexi Marensky, who's in town with his father for the summit. By the way, he asked if you'd be willing to meet over a drink with him and his two colleagues from *Aftenposten*. He understands your schedule's a bitch, but he'd sure be grateful if you could find half an hour."

Waterman wrinkled his brow. "I can't very well say no. Tell him tomorrow—your hotel at about five-thirty. By the way, is it far?"

"Just around the corner."

"Jay, you said Øve wants you to meet Alexi Marensky?"

"Yep. Day after tomorrow."

"You *do* know who he is, don't you?"

There was a knock at the door. Parisi let the waiter in, took the tray, tipped him, and eased the door shut. "Of course I know who he is," he said, obviously wounded. "He's the center-ring trapeze artist from the Moscow Circus. The one who coined the phrase 'Make sure you know what you're grabbing before you let go of what you've got.' I've got it tacked up on the wall of my office—it's practically the naval intelligence credo. Oh—he's also the only son of Novikov's chief adviser." They both laughed.

"I deserved that," Waterman said. He proffered a glass to Parisi and took one himself. "Skoal," he said.

"*L'chaim*," Parisi countered. "To life."

They touched glasses. Waterman sipped approvingly. "Good." He set his glass down. "Jay, did Øve say anything about Alexi or his father?"

"Just that Alexi was a big fan of Novikov's—quit his job at some research institute to start up a pro-Novikov periodical, wrote a lot of articles
defending *perestroika.* But Anders said he's become disillusioned with Novikov—thinks Novikov's conceding too much to the Old Guard these days.
I got the idea he's been in a kind of depression."

"Look, it may come too late to be much use, but any intelligence you can
get on Marensky Senior would be helpful. He's such a chameleon, we can't
get a line on him. Knowing more might give us some insight into Novikov."

"Leave it to me," Parisi said.

"How do you and I communicate?" Waterman asked. "The talks'll be at
Ainola, Jean Sibelius's former home. The Finns wanted it there for security
reasons. It's supposed to be beautiful—heavily wooded; rustic; picturesque.
The problem is, it's isolated—twenty-three miles from town. We'll have to
figure out some way I can contact you if you have a message from the
secretary or if I need to get in touch with him."

"Maybe this'll help," Jay said. He took a small black pager from his
pocket and handed it to Waterman.

"Where the hell did you get that?" Waterman asked.

"U.S. Navy Office of Congressional Liaison. They'll never miss it. When
you want to get me, you dial this number," he said, handing Waterman
a piece of paper. "If I need to get you, you'll feel the beeper vibrate—it
won't do to have it go *beep, beep.* I'll be standing by at Järvenpää train
station—that's a ten-minute walk from the Sibelius house."

"Whose phone number is it? Where's the transmitter?"

"Our friend the station chief was good enough to set it up at his apartment."

"Damn," Waterman said, with genuine admiration. "I knew you were
the perfect man for this job."

"I spent most of yesterday making the trip out to Ainola," Parisi said
with satisfaction. "I was worried the beeper might lack the range we need,
but it works just fine."

"Jay," Waterman said with some awe, "you're good."

Parisi grinned. "Let's not get me a swelled head—yet."

Helsinki, December 15, 5:45 A.M.

Waterman was up seventeen minutes before the 6:00 A.M. wake-up call came through, and uncharacteristically wide awake. It was the adrenaline, he thought, as he raced through his shower, toweled dry, and climbed into his clothes. As he dressed, he silently thanked Laura for the silk long underwear she'd remembered to stick in his suitcase. It was cold even though the Inter-Continental's rooms were heated according to foreign tastes. Minutes later he was on the phone to Mitchell Wallace, whose suite was on the floor above, hammering away at the NSC adviser about being included in the operational meetings.

Wallace told him to talk to the chief of staff, so he hung up and awakened an aide to Gary Burner, who groggily—and naively—said it would probably be all right with the chief of staff if General Wallace agreed. So he called Wallace again. "Burner says it's okay with him if it's okay with you," Waterman white-lied.

"All right, all right, Michael," Wallace sighed. "Ten-thirty in suite 1010."

He'd just hung up the phone when breakfast arrived: wonderful fresh-squeezed orange juice, a basket of dark bread and rolls with the sweet butter for which Finland was world-famous, and an extra-large silver carafe filled with strong black coffee. Flushed with his success, Waterman tore into the food with a vengeance. The waiter had barely departed when a thick packet of press clippings, faxed from bulldog editions of *The New York Times* and *The Washington Post*, then collated and photocopied in the State ops center down the hall, was shoved under Waterman's door. Nothing new, he thought with relief as he sipped and scanned. No news was good news.

Waterman was polishing off the last of the rolls and butter when an envelope from the White House was pushed under the door of the living room. He tore it open and read:

Memorandum: The White House
CONFIDENTIAL

TO: Summit Participants on the U.S. Team
FROM: White House Press Secretary
DATE: December 15
SUBJECT: Press Contacts

This memo will serve as formal notice that no one—repeat, no one—will have any contact with the press without prior personal approval from me, from Chief of Staff Burner, or from the secretary of state.

If you receive a request for an interview or a request to comment on any aspect of the summit whatsoever, you will not be interviewed, or speak a syllable of comment. You *WILL* refer it to the White House Press Office without delay.

I must remind you that "contact" *includes even casual conversation with the press.* Chatting in the bars or gossiping during bus rides to the summit site or anywhere else is absolutely prohibited. I plan to read all summit stories very carefully, and at the first sign of a leak I will personally search out the malefactor and send him or her home on the first available flight.

Waterman crumpled the memo in disgust. Across town the Russians were backgrounding the press like crazy. Indeed, the Soviet Press Office had been doing a land-office business arranging interviews, providing backgrounders, distributing—always in English—papers on every subject that might conceivably come up at the summit. Novikov wasn't scheduled to arrive until later today. But the propaganda apparatus had been hard at work for weeks. No U.S. spokesman had appeared on any of America's morning TV shows. The Soviets and their surrogates were booked on everything from *Good Morning America* to *Donahue.*

Waterman was scornful of the White House Press Office and especially of Alan Kirkwell for this dereliction. He knew there was only one reason Kirkwell didn't get his egocentric ass over to Helsinki to work the press in advance the way the Soviet spokesman and his aides did. Kirkwell wanted to fly on *Air Force One* so that he could be seen on TV screens all over the world coming down the stairs just behind the president. As a longtime anonymous Capitol Hill staffer, Waterman detested such performances, especially when they resulted in propaganda victories for the other side.

He looked at the inch-thick stack of handouts from the Soviet Press Office that lay on his bedside table, courtesy of Øve Anders. He'd read them before going to bed, expecting to be put to sleep. To his horror, Waterman had discovered they were deft and well written; the sort of stuff reporters regularly folded into their daily stories, thus becoming unwitting propagandists.

Waterman stood with the gag order in his hand and the last of his black-bread roll in the other, wondering whether Bennet had received the same message or whether, perhaps, this was some plot directed specifically at him.

Then he unballed the memo and pressed it flat with his hand, trying to rub out the wrinkles. *This* paper he'd save for his files. It was too good to throw away.

With the memo still in hand he called Anders's room at the Pasila. Parisi picked up the phone. "Sleep well?"

"Until the time difference caught up with me at about five."

"I got the talking points to Washington," Parisi said. "Bill Collins said he'd get them to SECDEF. Bill says, quote, the speedy service is much appreciated, end quote."

"That makes me happy." He shook Kirkwell's detestable memo. "Is Øve there?"

"In the shower."

"Pass him a message, will you, Jay? Say I have to request formal approval to meet with him and his friends. And from the tone of a note I've received, I doubt it'll be granted. Tell him I'm sorry—but I'll do the best I can to get it approved."

Helsinki, December 15, 6:00 A.M.

Three miles away the president still slept—on a bed that had been airlifted from the White House five days before his arrival—in the residential wing of the American embassy, a rambling brick building that occupied several splendid acres high on a wooded hill overlooking the city.

A hundred yards from where he slept, others had been at work all night. Indeed, even before *Air Force One* had touched down at Helsinki, a White House operations center had been established in the working offices of the embassy. Secure computers and Xerox machines, flown from military bases in Germany, clicked and wheezed as Top Secret schedules, confidential briefing notes, classified background papers, attendance lists, and the scores of other requisite documents began to pile up in the cramped quarters of an embassy that normally saw less activity in a year than would take place in the seventy-two hours of the Finland summit.

Communications gear was everywhere. Ceiling-high mountains of insulated equipment cases turned the corridors into lethal obstacle courses. Thick bundles of insulated cable, which connected a network of twenty-six workstations to the three microcomputers, were taped to the floors in clumps. Others, tangled as spaghetti, completed the phone, fax, and intercom network allowing the White House to maintain the same quality of communications in Helsinki as it did in Washington.

Back at the Inter-Continental, a similar office had been set up by the State Department Secretariat. With the worldwide flow of communications pouring into State's operations center, the thirty or so clerks, secretaries, communicators, staff officers, motor-pool managers, protocol officers, cipher operators, and Secret Service agents scurried like worker bees from one interconnected suite to another, carrying a never-ending stream of cables, faxes, telexes, and file folders. Around the clock they worked in both locations. The nerve center of the world, it seemed, had moved to the seventh floor of a hotel and a nondescript embassy on a hill overlooking downtown Helsinki.

There was a third operations center, too, Waterman knew—the Department of Defense's covert lonely outpost—manned by Jay Parisi, in the corner of Øve Anders's hotel room.

Helsinki, December 15, 6:15 A.M.

Waterman looked over the day's revised schedule, which had just slid under his door. The first of the operations meetings—he saw his name was included in the roster—was scheduled for ten-thirty. Late enough, he knew, to give the president an easy morning to recover from the trans-Atlantic journey while leaving a comfortable amount of time for final preparations before Wednesday's meeting with Novikov. A working lunch was set for noon, and a postlunch meeting with the senior advisers, to which Waterman was invited, was scheduled. It would be there that the president would go over the briefing materials in detail. Maybe not as much detail as Waterman would like: He frowned to see the meeting would be cut short by the president's traditional courtesy call on the Finnish government, which had been arranged for midafternoon.

The evening had been left free at the president's specific request. He had ordered, so the schedule said, an early dinner of broiled chicken, rice pilaf, and green salad, accompanied by one glass of California chardonnay, and followed by a private showing of the movie *North by Northwest*. The feature presentation, Waterman knew, would be preceded by a classified short subject—the CIA's twenty-minute psychological video on Novikov. It was just the sort of evening the president wanted before his first encounter with a Soviet leader twenty-three years his junior.

Waterman discovered to his dismay that getting into the operations meeting was at best a Pyrrhic victory. Nothing of substance was discussed, and the group (minus the president, who, at the last minute, wisely chose not to participate) wasted forty-five minutes on the sort of administrative trivia Waterman had spent a career in Washington trying to avoid.

The afternoon working session with the president was short—just an hour, much of which was spent going over the key arguments supporting the American position on each of the principal agenda items: human rights—we wanted more; strategic weapons—we wanted fewer; medium-range missiles—we wanted none; regional issues—we wanted the Soviets to stop supporting subversion in the Third World; trade and economic questions, and the like.

He listened carefully for signs that the president might have adopted new positions—positions influenced by State, or Gary Burner. He was gratified to hear none. On strategic defense especially, the president seemed as dedicated as ever to the proposition that the development of a Strategic Defense Initiative was a good thing. Then, with just a few minutes remaining, the president invited the advisers gathered around the table to make any comments they wished.

Waterman used his own time to caution against assuming Novikov was clearly and reliably committed to real reform. And despite the dirty looks he got from Dan Bennet, he plowed some new ground, explaining to the president that, typically, Soviet negotiators threaten to break off negotiations as a device for wringing concessions from those across the table.

"You shouldn't be surprised, Mr. President," he said, "if at some point Novikov says or implies an impasse has been reached; an obstacle of some kind threatens to stall any results from the summit. What you should remember when he says that is it's a bluff—he's playing poker. And, sir, the reason he'll be bluffing is that he knows you're holding the winning hand."

The president thanked him warmly. "Well, I've been through a lot of negotiations, Michael, and I've experienced every conceivable negotiating ploy at one time or another."

The president's eyes crinkled up in a paternal smile. "The toughest one I remember is, ah, the time I negotiated the end of the Peloponnesian Wars. Golly, that Pericles was a tough one—worse than Brezhnev." Everyone laughed, including Waterman. The Old Man really knew how to bring the tension level down.

"Well, son," he said to Waterman, "something else you might want to know about me, too—I'm a pretty savvy poker player when the chips are down."

Waterman laughed with the rest of the table as the president left the meeting. The group stayed behind to chat for a minute, and the consensus, with which Waterman agreed, was gratifying: The president was alert and at the top of his form. He'd given Waterman, at least, the firm impression that he was ready to resist any pressure Novikov might apply. Waterman left the afternoon meeting more confident than at any time in recent days.

CHAPTER TWENTY-ONE

Helsinki, December 16, 5:45 A.M.

A steady light snow fell gently in the predawn darkness, dredging the empty sidewalks in white and silencing the handful of cars that could be seen, headlights thrusting shafts of light, in the street below. Barely awake, Waterman peered through his drapes at the green uniformed police clustered together at the security barricades that blocked entry to the hotel. He let the heavy velvet panels slide closed, yawned, stretched, then phoned room service. Then he picked up his secure briefcase phone and his classified papers and trundled them into the bathroom. When he emerged half an hour later, showered, shaved, and wrapped in a thick terry-cloth robe with an Inter-Continental logo on the pocket, two pots—one filled with hot, strong coffee, the other with foamy steamed hot milk—were waiting on his coffee table.

He served himself, then sat down on the sofa to study the mass of material he would take to the meeting.

By the time he had gone to bed, the final version of the president's talking points had been reproduced and inserted in black ring binders emblazoned in gold with the presidential seal. Three-by-five cards had been prepared on the major points. Waterman took the time to check that they matched the talking points in the longer version. More than once during ministerial sessions he'd won battles over language only to lose book wars. A word-for-word scan was the only way to be sure that DOD's concerns had actually been inserted into the president's talking points. He was relieved to find that they were still there.

Then he picked up the blue trip book—the day's "bible." He was to ride in car number six in the motorcade, which would leave the front entrance of the hotel at nine-fifteen for Ainola.

The bible included the layout of the rustic country home. The floor plan was marked to indicate where the president and Novikov would meet—right down to an X where they would greet each other on the front steps for the first time, precisely at 10:30 A.M. It also showed the drawing room where the advisers to the two delegations would mill about waiting while their principals talked and negotiated—according to the book, coffee and pastries would be available—and showed Waterman how to get to the second-floor bedrooms, fitted out as temporary offices, where working space for the delegations had been set aside.

The president and Novikov would talk in the library, a large corner room with a solid wall of bookcases on one side and a wall of windows on the other. In the middle of the bookcase wall there was, Waterman saw, a large fireplace. Four chairs—"comfortable," according to the bible—had been arranged for the president, the general secretary, the Soviet minister of foreign affairs, and the American secretary of state. A quartet of smaller chairs was also indicated: a pair for interpreters and note-takers from each side. Waterman turned back to his homework.

By the time he drained the last of his coffee, the table in front of him was full of papers organized by categories into colored filing folders: red for talking points, blue for contingency talking points, yellow for background papers, green for biographical material, white for cables. Waterman dumped them all in an oversize aviator's briefcase that bore the legend PROPERTY OF THE DEPARTMENT OF DEFENSE, together with the beeper and spare set of batteries Parisi had supplied, some coins in case he had to make calls from pay phones, and a supply of writing paper and pens.

With everything in order, he dressed quickly and sat down at the desk in the living room to prepare a note for Jim Ryder. Parisi, who would take up his position at the Järvenpää station café later in the morning, would pick up the note after Waterman had left the hotel and send it backchannel through the CIA's Helsinki station chief.

It was a cursory report. Waterman included a summary of the final preparations, his reading of the president's mood, a précis of the working session at the embassy with the president, and his fight to be included in operational meetings. Its main purpose was not so much to inform, but to ease the secretary's pain at having been excluded from the summit by making sure he knew what was taking place.

At eight-fifteen he phoned Parisi to arrange for him to pick up the message. Fifteen minutes later he received a call from the State Department Secretariat: The departure from the hotel had been advanced from nine-fifteen to eight forty-five, as the road to Järvenpää was icy and the trip would take longer than anticipated. He hastily checked to make sure everything he'd need was accounted for, paused to remove the crypto key from the secure telephone (without the key it could be left in an unsecured hotel room), and headed downstairs for car number six.

A Secret Service agent stood by the hotel door handing enameled lapel access pins to authorized individuals and checking their names off a list. Waterman pushed the triangular red-and-green pin through the fabric on his lapel and attached the clip on the underside. Without the right pin, which changed daily, it would be impossible to gain access to the summit site.

Not even Waterman's preoccupation could diminish the beauty of the ride. Just outside the city, the motorcade made its way through a pine forest that covered most of the distance to Järvenpää. Even at nine in the morning the sky was still dark; but the falling snow and the snow-laden trees were visible in the light reflected from passing cars and farmhouses along the way. Undisturbed by urban traffic, the blanket of snow covering the fields astride the highway was pristine; without footprints or tire tracks it was smooth and silky. He sank back in plush leather and lost himself in thought.

" 'Whose woods these are I think I know,' " he recited as he stared into the forest, listening to the metronomic *click-swish* of the windshield wipers. And I have promises to keep, too, Waterman thought—and miles to go before I sleep.

From Järvenpää, where the motorcade turned off the main road, it was a short two kilometers to Ainola. Even before the villa itself came into view, Waterman could see the aurora borealis created by the scores of television lights. As he drew closer, he could make out smoke rising through the falling snow. The limo's studded tires crunched the firmly packed snow, and Waterman put his nose to the window to get a first look at the house where the leaders would meet. Designed at the turn of the century by Lars Sonck, a distinguished Finnish architect and friend of the Sibelius family, it was surrounded by tall trees, many of them bare and ghostly white in the relentless TV lights.

Before Waterman knew it, the motorcade had pulled up and stopped. General Wallace, Chief of Staff Burner, and Ambassador Ellis Moore, trailed by Waterman, Bennet, Bob Wellbeck, Phil Lanier, two of Burner's staff, the interpreters, and the note-takers, jumped from the limos and made straight for the door. Looking almost furtive, the Americans darted into the small house without responding to the barrage of questions shouted in half a dozen languages.

Inside, Waterman looked around quickly. Ainola was much more rustic than he'd imagined—the ceilings were accented by long beams; most of the walls had been built of unfinished wood that had softened with age and weather. He shed his coat, then joined Bennet, Wellbeck, and the others climbing the stairs to the second-floor bedroom that served as the American delegation's office.

The small, packed room had been filled to overflowing with summit furniture: two large desks, each with a word processor, several chairs, a telephone, a small Xerox machine, and a selection of mineral water and soft drinks crammed cheek-to-jowl on a Formica table. The delegation deposited its classified materials under the watchful eye of a Secret Service agent, then descended the wide staircase to the living room below to await the arrival of the president and the secretary of state.

The protocol had been worked out in minute detail. On this, the first day, the Americans were to be in place first. The president would greet Novikov on the front steps. That night viewers all over the world would watch as the president emerged through the front door and shook hands with the general secretary of the Communist party of the Soviet Union. For the second day the order would be reversed. The arrangement, which had taken days of negotiation, amounted to sharing the home-court advantage, with some slight edge—in which Gary Burner took great pride—for the American side.

From the window of the living room Waterman saw flashing red lights. Momentarily, the escorts—two police vehicles, half a dozen motorcycles, and a Secret Service War Wagon followed by the president's Cadillac limousine and two Secret Service chase cars, came into view. There was an explosion of strobe lights as the wall of still photographers recorded the president stepping from the armored limo, followed by the secretary of state. Both men waved to the press—more than two hundred men and women bundled up in down parkas and heavy overcoats spread out on a forty-foot-wide three-tiered stand.

"Mr. President, what are you going to say to Novikov?" one of the White House reporters shouted. "Can you get a deal with him?"

The president, a lapel of his dark-blue suit peeking out from under a gray topcoat, turned and paused briefly. "I've been looking forward to this meeting since the general secretary first broached the possibility of a summit," the president said. "We have a lot to talk about." Then he turned through the door into the house.

Gary Burner ushered the president inside. He took his coat, insisting on taking the president and Winthrop on a quick tour of the house. He looked, Waterman thought, much like a bellhop, turning on the lights and opening closets to show guests around a hotel room. Then they all stood silently in the entry hall waiting for Novikov to arrive.

With another round of flashing red lights, the Soviet delegation arrived. Waterman, in the background, watched as the two leaders posed for photographers in the doorway, smiling and shaking hands. The bareheaded president, tall and erect, towered above the diminutive general secretary, who wore a long black overcoat and a fur hat. Waterman was struck by how slight the Soviet leader was.

Behind Novikov followed the rest of the Soviet delegation: The foreign minister came first, then Novikov's top adviser, Yuri Marensky, followed by the Soviet chief of staff—Waterman noted that he wore full military dress and no overcoat. Last up the steps came half a dozen anonymous aides, interpreters, factotums, and security men.

As the pool of photographers and reporters watched, the two delegations mingled in the large entry hall, reticently shaking hands while introductions were made and greetings exchanged. It reminded Waterman of a junior-high prom, where shy adolescents had to be prodded to talk to one another. He edged toward Yuri Marensky and put out his hand. "Michael Waterman," he said, inclining his head formally.

"Yuri Marensky." The Soviet surveyed Waterman with clear gray eyes. "I have heard a lot about you."

"I've heard about you, too. We share a friend in Øve Anders."

"Ah, Øve." Marensky smiled. "Basically, he is a good man, although he is very tough on us. I wish he scrutinized your motives as thoroughly as he does ours."

"I think he's an equal-opportunity reporter," Waterman parried. "He's tough on both sides." He paused, uncertain how to proceed.

Marensky's eyes sensed something, and he turned away. "We will talk again."

"I hope so." Now, Waterman saw what Marensky had seen. A protocol officer was leading the press pool toward the library, where the leaders had been taken. Waterman followed behind and craned his neck so he could see into the room. There was a fire in the yellow brick fireplace, and the scent of burning pine filled the room. A crust of snow on the window mullions created a Currier & Ives Christmas-card scene of warmth and cheer—exactly what Gary Burner had hoped and planned for. The pool spread out along the line of bookcases and recorded the two leaders taking their places in opposing easy chairs, flanked by the secretary of state and the foreign minister and the note-takers and interpreters. They were allowed to remain for the exchange of greetings, then quickly ushered out. The double doors to the library were closed, and four security men—two Soviets and two Americans—stood guard outside. The Finland summit had begun.

Ainola, Finland, December 16, 10:00 A.M.

The president shifted in his chair until he was comfortable. He picked up his briefing book from the coffee table and withdrew a stack of notecards from a clear plastic envelope taped to the inside cover. He looked at the Soviet, who had settled into his chair, and began.

"Mr. General Secretary," he said formally, smiling broadly, "I'm pleased we have arranged this opportunity to meet face-to-face. Our staffs have worked diligently to frame the issues for our agenda. They have labored long and hard to create the circumstances in which we might succeed in finding ways for our two countries to develop a relationship of cooperation."

Pausing for the translation, the president looked down at the three-by-five cards in the palm of his hand, then across to the secretary of state, who opened the briefing book to the first tab. His eyes then traveled across the coffee table separating the Americans from the Soviets, darting from Novikov, thin, pale, and graying, to the foreign minister, ruddy with a smooth round face and white hair, immaculately dressed in a double-breasted Italian charcoal-gray suit. Novikov was leaning forward, his right ear cocked, to hear the translation whispered by a balding interpreter seated just inches away. The two note-takers scribbled rapidly.

"I don't believe that there is any problem—*any problem*—we can't solve if there is political will on both sides." He paused, looked at his three-by-fives, took the top one, placed it in the rear of the deck, then continued, "I pledge that the will exists on our side. We're ready to settle all issues, military, political, cultural, economic—all of them."

The president shifted cards again. "I know you've been critical of some of the things we're doing. It's true we've been rebuilding our defenses. I make no apology for that—for several years we neglected our defenses. I know you object to our decision to go ahead and deploy missiles in Europe. But these are to counter yours—and yours not only came earlier, there are many more of them."

Another card was turned over. "I'm ready to call a halt to all this. Or we can go on as we've been these last five years, mostly under your predecessors, of course. *We* can afford to go on spending, because we have an economic system that works: It grows, it produces unprecedented wealth, it pushes out the frontiers of technology. So we can go on . . . but we're ready to halt the military competition between us. I've got you on my dance card. That's why I'm here. But it takes two to tango."

The president paused. He looked at Anthony Winthrop and moved his head slightly as if to cue the secretary of state. When Winthrop didn't pick up his line, the president continued, "I suggest, Mr. General Secretary, that we work through the agenda our staffs have drawn up. The secretary of state has some ideas on how we might go about that."

Winthrop was about to speak when Novikov, who didn't wait for the full translation, responded.

"Mr. President," the Soviet leader began, "I, too, hope we can resolve our differences and put an end to this unproductive competition in the instruments of destruction. You know, we are attempting ambitious changes in our political and constitutional structure. A great deal has been accomplished since I launched plans to reform our economy and bring openness to our political structure. Still, a great deal remains to be done.

"We proceed from the premise that ending the Cold War is a vital element of our plans. And we are prepared to play our part. But we cannot act alone. You just said it takes two to tango. But this must be more than a dance—it must be a partnership. That's why I'm here today—to see whether we can become partners in ending the Cold War once and for all. It won't be easy; radical change is never easy. But we must try. We *must* try." Novikov spoke rapidly, without the benefit of three-by-fives, punctuating his words with staccato gestures, openhanded jabs at the air in front of him.

"Now," he continued. "Now—let us hear what the secretary of state has to say."

The Soviet listened intently as Winthrop outlined the prearranged talking points in the briefing book, proposing that the morning be spent on arms-control and security matters, the afternoon on regional and bilateral issues.

"This is acceptable to me," Novikov said after the interpreter finished whispering in his ear. "I trust that the minister for foreign affairs agrees with us, doesn't he?"

Fodor Glazov rumbled affirmatively in his distinctive basso profundo, "This would be an excellent way to proceed."

"Very well, then," Novikov said.

He looked at his foreign minister, then fixed the president in his gaze and smiled. "We would be pleased, Mr. President, to hear any new ideas you might have on how to resolve the impasse that has developed over nuclear-arms control, especially your effort to gain a strategic advantage by deploying missiles in Europe that can strike my country. And, of course, I expect you will wish to discuss your plans to build strategic defenses."

The president shifted in his chair, riffling through the wad of three-by-fives in his hand. He found the medium-missile card, read it, nodded to himself, then began to speak. "As you know, Mr. General Secretary, we have proposed the total elimination of all medium-range missiles. Thus far, we have been unable to gain your agreement. I know you argue that our deployment of missiles in Europe upsets the strategic balance. But you have been saying that for years now, and each year it is you who adds new missiles in Europe. I hope you're prepared to reconsider your position. The world supports the American proposal—the Zero Option. It would be a concrete indication that each of us is prepared to take a major step—"

Novikov interrupted. "We could agree to the elimination of all medium-range missiles in Europe. But we must insist on retaining some—not very many, but some—missiles in Asia. Perhaps a hundred. Would that be acceptable to you, Mr. President?"

"Eliminate them *all* in Europe?" the president asked.

"Yes, all," Novikov replied.

"Why, yes . . . I mean . . . of course." The president seemed taken aback. He had expected greater resistance than Novikov was showing. There'd hardly been an argument.

"Then we agree?" Novikov asked. "I want to be sure we understand each other."

"We agree," the president replied, smiling and nodding. "We'll eliminate all medium-range missiles—"

"In Europe," Glazov interjected.

"In Europe," the president repeated.

"Mr. President—" It was Winthrop.

"Tony?"

"Mr. President—" The secretary of state had an urgent tone to his voice.

"And each of us will be allowed a hundred missiles in Asia," Novikov interrupted.

"Yes," the president said. "Of course, we'll have to agree on verification. You have an old Russian proverb—"

" 'Trust but verify.' I know it well, Mr. President. Yes, indeed—we're as interested in verification as you are," Novikov said. "But I propose we leave verification provisions to the experts."

The president looked at the secretary of state. "You were saying, Tony?"

"Only that we still have to work out virtually all of the verification aspects, Mr. President."

Novikov interrupted again. "Then let's agree to instruct our staffs to prepare some language for the communiqué recording this historic agreement. It could even say the issue of verification will be left to the experts to resolve."

The president nodded agreement.

"There is a further point you might want to consider, Mr. President," Novikov said. "We see no reason why we should stop with the elimination of medium-range missiles in Europe. I propose that we eliminate short-range missiles as well."

"You mean . . . *all* short range missiles?" the president asked, incredulous.

"Exactly," Novikov said. "If we can agree to eliminate medium-range missiles, why can't we eliminate shorter-range ones as well? Let's agree, here, now, immediately, to remove *all* missiles from Europe."

The general secretary removed a typewritten page from the folder in front of him and handed it to the president. Winthrop read it over the president's shoulder. It was a communiqué stating the two leaders had agreed in principle to the elimination of *all* missiles of all ranges from Europe within twenty-four months. Novikov fell silent while the president studied the document, watching as his eyes moved across and down the page.

Winthrop hastily penned a note and, leaning toward the president, placed it in his hands.

Mr. President, can we take a minute to reflect on this? The British and French governments will object. NATO will balk because it will surely lead to the denuclearization of Europe and destroy the underpinnings of NATO strategy. And the hundred missiles in Asia—that's a problem, too. We have no place to base them.

The president read Winthrop's note. He turned to Novikov. "Mr. General Secretary, I suggest that we take a brief recess so that I might consult with the secretary of state."

The two Americans rose and walked to the far end of the large room.

"I don't understand your note," the president whispered. "You've been urging me to be flexible. Now, Novikov's come up with a proposal that would bring us closer to a world without nuclear weapons—and you seem reluctant to go along."

"Mr. President," Winthrop replied, "it's one thing to give up medium-range missiles. NATO's agreed to that. But they don't agree with abandoning nuclear weapons altogether. And he's demanding a hundred missiles in Asia. We have no place to deploy a hundred missiles. We'll end up with none."

"Tony," the president said, "I'm tired of getting jerked around by the Europeans. For months now, you've been sending me one paper after another arguing that we ought to give Novikov the benefit of the doubt. That's been the bottom line in every conversation we've had on the subject. Ryder and McCandless have argued the other way, just as passionately. We had endless meetings on this, and you—*you* carried the day."

The president shrugged his shoulders in bemusement. "Now, I can't think of a good reason for saying no to Novikov. If he's willing to give up *his* short-range missiles, I don't see why we shouldn't give up *ours*. There's a limit to how far I'm prepared to go just to keep the Europeans happy. Hell, they complain no matter what we do anyway."

"But, Mr. President," Winthrop said, "I—"

"The benefit of the doubt, Tony. If that's going to mean something, I can't say no to his proposal. As a matter of fact, perhaps we can go them one better. Just wait." He turned and left the secretary of state open-mouthed. Winthrop followed as the president crossed the room to where Novikov and Glazov sat.

"Mr. General Secretary," the president said, "we can accept your proposal. We agree to the elimination of short-range as well as medium-range missiles.

"But I have a better proposal." The president slid the deck of three-by-five briefing cards into his pocket. "You and I have both talked about what a wonderful thing it would be if we could agree to rid the world of the specter of nuclear destruction, if we could lift from the shoulders of mankind the burden of carrying arsenals of mass destruction.

"I know that's always seemed like a utopian dream. But why are we here if not to dream? What is our job if not to convert dreams into reality?

"That's why I say this: Why stop with medium- and short-range missiles? We've been proposing a fifty-percent reduction in the number of strategic weapons on both sides. Why stop with fifty percent?

"Mr. General Secretary," the president continued, his voice rising with emotion, "let us undertake to dream the impossible dream. Let us agree to eliminate all nuclear weapons."

Winthrop's face went white. The American note-taker paused, his pen frozen to the paper tablet in his hand. The interpreter's eyes widened. Had they heard correctly? Was the president of the United States proposing a total nuclear disarmament?

Novikov leaned forward in his seat, a satisfied grin on his face. "Mr. President," he said slowly, "the total elimination of nuclear weapons has been the policy of the Soviet Union for many years. We never believed that you or your allies would agree to such a scheme. We have listened for years to the excuses with which this Soviet position has been rejected by the United States.

"Now, the world will learn we've been sincere. We are ready to rid the world of nuclear weapons through a program of immediate radical cuts.

"Mr. President, we believe we should strive for total, comprehensive nuclear disarmament by the year 2000. In fact, we can move sooner than that. With goodwill on both sides, we believe this can be accomplished within three to five years. We are ready, Mr. President—we are ready to act."

Anthony Winthrop sat stunned. An agreement of incalculable importance was taking shape—an agreement he knew in the depths of his soul was fraught with danger of historic proportions. It was one thing to gamble with mainstream agreements, the kind that made minor adjustments of a political or military nature: a few more missiles here or a few less there, an abstention at the UN, a regional settlement somewhere in Africa—none of that mattered very much. But what of cosmic changes? For those, one would want to be certain. And Anthony Winthrop was anything but certain. He riffled the pages of the briefing book, but even as he raced from tab to tab, he knew there was no entry to cover the situation, no cautionary memo to deflect the president from his course. And what if—*what if the Soviets didn't mean it?* What if they'd decided to cheat already? He knew all too well there was no way to verify compliance with an agreement eliminating *all* nuclear weapons. No way. A million inspectors couldn't begin to do it. Nuclear warheads were small . . . some would fit in a small suitcase. Finding them all? It would be impossible.

He dashed off another note: *Can't verify no nukes.* He pressed it into the president's hand.

The president took the folded sheet and glanced at it quickly. Then he crushed it in his hand and shoved it into his jacket pocket. "Mr. General Secretary, I want to be certain we mean the same thing," he said, speaking rapidly and excitedly. "We are agreeing to eliminate all nuclear weapons of all types, land-, air- and sea-based, strategic and tactical. And we will do so within, should we say, three years? Is that agreed between us?"

Novikov nodded.

"Yes." The president stood up and walked to the seated Soviet leader. He extended his hand. Novikov rose awkwardly. The president took Novikov's hand and pumped it vigorously. "Mr. General Secretary, the world will not be disappointed at what we have done here."

"We will have to work out a great many details," Novikov said solemnly.

"There's time," the president replied. "There's time."

"Mr. President," the Soviet said, "two thousand years ago the great Chinese philosopher Sun Tzu wrote, 'The first factor in war is moral influence.' Today, you and I can say with assurance that the first factor in peace is also moral influence. Today, Mr. President, we have earned our place in history through the exertion of moral influence."

Winthrop, sitting motionless, was jolted. Sun Tzu—he'd heard that name before. That was the Chinese philosopher McCandless had quoted—something about Novikov's office. He couldn't quite remember, but it had something to do with warfare. Or tactics. Or deception. Dammit—he couldn't remember.

Novikov still had the president's hand in his own. "Mr. President," he said, "I propose we take a brief recess. With so much accomplished so quickly, we will both benefit from a chance to confer with our advisers."

"Oh, yes," the president said. "That's fine with me."

From his vantage point in the living room, Waterman saw the doors to the library open, and the president, accompanied by four Secret Service agents, head for the stairs. The secretary of state followed. He was so pale Waterman thought he might be having a heart attack.

"Fast," Winthrop said urgently. "Upstairs."

The American delegation office filled rapidly with advisers. The president grinned amiably. The secretary of state looked tense and uncomfortable but nevertheless managed a forced smile. The two men sat in two easy chairs near the window. Everyone else stood facing them, notepads at the ready.

The secretary of state spoke. "We have just completed an extraordinary session with the general secretary. I can get right to the bottom line by saying Mr. Novikov has agreed to a proposal by the president to eliminate all nuclear weapons from the arsenals of the United States and the Soviet Union, and to do so within three years."

There was an audible gasp, followed by a stunned silence. No one moved. No one spoke. The color drained from Waterman's face. General Wallace stood motionless at attention. Even Bennet, Wellbeck, and Lanier, who stood together to Winthrop's right, were clearly shocked by what was, in the annals of diplomacy, an event without precedent. Alan Kirkwell's mouth was moving as he recited silently to himself the phrases that might go into the press announcement.

It was Gary Burner who broke the silence with a bellow that reverberated through the small room. "Congratulations, Mr. President. What a fantastic, incredible accomplishment! No one would've believed it."

"Well, we're not home yet, Gary," the president said. "As Tony says, there's a lot to be worked out. Novikov proposed a short recess. I guess he thought things were moving awfully fast—and I suppose they were. Golly, we've been at this disarmament business for years without getting half this far. I mean, we did more in an hour and a half than we've managed in all the years since World War Two."

"Mr. President," the NSC adviser asked, "how are you going to proceed? This session only has another twenty minutes to run. Are you going to talk details, or do you want an expert group to start on the details while you and the general secretary continue talking in broad terms? Do you want simply to work toward a joint communiqué that lays out the principle and says that further negotiations will take place in diplomatic channels? We need some guidance."

Waterman felt a knot forming in his stomach. His mouth was dry. He was short of breath. Please, God, he thought, let the Old Man go for general principles. Don't get into details.

"Tony"—the president turned to his secretary of state—"what do you think—about proceeding, I mean?"

"Mr. President, I think we shouldn't attempt to go much beyond what's been said already. A general expression of agreement would seem to be enough. There's no time to work details, so there's not much point in going beyond the general formula."

Waterman spoke up. "What about strategic defenses, Mr. President? Was anything agreed on defensive systems?"

"SDI never came up," the president said. "Either they've abandoned the position that they won't limit nukes unless we give up SDI or they're waiting to raise it later. I think it's a pretty good sign that Novikov didn't raise it."

"I hope, sir," Waterman said, "that if Novikov raises SDI, you'll tell him there can't possibly be an objection to our continuing work on defenses as a kind of insurance against cheating. After all, if there are no offenses, there's no need to fear defenses."

The president beamed. "That's exactly what I'd planned to say, Michael. That's the argument Jim's been making for months. It's even in the talking points." He looked at the secretary of state. "I suppose that means that I have permission to say it?" The president laughed.

Winthrop coughed. "Mr. President, you should know that we've got a huge verification problem on our hands. Take the elimination of small nuclear warheads. We have no way of verifying whether they have, in fact, been disposed of or not."

"But, Tony, those weapons would be the last to go. We'd start with the big land-based missiles and submarines. As our confidence grew, then we'd go on to the smaller stuff. And of course we'll have SDI as a backup—that's crucial."

The secretary of state nodded. "But even so, Mr. President, the risks—"

"You know," the president interrupted, "Novikov said something important this morning. He quoted that old Chinese philosopher—Confucius—who said, 'Moral influence is the key to peace.' And the chairman went even further. He vindicated my historic strong positions about the Soviets, when he told me it was *American* moral influence that had brought about this change in world history." The president looked over at his secretary of state. "Didn't he, Tony?"

Winthrop blinked. "I think, Mr. President, what General Secretary Novikov was trying to say was—"

The president cut him off. "I know what he was trying to say. He was telling me that it's taken a long time to get to the point where the world's superpowers could talk realistically about getting rid of all nuclear weapons." He leaned forward in his chair and looked the secretary of state right in the eyes. "I know about risks, Tony. But we're not going to achieve anything if we don't take risks."

Waterman's gut was churning. Confucius quotations about moral influence? What the hell had happened in there—had they been reading fortune cookies to one another? This was Waterman's worst nightmare. He'd achieved a coveted place at the table, but he was powerless to deflect the president from his course. He was only an assistant secretary, free to comment when asked, maybe even to intervene on technical subjects wholly within the competence of the Pentagon. But this! How could he tell the president of the United States that the risk he was about to take was too great? He stood quietly, biting his tongue.

He looked at the others. Winthrop's discomfort was clear. NSC adviser Wallace's pasty face betrayed no emotion. But the way he cracked his knuckles, pulling on each finger in order, betrayed inner tension. Only Gary Burner, whose considerations stopped at the political, looked smug.

Even Dan Bennet, standing silently, his arms folded across his blue pin-striped vest, appeared to be unnerved by what he was hearing.

Waterman's reverie was interrupted by the secretary of state. "Sir," Winthrop said, "we'd better go back downstairs and wrap up this session. After lunch at the embassy we're due back here at three-thirty for the afternoon session. The staff will stay here—I think they've got their work cut out for them."

He looked at the NSC adviser. "Mitch," he said through clenched teeth, "we should pull together a 'next steps' paper the president can see before the afternoon session. Rather more has happened this morning than any of us anticipated."

The president got up and, with Winthrop close behind, headed downstairs to the study.

General Wallace spoke up as soon as the door had closed. "Incredible." He paused. "Well, I think the tasking from the secretary's pretty clear. Let's take a few minutes—say, half an hour—to digest what we've just heard. Then we'll start working on the 'next steps' drill. And let me emphasize that there will be no backgrounding, no whispering, no mention whatsoever—to anyone, under any circumstances—about what you've just heard in here."

Waterman quietly left the room and walked down the stairs. Heading for the front door, he paused to retrieve his coat, gloves, and a heavy wool scarf. Outside, braced by the cold, he pulled his collar up and headed past the phalanx of waiting reporters to the line of limos parked along the road leading to the house. The snow had stopped, and the skies were beginning to clear. The morning darkness had given way to a pale northern winter light. He got in the front seat of car number six. The driver had kept the engine running to keep warm.

"I have to go to Järvenpää station."

CHAPTER TWENTY-TWO

Järvenpää Station, December 16, 12:20 P.M.

The modern concert hall next to the station swarmed with reporters, its salons and corridors having been turned into an international press center. Hoping to avoid encountering anyone who might know him, Waterman walked briskly from the car, his collar up and head scrunched down. Inside, he looked for signs pointing to the makeshift café—just a few tables set up in the waiting room. It was crowded with press and sightseers. He peered around and spied Parisi at a table in the corner, munching on a sandwich and sipping beer.

"I'd have ordered you some lunch," Parisi said, "but I didn't know you'd be making social calls."

"Jay, this is no social call. The shit just hit the fan."

"When shit hits a fan, it is never randomly distributed." Parisi took a huge bite of the sandwich. "Sit down, Michael."

"Dammit, Jay, stop eating." Waterman pulled out the chair and dropped into it. He peered at what sat on the oval platter in front of his friend, who was paying him no mind. "What the hell is that, anyway?"

"You've heard of a Reuben? Well this is a Rudolph—reindeer and cheese on rye with mustard and mayo." Parisi saw the look on Waterman's face. He set the sandwich back on the plate. "What's happened?"

"Things are spinning out of control up there," Waterman said. "Take down what I'm going to say. You'll have to draft a message and get it sent."

Speaking rapidly but with precision, Waterman filled Parisi in on the morning's session. Parisi took careful notes as Waterman spoke.

"Jay, you've got to get this summary to the SECDEF, ASAP. Use McCandless's backchannel. Get Bill Collins on the phone and let him know it's coming. And copy the entire message to McCandless, Eyes Only, with this addition: Ask him to send me by return immediate cable the quotation from Sun Tzu that Novikov keeps on the wall of his office. Make sure someone's standing by to receive it. And beep me when the message has been received in Washington."

"What's the Sun Tzu business all about?"

"The president said Novikov quoted Confucius to him. I just can't believe that. Besides, we know Novikov used to keep a quote from Sun Tzu on his office wall. McCandless even read it to the president once—at an NSPG meeting a few months ago. The Old Man ignored it at the time. So this morning, Novikov threw another Chinese quote at him. Maybe I can jog his memory with the Sun Tzu quote from McCandless—it's about strategic deception, and I think it reflects the Soviet position pretty accurately." Waterman rose. "Gotta split."

"You're going back to Ainola?"

"Right away. There's a meeting in"—he looked at his watch—"less than ten minutes. I've got to try to slow things down. They'll probably discuss strategic defenses this afternoon. I'm praying the Old Man hangs tough, and Novikov overplays his hand. Maybe Winthrop will help."

"Winthrop?"

Waterman nodded. "Winthrop. I could see he was shaken; I've never seen him so taut. He knows that total nuclear disarmament is loony tunes. NATO will come unglued. The Chinese will go berserk. God knows what the Congress would do. There's no way it can be verified. The Sovs will cheat—hell, even Mother Teresa would cheat under the same conditions. We'd have a crisis on our hands that not even the State Department's smoke and mirrors will be able to obscure."

Parisi shook his head. "What a disaster."

Waterman nodded agreement. "And it's happening right now in a Finnish composer's country study."

Waterman stood up. He reached down, picked up Parisi's sandwich, and took a big bite.

"Not bad for a Rudolph," he said, snatching a napkin and wiping his mouth. "But don't count on much for Christmas. You've blown it with Santa."

. . .

By the time Waterman got back to Ainola, the morning session was over, and the president had already departed for the embassy. The last item discussed between the two leaders had been what to make public of the morning's discussion. To Waterman's great relief—and Gary Burner's immense anguish—they had agreed to say nothing. Alan Kirkwell confirmed it: Despite a barrage of questions shouted at them as they left, the two leaders departed Ainola without making any comment. It was, for Waterman, a tiny glimmer of hope: Once announced publicly, an agreement of such importance would be impossible to reverse.

On instructions from the president and Winthrop, the advisers began to pull together a paper on the issues that would need to be resolved before a general "agreement in principle" on total nuclear disarmament could be turned into a workable treaty.

Even before Waterman joined the discussion, the list was long: definitions, phasing, timing, verification, safeguards, the future of nonnuclear forces, third world countries, systems capable of carrying both nuclear and conventional warheads, treaty monitoring, withdrawal provisions, resolution of disputes—it went on forever. Agreements in principle were one thing, treaties quite another.

The postlunch strategy meeting with the president was chaotic, jammed into less than an hour between his return to Ainola and the start of the afternoon session. Issues that deserved serious discussion were reduced to ten-second quips and slogans. It was sound-bite diplomacy of the most dangerous sort. It seemed to Waterman the president didn't want to hear anything that might complicate the completion of a looming disaster.

Helsinki, December 16, 8:20 P.M.

It was windy and bitter cold by the time the motorcade returned to the Inter-Continental. Even the short walk from the limo to the main entrance—six cars back was well outside the protection of the canopy at the entrance—was enough to make Waterman's ears hurt. He was waiting for the elevator when the beeper in his pocket began to vibrate. Parisi was trying to reach him. He punched the "up" button a second time reflexively, knowing it wouldn't hasten the arrival of the elevator. He stopped at the control room on the eighth floor to pick up his room key from the Secret Service agent who oversaw keys and classified material. The agent handed him a thick wad of messages. With the exception of a message from Laura asking him to call, they were all from reporters covering the summit. They knew there was a gag rule in effect, but thought it worth a try anyway. Waterman was sure there was at least as large a pile of press calls waiting for the others. He shuddered to think of Bennet or Wellbeck breaking Wallace's rules and backgrounding them. Any remaining hope for turning things around would vanish if word of the day's negotiation leaked.

Inside his room he dumped his coat, briefcase, papers, and messages on the living-room sofa and went straight to the phone. He dialed. Parisi answered.

"Jay, I just got back," Waterman said. "Can you get over here and fill me in?"

"I'm on my way. Order me a beer."

"If you've got a copy of the stuff that went out, bring it along."

It took Parisi less than ten minutes to arrive, a wad of cables in his hand.

"Here—this went out at fifteen fifty-five. Bill called at sixteen-forty to say it was in the secretary's hands. McCandless's special assistant called to acknowledge that an 'Eyes Only' was delivered to the DCI at sixteen-fifteen. That's all Helsinki time." Waterman read the messages while Parisi took a beer from the minibar.

"There's a tin of foie gras in the bag on the table," Waterman said. "Open it, and I'll join you."

"You wanna talk about Act Two?" Parisi asked.

Waterman groaned. "You won't believe this," he said, "but it actually got worse. The only thing that saved us is they ran out of time. If we'd had another hour, we might actually have something in writing. As it happens, they spent most of the afternoon on SDI, and the mood began to sour a little."

"You mean—"

"Only a little. Not enough to derail the train that roared through this morning. Novikov demanded that we abandon SDI as part of the deal. The president argued SDI would be harmless, except as a hedge against cheating. They went round and round."

"So how did they resolve things?"

"They didn't. They agreed to continue tomorrow morning. They revised the agenda to allow time for it. Novikov said he could settle for agreement not to deploy SDI for ten years if we agreed to limit research and development to laboratory experiments and to ban testing in space."

"Jesus."

"During a recess we met with the president. He wanted to know whether we could continue the SDI program under those circumstances. I told him it would be impossible. He was clearly troubled. Then goddam Dan Bennet said they had done some work on that issue, and *he* believed SDI could continue even with the restrictions Novikov was demanding. He's apparently convinced himself that total nuclear disarmament is just what the world needs right now, and he's willing to go to the mat to defend his point of view." He snorted. "Just what I needed, right? Christ, neither Wallace nor Winthrop said anything. So I wound up having to argue with Bennet."

"Black-hat Waterman rides again," said Parisi.

"But not alone. I did get a little help from Moore. He's no fan of SDI—but he's honest. He said he personally would be prepared to give up SDI, but he doubted we could keep the program going if we couldn't test in space. And in a sense Winthrop and Wallace were helpful just by saying nothing. It's a slender reed—but the president's dream of a strategic defense may, just may, be enough to save us."

Parisi smeared a cracker with foie gras and put it in his mouth. "What about the rest of the agenda?"

"It's pretty clear they won't get around to discussing human rights, regional issues—or anything else."

Parisi shook his head. "So—either way we lose. If this deal goes forward, we're screwed. If it falls through, we're still screwed—we'll have opened ourselves to a massive worldwide propaganda campaign—how the Americans, fanatically devoted to SDI, refused to free the planet from the scourge of nuclear weapons. Even worse, the Soviet Army and the KGB will have proven their hard line works—they'll have shown the American president is ready to deal away our nuclear deterrent."

Waterman nodded. "You know, I think Novikov's one of them, completely comfortable with the Old Guard—as long as they're personally loyal to him. For all the talk of *perestroika,* he's a Communist to the soles of his feet. His reforms are intended to save the system, not replace it.

"I got into an argument with Bennet over where Novikov's heart is—with the reformers, neutral, or against; in favor of the bloated military budget, or against. But I don't give a damn where his heart is; I don't care about his head, either: It's his hand I'm interested in—the hand that signs the directives and approves the budget."

Waterman poured himself a mineral water and gulped it down. "There's one bright spot—Winthrop's worried. He knows we're in trouble. He's agreed to see me at seven tomorrow in his suite."

"I should probably cancel my dinner with Øve and young Marensky and stick around to help."

"No point," Waterman said dejectedly. "Besides, maybe you can pick up something useful at dinner—Marensky could have something to say."

Parisi looked at his watch. "Then I'd better get moving." He grabbed his parka from the bed. "Look, I'll swing by later if there's anything to report."

"Where you going, by the way?"

"The Alexander Nevski. Øve says it's the best Russian food in Helsinki."

"*Das veedahnya,*" Waterman said as Parisi closed the door behind him.

Waterman retrieved the briefcase phone and set it up on the desk in the living room. Then he took the crypto key from the inside pocket of his suit and inserted it in the compact instrument. In a moment he had Bill Collins on the line.

"We're in the clear, Bill," he said as he studied the green light on the control panel. "You ready to go secure?"

"Ready," Bill answered.

"I'll go first," Waterman said. He turned the crypto key halfway to the right. "Okay—now you turn yours." He watched the light and waited. In a few seconds it went red. The secure circuit had been established.

"Bill, can you hear me?" Waterman asked.

"The sucker works." Bill's voice came through the headset. "We're secure. Can you hear me?"

"Perfectly," Waterman replied.

"The boss is apoplectic. He wants to talk to you—I've got him standing by. Hang on while I get him."

"Michael?"

"Mr. Secretary."

"Thanks for the message. What more can you tell me?"

Ryder listened without comment as Waterman briefed him on the afternoon session.

"What's your sense of where Winthrop's headed?" the secretary asked. "You really think there's a chance he might help slow this down?" There was a note of incredulity in his voice.

"I can't be sure," Waterman replied. "I know he was uncomfortable. For example, the president seemed impatient—even annoyed—when we gave him a long list of issues that would have to be studied and negotiated before we'd arrive at a treaty. Winthrop seemed almost relieved. My guess is he doesn't want to be out there by himself."

"I suspect you're right," Ryder said. "Maybe we can complicate the picture by introducing some facts."

"I was about to put together a short paper—just a page of key points— on the technical impossibility of carrying out SDI under Novikov's conditions. It would help a lot if you could make sure the Joint Chiefs don't comment separately. That could really undercut your position, and I wouldn't put it past State to go to them for a dissenting view."

"I'll have a word with the chairman," Ryder said. "Look, you'll need all the ammunition you can get. I'm going to send you a copy of the note I got from McCandless—the one I showed you—on the secure fax. But you'll have to be extraordinarily careful using it. You mustn't discuss it, not even in the bubble. I'll write a note to the president saying I've asked you to bring it to him. Let him read it. But be careful not to talk about it. There's a life at stake, and I don't want to learn later that the room in which it was discussed was insecure. We've got to keep reminding the president we're not dealing with the Chevy Chase Garden Club."

"That should help," Waterman said. "The president was really rooting for the young guy. He'll be furious to know what happened to him—how we were had."

"It won't be enough, but it's all we've got right now." There was a pause. Then Ryder's voice resumed. "You know, Michael, the president's had this thing about total nuclear disarmament for years. There was never an occasion to argue it out—it was always so farfetched. I wish we'd had to confront it sooner. . . ." His voice trailed off, and for a long moment Waterman thought the connection had been broken. Then the SECDEF spoke again. "One last thing. If we fail to dissuade the president, if he's determined to go ahead, I want you to try to do two things. First, keep any statement as general as possible, so we can seek some protection later in the details. Second, I want you to give the president your full support. We may think what he's doing is unwise, but he's the president. We'll use all the influence we can muster. But when his mind's made up . . . so is ours."

"Understood, sir."

"When will you be back in touch?"

"I'm having breakfast with Winthrop tomorrow morning. It'll be the middle of the night in Washington. . . ."

"Call me as soon as you see him. Whether he's alarmed enough to help is crucial. Don't worry about waking me up—I don't expect to do much sleeping tonight anyway."

CHAPTER
TWENTY-THREE

Helsinki, December 16, 9:55 P.M.

Øve Anders was already seated at a cramped table for four in a small private room as Jay Parisi threaded his way through the crowded main salon of the Alexander Nevski.

"Ah, Jay," Anders said, rising to greet him. "I'm glad you've come."

"Sorry to be late, roommate."

"Not to worry. The others are running behind, too. Alexi just called to say he'd be late. So let's have a drink." He summoned the waiter, a rather stiff but efficient-looking fellow whom Parisi had seen ferrying back and forth to the kitchen carrying heavy trays of marinated salmon, pickled garlic, beets, lamb's tongue, smoked fish, eggs, caviar, and black bread—the traditional *zakuski*, a variation on the Scandinavian smorgasbord brought back to Russia by Peter the Great.

"This is quite a place," Parisi said, looking around. "Were those the old czar's eagles in the windows?"

"Romanov double eagles—the imperial crest—made from stained glass. And the best Russian food in Helsinki." He spoke to the waiter in rapid-fire Russian. "Let's see if they live up to their reputation tonight." He winked at Parisi. "You know, Indian food is better in London than New Delhi, English cuisine is better in New York than London, and I can assure you that Russian cooking is better in Helsinki than in Moscow. This is also

Alexi Marensky's favorite place, which is why we're here. It's sort of a reunion, really."

"Oh?"

"Alexi's bringing an old friend—an American named Andrew Weston."

"What does he do?"

"Weston? Professor at Stanford—advanced Soviet studies."

"Is he here for the summit?"

"Don't know," Anders said. "I've seen him in Moscow once or twice— he runs an exchange program, so he gets there a lot." He drained the red vodka in the glass in front of him.

Parisi did the same. It burned his throat. "That's terrific. What the hell is it?"

"Pertsovka," said Anders. "Vodka flavored with chile peppers."

Parisi refilled his glass from the bottle, which was embedded in a block of ice. *"Nazdrovya."*

Anders returned the toast.

They were well into their third Pertsovka when Marensky arrived with the American, a tall, ruddy man who wore a Russian fur cap at a rakish angle.

"Andrew, Alexi, meet Jay Parisi, visiting from the States," said Anders, rising to make the introductions. He stepped out from behind the heavily laden table and embraced the newcomers. "We go back a long time," the Norwegian said, enfolding Marensky in a massive bear hug.

"I understand you're from Stanford," Parisi said to Weston. "You here to research the summit?"

Weston winced as he swallowed his vodka in a gulp. "Actually, I'm here at the invitation of the secretary of state. Dan Bennet, his top aide, is an old friend. We were roommates at Dartmouth. Since I've spent a fair amount of time in Moscow, I was put on the American delegation as an adviser. How about you?"

Parisi sensed Anders was about to say something about room-sharing, so he cut the Norwegian off. "Oh, no, just a tourist. I always wanted to see this part of the world, and I had to use a bunch of frequent-flyer miles. Did you know that in the off-season it's only thirty thousand miles' credit for a first-class round trip here?" He peered at Marensky. "You part of the official Soviet delegation?"

"My father is. I work as an editor at a sociological journal. In the Soviet Union that means a political journal as well. I'm writing about the summit."

"You're not the only one," Anders said. "But news is moving like molasses. There hasn't been a word from Ainola. We've all been reduced to studying videotape of Novikov and the president entering and leaving to see whether they're smiling." He fixed the Russian with a wry smile. "You didn't happen to bring any Russian-speaking lip-readers with you?"

Marensky didn't take the bait. "I wish I had," he said. "But I don't know any more than you. My father spent the whole day at Ainola—I only saw him for a few minutes at the hotel, and he was racing to get ready for the official dinner—and he didn't tell me anything. But I can say he was smiling, if that's any help."

"Dan Bennet was smiling, too," said Weston. "I saw him just before I left to meet you, Alexi."

"Did *he* say anything?" Anders asked. "I've got editors waiting by the phone in Oslo ready to pounce on any scrap."

"Nope. Just that it had been a productive day. You know how diplomats are—never a careless word."

"It must be exciting," Parisi said, "being at the summit."

"Unbelievable," Weston said. "Getting to watch as history's made." He slapped Alexi on the back. "We'll have stories for the grandchildren, won't we, old friend?"

The troika of old Moscow hands fell easily into a conversation about mutual friends, the political landscape in Moscow, the problems of daily life in the Soviet capital. After almost an hour of vodka and *zakuski*, followed by an entrée intriguingly labeled "roast bear in pot" and two bottles of a strong red Azerbaijani wine called Matrassa, Parisi saw that Marensky was becoming increasingly troubled and preoccupied.

Anders looked at his old friend and poured some wine. "Tell me, Alexi, is it true—and I have this on good sources—that Novikov's planning to appoint a group of hard-liners to the Politburo?"

"If he does," the Soviet said, "it will be a mistake for which the whole world will pay."

"What about Novikov?" Parisi asked. "What sort of man is he?"

"Once, probably our best hope," Marensky said morosely, draining his glass. "He knew how badly we'd failed, how much needed to be done. He gave us our first real breath of fresh air since the great patriotic war— World War Two, as you call it. Oh, it's true there was more talk of reform than action. But that was only to be expected. After all, the party apparatus and the bureaucracy fought him from the very beginning."

"You're talking about him in the past tense. Are you saying he's changed?"

"A good question, Jay." Marensky held his glass out for more. Parisi obliged him. "I don't know. Our problems are so deep. . . .

"You know, Andrew," he said, turning to Weston, "you made a big mistake when you didn't jump on Novikov at the first sign that things were slipping. He's a man who responds to pressure."

"But, Alexi," Weston interrupted, "you and I both know that the Soviet Union has never historically responded to pressure."

"Maybe that was the case with Stalin," Marensky said. "But Kennedy learned fast enough. After Khrushchev steamrolled him in Vienna, he developed backbone for what you in the West call the Cuban Missile Crisis. That convinced Khrushchev the Americans meant business." He gulped a glass of vodka. "I could give you chapter and verse—but forget that. It's Novikov we're talking about. Novikov's a different case altogether. With some people it's a question of who talked to them last. With Novikov it's who talks the loudest. God, if you only knew how much leverage you've got. Novikov needs you. He needs Western capital, Western know-how, Western technology. He needs the West to avert its eyes while he tightens up on the growing nationalism."

"He needs time to develop *perestroika* and *glasnost*," Weston insisted.

"Bullshit!" Marensky slapped his hand on the table. "Novikov is a political animal. He grew up as a protégé of Andropov, the man who headed the KGB. He understands that if the West is soft, he can be hard, but if you're tough, he'll have to be pliable."

Parisi listened, fascinated. Here was the son of a senior Soviet diplomat, virtually pleading with two Americans and a Norwegian to be tough on the general secretary of the Communist party of the USSR. It was true he'd drunk his share of the wine and vodka. But it was extraordinary all the same. Certainly, it would make an interesting—perhaps even significant—report for Waterman.

It was well after midnight when Anders suggested they adjourn to the bar of the Kalastajatorppa Hotel. Parisi demurred, saying he was tired.

"If you don't mind, I think I'll turn in," he said. "I'm still a little jet-lagged." He tried to cover his share of what he was certain was a substantial bill, but Anders wouldn't hear of it. "You're the guests of *Aftenposten*," he said.

The Norwegian surveyed the table, laden with empty wine and vodka bottles. "My expense account'll describe all this as research materials," he said with a wink.

Helsinki, December 17, 1:00 A.M.

Waterman was puzzled. He studied the blue trip book closely. No Weston. No Andrew anything, for that matter. "But the name, Jay—the name. I know the name."

"He told me he'd been invited by the secretary of state," Parisi said. "And I'm certain he said he was Dan Bennet's roommate at Dartmouth."

"Of course!" Waterman cried. "That's the guy who came back from Moscow saying Novikov wanted a summit. He's a big pal of Yuri Marensky's, and a big apologist for Novikov. It's gotta be the same one."

"Uh-huh," Parisi said. "But he's not Yuri's friend, he's Alexi's—the son. He goes to Moscow all the time. From the way they were jabbering, he's conversational in Russian. He's obviously—"

"Jay," Waterman interrupted. "Listen—at the meeting when the president agreed to a summit, the backchannel was an Andrew Weston. But the only thing Winthrop told the president about Weston was that he was a professor friend of Yuri Marensky's who got to Moscow on a regular basis, and that he'd been used as a diplomatic backchannel before. Now he turns out to be Dan Bennet's college roommate. And he turns up here—but not on the official deregulation list."

"Well, if he's Yuri's friend, he never mentioned it. This guy is an asshole buddy of Alexi—the son. Evidently, they met when Yuri was ambassador here and stayed close ever since."

"You're a trained intelligence officer. Do you see a setup?"

Parisi wrinkled his forehead. "I just don't see . . ."

"I'll draw it," Waterman said. "Bennet used Weston to set up the summit. Winthrop told the president the idea was Novikov's. I'll bet Weston told Marensky the idea was the president's."

"Sure." Parisi shook his head. "It was a no-lose situation so far as Bennet was concerned: If Novikov said no, no one would have known. But he said yes—and look where we are tonight."

Helsinki, December 17, 7:55 A.M.

Waterman reread the handwritten memo to make sure there were no important errors. Finding none, he extended it toward Parisi, who stood by the door fumbling with a handful of double-A batteries and Waterman's beeper. "Here—get moving."

Parisi tucked the message under his arm while he shoved the beeper and batteries into the pocket of his hooded parka. Securing the message in his breast pocket, he pulled on fur-lined gloves and opened the door. "I'll see you at the station café," he said. "I'm going to stop by my hotel to change clothes after I send this." Parisi had spent the night on Waterman's couch.

"Let me call you a cab."

"Don't need one. Got a car waiting outside."

"Car?"

"Biggest Mercedes stretch limo you've ever seen. How else does a tourist get around Finland in the dead of winter? Pulled by Dasher, Dancer, Donner, and Blitzen?"

Waterman was dubious. "Who's paying?"

"Cabs are unreliable," Parisi said. "And the train to Järvenpää station never runs on time."

"But who's paying?"

"It's only four hundred bucks a day—plus overtime."

"Jay, who's paying?" Waterman asked again.

"You are, sir," Parisi answered. "I charged it to your Gold Card."

Waterman never even considered how Parisi had got the number. "Why of course . . . how stupid of me. When the bill comes in, and Laura says, 'What's this two thousand bucks for limo service?' I'll just tell her Finnish trains and taxis are unreliable."

"You can tell her it was your contribution to save the Free World."

"I gave at the office." Waterman looked at Parisi. "Get the hell out of here."

"Roger, roger." He cracked the door open and shook the folder in Waterman's direction. "By the way, is it okay if I read this?"

"Would it make any difference if I said no?" He waved Parisi away. "Shut the door."

"I love you, too." Parisi saw the elevator doors were just closing. He launched himself at the "down" button and caught it just in time. He climbed aboard to see Andrew Weston, bleary-eyed and unshaven, at the back of the crowded elevator standing next to an immaculately attired Dan Bennet. Weston looked as though he'd spent the night sleeping in the clothes he was wearing. He had both hands clutched around Bennet's upper arm. Parisi couldn't make out what they were saying, and he didn't want to be noticed by Bennet. He left the elevator quickly when it reached the lobby and walked briskly out the main entrance, and around the corner to his waiting car.

Once safely ensconced in the back of the limo, Parisi turned on the light and began to read:

Memorandum: Department of Defense
SECRET

TO: The Secretary
FROM: ISP/Michael Waterman
DATE: December 17
SUBJECT: Developments at the Finland Summit

I met this A.M. with SECSTATE. He told me he spent a sleepless night worrying about the turn of events yesterday. He never expected anything like the president's response to Novikov. He told me total nuclear disarmament is a "dangerous leap in the dark." He says he "regrets" having failed to argue against the president's endorsement of a nuclear-free world in his UN speech and on other occasions. He says he thought at the time it would help get the peaceniks off his back without doing any real harm since it was so unrealistic.

I asked whether he would try to get the president to back off. At that point he motioned to me to follow him into the bubble installed in his suite—it houses his secure phone and is not much bigger than a telephone booth.

Once inside he told me he'd tried last night, but the president was "euphoric" at the prospect of going down in history as the man who "removed nuclear weapons from the face of the earth."

I told him I'd be getting a paper showing that SDI couldn't survive the limitations Novikov's insisting on. He said he thought Novikov might settle for fewer restrictions on SDI in order to get us committed to abandoning all nuclear weapons. He promised to make sure I had time to present the facts on SDI at a briefing with the president later this morning.

Winthrop is also worried about NATO reaction to news that we've agreed to abandon nuclear weapons. (He does, incidentally, think that the whole thing will eventually fall apart over verification—but not until after we've destroyed NATO.)

I asked him about our prospects. He said the situation was "grave" and that he "doubted it could be turned around unless Novikov makes a serious mistake in the session this morning."

He also told me that at the formal dinner last night Novikov took the president aside and asked him as a "personal favor" to agree to what he called a moratorium on the human-rights issue. The Soviet said he needed breathing space to deal with the political unrest that the deteriorating economy and his reform program were causing. To Winthrop's dismay, the president agreed, and human rights has been dropped from the agenda. (This will, incidently, free up some additional time for further discussion of arms control.)

I'm sorry to send such a gloomy report. The only good news is that I think Winthrop's with us, at least for the moment.

Forest is beautiful. Wish you were here.

Helsinki, December 17, 8:35 A.M.

The incoming traffic from Washington was waiting by the time Parisi arrived at the CIA station. He put the double-sealed envelope in his pocket, handed Waterman's memo over for transmission, then headed back to his hotel.

Parisi saw the note as soon as he entered the hotel room. It was written in Magic Marker and taped to the headboard of his bed.

JAY—URGENT!! URGENT!!! YOU CONTACT ME IMMEDIATELY AT AFTENPOSTEN HELSINKI BUREAU, TELEPHONE 142-864. ØVE.

Reflexively, Parisi grabbed the bedside phone and dialed the number. He got a busy signal. "Damn," he said. "Okay, Øve—I tried." He stuffed the note in his parka pocket, changed clothes faster than Clark Kent, grabbed his electric razor, and was out the door in three and a half minutes.

Helsinki, December 17, 8:45 A.M.

The snowy reflection of flashing red and white lights from motorcycle outriders and security vehicles resembled an onstage thunderstorm as the motorcade taking the American delegation to Ainola moved rapidly down the deserted highway.

Waterman read through press clippings faxed from Washington. The *Times* and the *Post* were thin on hard news, although both gave extensive coverage of the toasts at the dinner hosted by the president of Finland. Waterman breathed a sigh of relief. Despite the presence of five thousand journalists, the press had failed to ferret out the summit's truly astonishing developments. For whatever reason—perhaps they feared that premature exposure would lead to pressure on the president to back away from the position he'd taken on Tuesday—the Soviets had kept to the agreement not to go public. Even better, Dan Bennet had kept his mouth shut.

By 8:45 the delegation arrived at Ainola and assembled quickly in the upstairs delegation office to discuss strategy for the final negotiating session between the leaders. Mitchell Wallace, in his most officious manner, announced that the president had decided to defer any discussion of human rights. "The president and the general secretary spoke privately last night at dinner and agreed we'd prepare for a midyear summit at which human rights and other issues will be discussed," he said. Then he dropped a real bomb: "The president wants to leave ample time to conclude the arms-control portion of the current discussions. In light of the amount of work remaining, he and General Secretary Novikov have decided to extend this summit with an additional afternoon session."

Waterman's heart sank.

"What about SDI?" he asked numbly.

"We'll want to discuss that at ten. He'll want to hear the pros and cons. Michael, I'd like you and Dan to take the leads on that issue. Boil your points down to five minutes apiece."

Five minutes, Waterman thought. Five lousy minutes to dispose of the nation's most important strategic program. His anger rose as he thought back to the countless hours of work he'd put in on strategic defenses—the days and nights away from his wife and child; the meetings, conferences, testimony; the articles, backgrounders, cables, deadlines. All that effort, he thought—only to have it scuttled here in nanoseconds.

"What about verification?" Waterman asked. "We've got to talk about that. And NATO. Surely the president will want to hear about the implications for NATO?"

The national security adviser cut Waterman off. "This is neither the time nor the place for micromanagement, Michael. We're here to support the president, not complicate matters."

Waterman's contempt for Wallace welled up. What the president needed most of all from his national security adviser was honesty and clarity. Saluting was what Mitchell Wallace did best.

"I'll be back," Waterman said. He turned on his heel and left.

Järvenpää Station, December 17, 9:30 A.M.

Waterman climbed out of the car at the Järvenpää station and was about to head for the café when he felt a hand on his shoulder. It was Parisi.

"Let's talk in my car."

Waterman followed Parisi to the station parking lot, where an enormous stretch limo occupied two spaces, its liveried driver standing at attention as they approached.

Waterman whistled, impressed. "Now that I've seen it, I feel better—this is a steal at four hundred bucks a day," he kidded Parisi.

They climbed into the cavernous passenger compartment. Parisi took three sheets of paper from his pocket. There was a crisp, clear, well-composed set of key points on the impact of Novikov's proposals about SDI. It bore out Waterman's seat-of-the-pants advice that SDI couldn't go forward under the Novikov restrictions. Thank God for Scott Bracken, he thought. The second sheet held the quotation from Sun Tzu that sat above Novikov's desk. The third was a facsimile of the note from McCandless to Ryder relating the fate of the would-be defector, Kostiv. Three slim arrows in Waterman's quiver.

"Good work," Waterman said.

"I was shocked," Parisi said. "I had no idea—"

"None of us had."

"What are you gonna to do?"

"I wish I knew," Waterman said. "God, Jay, I just feel terrible."

"Speaking of terrible," Parisi said, "I saw Andrew Weston in the elevator this morning, absolutely hanging on to Dan Bennet. He looked in horrible shape."

"He couldn't look worse than I feel," Waterman said. He folded the papers and slipped them in his pocket. "I've gotta get back before they close the road for the president's motorcade. We brief him in about twenty minutes." He tapped his chest where the papers sat. "It's our last shot, Jay."

Ainola, December 17, 10:00 A.M.

This time it was Viktor Novikov who waited at the open door as the president, accompanied by Winthrop and Burner, arrived at Ainola precisely on the hour. The press pool—the reporters and photographers allowed past the security perimeter to a press stand outside the house—numbered a hundred. So hungry for news were they that, even standing in the second-floor bedroom office behind two sets of storm windows, Waterman could hear the barrage of questions as the president emerged from his car, waving his characteristic, convivial two-armed wave to the shouting mob without responding. He paused just long enough to be photographed shaking hands in the doorway.

In his talk with Waterman, Winthrop had described the president as euphoric. Now, as the Old Man literally bounded eagerly into the bedroom office to be briefed, Waterman saw that Winthrop's characterization had been an understatement. The president was exuberant, bubbling over with enthusiasm. He was full of praise for Finland, ebullient about how well he and the general secretary had got along at last night's dinner, delighted about what he called Novikov's "obvious sincerity," and elated by the historic turning point that had been reached the day before.

For half an hour they went through the motions of considering the issues that would dominate the morning session. Then it was Waterman's turn: his five minutes in the spotlight.

Using the memo from Washington, Waterman gave a clear, disciplined exposition about the dire impact of curtailing SDI testing. The bottom line was stark: Without testing in space, there would be no way to demonstrate the feasibility of strategic defense. And without hard proof that SDI worked, Congress would surely reduce—and eventually halt—funding.

He looked around and saw a room full of blank faces. They don't give a damn, he thought. All they want is an agreement—and any agreement will do.

He concluded with the argument he thought most powerful and most likely to influence the president. "Sir," he began, "if we were to sign a treaty promising to eliminate all nuclear weapons, we would implement that pledge absolutely. But it's virtually certain the Soviets would hold some back."

He saw the president nod slightly in agreement and pressed on: "You or your successor would have to face the moment when we destroyed the last remaining nuclear weapon in the American arsenal and Mr. Novikov or his successor informed us that they had done the same. But suppose they cheated. Suppose they squirreled away a few hundred, even a few dozen? What then? Even if we managed to achieve parity of nonnuclear weapons, we'd still be hopelessly vulnerable.

"At the very least, Mr. President," Waterman pleaded, "keep the right to test and deploy SDI as a hedge against Soviet cheating."

Waterman's words obviously made an impression. The president was listening carefully. For a moment it was like the old days, the president nodding at all the right places.

Then his five minutes were up, and Bennet argued the case for accepting limits on SDI. It was a slick presentation, calculated to heighten the president's appetite for a nuclear-free world while relegating the Soviet proposed limits on SDI to a "minor encumbrance that technicians could work around."

Bennet spoke directly to the president, his voice compelling and urgent. "There is no doubt in my mind, sir, that a certain amount of risk is involved here. The Soviets have the capability to cheat—technically, so do we, of course. But at the core of this issue is something that has only been dreamed about ever since the start of the Cold War: peace. Real peace." He cast his eyes around the room. His glance stopped momentarily on Waterman. "I believe we can work around the technicalities and achieve that incredible goal without giving up one iota of our security. I believe, Mr. President, that the end here is worth the means."

Waterman watched Bennet watching him. He knows, Waterman thought—he knows he's won. He raised his hand in the president's direction, so that he could rebut Bennet. "Mr. President—"

Gary Burner broke in quickly. "The president's going to need a minute to compose his thoughts," the chief of staff said. "I don't think we're gonna resolve this technical dispute here anyway. Unless someone has something urgent to say, I think we should adjourn."

"There's something else," Waterman said. He pulled the two remaining sheets of paper from his pocket. "It's important—"

He was interrupted by Burner. "What's important is that the president gather his thoughts together for the earthshaking event that is about to take place."

The president nodded his agreement.

Waterman couldn't believe it. It was over. Finished. Done with. He felt like shouting, screaming.

He didn't. Instead, as the room emptied, he took the secretary of state aside. "I need a minute alone with the president," he pleaded.

"There's no time," Winthrop replied. "He's got to head downstairs right now."

Waterman's left hand held his arrows: the trio of folded documents. He shook them in Winthrop's face. "Mr. Secretary, there's something he's got to know."

"I'm sorry, Michael," Winthrop said. "It's too late."

CHAPTER
TWENTY-FOUR

Järvenpää Station, December 17, 10:30 A.M.

Jay Parisi bundled up against the cold and went for a walk to kill
time. For twenty minutes he watched his footprints in the snow,
lowering his head against the chill easterly wind that swept across
the open space behind the Järvenpää station.

It was getting too cold, he thought as he headed back. He plunged his
gloved hands into his pockets to get a better hunch against the wind and
felt the crushed note from Anders. Damn, he thought, I forgot all about
Øve.

He walked briskly back to the station waiting room, inserted a coin in
the pay telephone near the ticket window, and dialed. The line was busy.
He called three times. Finally, a voice came on the line.

"Hello?"

Before he could say anything else, the phone was loudly set down. He
could hear voices in the background. He waited. "*Aftenposten*—Anders."

"Øve, it's Jay."

"Thank God." The Norwegian spoke quickly in his Scandinavian accent.
"Jay, I have to see you at once. It's a matter of the utmost urgency. Where
are you?"

"In the phone booth at the Järvenpää station."

Anders said something Parisi was sure meant "shit" in Norwegian.

"Stay there," Anders said. "I'll be there as fast as possible."

"Can you say what it's about?" Parisi asked.

"Not on the phone. But I promise you it's vital we speak. I'm on my way."

The phone in Parisi's hand went dead.

Ainola, December 17, 11:15 A.M.

The Soviet and American advisers milled around the living room, drinking coffee and chatting aimlessly while the president and Novikov, together with Winthrop and the Soviet foreign minister, were closeted in the study.

Alone in a corner of the room, Waterman prayed for a recess so he could attempt to gain a brief audience with the president. His hand rested on the quotation from Sun Tzu. Surely, that would jar the president. And he had McCandless's letter to Ryder. How could the president fail to be moved by it? Waterman was sure he'd be enraged to know the Soviets had both deceived him and caused the death of a boy whose only crime was to jump for freedom. But unless there was a break, he'd never have the chance to tell the president.

Järvenpää Station, December 17, 11:30 A.M.

Parisi was looking out the window when a taxi screeched to a halt at the main entrance to the station, the door flew open, and Øve Anders, without coat or hat against the cold, jumped out. Parisi rushed to the curb. The two men walked into the station. "Jay," Anders said, "you've got to get a message to Michael. There's no time to lose."

"What's going on, Øve?"

"Last night, after you left the restaurant, Marensky, Weston, and I went for a drink. Marensky was nervous. I don't know whether you'd noticed."

"Yeah, he was uneasy during dinner. The vodka seemed to relax him, though."

"Frankly, Jay, Alexi never drinks."

"Very atypical Russian."

Anders continued to look grave. "We went out for a nightcap. About two, Alexi really went off the deep end—crying one moment and laughing the next. He was incoherent for a full fifteen minutes. I thought he was having a nervous breakdown. Weston and I worked hard to calm him down."

Parisi shook his head. "Sounds like something out of Dostoyevski."

Anders pulled his pipe out, lit it, sucked the smoke in deeply, and exhaled. "Suddenly, he pulled himself together. Calmly, he led us outside. He told us that just before dinner he'd been taking a nap in the second bedroom of his father's suite. His father and General Zalinski, chief of the Soviet General Staff, came back from Ainola. Evidently, they didn't know Alexi was there. They turned on the radio, probably to drown out listening devices. But they sat talking next to the central-heating duct, and the conversation carried clearly into the bedroom, where Alexi heard everything.

"He said they were drinking vodka, toasting each other—ecstatic about the way the summit was working out. He says Zalinski told Marensky he'd never have believed it possible for an American president to agree to nuclear disarmament. Then Zalinski told his father the army and the strategic rocket forces had finished Operation Deep Sleep a week ahead of schedule."

"What the hell is that?" Parisi asked.

"It is a plan to hide nuclear weapons. Four hundred of them, and components for hundreds more. Zalinski boasted they'd never be detected."

"Jesus."

"Then they congratulated themselves on their success in getting Novikov to authorize Deep Sleep. Alexi got the impression Novikov had resisted at first—but if he wanted to remain general secretary . . ."

"In the end he gave in," Parisi said.

"Involuntarily, it seems. But it amounts to the same thing."

"In a way it's just what Alexi was saying at dinner: Novikov making concessions to stay in power." Parisi took Anders by the shoulders. "Do you believe him?"

Anders nodded grimly. "Yes—Alexi would have no reason to lie to me or Andrew. We're like family, Jay."

"Who else knows?" Parisi asked anxiously.

"Dan Bennet."

Parisi was dumbfounded. *"Bennet?"*

"Marensky was desperate. I know you're working in some capacity for Michael, but I didn't want to—how do you say?—blow your cover. Besides, Alexi wouldn't have trusted you—he doesn't know you. Anyway, he asked

Andrew Weston to tell Bennet. But Andrew insisted Bennet hear it directly, so at about three-thirty this morning he pulled Bennet out of bed and let Alexi tell his story all over again."

"Then the president and the secretary of state know what Alexi says."

"I'm not sure," Anders said. "Bennet's reaction was strange. I'd have thought he'd go, you know, 'I must go immediately to wake up the secretary,' or something like that. But he didn't. He just said he'd handle it. Weston went to see Bennet again first thing this morning. He told me afterward Bennet seemed skeptical—he's not sure he believed Marensky. How could he not believe Alexi? He's put his life in jeopardy—if they find out, he's dead. As soon as I learned that, I tried to call Michael—but there was no answer, so I tried to get hold of you. Thank God you found me."

"I'll get Waterman," Parisi said. "He has a beeper." Then, suddenly, he turned white. The moment he'd said it, he'd hit his left-hand pocket. Inside was a beeper and four batteries—Waterman's beeper. He remembered he'd picked it up to change them. "Shit."

"What's wrong?"

Parisi pulled the beeper from his pocket. "This is Michael's," he said ruefully. He thought for several seconds. "Øve, do you have press credentials?"

"Of course—but not a pool pass. I can get into the press center, but without a pool pass I can't get to Ainola."

"How can we get a pool pass?"

"Lars Hammarstad—he's one of my colleagues—is Scandinavian pool for the morning session. I can reach him on the mobile phone."

"Do it!" Parisi cried. "Tell him to get his ass down the road and to bring his pool pass with him. Tell him there'll be a big goddam stretch Mercedes limo waiting on the road just below the security barrier. Tell him to give his pool pass to the guy in the limo."

Parisi headed for his limo in a dead run. "Let's go," he shouted to the driver as he slid into the front seat.

━━━━━━━━━━━━━━━━━

Ainola, December 17, 11:50 A.M.

Hammarstad was standing at the side of the road when the limo pulled up and the door flew open. "*Aftenposten?*" Parisi asked.

"Yes," Hammarstad said. "Lars Hammarstad."

Parisi shook the man's gloved hand. "Pool pass."

Hammarstad removed an octagonal, bright yellow cardboard disk from around his neck and handed it to Parisi. On it, written in large crimson English and Cyrillic letters, were the words PRESS POOL 17/USA-USSR. Parisi slipped the chain over his head.

"Do they log you in and out?" Parisi asked.

"No," the reporter said. "They don't even look at your face—just the shape and color of the pass."

"Do you have a notebook?" Parisi asked.

Hammarstad pulled a reporter's spiral notebook from his pocket. "I'll need it," Parisi said, taking it from his hand and ripping out the pages that had been written on. He handed them to the reporter and shoved the blank notebook in his pocket. "A reporter's got to carry a notebook. You wait here. I'll send the limo back for you as soon as he drops me off at Ainola. Anders is waiting for you at the station."

"What's going on?" the bewildered reporter asked.

"Anders'll explain," Parisi said, knowing full well that Anders wouldn't.

The Finnish guards examined Parisi's pool pass and allowed him, but not his car, in through the security checkpoint. Cursing in Italian, he got out and jogged the last two hundred yards, chugging breathlessly up to the crowd of reporters and cameramen staking out the house.

There was one hurdle left. The pool pass entitled Parisi to stand with the others but gave him no access to the site itself. He caught his breath, ducked under the rope barrier, and headed straight for the front door. Ten yards from the entrance a pair of U.S. Secret Service agents and KGB security officers stood with a cluster of uniformed Finnish security police. A Finn blocked his progress. "Sorry, you can't go farther."

Parisi flashed his pass. "Can you help me, please?" he asked. "I have to get an urgent message to Assistant Secretary of Defense Michael Waterman. He's part of the American delegation inside."

"I'm sorry," the guard said. "We're not allowed to pass messages."

"But this is an emergency," Parisi said.

"Talk to the Secret Service if you want. I have no authority to pass a message into the house." The guard motioned to an American security officer.

"Excuse me, sir," Parisi said. "This is an emergency, and I need your help. I must get a message to Michael Waterman—the assistant secretary of defense. It's urgent."

"What's so urgent?" the agent asked in an unmistakable Boston accent.

"We just got word on the wire that Secretary Waterman's father died. Killed in a plane crash outside Gloucester, Massachusetts. He's got to contact his family immediately."

"Oh, Christ," the agent said. "Look—you write a note and I'll send it in to him." He stomped his booted feet in the cold. "Jesus, what a time for it to happen."

Parisi took out Hammarstad's notebook and scrawled a note:

Bad news, Mike—your father was killed in a plane crash last night. I'm outside the house with the press pool. Please contact me ASAP for further urgent details. I'm terribly sorry. Parisi.

He handed the message to the agent, who read it and then went inside. A moment later he emerged and gave Parisi a thumbs-up. Parisi returned the gesture. Then the front door opened, and Waterman stood there, looking wildly around.

Parisi waved. "Over here, Michael—over here." God bless the memory of Sam Waterman, Parisi thought—he'd always been there when Michael needed him, and he was there for him this time, too.

Coatless, Waterman stood, teeth chattering with cold as he listened to the account of Marensky's revelations.

"Jay," Waterman said. "Are you sure—absolutely, positively sure— Bennet knows about this?"

"That's what Anders told me," Parisi said, "and he was categorical. He was there when Marensky told Bennet. He heard every word. There's no doubt."

"I'd better get inside," Waterman said. "Jay, you get this to SECDEF and McCandless as soon as you can. Then stand by in my room at the Inter-Continental."

He grabbed Parisi in a bear hug. There were tears in Waterman's eyes. "Goddam, Jay, you do great work."

Waterman bounded up to the delegation office. The morning session was due to end any minute. Waterman wanted to be waiting, in position, when it broke and the president came upstairs.

The office was empty. Everyone was still downstairs, outside the library doors. Waterman sat at a desk and began to outline the points he would make to the president if he got the chance. He heard someone and looked up from his notes to see Dan Bennet in the doorway.

"The secretary just came out of the meeting to say they've decided to go past the twelve-thirty lunch break. Looks like they're getting down to the short strokes, Michael."

"Did he say what's happened substantively?" Waterman asked.

"They're still hung up over SDI, but I don't have any details. If I had to, I'd guess the Old Man's gonna give it away."

Waterman turned his page of notes facedown on the desk. "You can't tell me you're happy about what's happened, Dan. You know damn well total nuclear disarmament is dangerous nonsense."

"Risky? Sure," Bennet said. "But so's an arms race. For centuries the world's been run by men with guns and powder. I think it's worth some risk to try pens and ink instead."

"You'd better pray you're right, Dan. You're betting the store."

"Am I?"

Waterman looked at him evenly. "You know you are."

Bennet's silence told him everything he had to know.

"What if they cheat, Dan?" he asked, finally. "What if they have no intention of totally disarming themselves?"

"I told the president this morning—they're perfectly capable of cheating, Michael. Nobody would argue with that for a minute. But you've got to have faith. In the absence of any hard evidence—absolutely indisputable evidence—I'll take my chances with Novikov."

Ainola, December 17, 12:45 P.M.

Waterman had positioned himself as close as he could get to the study, when its heavy doors swung open, and the two leaders, flanked by their interpreters, shook hands as they moved into the center vestibule. The secretary of state and Soviet foreign minister led the way.

Dan Bennet, too, waited. He edged alongside Winthrop as if to speak to him. Waterman threw a hip and nudged Bennet out of the way. He fell in alongside Winthrop and took hold of his arm. "Mr. Secretary," he said urgently, "I must see you in private. It's a matter of the utmost importance."

"We're very far along the road for last-minute appeals," Winthrop said. "I know how strongly you and Jim Ryder feel about SDI, and—"

Waterman walked the secretary of state into a corner of the central hall. He spoke in a low but insistent tone. "This isn't about SDI, sir. Please, Mr. Secretary, can you get me five minutes alone with him? I have information he must hear before he goes back in."

Winthrop pulled free of Waterman and tried to go around him so he could start up the steps to the second floor. Waterman blocked his way. "Mr. Secretary," Waterman whispered in his ear, "I have a very sensitive message from the secretary of defense. It's my duty to see that it reaches the president. But I also have reliable information that the Soviets have hidden nuclear weapons in anticipation of an agreement banning them. You must let me report this to the president."

Winthrop stopped in his tracks. He looked at Waterman as if he were crazy. "You can't be serious."

"It's true, I swear it—"

Winthrop looked up into the younger man's eyes. The look left no doubt that Waterman's career was on the line. Then the secretary of state took Waterman's arm. "Come with me," he said curtly.

At the second-floor landing he turned. "Wait here," he ordered. Waterman complied, his heart pounding. He was sweating profusely. Finally, the door opened, and the secretary beckoned him forward, holding an open hand in Waterman's direction. He'd have five minutes.

The president was seated in a comfortable wing chair that afforded him a clear view of the forest. Pages of drafts and notes were spread out in his lap. Winthrop took a seat on a wooden chair with a woven rush seat, his legs primly crossed at the ankles.

"Come on in, Michael," the president said warmly. "Tony says you have something important to tell me."

Waterman took a deep breath. "Mr. President," he began, "I appreciate your giving me this time. First, the secretary of defense asked me to give you this." He walked to the president's chair and handed him the copy of McCandless's note to Ryder about the real fate of the young Ukrainian defector, Kostiv. The president read it carefully. Waterman could see his eyebrows raise.

"Neither the DCI nor SECDEF wanted to upset you unnecessarily, sir," Waterman explained. "But under the circumstances the secretary felt you needed to see it today." He watched as the president shook his head slowly while pursing his lips. He noticed the president's left hand tighten into a fist.

"Second, Mr. President, when I heard you say General Secretary Novikov quoted a Chinese philosopher to you, I took the liberty of obtaining the quote from Sun Tzu's book *The Art of War* we know he kept framed on his desk before he became party secretary. You may not recall the contents—it was several weeks ago when DCI McCandless referred to it during an NSPG meeting—but the DCI thought it was important for you to see it again today." He handed the fax over and watched the president's eyes move from line to line:

When able to attack, seem unable; when active, seem inactive; when near, make the enemy believe you are far; when far away, make him believe you are near; when organized, feign disorder; if weak, pretend to be strong, and so cause the enemy to avoid you; when strong, pretend to be weak, so that the enemy may grow to be arrogant.

The president put the sheet of paper on his lap and looked calmly at Waterman. "I want you to know I would never base any policy of the United States on the idea that we can trust the Russians. They're all capable of deception, there's no doubt about that. They even deceive one another. I'm not ready to take anything on trust. Remember the old Russian proverb, Michael. 'Trust, but verify.'"

"I understand, Mr. President."

"But at summits, Michael, things happen between leaders. Call it what you will—empathy, rapport, or whatever. The way Roosevelt and Churchill got along when they first met wasn't guaranteed. Certainly, it was a meeting of great minds. But it was more—it was chemistry. And those moments of chemistry between the leaders, something that cannot be predicted, are what become great moments in history."

"In that case, Mr. President, the opinion you form of Mr. Novikov assumes very great importance."

"That's right, Michael."

"And . . ."

"And I can say that our chemistry has been, well, very good. He's a likeable man, Michael. He's easy to talk to. I believe that he wants to do something positive. And yet, well, as Bill McCandless said . . ." The president shook the fax in Waterman's direction.

"There's something more." Waterman took a deep breath. "Mr. President, last night, Yuri Marensky's son, who is here with the Soviet delegation, overheard his father talking to General Zalinski. He believes General Secretary Novikov was pressured to allow the army and the strategic rocket forces to hide nuclear weapons so they'd be retained covertly after any treaty banning them."

The president's eyes went wide. "What?"

"I know it sounds fantastic, Mr. President. But that's what Alexi Marensky says. And I believe he's telling the truth."

The room was suddenly very quiet. Waterman studied the intricate patterns in the wood floor. Outside, the sky had turned ominous; gray angular clouds that promised snow were moving quickly to block the sun. To Waterman it was an omen.

He shook his head to clear it, and continued his narrative. "Young Marensky was stunned—horrified by what he heard. He's a passionate reformer, a supporter of *glasnost* and *perestroika*. But after listening to his father and Chief of Staff Zalinski, he became convinced Novikov succumbed to the hard-liners. He put his life on the line to tell us."

All the color drained from the president's face. He looked suddenly vulnerable and very, very old. The president had always appeared to Waterman a robust man whose age was belied by his constant motion and ceaseless activity. Now, pallid, silent, and motionless, he seemed abruptly to have developed the translucent, brittle fragility of the elderly.

Finally, Winthrop spoke. "Michael, these are grave accusations. But there's no way we could hope to confirm them in the time available to us. It just can't be done." The secretary rose. "Thank you, Michael, you—"

"I'm not alone in knowing this, sir!" Waterman shouted.

Winthrop turned. "Who else has this information?"

"Dan Bennet. Alexi Marensky told him last night. Andrew Weston was in the room, too."

Winthrop opened and closed his eyes several times rapidly as if to blink away the reality of what he'd heard. He walked to the door and opened it. "Get Dan Bennet," he said to someone in the hallway.

He crossed the room and looked out the window at the snow-covered forest. "Mr. President, if Dan confirms this, I don't see how we can go forward—at least not now. We'd have a tough time trying to get Senate ratification of a sweeping disarmament treaty in any case. But if there's any evidence of Novikov's going into this thing with the intention to cheat, it would be enough to sink any treaty."

"Get word to McCandless immediately," the president said, shaking his head in disbelief. "I want Bill's judgment on whether it's possible for them to have fooled us so completely."

"There may not be time, Mr. President," Winthrop said. "But I'll see that he's contacted at once. It's"—he looked at his watch—"six in the morning in Washington. There's not much he'll be able to tell us in the time we have left."

There was a knock at the door. Bennet walked in with his usual confident gait. He was about to greet the president when he saw Waterman. His smile evaporated.

"Dan," the secretary of state began, "Michael has just reported to the president that General Secretary Novikov has authorized the army to hide nuclear weapons in violation of the treaty. Moreover, he says, you received similar information as well—from a reliable source."

Bennet looked as if he'd been gut-punched. "Yes, sir," he wheezed.

"I—I—wanted to be certain . . . it's such a grave accusation," Bennet stammered. "I've been thinking about it all morning, trying to come to a conclusion I could present to you. At first, I was inclined to disbelieve it.

I thought the source well meaning, but colored by his passion for reform. He hates the army and the KGB, you see—and . . . well, but I think now I'm inclined to accept what he said."

"Is it true you learned this from Yuri Marensky's son?"

"Yes, sir."

"And Andrew Weston was also present?"

"Yes, sir, he was."

"And did Weston give Marensky's story credibility?"

"He did, Mr. Secretary," Bennet said formally.

"And do you have any doubt about the reliability of Mr. Weston? He evidently knows Mr. Marensky rather well."

"No, sir, I have no doubts about Andrew Weston."

Winthrop took on the role of prosecutor. "Is there anything else you learned from Marensky or Weston that the president ought to know?"

Bennet straightened up. Normal color returned to his cheeks. He seemed to regain some of his confidence. "Mr. President, Marensky told me he overheard General Zalinski talking to his father. What he gleaned from this is that the army has forced Novikov—against his will—to go along with the scheme to conceal weapons. Of course, now that we know this, we should be able to negotiate suitable verification arrangements. I also think—"

Winthrop stopped him abruptly. "Dan, if you'd join the others downstairs, I need a few minutes alone with the president."

Bennet wheeled and left the room.

Waterman stood transfixed. The secretary of state looked at him. "Michael?" He got no reaction. Finally, he walked over to the younger man and tugged at his sleeve. "Michael? The president and I have to talk."

Waterman nodded. "Yes, sir."

"Alone," Winthrop said, placing his hand in the small of Waterman's back and shoving him gently toward the door. "The president and I have to talk *alone.*"

Waterman closed the door behind him. Dan Bennet was standing outside, staring into space. Together, they descended the wide, creaky staircase in lockstep unison, neither man speaking as they made their way to the rustic living room.

Waterman surveyed the roomful of advisers as they stood making small talk. They didn't know it yet, but it was all over. He placed his coat over his arm, retrieved his briefcase, and walked toward the door as if in a trance.

Outside the press waited for some word. They didn't know it, either, but there would be no word.

Waterman felt light-headed, and yet strangely deflated. What an incredible turn. All the work, the infighting, the leaks, the back-stabbing. And what had it come down to? A Russian dreamer with a conscience.

And a Norwegian newsman who, God bless him, had a conscience, too. Poor Øve—what a story he'd blown. The story of a lifetime.

Waterman walked outside, coatless in the frigid air, as oblivious to the volley of questions shouted from the press pool behind the barrier as he was to the subzero temperature. He walked to car number six, collapsed in the backseat, and told the driver to head back to Helsinki.

The Finland summit was over. All that remained was for Bennet and the rest of the State Department team to draft a vacuous communiqué saying the two leaders had met and exchanged views and would meet again sometime in the future for further discussions.

There'd be nothing to sign. No earth-shattering agreements. No finely worded documents to take their place in the annals of diplomacy.

Nothing. Just a long flight home.

He put his head back and watched the forest go by, a green blur through the tinted glass. He closed his eyes. He thought of Jim Ryder, the McCandless note in his hand and tears in his eyes, standing by his office window. He thought of the DCI tracking down a quote from Sun Tzu, probably in the middle of the night. He thought about what had happened to Kostiv— and what might have happened here today without Jay Parisi and Øve Anders in his corner. He thought about his wife and his son and wondered just how much about the day's events he'd ever be able to tell them.

He opened his eyes and wiped away tears. The forest was still a green blur outside. The promises had been kept, he thought. But it would still be miles before he'd sleep.

December 17, 5:45 P.M.

The flight from Helsinki to Brussels, where the secretary of state was scheduled to brief the NATO foreign ministers, was scheduled to take less than two hours. Even with the evening arrival, Dan Bennet knew a mob of reporters would be waiting in the Belgian capital to hurl questions at Winthrop, so he set to work immediately outlining talking points in a memo for him.

He perused the pages in front of him, chewed on a green Uni-Ball, and pondered the lackluster denouement of the Ainola summit. There had been no high-flown communiqué, no adulation from the world press—just insistent questioning as to what had gone wrong. What *had* gone wrong? Bennet wondered. He'd tried his best—they'd all tried their best—and yet, it had just . . . collapsed.

Indeed, the entire world—at least those with access to a TV set—knew it, too. The pictures of the president and Novikov leaving Ainola without comment, climbing into their respective limousines without pausing to shake hands or smile for the cameras, was seen live all around the world. Those stark images left no doubt the summit had ended in failure.

In fact, before the president had left Helsinki for an overnight visit to London and then home to Washington, before Winthrop's aircraft took off for Brussels, the precise nature of that failure was already becoming a matter of controversy.

Even as General Secretary Novikov's limousine was driving the thirty-eight kilometers from Ainola to Helsinki, the Soviet press operation went into overdrive to explain that the promise of massive nuclear disarmament had foundered on the American president's insistence on continuing work on SDI. Before the president had reached his quarters at the U.S. embassy in the Finnish capital, Anthony Winthrop was making a statement at the international press center blaming the failure on overreaching by the Soviets. Having been unable to agree about peace, the superpowers waged an undeclared and unrestricted war of words.

Almost unrestricted: The president, after a secure conference call between himself, Winthrop, Ryder, and McCandless, decided nothing would be said about what they had learned of Novikov's plans to retain nuclear weapons even after an agreement to abolish them.

Bennet found a typo and circled it. "Damn," he said aloud. He wondered how he'd fare now that the summit was over. All that work for nothing. He sighed. It was going to get boring at Foggy Bottom. Maybe it was time for an ambassadorship. Rome? Perhaps. Paris? Even better. He edited a sentence he found too windy. After staffing him for several years, Bennet knew what Winthrop required: crisp talking points that NATO foreign ministers would understand and approve.

Bennet was just handing the memo to Bob Wellbeck, who would see to having it typed and circulated, when Winthrop's security officer summoned him forward to the secretary's cabin. He pulled his suit coat down from the overhead, straightened his tie, and strode forward.

Winthrop sat in a high-backed leather judge's chair, his collar open, his tie off. He wore his tattered old cashmere cardigan, so worn it had suede patches on the cuffs and elbows. He was absorbed in a leather-bound briefing book.

"Mr. Secretary," Bennet said, pulling the curtain halfway shut behind him, "I've completed a memo with talking points for the ministerial and Q's and A's for the press. Renalda's typing it up now."

The secretary of state looked up. "Sit down, Dan," Winthrop said, closing the book on his lap. "I have something to say."

Bennet sank into the L-shaped banquette opposite the secretary of state. He tucked his feet under the trapezoid-shaped leather-covered table and scrutinized the secretary of state. He didn't much like what he saw: Winthrop appeared washed out, drained, tired.

"Dan," Winthrop said, "I'm not happy, not at all happy, about your failure to keep me informed on important matters. You've been dilatory in reporting information that, as secretary of state, I needed to know and that you had an obligation to make known to me."

Bennet was taken aback by Winthrop's icy, quasi-legal tone, made all the more menacing because he'd never before spoken to him in that way. Bennet wished the curtain drawn across the entrance to the compartment would part, and Renalda would come in with the talking points. Having his talking points in front of him would remind Winthrop of how invaluable Bennet's assistance was, how Bennet was always on top of every requirement, paper in hand whenever it was needed. Dan Bennet was never without an answer. He hoped the secretary appreciated that.

"I should have been able to weigh the full implications of the information you chose to keep from me," the secretary repeated.

"It won't happen again," Bennet promised earnestly.

"Indeed it won't," Winthrop responded. "Dan, you obtained information about Novikov that was of the utmost importance. It was passed to you by a courageous man in the belief he was warning the president of the United States. I should have been informed immediately. If you'd been concerned about weighing the reliability of the information, you could have passed it to me with caveats. If young Marensky hadn't seen fit to establish a second backchannel, if the word hadn't gotten to Waterman, his story might never have come to light."

"Mr. Secretary," Bennet protested, "I—"

Winthrop waved a finger in Bennet's face. "Let me be blunt. You showed poor judgment in not getting to me immediately."

Bennet began to speak. "But, Mr. Secretary, I think—"

"My interest in what you think came to an end in Sibelius's bedroom. There's no point in further discussion. As the secretary of defense is fond of saying, 'If I say any more, I would only be repeating myself.' "

Winthrop pulled a pair of half-glasses from his breast pocket, opened the book on his lap, and idly scanned the pages. "I think it's time to talk about what you'll be doing next, Dan. How's your French?"

Bennet's pulse quickened. "It's passable, Mr. Secretary. With a little work I could be fluent."

"Good," the secretary said. "Burkino Faso is open. I'm going to nominate you as ambassador there."

Bennet's jaw dropped. "But—"

"That will be all, Dan," Winthrop said without looking up.

Bennet got to his feet just as Renalda, carrying the freshly typed talking points, pulled back the curtain to the secretary's cabin. She held it in front of her like a bullfighter's cape as Bennet withdrew.

December 18, 5:00 P.M.

Air Force One taxied as close to the press stand as it was safe to go. When the doors opened, the president emerged, smiling and waving. In his pocket was the draft arrival statement that Gary Burner, General Wallace, and Alan Kirkwell had written during the flight from London. After a cursory walk down the receiving line of dignitaries and a quick review of the honor guard, the president made his way to the podium.

The vice president's introduction was brief—he'd been instructed by phone from the presidential aircraft to keep it low-key. He did. Then the president raised his arms in his familiar two-handed wave, turned toward the cameras, and began to speak. "Mr. Vice President, all our good friends from Congress who've turned out to welcome us back in this great country of ours, and my fellow Americans all across the nation . . ."

While the president made his statement, Waterman made his own way down the steps pulled up to the aft hatchway of the huge blue, silver, and white 707. He stopped halfway down to scan the crowd of dignitaries, well-wishers, and onlookers who lined the chain-link fence at the edge of the tarmac.

Laura and Jason saw him just as he saw them. Jason pointed, then waved excitedly. Waterman ran across a hundred yards of tarmac and through the gate, dropped his bags, and swept his wife into his arms. "God, I love you," he said.

Then he picked up his son and squeezed him tight. "Hi, goose—what do you think of *Air Force One?*"

"It's so big. We saw the president. He waved at us."

"That's because he likes gooses like you." He gave his son a kiss on the cheek and tossed him playfully in the air.

"Daddy, what did you bring me?"

"Have I got something for you, goose?" Waterman knelt down and burrowed in his shoulder bag. He retrieved a small, soft package. "Have I ever." Jason tore open the wrapping and let a blue cotton T-shirt unfold.

"Who's that, Daddy?" the boy asked, staring at the unfamiliar face silk-screened on the front of the shirt above the legend I LOVE FINLAND.

"His name's Jean Sibelius, a Finnish composer," Waterman said. "I visited his place in the country."

About the Author

RICHARD PERLE was assistant secretary of defense for international security policy from 1981 to 1987. Now a consultant and commentator based in Washington, he is a fellow at the American Enterprise Institute. He lives in Chevy Chase, Maryland.

About the Type

This book was set in Photina, a typeface designed by José Mendoza in 1971. It is a very elegant design with high legibility, and its close character fit has made it a popular choice for use in quality magazines and art gallery publications.